Jules Claretie, Frances Cashel Hoey

Camille Desmoulins and His Wife

Jules Claretie, Frances Cashel Hoey

Camille Desmoulins and His Wife

ISBN/EAN: 9783337813000

Printed in Europe, USA, Canada, Australia, Japan

Cover: Foto ©Raphael Reischuk / pixelio.de

More available books at **www.hansebooks.com**

Dedicated

TO THE MEMORY

OF

J. MICHELET

MY REVERED MASTER

J. C.

PREFACE.

Scribitur ad narrandum veritatem.

THE following history of the most dramatic and touching episodes of the French Revolution has cost the author many years of labour, which he regards as the best employed period of his life. Just as he had terminated his researches into the life and character of the men on whom he proposed to form a judgment, the late war between France and Prussia broke out, and the terrible days which led France for a moment to the brink of destruction ensued. Not until after those dark days of cruel trial had come to an end did the historian resume his interrupted task, bringing to its fulfilment greater calmness of mind and increased certitude of experience; for, by the light of events of which he has been the sorrowful eyewitness, he has contemplated the facts of an eventful past not yet a century old.

Such periods of national trouble as that through which we have just passed have one element of consolation amid their bitterness; they force the least reflective minds into attention and thought. They are the hours of 'examination of conscience' for peoples. The

nations, and every thinking being among them, ask
themselves whence has ruin come, and where has the
sin been ? Only by comparing the tempests of the
past with those of the present can we study them
scientifically, and define their causes and their results.
No study is more useful at the present day than that
of the French Revolution, undertaken in a free spirit,
untrammelled by any sectarian tradition, or traditional
idolatry, animated solely by the ardent love of liberty,
and of justice. Either the time has now come, or it
will never come, to press the experiences of yesterday
into the service of the realisations of to-morrow ; to
exhibit in their true light, with all their greatness,
and all their weakness, the men who, in the space of
three years, from 1792 to 1795, accomplished a task
which eight centuries of monarchy had failed to
achieve; who restored its natural boundaries to our
country, but who also set a Cæsar over the aggran-
dized land. The right moment has come at which
to show the world how Republics perish, in order that
it may learn how Republics may be founded.

The author has attempted such a task. He knows
that a writer who ventures to tell the truth, without
making phrases, in troublous times like the present,
when parties are fighting almost at haphazard, like
sharpshooters at night, exposes himself to no small
obloquy. He knows that a work of historical criticism,
such as the present narrative, is likely to be equally
displeasing to friends and adversaries. The knowledge
does not disturb him. In the 'interior judge' of whom
Fénelon speaks, the writer has a sovereign adjudicator
—his conscience—placed above all other judges ; and

the law which he holds dominant over all laws is that of respect for the truth as he believes it to be. 'I bend no more before the red heel than before the red cap,' said the Russian patriot, Alexander Herzen, one of the manliest and most independent men of this century. Like him, the author despises courtiership of every kind, to whatever rank or power it may address itself.

This history may then be read with confidence. In it will be found nothing insincere, nothing which is not borne out by facts, based upon a document, or proved by some written evidence, whether already known, or published for the first time in this volume. Our era is that of exactness and of patience in the matter of historic research. It does not boast the lofty flights of genius, but it has at least the virtue of respect for truth; which is, perhaps, the most praiseworthy of virtues, for, to our mind, it leads to all the others.

It was no easy task for the author to make up his mind to close this work, which was the joy and the hope of his youth. What bright and happy dreams he had dreamed over it! With what intense pleasure he had turned over the faded yellow papers of the Archives! With what emotion he had opened the records of the revolutionary tribunals! With what pain he had watched the falling, one by one, of so many noble and intellectual heads! How he had rejoiced to find in those faded pages the memory and the echo of many glorious days! When the following chapters shall be read, a gloomy contrast must necessarily be drawn between that past and the present, or rather, between the past of eighty years ago and the past of yesterday. How great France then was, soaring above the world, and, better still, illuminating it with her lustre, over-awing it, astonishing it rather by her ideas than by her arms ; offering the unique spectacle of a single nation repelling the invasion of a world, and distributing the standards captured from the enemy in its external strife, to serve as bandages for the wounded in its civil wars.

That was a proud and lofty spectacle, even for the conquered—aye, for the conquered above all ! Perhaps it will make us reflect more seriously on our brief humili-ation. If France is to be saved, and reconstituted, for which I hope with all the strength of my being, it will be by the picture of her past greatness, of the devotion, the dissensions, the martyrdoms, the sufferings, and the glories of other days. In them there is twofold profit, twofold teaching. We learn at once to avoid the sanguinary excesses into which our fathers fell, and to imitate the self-denying examples by which they effaced their severe measures, their faults, and their errors. May the perusal of these pages strengthen minds who feel what republican virtue ought to be, in devotion to liberty, respect for law, love of justice, obedience to duty, and love of country—that sublime love for France which sustains, engenders, and quickens all other virtues.

This historical essay has no other aim. The author's task will seem light to him if he shall have succeeded in making his readers love, not only the men whose tragical fate he narrates, but those great things which rise above the men—Liberty and Country.

JULES CLARETIE.

CONTENTS.

CHAPTER III.

CHAPTER IV.

CHAPTER V.

ILLUSTRATIONS.

CAMILLE DESMOULINS

AND HIS WIFE.

———•◦•———

CHAPTER I.

CAMILLE DESMOULINS AND THE DANTONISTS.

A MAN always retains a little of the natal air which he has breathed in childhood and in youth. In many instances the temperament and the life of an individual may be explained by the soil on which he was born. Why should we not ask a village, a street, a paternal dwelling, whether they have not preserved some secret remembrance of the celebrated person whose first utterances they have heard, whose first dreams they have silently witnessed ? Inanimate things, it seems to me,

B

may have their regrets, and we may find traces in them of the beings whose birth, development, and death they have beheld. Besides, the eager need of knowing everything which belongs to our time requires that the historian shall study the scenery and decorations of his drama before he begins to unfold its action.

It was on an April morning, while the cannon of the civil war was roaring around Paris, that I resolved to go to Guise and ask the little town for recollections of Camille Desmoulins, the '*gamin* of genius,' whom Paris attracted, seduced, and kept for ever. It was not without emotion that I undertook this journey. It seems to me that the shades of the famous dead return to the places where the memory of them dwells. I was eager to see and to interrogate Guise, that quiet city of the Vermandois, which Camille invoked, in the wildest hour of the revolutionary tempest, as an asylum too soon abandoned, a humble paradise for ever lost. Had the town faithfully preserved the memory of one of the most famous of her sons? Was this district of Picardy, formerly so far advanced in literary culture, grateful to Camille Desmoulins for the literary renown which he had reflected upon it? The spirit of the soil has changed within the last fifty years; the sharp, satirical, mocking, gossipping spirit, that of the *littérateur*, and of the story-teller after the fashion of the *fabliaux*, has been gradually silenced by the opposite spirit of speculation and industry, which has invaded the whole country. At Vervins and at Guise there are to be found at present only a few specimens of those old provincial scholars, deeply learned, laborious *savans*, who toiled in semi-obscurity at some patient task, far from the central light indeed, but perhaps near to the truth. In all probability I was destined to disappointment, and should not find even the phantom of Camille Desmoulins at Guise.

The way from Saint Quentin to the hard-working little town of Guise lies through a rich, productive, un-picturesque country, where cornfields stretch away to the horizon on either side of the road. Guise does not announce itself in any way to the traveller, who hardly sees the high tower of the château as he approaches ; but, on descending a sloping road, which passes through a kind of faubourg composed of houses with thatched roofs, is surprised to find himself in a city of the past— of strange, calm, sleepy aspect. The fortified château stands, firm and imposing, upon the summit of a steep ascent, and the houses, almost all dating from the seven-teenth century, seem to nestle beneath it for shelter.

There are two distinct towns in this little city of Guise : the old and the new ; but the old still maintains its sway. The old town of the fifteenth and sixteenth centuries, built upon the hill hard by the château, that town which we see in the etching by Johannis Peeters Delin (1572) with its ancient donjon and its ramparts, it is true, no longer exists. The whole of Guise seems contemporary with Desmoulins, with the early years of the Revolution. But its quasi-antiquity was sufficient for me. I was seeking only for traces of the manners and the memories of the eighteenth century.

The tall roofs are covered with slates ; the streets look as they looked in 1750. The dwellings of the bourgeois and the small tradesmen bear the dates of their construction, inserted into the building in figures made of iron rods. As one walks along the narrow but regular streets, one's fancy reconstructs the life of the past ; and sees, in the traders of to-day, the merchants and shopkeepers of former times, the mercers and the drapers. Not for many a year has the slated belfry of the little Town Hall resounded with the peal of its tenant, but, though hushed, the tongue is still there which celebrated all the joys and announced all the mournings of the community. How small and humble this little Town Hall looks, standing at the foot of the château, frowned on by the citadel and menaced by its guns. It exists, it might be said, only under favour of this perpetual threat, and the château could destroy it at a single blow. But the huge pile of stone represents nothing more than brute force, mere strength. The little building contains the papers of the city, the certificates of births and marriages, registers, deeds—this old house represents the law. The lofty tower, leprous and unsightly with its yellow stains of time, rears itself up, formidable, indeed, but useless, like a giant disarmed by old age. This colossal construction, for all the thickness of its mighty walls, could not have arrested the German invasion in 1870 for two hours. Its sonorous arches, its great gates with arms blazoned in sculpture on the rock above them, its gloomy galleries, are of no avail against modern warfare waged with guns of steel. When I passed by, the Gardes Mobiles were at their drill in the shade, while the wind blew merrily over the height, whence I could see distant fields, the rivers Aisne and Somme, groves of trees, villages half hidden in verdure, or by the undulations of the ground. On the horizon was Wiége, where sleep the humble ancestors of Camille, and at the foot of the citadel was Guise, with its lofty roofs, its promenades, its trees, the buildings of the Famislistère, wearing the gay and prosperous aspect of a small industrious town. I came and went, I looked about, I sought out every association, and I pictured to myself Camille Desmoulins, going to and from the Picard town, following the course of the little river, book in hand, reading, dreaming, exhaling his youthful enthusiasm. Methought I came upon him once more at the corners of the narrow streets, or in one of those quiet old houses, full of books and the talk of old times, or on the road to the château, climbing the steep ascent to the citadel, stopping on his way to listen, smilingly, to the music chanted in the church; reciting verses from Voltaire before the chapel, and quoting Tacitus in front of the fortress.

The house in which Camille Desmoulins was born stands in the High Street of the town, called in the documents of the time 'the street of the Grand Pont, in front of the Place d'Armes.'[1] It is a small, clean-looking, cheerful house with a slate roof, and walls of dazzling whiteness, manifestly the house of a bourgeois family, honest, estimable people, accustomed to daily labour, to the patient and uncomplaining endurance of the cares and needs of life, and fain to accept with gratitude the rest which succeeded to each day's work well done. Not rich, of a surety, but content with

[1] The following particulars have been obtained from the present proprietor of the house :—

Last deed of sale (1852). A house at Guise, in the Grande Rue, opposite the Place d'Armes, roofed with slate, with garrets and cellar, stable, coach-house, yard, and garden ; the building facing the Grande Rue, and extending backwards to the Place Lesur.

Preceding proprietors :—

1. Jean-Joseph-Benoni Ducrot, formerly advocate of the Cour Royale at Paris, and Henriette-Florence Alix, his wife.

2. Pierre-Alexis Hennequierre, deceased, landowner at Guise, and Geneviève-Laurence-Virginie Teffin, his widow.

3. M. Philippe-François Hennequierre et Màdame Marie-Louisa-Victorie Merlin, his wife.

4. Jean-Benoît-Nicolas Desmoulins.

their fate, satisfied with the lot that had fallen to them, and prouder of their reputation for honesty than of their narrow fortune. Not theirs, repose with dignity, the *otium cum dignitate* of the ancients, but a better lot, that of toil with dignity. The whole house tells of habitual work, and it is easy for one's fancy to refurnish those rooms, with their ceilings supported by beams of wood, and their plainly carved panels; to reconstruct the lawyer's study, with its great table laden with papers, its bookshelves filled with learned books, and heavy treatises on law; and to discern the housewife's favourite corner, the work-table and the chair which were Madame Desmoulins'.

The front of the house facing the street has been partly taken down; it was in that portion that the young pair lived at first after their marriage. The small house in the garden, with the date of the year 1772 cut upon its walls, was no doubt built when the former dwelling had been outgrown by the children born to them and then growing up. In the second building, erected during the childhood of Camille, we find the shadows of many things of the past; some peaceful and some sad. There are the stairs which resounded to the children's noisy tread; the kitchen, like one of Chardin's pictures, which was so busy and bustling on days when that important personage Cousin de Viefville des Essarts visited the house, or when the Prince de Conti sojourned beneath the roof of the Lieutenant-general. The past revives between these white walls, in the flowery little garden, in this corner of the world which seems to have preserved the memory of the former dwellers in it, long after that memory has died away from among the living; a vanished past, a humble and gentle past, calm, peace-

ful, simple and severe, like the upright life of the elder
Desmoulins, sad and tear-stained like the destiny of an
honest man.

In one story of this house, which is at present the
property of M. Bailly, there lives an old man, who was
formerly a dancing-master. He is an amiable old
man, very smiling, polite, and odd. Since 1810 he
has never quitted his abode, which is filled with old
engravings and mineralogical curiosities of his own
collecting. I tried to awaken in the memory of this
charming little old man an echo of the noise which
Desmoulins made here formerly ; but in vain. M. Fey-
deau gently shook his head, whitened with the snows
of ninety years, a head like one by Holbein for sagacity and wrinkles, as he answered to my prompting.
'No,' he said, 'I do not know, I have never heard ;
the last time any one spoke of Camille Desmoulins
at Guise'—then, correcting himself,—'spoke of *the
Citizen Camille Desmoulins*, was when our Prefect, M.
de la Forge, came here to review the Mobiles. I have
no remembrance of anything else.' The inhabitants
of Guise are all like this old man. They have forgotten their unfortunate townsman, the generous fool,
the mad-cap of genius, who gave his life to the Republic ;—they have forgotten, after having misunderstood
and perhaps calumniated, him.

I had been informed that an interesting portrait of
Camille existed in the Town Hall at Guise, and was
to be found in the municipal council chamber. I went
thither and asked to see the portrait. Two officials
who accompanied me pointed to some portraits of certain great personages of former times, clad in cuirasses
and wearing long curled wigs. 'It must be that one,'
said one of my guides, indicating a portrait of big, fat

M. de Beaulieu, who defended Guise in the brave
days of old.   Evidently this man thought I could
not be anxious to see any but a great personage.
The portrait of a small attorney, and a poor writer,
indeed! 'It may be here, after all,' said the man, as
he opened a sort of dark press in the wall, where the
shiny black gowns and caps of judges, lawyers, and
officials of the court were hung up in dusty obscurity,
and the firewood destined for municipal consumption
was also stored.   There, in a dark corner, heaped
together, were a number of blackened and worn gilt-
frames, old portraits, and busts of dethroned personages, kings and queens.   These were the detritus of
our revolutions ; all that our poor France has by turns
welcomed with acclamation and then renounced and
repelled; carried to the Pantheon with blind admiration
or flung into the gutter with mad fury; all the fallen
and faded royalties, all the beaten ones lay there together, brought into incongruous contact by the
ironical community of destiny.   A plaster bust of
the late Emperor faced a bronze bust of King
Louis Philippe.   My guide dived among the heap of
frames, and brought up in succession a lithograph representing the Duke of Orleans; an engraving of the
Duke and Duchess de Berry ; Napoleon I., in an im-
perial mantle spotted with flies, and then a portrait
of Cavaignac.   The glass frame of the latter was
broken.   At last, he came upon Camille Desmoulins,
a lithographed portrait, after the painting by François
Bonneville, without any artistic merit.   There it lay,
dusty, dirty, forgotten, exiled, as it had lain for
years, in the dust and darkness of the past.   'Born
at Guise' was written beneath the figure.   Who knew,
or cared anything for that, in the little town in Picardy ?

No one is a prophet in his own country, it seems, not even a martyr.

II.

Camille Desmoulins was born at Guise on the 2nd of March 1760, and not, as several historians have affirmed, in 1762, though he supported their statements himself by his reply to the President of the Revolutionary Tribunal, when, on being asked how old he was, he said : ' I am *thirty-three*, the age of the *sans-culotte* Jesus.' In 1794, Camille Desmoulins was thirty-four.[4] He must have remembered this on the day after his condemnation, for he wrote in his last letter to his wife—' I die at thirty-four.'

Picardy, whose vigorous soil produced the human plant, so to speak, more full of sap and vitality than elsewhere, counts her fighting-men by tens. Picardy is the country of Condorcet, who was born at Ribemont ; of Babeuf the dreamer of equality, a native of Saint-Quentin ; of old Calvin, of the Saint-Simons, and the Guises ; and, in more ancient times still, of the preacher of the Crusades, the enlightened and ardent Peter the Hermit. The violent struggle for the emancipation of the commons which the Middle Ages witnessed was most desperate and most decisive in Picardy. One

[1] 1760. ' On the second day of the present month was born, and on the third day of March was baptised, Lucie-Simplice-Camille-Benoist, son of Maistre Jean-Benoist-Nicolas Desmoulins, civil and criminal lieutenant-general of the bailiwick of Guise, and of dame Marie-Magdeleine Godart, his wife ; godfather, M. Joseph Godart, maternal uncle, of the parish of Wiége ; godmother, dame Magdeleine-Elizabeth Lescarbotte, also of that parish, who have signed, together with us, the present act.'— *From the register of the parish of Guise.*

Camille was baptised in the church of St. Pierre and St. Paul at Guise (diocese of Laon). It is an odd coincidence that he and his wife were both called *Lucie.*

might believe that Picard blood boils and beats more readily than elsewhere; heads are hot there, and M. Michelet, a Picard himself, calls his country 'choleric Picardy.'

With all this, however, Picardy is the country of reason and common sense, fortified by a prudent and sagacious humour, which becomes cunning in the peasant, and wisdom in the educated man. In the Desmoulins family, we find in M. Desmoulins, lieutenant-general of the bailiwick of Guise, a striking example of calm reason, as opposed to the quick temper and ardent impulse of the Picard. He was a grave and industrious man, highly esteemed by his fellow townsmen, whose interests he administered with strict honesty; he was faithful to his public duties, happy in his private life, and he lived free from care and envy in the quiet dwelling, where, when I visited it, I beheld the blue uniforms of the Saxon dragoons. I picture to myself M. Desmoulins in his modest, well-kept house, like one of those legists, numerous enough in former days in the country parts of France, who lived in obscure retirement, labouring noiselessly at some profound and valuable work. Many a time were men of brilliant renown, the pride of the Parliaments of Paris, obliged to bow before the learning of these unknown scholars, and respectfully to beg their aid. These laborious seekers after knowledge, living in silence face to face with their own works, took no pride in being consulted by famous men, but, when they had spoken, quietly resumed their interrupted tasks. Thus M. Desmoulins undertook an 'Encyclopædia of Law,' which was never destined to see the light of publicity. His manuscripts have all been dispersed and lost.

M. Desmoulins was not rich. His wife, Madeleine Godart, of the village of Wiége, brought him a small portion, which partly paid the expenses of the education of the children born during their union, which was one of true affection and tranquil happiness. They had five children : three sons, of whom Camille was the eldest; (the others, named Dubuquoy and Sémery, became soldiers;) and two daughters. One of the daughters · became a nun ; the other was still living, when in 1838 M. Matton, a relative, published an edition of the works of Camille Desmoulins for her benefit.[1]

Camille, the eldest son of M. Desmoulins, inspired his parents with the greatest hopes for his future by his intelligence, by the light in his brilliant black eyes, by the precocity of his repartees, and the general liveliness of his mind. The father was so proud of the child that he was prepared to make heavy pecuniary sacrifices in order to develope his fine qualities. He should be a man of law, an advocate at the Parliament of Paris ; this fiery and resolute child should attain to that which his father had renounced the hope of ever reaching. Unhappily a complete education cost much money in those days ; and, but for the aid of

[1] Paris : Ebrard, publisher, 2 vols. in 8vo, Matton's edition, compiled by a sincere admirer of Camille, and an educated and excellent man, has been adopted as the type of all succeeding editions. On May 6, 1807, one of the brothers was still living. This is proved by a deed of that date in which the relatives of M. Desmoulins are named as follows :—

Jean-Louis-Deviefville des Essarts, conservator of woods and waters at the residency at Amiens, residing at Guise, executor.

Nicolas-Sémery Desmoulins, gendarme in the company of La Stura, at the residence of La Chiesa.

Dame Anne-Françoise-Marie Bosdeveix, widow of M. Claude-Etienne-Larridon Duplessis, guardian of *Horace-Camille Desmoulins,* *son of Benoist-Camille Desmoulins,* and of dame Anne-Lucile-Philippe-Larridon Duplessis.

a distant relative, his parents could never have made of
Camille Desmoulins the wonderfully erudite scholar
he became. M. de Viefville des Essarts, formerly
an advocate at the Parliament of Paris, and subse-
quently deputy from Vermandois to the States-General,
obtained a 'bourse' at the College of Louis-le-Grand
for the young Camille.[1]   There, in the old school where
his memory still survives, Camille Desmoulins set himself to severe and ardent study, giving himself up,
body and soul, to that antique world which he never
ceased to love; feeding on Athenian honey and
Roman marrow, learning from the great past a juvenile love for the great word Republic, whose meaning
he perhaps only half comprehended. He loved it
better than he understood it; his whole soul glowed
with enthusiasm at the word, spoken in a harangue
of Cicero's with grace, in a tirade of Lucan's with boldness, and in a chapter of Tacitus with clear precision.
At a later time, when he was wont to boast that he
had been the first to utter that word aloud, he must
have evoked the memories of those schooldays, of
that period of moral and intellectual incubation during
which the Republican germ was growing within him.
When still a youth, he was already one of the *ten Republicans*, whom, he said, it would have been hard to
find in Paris in 1788. 'That which constitutes our
glory,' says Camille Desmoulins, 'is that we undertook the Revolution with such small beginnings. Our

[1] The untruthful Leipzig 'Biography,' whose errors I shall have
frequent occasion to correct in the course of this history, affirms, contrary
to the facts, that Camille Desmoulins was educated at the College of
Louis-le-Grand at the cost of the chapter of the cathedral of Laon. M.
Edouard Fleury, the author of a severe and often inexact 'History of
Camille Desmoulins,' does not venture to affirm the authenticity of this
tradition.

Republicans were, for the most part youths, who, having fed on Cicero at school, had conceived a passion for liberty. We were educated in the schools of Rome and Athens, and in the pride of the Republic, that we might live in the subjection of monarchy and under the rule of Claudius and Vitellius. What an insensate government, to imagine that we could be inspired with a passionate admiration for the fathers of the Roman republic, the men of the Capitol, without a corresponding horror of the men-eaters of Versailles ; that we could admire the past without condemning the present, *ulteriora mirari, præsentia secuturos.*[1]

In the above passage the secret of this independent spirit is revealed. Camille was evidently from his earliest years, and always remained, a political *littérateur,* if I may use the phrase ; and his admiration for antiquity, which was to a certain extent artistic, largely inspired his preference for a form of government under which his dreams of an elegant democracy and an ideal liberty invariably clothed themselves in the garb of Greece or Rome. Besides, the scholar was always uppermost in him, and until his last hour

---

[1] M. Eugène Despois, in a remarkable essay upon Camille Desmoulins, gives a curious extract from a collection of deliberations of the College of Louis-le-Grand, page 211 :

January 19, 1781.

'Upon the report rendered by the Principal of the eminent talents of the *Sieur de Robespierre,* boursier of the College of Arras, who is about to terminate his course of study ; of his good conduct during the past ten years, and his success in his classes, both with respect to the distribution of University Prizes, and in the examinations in Law and Philosophy :

'The Council have unanimously accorded to the said *Sieur de Robespierre* a gratification of 600 livres, which shall be paid to him by the treasurer of the College of Arras, and the said sum shall be allowed to the treasurer in his account, on his reporting the expedition of the present deliberation, and the quittance of the said *Sieur de Robespierre.*'

In the same register we find, under a later entry, 'a bourse granted to Desmoulins, *for services rendered by his father.*'

he was the same man who was seen, one day, in transports of delight over a passage in the Book of Ezekiel, in which he discovered that the Revolution was predicted word for word.

At the College of Louis-le-Grand, where several boys from Guise were studying at the same time—the future author of the 'Annuaire' among the number—Camille Desmoulins met a youth of his own age, also a 'boursier' like himself, who was maintained at Paris by the College of Arras. This was Maximilian Robespierre. We can imagine the juvenile talks of the thoughtful, fervid, precocious youths, the clashing sentiments of two such opposite natures, the one ardent and fanciful, the other meditative and severe. What confidences, what hopes, what chimeras must have been given to the wind under the trees in the college gardens! What dreams must have been dreamed in that small room on the fourth floor, where Gresset, the master, had composed his 'Chartreux,' and where Camille was in the habit of shutting himself up alone to concoct epistles! 'I was born to write verses,' said the unfortunate Camille, at the foot of the scaffold, doubtless remembering, not without emotion, the 'Epistle' which he addressed to MM. les Administrateurs du Collége Louis-le-Grand. In that epistle he mentions, with an expression of gratitude which the future bore out, the name of his best-beloved teacher, the Principal of the College, whom he calls 'the good Abbé Bérardier,' a man of superior intellect and excellent heart, a friend who was destined to be his adviser in later days, and to survive him.

In the 'Année Littéraire' for 1784, we find the lines in which Camille bade his teachers adieu in sincere and touching language. The verses, quoted with just praise, for their tone and sentiment (we are not now considering their form), are as follows :—

> . . . . J'oserai faire entendre une voix
> Faible, mais qui, du moins, ne sera point vendue.
> Désormais, ô ma lyre, à jamais détendue,
> Tu ne charmeras plus mes maux et mon ennui !
> Mais, cher à l'innocence, et du faible l'appui,
> Je pourrai quelquefois goûter ce bien suprême :
> Je ferai des heureux.   Eh ! qui dans ce séjour,
> Elevé près de toi, n'en veut faire à son tour,
> Bérardier ? Ce lieu même, où, sur les rives sombres
> Gresset, avant le temps, crut voir errer nos ombres,
> Je l'ai vu sous tes lois, trop tard pour mon bonheur,
> Retracer bien plus tôt le séjour enchanteur
> Des bosquets d'Académe ou l'heureux Elysée.
> Que dis-je ?   Près de toi, doucement abusée,
> L'enfance ici se croit sous le toit paternel.
> O Bérardier, reçois cet adieu solennel ! [1]

[1] The Abbé Bérardier, Principal of the College of Louis-le-Grand, and whom Camille Desmoulins especially loved, was revered and beloved by all his pupils.   In the 'Journal de Paris' of May 13, 1788, we find a letter signed *Brocas, curé de Saint-Benoît*, addressed to 'the authors of the journal,' and dated January 10, which relates that in October the pupils at the college, threatened with the loss of the Abbé Bérardier, and desirous of giving him a last proof of their attachment, resolved to anticipate his birthday, and celebrate it before he should have quitted his post.   They accordingly collected a sum of 696 livres.   But the Abbé Bérardier refused to accept it, and requested them either to take back their subscriptions or to devote this sum to 'some more useful good work.'   'They have,' says the Abbé Brocas, 'willingly adopted the second alternative. In consequence, they have placed in my hands the sum of 696 livres to be employed in procuring the liberty of poor and honest persons in my parish who were threatened with captivity, or already assessed for small debts, and in such other good works as I shall select.'

I have also found in an article by M. Despois this curious indication, that Camille Desmoulins obtained in 1778, at the great *Concours*, an accessit in *Amplification française* (which was the title given to speech-making in the old university).   The *Palmarès*, which was in Latin, according to the ancient custom, cites : *Camilla Benedictus Desmoulins, Guisius, è Collegio Ludovici Magni.*   In the same year the first prize for 'Amplification' was awarded to André Chénier, *Andreas Maria de Chénier, Constantinopolitanus, è Collegio Navarræo.*   Here were two

We are not led by this epistle, of which an account is given in the ' Journal de Paris ' of August 12, 1784, to believe that Camille Desmoulins would have been a poet. His early verses are simply those of a rhetorician ; only valuable from a psychological point of view, as revealing to us the condition of this young mind in the midst of the college of which Camille draws an idyllic picture after the fashion of Gessner :

> Là, du patricien la hauteur est bannie,
> Et la seule noblesse est celle du génie.
> Tous cultivent les dons qu'en eux le ciel a mis ;
> En comptant leurs rivaux ils comptent leurs amis ;
> Leurs talents nous sont chers, leurs succès sont les nôtres.
> Et le laurier d'un seul couronne tous les autres.
> Je vis avec ces Grecs et ces Romains fameux,
> J'étudie une langue immortelle comme eux.
> J'entends plaider encor dans le barreau d'Athènes :
> Aujourd'hui c'est Eschine, et demain Démosthènes.
> Combien de fois, avec Plancius et Milon,
> Les yeux mouillés de pleurs, j'embrassai Cicéron ! [1]

An enthusiast of this sort, on quitting Paris and the class-rooms, must have appeared eccentric and exaggerated to the good people of Guise, and, indeed, he never quite got over the resentment with which their surprised reception of him inspired him. He shows this in many of his letters. He arrived in high spirits, bringing his student's humour and recklessness to the little town ; and he soon found that, with change of place, these had become unseemly. The only recollection he has left in his natal town is of this kind, a not uncommon experience, it must be admitted, in the case

fated laureates. (See M. Despois on Michelet, ' Revue politique,' August 15, 1874.)

[1] M. Ed. Fleury quotes these verses, but his quotation contains two unpardonable errors which are rectified here.

of men whose ideas are in advance of those of their fellow townsmen, and their former friends. Some years ago I received a letter from M. Chérubin, a resident at Guise, which contained some recollections of a very old lady who belonged to one of the most ancient families of Guise, and who had preserved her faculties intact to the extreme limits of human existence. This lady retained a distinct recollection of far distant events, and, when she mentioned Camille Desmoulins, always commented severely on what she called his levity in social relations. In her old age she still resented some of the *risquées* jokes which he had played off in her salon when she was a young woman.

This is probably the tradition that M. Edouard Fleury echoes in his work on 'Camille Desmoulins and Roch Mercandier,' when, in his first volume (page 15), he exhibits Camille as not only frolicsome, jesting and given to levity, but violent, and passionately impatient of all discussion.

'A strange circumstance,' says M. Fleury, 'is related in connection with Desmoulins' enthusiasm. It occurred during a vacation, when he had been passing a few days at the house of a relative. A dinner was given in his honour, to which the local notabilities were invited. A person who was present was aware of the readiness of the young student to be carried away by any discussion upon his favourite heroes, upon the perfections of democratic government, or the sublimities of republican metaphysics ; it was quite an after-dinner amusement to rouse Camille into one of his ready fits of anger by furnishing him with an active, eager, and sincere antagonist. An opportunity offered, and the young man fell into the trap. At first he replied politely and with tolerable calmness ; but when his adversary shook his head ironically as Camille developed what he called new principles, he first became compassionate, then tried to jest, and afterwards, firing up, gave way to his irritation, flinging himself against all obstacles and arguments.   Sarcasms drove him frantic, and "heresies," as he called them, made him lose every atom of self-control.   With eyes aflame, trembling in every limb, and with insult in his words, he rose, flung his dinner-napkin at the head of the obstinate royalist who denied the glory of the Republic, bounded upon the table, smashing all before him, and turned it into a tribune, thus anticipating his future triumphs at the Café de Foi. Thence, undeterred by shouts of laughter from some of the company, the reproaches of others, and the distress of his relatives, he spoke long and excitedly, declaring his convictions, denouncing tyranny, lauding to the skies his ideal idol, repeating all the common-places which had hitherto been relegated to the domain of theory, and which he was speedily to remove into that of practice in the political life of the nation which he helped to push into its excesses.   Streaming with perspiration, and heated with anger, he at length descended from the table, amid a dead silence on the part of some of his hearers, the openly expressed anger of others, and the regret of all that such a scene had taken place.'

The writer from whom we borrow this anecdote was anxious to prove that the natural violence of Camille was such as to lead to those excesses of the pen which we ourselves shall have to condemn.   But M. Fleury is too hasty in his anxiety to paint Camille in dark colours ; he has exaggerated a mere burst of juvenile enthusiasm into which the boy was provoked by the teasing of Madame Godart de Wiége one day during the vacation of 1784, when she had invited Camille Desmoulins tò dinner.   M. Matton the elder, the editor of the works of Camille Desmoulins, gives a much simpler and more veracious account of this scene, which convicts the young student, whose head was full of the ' Philippics of Cicero,' and the ' Révolutions Romaines' of the Abbé Vertol, of nothing more serious than vivacity which was at all events generous.

The 'Révolutions Romaines' of Vertol filled him with admiration. He was completely carried away by those terrible dramas in which the austere face of Brutus and the death-doomed heads of the Gracchi appear each in its turn; by the astonishing and super-human (also inhuman) procession, in which Virginius carries his poniard, Curtius spurs his horse into the gulf, the Fabian brothers fight like the Maccabees of Rome, and Cato falls upon his sword that he may not survive defeat. That long martyrology of heroes had accustomed Camille, and many others, to discern nothing but a pompous tragedy in the eternal strife of humanity. Rome, that antique she-wolf, whose milk we have all drunk, does, in truth, feed an ideal of fierce virtue in man, very different from humble, sound, every-day goodness. In our day, humanity is weary of theatrical heroism, and desirous only of patient labour, of enduring devotion, and of sacrifices to civic duty in which there is nothing sculptural. It is better so. We do not desire to reduce virtue to *bourgeois* proportions, but we think it is time that it should be left to those which are simply human. By this means it will be more surely attained and diffused.

Camille, in all the intoxication of his favourite studies, was in the stage of antique virtue—of the Roman, indeed, the marble kind, if I may say so. He congratulated himself that his parents had given him in his baptism three Roman names, *Camillus, Sulpicius, Lucillus*. He had worn out, or lost, at least six copies of the 'Révolutions Romaines,' by Vertol, and invariably had a volume of the book in his pocket. A copy of the 'Philippics of Cicero' covered with manuscript notes, in which Camille recorded his correct impressions as he read, has been preserved. These two books he was never without.

Thus, hard-working and passionately devoted to learning, Camille concluded his studies brilliantly. He left the College of Louis-le-Grand with regret, which he expresses in his verses, commenced his legal studies immediately, took his bachelor's degree in September 1784, became a licentiate in March 1785, and was sworn in, the same year, as an advocate of the Parliament of Paris. He was then twenty-five years old. We have found but few traces of Camille's beginnings at the bar. He was not born an orator. Admirably gifted as a writer, with a truly astonishing rapidity of thought and of expression, bold, pointed and ready, he was an indifferent speaker, and easily put down. And then he stammered, though not after the ordinary fashion of a stutterer; his was rather the hesitation of a man endeavouring to overcome emotion. He began his phrases, started himself, so to speak, with a reiterated hon! hon! (Lucile gave him the name of Monsieur Hon.) M. Moreau de Jonnés, who died in 1870, aged ninety years, has often told me about Camille Desmoulins' manner of speaking, which he remembered perfectly. At first he was unpleasant to hear, his voice was hard and hesitating, but little by little the stammer lessened, as the orator warmed to his subject, until, when he was fully inspired and carried away by his subject, Camille stammered not at all. He pleaded seldom, and without brilliancy; but the sacred fire of authorship was always alight within him; he incessantly felt the irresistible impulse which puts the pen into the hand as it would put a sword; he flung his projects and his hopes on paper, and lived poorly enough on the product of law-copying which he did for attorneys. We find him composing rhymes for songs, or fabricating epigrams, wandering hither and thither in that great Paris where he dreamed of making a place for himself; to-day he is listening to Beaumarchais' Figaro, in the pit of the theatre, to-morrow seeing Ginguené or Chamfort. Thus he was polishing his arms, he was preparing for the coming assault, he smelt powder in the air; and, perhaps, in his obscurity, in his garret-room, from the gloomy depths of his unknown life, he already told himself, ' I too shall shed my thoughts upon the world !'

III.

The hour had come when the world, shaken, agitated, and giving way in all its parts, began to feel a new germination within it. The task at which the philosophers of the eighteenth century had wrought so ardently was bearing its fruits in the old age of that century. The revolution which had already com-menced in the minds of men was about to enter into the domain of facts, never again to be arrested in its course. In vain should the partisans of the past engage in the strife which still endures; the movement, accele-rated or retarded by turn, according to circumstances, could never thenceforth be impeded. Voltaire, Diderot, the encyclopædists had not vainly sown the seed of their thoughts on barren ground. The harvest was near.

At that time every true French heart hoped for, and desired, a peaceful development of the new and inevitable problems ; but events were about to turn this

fair dream into a tragedy. At the dawn of the year
1789, the nation had only reached the stage of hope ;
and a deep breath of relief was breathed throughout
all France, when Louis XVI. convoked the States
General.[1]

This convocation of the States General—demanded
at the assembly of the Notables, which closed on the
25th May, 1787,—had been formally promised by Louis
XVI. at the Bed of Justice which he held, on the 24th
November, 1787, for the registration of two edicts.
It happened strangely that the king promised this
convocation in the year 1792, and 1792 was the year
which witnessed the destruction of the monarchy.
France, however, was thirsting for many reforms ;
she could not wait five years : 1792 lay too far in
the future.   The date of the convocation was hastened.
The king, yielding to the national will, resolved
to assemble, in January 1789, those States General
which had not met for a period of 175 years (1614), so
that, in the *Dictionnaire universel de la France*, published in 1771, R. de Hesseln, quoted by M. L. La-
lanne, had said, under the heading *Etats* : ' The
States General are obsolete.'   We may therefore imagine with what joy the nation learned that twelve
hundred and seventy-four deputies, three hundred and
eight of the clergy, two hundred and eighty-nine of the
nobility, and six hundred and eighty-one of the commons, or *tiers état*, were about to discuss its interests,
and regulate the new life to which it aspired.   Many
were the dreams of happiness to which this intelligence gave rise.   Nowhere did hope spring up more

---

[1] For information on the condition of Picardy before 1789, it would
be useful to consult a ' Notice sur les Archives civiles de l'Aisne,' compiled by M. Matton, Archivist to the department.

vigorously and brightly than in Picardy (especially in Vermandois and Soissonnais, which had been reduced to great poverty by the severity of the past winter); all the poor people believed that their burthens were immediately to be lifted off their bowed shoulders.

The statements, or *cahiers*, of the provinces, those eloquent voices, the plaints of the multitude, were at length to reach the ears of the king. The peasants, bent, like La Fontaine's wood-cutter, beneath the weight of their load, were to be permitted to appeal and complain, without having to dread death as the only reply to their lamentation. We may picture to ourselves what happy dreams illumined the smoky cabins. ' The king is at length going to learn what we suffer. Our *cahiers* will tell him, and our deputies at Versailles will not fail to repeat it to him. The king informed is the nation saved.' What visions!

This history must confine itself to that spot on which Camille Desmoulins was born. The preparation of the *cahiers* and the nomination of the deputies to the Assembly of the three orders were to take place at Laon, on the 16th March.

At Guise, the first electoral assembly took place on the 5th, and was presided over by M. Desmoulins, lieutenant-general of the bailiwick of Vermandois; M. Saulce was the Procureur du Roi, and M. Mariage, keeper of the records, was the secretary. The roll of the commissaries of parishes showed that two hundred and ninety-two were present.

The second assembly took place in the church of the Friars Minors at Guise. There seventy deputies from Laon to the Assembly of the three orders were nominated. If Camille's father had chosen, he might have been one of those to figure at Versailles.

'The lieutenant-general,' (I quote from the Records-office archives at Laon) 'having been unanimously elected, with the exception of one vote from the parish of Bernot, "applauded that vote as the symbol of liberty," but declined on account of his health, after having testified his sense of the honour done him by such a trust.' Thus, from the commencement, we find this unpretending, wise, and liberal man, refusing those honours which his son was eagerly to desire, and which were destined to cost not only that son, but both, so dear.

On the list of the seventy-five commissaries, deputies to Laon, I find the following names, in the order of their election.

No. 1. Jean-Louis Deviefville des Essarts, advocate, and sub-delegate at Guise.

No. 2. Adrien-Jean-Louis Deviefville, mayor of Guise.

No. 24. Lucie-Simplice-Camille-Benoît Desmoulins, advocate at Guise.[1] Together with these names are those of attorneys, millers, sheep-salesmen, and especially labourers. The man who belongs to the earth, the man of the soil, the *peasant*, comes up out of his furrow for the first time. These were only the preliminary elections, preceding the decisive elections of the deputies to the States General. The report of the assembly of the third estate at Laon registers a letter from the Marquis de Condorcet, who 'demands that a desire for the abolition of the trade in negroes may be introduced into the *Cahier.*' On March 16, 1789, that assembly

---

[1] Therefore Camille will presently sign his 'Ode to the States General,' 'Camille Desmoulins, *advocate*, deputy from the bailiwick of Guise.'

took place at Laon, 'in the hall intended for the public exercises of the College of St. Jean de l'Abbaye.' It was presided over by Caignart du Rotay, lieutenant-general of the bailiwick of Vermandois. Some generous impulses were already perceptible among the members present at these meetings. Caignart du Rotay, in his presidential address, when replying to a deputation of the clergy to the *tiers*, gives us a glimpse of that unhappily brief sacrifice which the electric sitting of the 4th August was to produce. 'We had read your hearts aright,' said he, ' when at the assembly of the third estate on the ninth of this month we announced that it should soon witness the greatness of soul of the two first orders; that it should most infallibly see them hasten to lay the voluntary tribute of their pecuniary privileges at the foot of the throne; that it should behold *this honourable offering to the country!*' Thus it was that several persons, on leaving the place of meeting, hoped that not only the abolition, but the voluntary renunciation of privileges might result from this decisive stroke.

On March 20, 21, and 22 the nomination of deputies to the States General took place : the assembly electing M. Le Carlier, Mayor of Laon ; Viéville des Essarts, deputy from Guise ; Devismes, advocate at Laon ; Bailly, labourer at Crésy-au-Moth ; l'Eleu de la Ville-aux-Bois, councillor to the king, elected in the election at Laon ; Leclare, labourer at Lannois.

We shall speedily find Camille Desmoulins regretting that his father has not just a little spark of ambition,[1] but finding some consolation in reminding

---

[1] Afterwards his memory dwelt upon those days. ' Remember,' he wrote, ' the tears which I have seen in every eye while you were

himself that the deputy from Guise is Viéville, or rather Deviefville des Essarts, sub-delegate from the bailiwick of Guise, his cousin.

The deputies were nominated,—but were their complaints about to be listened to at Versailles ? The *Cahiers* of their corner of French soil contain and repeat the greater part of those complaints which were uttered in common by all France ; and when the entire collection of the statements to the States General shall have been published, we shall be surprised at the unanimity of the protests made by the various portions of that vast, suffering, and oppressed body. It is indeed that 'same cry,' the 'Universal cry' of which Camille was afterwards to speak in his 'France libre.' The *Cahiers* of the States General resemble each other, and demand, for example, 'What purpose does the farm system serve ? That of ruining the people.' Or again ; they complain : 'The distribution of taxes is made by favour. The ecclesiastical estate has all the goods of France and the nobility, and it pays no subsidy either to the State or to the king.' (Complaints and grievances of the commune and inhabitants of the parish of Wissignicourt to be laid before our lords the deputies of His Majesty to the States General, at Laon, 16th March, 1789.) 'If the number of lacqueys and of persons employed in farms were reduced,' said a voice from the district of Monaigu, 'agriculture would be the gainer.' The resigned tone of these almost submissive protests is worthy of notice.

The small parish of Berrieux complains that it has to pay taxes to the amount of 4,545 livres, though it

speaking, when, in your capacity as president, you opened the assembly of your secondary bailiwick ; remember the 297 votes for the deputation which were given to you, out of the number of 298 electors.'

reckons only *one hundred and ten fires*. Many equally glaring cases of injustice existed, and had struck clear-sighted men, long before 1789. 'I know a village, three leagues from Paris,' wrote Grimm, in 1763, twenty years before the general movement of the nation, 'I know a village composed of two hundred fires, in a wine-growing country, and consequently poor,—this village pays to the king, every year, 15,000 livres tollage and capitation tax; the twentieths, the aids, the control, and all the farrago of rates which make up another sum of 15,000 livres. So that the king of France extracts 30,000 livres yearly from one wretched village. There are many princes in Germany who do not receive so much from an entire bailiwick.'[1]

But, perhaps from all France, there arose no cry so tragic, so deep, so grief-laden as that uttered by the inhabitants of the parish of Chaillevois. This dark page merits to be quoted entire.[2] *Ab uno disce omnes.*

---

[1] The bailiwick of Vermandois comprehended in 1789, 274 communes. See Matteville's 'Histoire de Laon.'
The presidential bailiwick was composed as follows :—

> M. Caignart du Rotay, Lieutenant-General.
> M. Dogny, Lieutenant of Police.
> M. Pelée de Tréville, Criminal Lieutenant.
> M. François, Lieutenant Assessor.
> M. L'Eleu,
> M. Laurent,
> M. De Martigny,
> M. De la Campagne, } Councillors.
> M. Dagneau,
> M. Romain,
> M. Fouant, Procureur du Roi.
> M. Delattre de Motte, King's advocate.
> M. Dumoutier, Clerk.

[2] 'If, at harvest time, and after the gleaning,' say the complaints of Berrieux, 'a poor person who has a cow and no litter to give it, should be found gathering the stubble stalks, he is mercilessly punished; and if,

'The community of Chaillevois is composed of about 200 persons, fathers, mothers, children, and grand-children. The most part of the inhabitants have no property whatever, those who have any possess so little that it is not worth talking about ; they are almost all vine-growers—that is to say, they work at the vines as labourers. A vine-grower may cultivate an acre of vines at most ; he pays for the cultivation of an acre of vines of one hundred rods the sum of fifty livres, beside five livres for the dressing of the vines until the vintage, after the principal culture, and five livres for digging after the vintage, sum total sixty livres. The vine-grower is occupied in this culture from February 15 until the middle of November, nine months of the year ; it is true that anyone who is capable of harvesting work may do it in this interval ; if he be a good workman his harvest work will be worth forty francs : if he finds opportunity for doing some other day-work in the other three months it will be so little that it is not worth reckoning in the account, and thus it is evident from this statement that the entire gain of a vine-grower is reduced to one hundred livres a year. Supposing that the wife earns one-half that sum, which cannot be supposed if she has several children, their earnings will amount to 150 livres, with which they and their children must be lodged, fed, and clothed. The ordinary food is bread steeped in salt water ; it is needless to say the bread is not buttered ; as for meat, it is never tasted except on Shrove Tuesday, Easter Sunday, and the feast day of the patron saint, at a wedding,

in winter, a man kills a crow, he is severely punished under pretext that by firing a gun he might set the village on fire, and that he is forbidden to carry arms. But if a servant of the great house wants his diversion, shots may be heard all over the village, and there is no pretence of danger. We know that the gentry have their rights of the chase, but we doubt whether the privilege extends to their servants.'

'At the time in question, wine not being always consumed on the spot, and means of transport being scarce, the barrels were emptied over the fields to preserve the casks. We have seen the same thing done in our childhood at Perigord. Since then railroads have turned the vine-growing countries into wealthy districts.' (J. C.)

'Correspondance littéraire et philosophique,' vol. iii. p. 411, concerning a paper entitled 'La Richesse de l'Etat,' by M. Roussel, councillor to the Parliament.

or when a man works at the wine-press for his master. A man may sometimes eat *haricots* and beans when the master does not forbid them to be grown among his vines. The king's charges in tollage and capitation tax amount to six livres, not including the *corvée* ; and he who has absolutely nothing is obliged to pay for a pound of salt fourteen or fifteen sols, according to the number of his children.

' One year he must buy a pound each week, another year a pound each fortnight ; one year more, another less ; this price is enormous, and causes many to be unable even to eat what is called soup. If, unhappily, either the husband or the wife have contracted the habit of using snuff, it is only by' depriving themselves and their children of bread that they can procure a few ounces from time to time. If a poor vine-grower falls sick, all his means fail ; if he sends for a surgeon, he will charge him more than he can earn in a week for a journey, for bleeding him, for a dose of medicine ; if he be summoned by anyone for a debt or any other cause, he must pay the process-server more than he can earn in two weeks, and a sentence of any kind must utterly ruin him ; his greatest scourge is justice. If he makes a piece of wine he must not sell it by the bottle, and he may die of hunger while waiting for a customer to purchase it in the piece ; and even if he sells it so, he must give seven or eight livres to the farmer. This is how the common people live under the best of kings, and in the midst of a nation which boasts to be the most generous of all nations, in an age in which nothing is talked of but humanity and beneficence ; and nevertheless the common people are the most precious portion of the nation, because it is they who do the most work ; but the fate of working people is almost the same everywhere, they have barely bread to eat, water to drink, straw to sleep on, and a hut to shelter them. Their condition is worse than that of the savages in America. If the king did but know the value of three sols, and that there are millions of inhabitants in his kingdom who, by working from morning to night, cannot earn three sols to live upon, for that is evident from the calculation just made ! Such are the griefs of the inhabitants of Chaillevois. May God grant that their complaint may touch the hearts of

His Majesty and of the States General who are about to be assembled to work the regeneration of France.

'In which faith we have signed :

'Joseph Flamant ; Balidoux ; Flamant ;

'Aubin ; Druet ; Joseph Payen.' [1]

Was this touching complaint ever read, this lamentation of the 'common people,' so fitted to 'touch the heart of His Majesty,' and to give to the future a true picture of the lamentable state of things which the Revolution was about to destroy ? We often speak, from the depths of our national trouble—(and without correcting ourselves in order that we may attain to it),—of the *regeneration* of France ; but they had a better right than we to talk of it, they, who like the poor people of Chaillevois had ' barely bread to eat, water to drink, and straw to sleep upon,' and who contented themselves by uttering in the hearing of Louis XVI. those words, solemn as a passing bell, ' *If the king did but know the value of three sols.*'

When we have read the Mémoires du Marquis d'Argenson, there is nothing to astonish us in complaints like these. For a long time the government of France had been, as D'Argenson said. in 1751, a ' *spendthrift anarchy*,' and the Court also, according to the Marquis, the 'tomb of the nation,' the tomb of those poor creatures of whom La Bruyère speaks, who creep of nights into their lair, and live on black bread, roots, and water.

Poverty, mortal, hideous, incredible, rose like a tide.

---

[1] M. Claretie gives this touching and terrible document in the original form, and with the extraordinary orthography, which makes it difficult to read. The directness, simplicity, and good sense of the statement contrast strangely with the ignorance of the undoubtedly capable men who drew it up. (Translator.)

This complaint will be found in the original among the complementary documents.

The curé of a village writes in his parish register in 1709 : ' I certify to all those whom it may concern, that all the persons who are named in this parish register have died of famine, with the exception of M. Discrots and his daughter.' And then he adds a note to this effect: ' The people have been eating dead carrion for a fortnight past ; there is no corn, and women have smothered their children for dread of having to feed them.'[1]

Thirty years later, D'Argenson writes that want and misery advance within the kingdom to an unheard-of degree ; men die, he says, ' as thick as flies, of poverty, and the living are eating grass.' The first president of the Court of Taxes, Le Camus, in his harangue to the king, ventured to bring under the eyes of His Majesty ' the people who were groaning in their wretchedness without food or money, obliged to dispute their sustenance with the beasts of the field.' D'Argenson was yet to say in his glowing emphatic manner that 'the peasants are no longer aught but poor slaves, beasts of burden fastened to a yoke.' In ten years, pestilence having come to the aid of famine, the population of France had diminished one-third, and the two remaining thirds were bowed down with want. In 1752, on a certain occasion when the king and queen and the dauphiness were going to Notre Dame, a poor man clung to their carriages and held out a loaf of black bread for them to see. ' Misery, famine !' he cried ; 'see what they make us pay three sous a pound for.' Was not this like a prologue to those days when the people should go to Versailles to seek the

---

[1] See ' La Famine de 1709 dans le val de la Loire' (*Mémoires de la Société d'Emulation de Moulins*).

Ed. Scherer, ' Etude sur d'Argenson et la France sous Louis XV.'

'baker,' the 'baker's wife, and the 'little baker's-man.'
The starving multitude was already exasperated.
'When the people no longer fear anything, they are
everything,' said D'Argenson, and added in a tone of
true prophecy : 'All these materials are combustible.'
Again he said, after 1751 : 'A disturbance may give
place to a revolt, and the revolt to a total revolution,
when real tribunes of the people may be elected, and
the king and his ministers be despoiled of their *excessive
power to do harm.*'   And again, later : 'The revolution
is certain ; there is nothing left *but to detach oneself
from one's country*, and to prepare to pass under the
rule of other masters.'   The revolutionists, at least, so
far from detaching themselves from their country,
attached themselves to her more closely and stronger
than ever, and would have none but her for their
sovereign and mistress.

But in the meantime expiring France was uttering
poignant lamentations.

While the poor people, La Bruyère's '*animals
with human faces,*' lived, or rather languished thus, a
heartless, frivolous, worthless society, steeped in pleasure, whirled about the summit of the weird edifice of
which the suffering multitude formed the base.   The
time was not far off when the publication of the
'Livre rouge' was destined to disclose into whose hands
the public money passed, and for whom the toiling
masses worked.[1]   Mistresses, abbés, marshals, nurses,

---

[1] The 'Red Book,' or list of secret pensions paid by the Treasury,
contained the names and quality of the pensioners, the nature of their
services, and observations upon the motive which had led to their being
pensioned.   It was printed at the Royal press in 1790.   This book,
printed in red, appeared in sections.   It gave rise to the publication of a
Cahier, in 8vo, entitled 'Coup d'œil sévère mais juste sur le livre intitulé
le Livre Rouge.'   The author writes : 'These are vengeances unworthy

procuresses, pimps, readers to the queen, croziered and
mitred personages, received pensions, some of them
enormous ; many reversionary, or else gratuitous
donations, and wealth in kind. 'M. Ducrot, hair-
dresser,' Camille Desmoulins tells us, 'received a retiring pension of 1700 livres, for his services as hair-
dresser to Mademoiselle d'Artois, who died at three
years old, before she had any hair, and Mademoiselle
X—— enjoyed 1500 livres per annum, because she
once washed the late Dauphin's ruffles. (' Révolutions
de France et de Brabant,' No. 20, page 227.) [1]   All this

of a National Assembly. Nevertheless it is only by letting light in
everywhere that truth is reached. 'Truth, that is my god !' was the
motto of the editor of the 'Livre Rouge.'

[1] This is no calumny on the part of Desmoulins ; all historians, worthy of
credit, agree upon the point. (Lacretelle, 'Histoire du dix-huitième Siècle,'
vol. iv. p. 274 ; Droz, vol i. p. 66 ; Henri Martin, 4th edit. vol. xvi. p. 298 ;
Michelet, 'Révolution Française,' vol. i. pp. 76, 126, 270.) We will
be satisfied with quoting Droz, who is certainly not to be suspected of
exaggeration :

'Terray prohibited exportation in a certain province, and grain fell in
price ; then he bought a quantity, and sold it again in a certain other
province which he had starved by exciting exportation from it. Louis XV.
resorted to the same kind of traffic to increase his private wealth.
Louis XV. was subject to a curious aberration of mind, which led him to
regard himself as two distinct personages, the man and the king, and the
man frequently speculated, and gambled in stock-jobbing against the
king and against France. The 'Almanach National' for 1774 disclosed
the name of an individual designated as *Treasurer of grain on the king's
account,* and thereby excited horror. The indiscretion of the printer
was punished, but the manuscript page had been read at the General
Controller's office, and, doubtless, a clerk, worthy of Terray, had seen
nothing to be surprised at in the fact that Louis XV. traded on the bread
of his subjects.

In 1781, Mirabeau loudly stigmatised this infamous speculation by
Louis le bien aimé. 'The king,' he said, 'horrible to think of, the king,
not only authorising, but practising a monopoly at the expense of the sub-
sistence of his people.'—*Lettres de Cachet,* chap. xii. p. 303.

And again in Note 35, p. 317, he quotes, as proof, the express official
mention which is made in the 'Almanach Royal' of 1773, of the *sieur*
Mirlavaud as *Treasurer of grain on the king's account.* On this indication,
afforded by Mirabeau, incredulous persons have searched the ' Almanach

is apart from the fact that the king, as stated in ' La France Libre,' publicly claimed the monopoly of grain ! ' Oh, a fine time, and a splendid reign ! ' exclaims the annotator, ' but what will posterity say ? '

Posterity will remember favourably for the king that when he signed the ' Decree concerning the Convocation of the States General of the Kingdom,' July 5th, 1788, his desire was to try to give a more liberal form to the government of France ; but posterity will likewise remember, with reproach, how this same monarch yielded to those who pursued the new ideas with hatred as active as it was stupid.   Posterity will declare it deplorable that from 1789, the country, suffering and dislocated, but unanimous in its desires, was not permitted to hail the advent of the definitive reign of liberty.   Guilty indeed are they who oppose to such desires their private repugnance and resistance. Malouet, who was averse to excess of any kind, who was one of the most moderate men in the National Assembly, of whom Burke said that he was the best ' who had watched by the bedside of the dying monarchy,' pointed out to the ministers of Louis XVI, the line of conduct which they ought to have adopted. ' The will of France,' said he, ' has summoned the States General ; it is indispensable that that will should be obeyed.   You have been forced to invoke the counsel and the succour of the nation, *you cannot go on any longer without the nation* ; from its strength you must

Royal ' for 1773, and not having found any such entry, have pretended that the fact alleged by him was false.   They are correct in stating that the almanack for 1773 does not contain the important item, but they would have only had to look in that for 1774, the last which appeared under Louis XV., to discover it.   The table of contents also includes (p. 571 B) the title of the office : *Treasurer of grain on the king's account.* The almanack for 1773 does not include it.—See Prudhomme, Introduction to ' Révolutions de Paris,' p. 34.

draw your own.' The monarchy might, perhaps, have been saved, if the advisers of the king had comprehended that, thenceforth, agreement between the king and the nation was necessary, and that neither material nor moral forces were on the side of the past. But it is bootless to speculate upon the point. It was fated that Louis XVI. should allow himself to be dragged to his destruction by her whom *Monsieur* (the Count of Provence), and the pamphleteers inspired by him, dubbed *The Austrian*, before the people, imitating the court, gave her that name ; and by men who, like M. de Montmorin, seemed bent on ruining that monarchy which, in their blindness they believed they served.

Great political excitement had been caused by the convocation of the States General. Pamphlets cropped up in all directions. Did not the Decree of the 5th of July, 1788, say: His Majesty 'invites all the learned and instructed persons of his kingdom, and especially those who compose the Academy of Inscriptions and *belles-lettres*, to address information and memorials on the objects of the present decree to the Keeper of the Seals' ? Men's brains seem to have taken fire like gunpowder. All the 'heads big with folios,' as Camille Desmoulins says, began to bring forth. Mangourit, with his 'Tribun du peuple au peuple,' sounded the first drum-tap. Count Avenel d'Entraigues published a quasi-republican 'Mémoire.' The writings of Necker, Mirabeau, and the Marquis de Beauvau, in which they put the ideas which were common to the great mass of the nation in circulation ; —such as the equalisation of taxation, and abolition of exemptions—were re-printed, or re-read. •The work of Linguet, the adversary of the Bastille, in which he attacked privileges, apropos of the land tax, and fiercely combated the fiscal system of the old régime, was warmly discussed. The famous pamphlet by Siéyès, ' Qu'est-ce que le Tiers Etat ? ' was, it may be said without exaggeration, in almost every hand. Thirty thousand copies of it were sold in three weeks. Cérutti, Target, Rabaut Saint-Etienne ; Servan, Thouret at Rouen ; Volney in Brittany ; Clavière, Condorcet, Brissot, all brought their contingent of militant pamphlets to swell the mass of writings which were read and commented upon everywhere, with feverish eagerness. Carra already ventured to write, in the ' Orateur pour les Etats-Généraux,' ' The People is the true sovereign, and the King is only his head clerk.'

What was Camille Desmoulins doing at this time ? Had his spirit not taken fire at such a spectacle ? In the list of the most influential of the political writings which preceded the opening of the States General, I find (see the ' Introduction Historique' to the ' Moniteur ') a pamphlet enumerated : ' La Philosophie au Peuple Français,' par M. Desmoulins, 1788.

A thought of Seneca's forms the epigraph to this essay : *Expergiscamur ut errores nostros coarguere possimus. Sola autem nos philosophia excitabit, sola somnum excutiet gravem.*—Seneca, *de Philosophia.*

The ' Moniteur' quotes a passage from this essay, which enables us to judge of the whole.

' It is time that you should lift up your head, and keep it uplifted ; it is time that you should re-enter into your rights, and recover your original liberty (this phrase is fine, and denotes the Desmoulins of " la France Libre ") ; the enterprise is formèd, the first movements are made ; but that is not enough ; you must resist until you shall be certain of your triumph. Ah, how much to be pitied you would be, if you should ever give way before your enemies! You would then be a hundred times more miserable than, you were before you ever dreamed of shaking off your chains. You would fall back into the sad and shameful servitude of your ancestors,' &c.

'The author,' adds the 'Moniteur,' 'proceeds to develope the principles of a plan for a Constitution.'

Is this pamphlet really written by Camille? In my opinion, it is impossible to doubt it. In 1788, Desmoulins was twenty-eight years old; he was still un-known, and 'disposable;' active, and a ready writer. How can it be supposed that the general fever had not infected him, impelling him to write, and proclaim his ideas upon the future Constitution? It would have been difficult for an advocate, and a man of letters, to keep silence at a moment when all France was talking.[1] Almost at the same time, Camille's enthusiasm for the States General, who would—as, in common with the majority of the nation, he believed—secure the welfare of the country, Camille's admiration of the 'tribunes' inspired him with an Ode, which for a long time defied all my researches, but which at length I had the good fortune to find, and which I have reprinted in my edition of the 'Works of Camille Desmoulins.' The ode is but indifferent poetry, like all the verses which bear the signature of Desmoulins, but it has the interest of a symptom, and it indicates the position, in 1788, of those rare spirits which an exclusively classical education had prepared for the love, if not for the clear conception of the Republic.

---

[1] The author's phrase, 'en un moment où la parole était à la France toute entière,' is untranslateable. It is equivalent to our parlia-mentary expression, 'catching the Speaker's eye.' (Translator).

In the Ode, Camille Desmoulins lauds the king, whose desire is to put truth in the place of falsehood.

> ' Cher prince, des rois le modèle,
> Eh bien nous doutions de ta foi,
> Et qu'au-dessus de Marc-Aurèle
> La France dût placer son roi ! '

Satire, bitter and sad, upon the condition of the nation, has, however, a larger place in the poem than the praises of the sovereign who has hearkened to the prayers of the people :—

> ' Pour les nobles, toutes les grâces,
> Pour toi, peuple, tous les travaux,'

says Camille, and continues in the same key :—

> ' L'homme est estimé par les races,
> Comme les chiens et les chevaux.
> Pourtant, au banquet de la vie
> Les enfants qu'un père convie
> Au même rang sont tous assis :
> Le ciel nous fit de même argile,
> Et c'est un fil aussi fragile,
> Que tourne pour eux Lachésis.
>
> L'impôt prend sa course incertaine :
> Dans le parc et dans le château
> Il ne pose son pied qu'à peine,
> Et foule vingt fois le hameau.
> Ton glaive trop longtemps repose :
> Du pauvre prends enfin la cause,
> Venge Naboth, Dieu protecteur ! '

Necker 'comes down from the mountain,' accompanied by Reason, and with the tables in his hand, like Moses, he is about to overthrow the golden calf :—

> La peuple sort de dessous l'herbe :
> Déjà, de ses mille cités,

Il voit, plein d'un espoir superbe,
Partir ses mille députés.
La Prière lente et boîteuse
De son succés, n'est plus douteuse,
Elle a monté devant Louis.

Then Camille addresses the deputies in conclusion :—

Tonnez, et tribuns de la plèbe
De l'esclavage et de la glèbe,
Effacez les restes honteux !

These were not the only verses written at this period by Camille Desmoulins. The collection entitled 'Satires, ou Choix des meilleures Pièces de vers qui ont précédé et suivi la Révolution (32 p., in 8vo., à Paris, l'an I de la Liberté, avec gravures),' contains several pieces signed with the name of Desmoulins. There are some infamous verses among the number ; and Camille's biographer, M. Ed. Fleury, does not hesitate to accuse him of them, although Camille, in the twenty-ninth number of his 'Révolutions de France et de Brabant,' vigorously defends himself against the charge of having written them. He denounces these verses as 'shameless' and 'cynical,' and adds, 'some of them are disgustingly gross.' And he concludes thus :—

'The libeller has adopted an epigraph taken from Voltaire, but he would be better fitted with the saying of Desfontaines : "Every one must live." When shall we have a good law on the liberty of the press ? However great my regard for liberty, I am forced to feel how much danger it may conceal when I see my name set down three times at the bottom of sets of verses in this infamous collection.'[1]

The 'Ode to the States General' attracted very

---

[1] There is, however, in the 'Recueil,' a set of verses in which it is impossible not to recognise the peculiar turn of Camille's humour, when cured of his affection for Louis XVI., whom he no longer compares to

little attention, and Desmoulins was probably somewhat piqued. The epoch was coming, however, which
was to bring him his hour. I can see Camille wandering about Paris, which already began to smell of
gunpowder ; coming and going to and fro ; rushing
off to Versailles, where the deputies were assembling,
his imagination excited by the solemn procession, on
which the May sun shone brightly, on the eve of the
opening of the States General ;[1] returning to Paris,
where every one was in a ferment ; listening to the
talk in the streets, and the discourse of the politicians
of the café Procope ; gliding among the excited groups
which thronged the Palais-Royal ; then going to the
clubs, and cafés, attracted by the pleasure of listening
to 'the admirable plans of the zealous citizens.' How
high must the pulses of the young man have bounded!
for he was certain of his strength, full of spirit and
talent, burning with ambition, 'inflaming others' (to
use his own expression,) and 'inflaming himself.'

Marcus Aurelius. Two years later, in 1790, Desmoulins wrote a satire
upon the King and Queen. (See 'Complementary Documents.') These
verses contain mere amenities compared with those which the 'Recueil
des Satires' attributes to Camille and to Marie-Joseph Chénier.

[1] 'Yesterday was one of the brightest days of my life,' wrote Camille
to his father, May 5, 1789. 'One must have been a very bad citizen not
to have taken part in the festivity of that sacred day. I think if I had
come from Guise to Paris only to see the procession of the Three Orders,
and the opening of the States General, I should not grudge the pilgrimage.
I have only one regret, that you are not among the deputies. One of my
school-fellows has been more fortunate than I—De Robespierre, deputy
from Arras. He has been wise enough to plead in his own province.'
And again, ' I have felt very spiteful towards you, and your gravel. Why
have you shown so little eagerness to obtain so great an honour? That
was the first of my griefs.'

Camille adds afterwards : ' I wrote yesterday to Mirabeau to get
myself made, if possible, one of the staff of the famous gazette of all that
is about to take place at the States General. They are subscribing to it
here by thousands, and it will bring the author 100,000 crowns, people
say. Shall I subscribe for you ? '

Châteaubriand, who saw him at this time, paints him for us in his ' Mémoires d'outre Tombe ' in repellant colours, as ' sallow, shabby, and needy.' Things were indeed going hard, just then, with Camille. This was a time of darkness, uncertainty ; of hope suddenly cast down, of despondency, followed by nervous excitement. He had already in his head his first successful pamphlet, ' La France Libre,' and he wrote to his father that it occupied him wholly. I see him, in my mind's eye, at Versailles, during the two days, Monday, the twenty-second, and Tuesday, the twenty-third of June, 1789, when the deputies, shut out of the hall where the ' séances royales ' took place, were running about the streets in search of a room where they might assemble. What fiery anger must have filled his Picard soul on seeing the representatives of the nation so treated ; but what enthusiasm must have succeeded to that anger when he heard them take their famous oath, never to separate until they should have founded the liberty of their country !

' They all exhibited ' (he writes to his father, in his letter of June 24) ' a Roman firmness, and are determined to seal our liberties with their blood. All Paris is aflame. The Palais-Royal is as full as an egg ; the Duke of Orleans is received with transports of applause. The King passes by, but all is silence ; M. Bailly, President of the Assembly, appears, the crowd clap their hands and cry, *Vive la Nation !* '

In these letters we follow the revolution step by step. We feel the pulse of feverish Paris. Very soon Camille will write : ' The conflagration is spreading. *Jam proximus ardet Ucalegon.* The guards, who have fraternised with the people, are torn away from the prison of the Abbaye. Already, even in this very month of June, the question of marching on the

Bastille and Vincennes is mooted.' Camille, who is carried away by the current, writes to his father, a friend of the Prince de Condé, who dined frequently at M. Desmoulins' house at Guise : ' *Your Prince de Condé dares not appear.* He is reviled, laughed at, hissed, lampooned.' In the same letter, Camille draws a picture of Paris in those days, which he himself afterwards called '*the dog-days,*' with a quick, skilful, picturesque, thoroughly French touch :—

'A few days ago a Countess was whipped in the Palais-Royal, where she was holding forth against M. Necker. Relays of talkers with stentorian voices succeed each other there every evening. They read the strongest things that have been written each day about the business of the time. The silence is only interrupted by *bravos* at the most powerful passages. Then the patriots cry *Bis!* Three days ago a child of four years old, full of intelligence and well-taught, was carried round the garden at least twenty times, in broad daylight, on a porter's shoulders, crying out, " By decree of the French people, Polignac is exiled to one hundred leagues from Paris ; Condé, *idem* ; Conti, *idem* ; D'Artois, *idem* ; the Queen "—but I dare not go on ! '

This ferment of the populace produced some terrible results. Presently we find Camille relating the *exemplary punishment* inflicted at the Palais-Royal on a police spy.

'He was stripped, and found to have been whipped and branded. The people found a whip on him, one of those whipcord handcuffs which these wretches use. They flung him into the basin, and then forced him like a stag in the water ; they flung stones at him, rained blows of their canes on him ; one of them struck his eye out of the socket. At last, notwithstanding his cries and entreaties for mercy, they flung him back into the basin. His sufferings lasted from midday to half-past five, and he had fully ten thousand tormentors.'

What furious madness that must be which seizes on a crowd at certain times, when Camille Desmoulins could be infected by it to such an extent that he experienced none of the rage and disgust with which this hideous crime ought to have inspired a man like him. He was carried away by the frenzy of the 'ten thousand tormentors.' A little later, and he will see that the *punishment* inflicted upon the police spy is but the prologue to other crimes of the same kind. Who can tell but that there were some of the future 'September murderers' among the people who expended their rage for five hours upon a half-dead wretch?

In the meantime the war was going on and organising itself. On the one side, three camps were formed around Paris, with parks of artillery, like that at the bridge of Sèvres; on the other, motions were made, and speeches delivered. 'It rains pamphlets, each more bright than the others,' writes Desmoulins. 'The soldiers are mingling with the people. The universal cry is *Vive le tiers état!*' Camille, having worked hard at his pamphlet 'La France Libre,' handed it over to his publisher on the twentieth of June. This man, whose name was Momoro, already styled himself *the first printer of the national liberty.* He was nevertheless a very prudent printer, and he, who was afterwards to accuse Camille of being a 'moderate,' and to become a Hébertist in '93, refused, in '89, to publish Desmoulins' work. He declared that it was too venturesome. Poor Camille was wild with anger. 'If I had the means,' he writes to his father, 'I would buy a printing-press, so much am I disgusted at the monopoly of these rascals.'

Momoro, however, the honest tradesman, who, we are told by Arnault, loaded pistols, saying, 'these are for people who bring bills,' though he hesitates and trembles on the eve of the fourteenth of July, when the patriots are menaced by Swiss and German regiments, will be totally free from nervousness after the taking of the Bastille ; and ' La France Libre,' printed since the beginning of June, 1789 will be sold freely after July 18, when the people have won.   This prudent Momoro was essentially one of those who, according to the sage precept of Mathurin Regnier, knew how to trim his sails according to the wind.

The taking of the Bastille was about to confer sudden popularity upon Camille Desmoulins ; he was soon to climb upon the table in the garden of the Palais-Royal and to make it the pedestal of his fame.   The Palais-Royal was, as we have seen, the burning centre, the very heart of the Paris of '89.   Newsmongers, suggesters of motions, speechifiers, and agitators elbowed each other around the Cracovian tree. There, where Diderot had formerly conversed with Rameau's nephew, Saint-Huruge now disputed with Fournier the American ; and the feverish, excited crowd gathered about, every one who had anything to tell or to say, in the busy, nervous, easily-moved groups which always collect in stormy times.

The relative situation of the court and the nation was, in July 1789, very much ' strained.'   Necker, who was popular, and at that time devoted to the interests of the people,[1] was endeavouring to withdraw the king

---

[1] Necker, the favourite of the nation, had also been a favourite with the nobles.   The general liking for him was of long standing. A few days after he was, for the first time, dismissed from Calonne's Ministry (May 1781), the Duchess de Lauzun, who was the gentlest of women, and remarkably timid, was seen to attack an unknown individual in a public garden, whom she had overheard speaking ill of Necker.

from that '*buzzing of counsel, violent of project, but without capacity of execution,*' of which Malouet speaks.

Louis XVI., instead of yielding to the superior wisdom of Necker, leaned, quite evidently, to the side of those who talked of using severe measures ; or rather, the king was, to use the expression of his brother, the future Louis XVIII., to the Count de la Marck, like a *ball of oiled ivory*, which would slip through one's fingers.

'The disdain with which the popular party was was talked of at court,' says Malouet, 'persuaded the princes to believe that they had only to put on their hats to disperse it, and when the moment came they did not even know how to put on their hats.' The king, who sometimes actually pretended to sleep while his councillors were talking, in order to disguise his feebleness and hesitation, did, however, for once, take the more violent course : he did put on his hat. Necker was sacrificed ; the dismissed minister was even required to leave France.

When Paris learned that its favourite had been exiled, the popular wrath was great. The Palais-Royal fever redoubled. It was no longer ferment, it had become fury. Sunday, the twelfth of July, was destined to cost Royalty dear.

Camille Desmoulins, angry and resolute, in the midst of a fiery group, and fiery like themselves, stimulating his neighbours, and stimulated by them, alive to every symptom of the anger of the multitude, and impelled by those who immediately surrounded him, made himself the mouthpiece of all. He jumped upon a table, and addressed the mob, conquering his habitual stammer in the enthusiasm of the moment. 'Citizens !' he cried, 'you know that the whole nation had demanded that Necker should be preserved to it! I have just returned from Versailles—Necker is dismissed! This dismissal is the tocsin of the St. Bartholomew of the patriots. To-night, the Swiss and German battalions will come forth from the Champ de Mars to massacre us. There is not a moment to lose! We have only one resource; it is to arm ourselves instantly, and to put on cockades by which we may recognise one another.' 'I was choked by a multitude of ideas which surged up in my brain all at once,' wrote Desmoulins two days later, 'and I spoke without any method, but my burning words went straight to the heart of the crowd.' So then, this unknown young man, black haired and with keen black eyes, sparkling with life, entered suddenly into history by a fiery improvisation, giving voice in his ardent vehemence to all the anger pent up in the breasts of the six thousand citizens who stood around him. The outrage had been inflicted upon all, but one single voice uttered the cry of protest in the name of the entire nation.

'What colours will you have for our rallying signal?' continued Desmoulins. 'Will you have green, the colour of hope, or blue, the blue of Cincinnatus, the colour of American liberty, and of democracy?' The crowd responded, 'green! green! green cockades!' And so the Revolution commenced, as the Spring commences.

Camille was the first to fasten a green ribbon into his hat. The trees of the garden, stripped of their leaves in a twinkling, furnished the electrified citizens with cockades. It was like a shower of verdure under the lime trees. The sun shone upon this new summer fashion, and Camille, animated, brilliant, still standing on the table, above the heads of the shouting crowd, drew two pistols from under his coat, and showing them to the people, cried : ' My friends ! the police are here ! They observe, they watch me. Well then, it is I who call my brethren to liberty ! But I will not fall alive into the hands of the police ! Let all good citizens imitate me ! To arms ! To arms ! '

The spark had been struck out ![1] It had fallen from the table which citizen Beaubourg, who was showing Camille up at the back, was afterwards to call *the magic table*. Camille crossed the garden, followed by the crowd, who formed an escort for him. This young man of twenty-nine years old, with the green ribbon in his hat, draws them after him ; henceforth, they shall follow him whithersoever he leads them ; in him are incarnate now, and shall be incarnate for the future— the Revolution and Hope.

All Paris was on foot. The Prince de Lambesc added to the popular ferment, by sabreing the exasperated crowd at the Pont Tournant ; and several charges of the Royal Allemand regiment helped to drive the people into insurrection. The soldiers were received on the first occasion with showers of stones, on the next they will have to encounter swords and guns. Camille scoured the boulevards, sweeping along with him a growing torrent of furious men. The playhouses were closed, as a sign of public mourning. The crowd invaded the Opera, and insisted on having the curtain put down. Some went to the sculptors' waxwork galleries, and carrying off the busts of Necker and the Duke of Orleans, they covered them with black

---

[1] ' I got down from the table half smothered with embraces ; some pressed me to their hearts, others bathed me with their tears ; a citizen of Toulouse, fearing for my life, declared that he would never leave me.'—Camille Desmoulins, *Le Vieux Cordelier*, No. 5.

veils, and paraded them through Paris. The artist-
people of Paris must always have a *mise-en-scène.*

The night fell. The great city, patrolled and
guarded by divisions of soldiers of the watch, of
gardes-françaises, and of the corps of armed citizens,
rested but badly, being disturbed by shots fired at in-
tervals. What did they mean? They meant that the
respectively inimical patrols, meeting in the darkness,
had come to loggerheads. On all sides were heard
dismal sounds, the threatening cries of night warfare,
and heavy blows were struck upon the shutters of the
shops. These were the appeals of the patriots to the
gunmakers, whom they forced to open their establish-
ments, and furnish arms to the first-formed battalions
of the urban guard. Camille Desmoulins, with General Danican, was at the head of those troublers of the
night. ' I had,' says he, in ' Le Vieux Cordelier,' ' at that
time all the daring of the Revolution.'

Meanwhile, Versailles was preparing for the strife.
The king's body-guards passed the night in battle ar-
ray. The bridge at Sèvres was protected by cannon.
Orders were issued to blow it up if it could not be defended. On Monday morning, 13th July, Paris was
swarming with men armed with guns, sticks, pikes,
swords, and pistols. The armourers had given up everything, even their old halberds. All these did not suffice,
and it became known that on the 14th the mob would
go to the Hôtel des Invalides, to seize the arms. So
large an armed force, let loose in Paris, might prove
terribly dangerous. Among the frantic multitude
were many who talked of setting fire to the hotels of
the aristocrats. The Hôtel de Breteuil and the Palais-
Bourbon were already menaced. The Electors, assembled at the Hôtel de Ville, protected the city from

this pressing danger ; they made order out of disorder itself, by creating a corps of citizen-militia consisting of 78,000 men, divided into sixteen legions. The Marquis de la Salle was elected commander-in-chief, and the Chevalier de Saudray second in command of this militia, which afterwards became the National Guard.

This citizen-guard admirably comprehended the part it had to play. On the same evening, it disarmed forty men, who could not give an account of themselves, but the greater number of whom had pillaged the house of the Lazarists that morning, and under pretext of finding corn hidden in the cellars, had broken into them and gorged themselves with wine.[1]

Now come citizens, ' of every rank, of every order, of every age,' to inscribe their names upon the list of the ' soldiers of the country,' and to adorn themselves with the green cockade which Camille Desmoulins has just invented, as though he were the poet of the Revolution. This cockade will speedily be replaced by blue and red cockades and ribbons, the colours of the good city of Paris, the green being rejected because it is the colour of the Count d'Artois. A little later, when white, the king's colour, shall have been added, the tricolour cockade will have been invented, that tricolour which accompanies our standards all over the world, and, linked with the destiny of our dear France, shares all its glory, and all its humiliation. The standards of the city are unfurled, the tocsin rings out, salvos of artillery are fired, the faubourgs are barricaded (how long before had D'Argenson predicted those

---

[1] Thirty wretched men and women were found the following day drowned in promiscuous heaps, or expiring in floods of wine.—See ' Le Moniteur' (July 17-20, 1789).

barricades ?), three thousand of the ' Gardes-françaises ' go boldly over to the ranks of the people ; every bit of iron in Paris is turned into a weapon; lead is melted down into bullets, and the Permanent Committee of Electors continues to watch over the city, which is filled with tumult and the stir of arms.

During the strife of those terrible days, many magnificent deeds of heroism were performed, which are now forgotten. At two o'clock in the morning of July 14, some people came to the Hôtel de Ville and announced that 15,000 men from the faubourg were coming along the Rue St. Antoine, towards the Place de Grève, to take possession of the Hôtel de Ville.

'They shall not take it,' said Le Grand de Saint-René, one of the Electors, 'for I will blow it up first.'

He made the city guards roll six barrels of powder into the cabinet which adjoined the great hall, and there he waited quietly until an attempt should be made to attack the Hôtel de Ville. Before such calm intrepidity, the mob fell back, not one dared to lift his hand against the Communal Palace.

The fourteenth of July was destined to witness the fall of the Bastille.

Un beau soleil a fêté ce grand jour,

says Béranger, who walked, when a child, upon the remains of the towers, while yet the rubbish cumbered the ground. The truth is that the sky was dull and cloudy during the greater part of the day.[1] On the preced-

---

[1] See the 'Journal de Paris.' The lamps, lighted at fifty-five minutes past eight, would, at that time of year, have been burnt out by midnight.

ing day a great deal of rain had fallen, and a violent
thunder-storm had taken place in the evening, which
would have have driven all the Parisians back into
their own houses, if Pétion's *mot* had been invariably
true. But the matter in question now was not a
disturbance. It was a revolution which all Paris was
turning out to see.

It has been said that the Bastille was defended by
only a handful of men, eighty-two invalided soldiers,
two of whom were cannoneers of the company of Monsigny, and thirty-two Swiss, of the regiment of Salis-
Samade, commanded by a lieutenant of grenadiers,
Louis de Flue, who made his men swear that they
would fire upon the invalids if those veterans should
refuse to obey the Governor. In all, less than one
hundred men. But, behind the walls of the fortress,
these few men with their fifteen pieces of cannon
turned upon the ramparts, three field-pieces in the
great square, fourteen chests of bullets with their
cartridges attached, fifteen hundred cartridges, and
heavy shot, and two hundred and fifty barrels of
powder containing twenty-five pounds each; might
surely have successfully resisted the attack of a
mob. M. de Launey, the Governor, had had twelve
rampart guns taken out of the magazine of arms; these
guns were of a kind called *amusettes de Saxe* and each
carried a pound and a half of balls. Besides, the
great ditch of the fortress sufficiently defended the
approach to the castle, 'which, without being very
strong,' wrote Saint-Foix, 'is one of the most redoubtable in Europe.'

We must not, however, exaggerate the military
importance of the Bastille. In 1578, the garrison of the

Duke of Guise had capitulated there, speedily enough,
before Henri Quatre. In 1649, the gunners of the
Fronde sent one ball among the royal troops,—one
only—and the twenty-two men who formed the garrison surrendered without firing even one shot in reply.
The cannon of the Bastille was better served in
1651, when Mademoiselle de Montpensier put the
match to the guns with her own white hands, in order
to create a diversion for Condé when he was closely
pressed in the faubourg. But these are not very great
feats of war, and July 14 marked the most famous date
in the history of the Bastille, whose demolition began
two days later.

Since the morning, a great cry had rung through
Paris, 'To the Bastille!' The population wished to
make an end of it. The guns of De Launey, turned
upon the faubourg, looked like provocation. Thuriot
de la Rosière, deputy from the district of Saint-
Louis de la Culture, demanded of the Governor
that they should be dismounted. De Launey refused; but his officers swore that they would make
no use of their arms unless they should be attacked.
Meantime the people and the Gardes-françaises
assembled in vast, muttering, and menacing masses in
front of the Bastille. When Thuriot came out, a great
number of unarmed citizens presented themselves,
demanding arms and ammunition. The Governor
ordered the drawbridge to be lowered, and the crowd
swarmed in; but the bridge was immediately raised (by
whom was that order given?), and the citizens, who
had penetrated into the outer square, were received
by a rolling fire of musketry. They were literally
shot down; and their exasperated comrades on the

outside rushed off to the Hôtel de Ville crying aloud for vengeance.

From that hour the multitude was unchained. Thousands of men armed with sabres, swords and hatchets, rushed upon the Bastille with all the vehemence of fury. Women and children swelled the human torrent which surged around the walls of the fortress. 'Soldiers, workmen, firemen, officers, *abbés*,' says the 'Moniteur,' 'all were moved by one common impulse.' The strife commenced quickly. A former soldier of the Dauphin's regiment, Louis Tournay, and an ex-soldier of the Royal-Comtois regiment, Aubin Bonnemère, staved in the outer gates, and the fight raged around the drawbridge. One of the assailants, named Bernard, fell, with thirty-three wounds in him, no doubt from an *amusette*. A second who was carried off said to his companions, ' Hold firm, my friends ; I die, but you will take it.'

When deputies from the Hôtel de Ville, carrying a white flag, reached the scene of action, it seemed for a moment as if the strife might be arrested. But this only caused a lull in the storm of the popular fury. The fortress three times refused to ' treat,' and continued its fire. We can quote here only a few of the consolatary traits which testify at once to the rage and to the heroism of the assailants in the fierce strife which grew fiercer with each moment of its duration. In the court of the Bastille the crowd seized a young girl whom they dragged away to the first bridge, while furious cries were raised of, ' Kill her, kill her ! She is De Launey's daughter ! Let him surrender the place, or see his daughter killed ! ' Some wretches flung the girl upon a heap of straw, and were about to set fire to it when

Aubin Bonnemère rushed forward, tore the girl from
their grasp, handed her over to the soldiers, and continued the fight. Less than a year afterwards
(February 5, 1790,) Aubin Bonnemère received a
sword of honour, and, from the hand of the girl herself (she was Mademoiselle de Monsigny), a civic
crown, which she placed upon her deliverer's head
with tears.

The narrative of the 'Moniteur,' the most complete
and important account we have of the events of that
memorable day, gives us a vivid picture of the physiognomy of the obstinate, fierce, heroic fight. It
shows us the Governor, De Launey, waiting for the aid
promised by M. de Bezenval, and M. de Flesselles,
hesitating, temporising, and 'taking the most dangerous line of all, none.' For a moment, when the
fortress was plainly in the hands of the assailants (the
first to climb the tower was J. W. Humbert; Hérault
de Séchelles followed him), M. de Launey, distracted
with rage and grief, resolved to blow up the Bastille.
An officer prevented him from going down to the
powder-room and setting fire to it. The exasperated
Governor went hither and thither, seeking for a barrel of
powder, repeating to his soldiers that they must bury
themselves under the ruins of the fortress; but the
'parley' was already sounding, and the white flag of surrender was hoisted upon the tower of La Bazinière.
A moment more and the besiegers would have thrown
themselves into the arms of the invalids and the Swiss,
who cried *Bravo!* as they rushed in; but unhappily
this fraternisation did not last. A fresh discharge of
musketry, a fierce panic, and the crowd which swarmed
over the Bastille resumed all its former fury. They
fought no more, indeed, but they killed. Béquart, the

same officer who had just before hindered the Governor
from blowing up the fortress, fell, pierced by several
sword-thrusts, his hand was struck off at the wrist by
a sword-stroke, and 'that hand to which so many citizens owed their safety' was carried by the crowd
in triumph through the streets of Paris, while the
unhappy Béquart was fastened to a gibbet on which he
died, by the side of one Asselin, his companion in arms
and in suffering.

M. de Launey, resolved not to survive, endeavoured
to pierce his heart with his sword cane (he was not in
uniform, but wore a gray frock with a ponceau ribbon) ;
but Arné, a grenadier, one of the conquerors of the
Bastille, snatched the weapon out of his hand. While
the crowd were clutching at the Governor's grey hair,
and threatening him with their swords, he turned to
Arné and Hullin, who had hold of him, and were protecting him, and said : 'Is this what you promised me ?
Do not forsake me.'

A short time later (but when his agony had been
too long and too sharp already), M. de Launey was
killed upon the steps of the Hôtel de Ville, whither he
had been taken. We have discovered the name of the
chief of his murderers,—for many hands struck him at
once. The man was one Dénot, a cook, who had
come thither by chance, and who told of himself
that, 'seeing a man pass by whom they were dragging
up the steps of the Hôtel de Ville, and "larding" with
shortened bayonets, he just hit him in the back, and
cut his head off with his knife.' [1]

---

[1] 'Documents inédits.' Examination of the said Dénot. 'Being
asked if it was with this knife that he had mangled (travaillé) the head of
the Sieur de Launey, he answered that it was a black knife, a smaller one ;
and on its being observed to him that it was impossible to cut off heads
with so small and weak an instrument, he answered that, in his capacity of

A latent ferocity suddenly developed itself—a phe-
nomenon which occurred only too frequently at the
time—in this humble actor in a great drama.

The fury of the populace was terrible. M. de
Launey's 'Major,' M. de Losme, was killed, and his
head was stuck on the end of a pike. M. de Méray,
the 'assistant-major,' was killed, in the Rue des Tour-
nelles ; M. de Persan, lieutenant of invalids, on the
Port-au-blé, and M. de Montbarey, a former Minister of
War, were also massacred. Nevertheless a great cry
was arising from thousands of breasts ; a great cry of
pity and clemency. 'Grâce!' cried the Gardes-françaises, 'Grâce, grâce!' One of the heroes of the day,
Elie, a hero in goodness as well as in courage, hit
upon the true word wherewith to end the massacre.
'*Mercy for the children !*' he cried, to those who were
dragging away young lads among their captives.
Standing proudly before them, his hair bristling upon
his sweat-bedewed brow, a bent sword in his hand, this
man's words sent a thrill of pity through the crowd.
'Let not our hands be stained with blood,' he said,
'before the turrets of the Bastille fall, for to-morrow's
sun shall shine upon that fall. Let all these prisoners,
who are unfortunate rather than guilty, swear, in this
place, to be faithful to the Nation !'

The blood and powder stained multitude applauded this sentiment, and the prisoners of the
Bastille, swore, standing before Elie, to give their
lives, in the future, no longer to the King, but to
France.

---

cook, he knew how to manage meat.' At a later period of the interro-
gatory he said : 'In acting thus, he thought he was doing a patriotic act,
and that he deserved a medal for destroying a monster.' Dénot also
accused De Launey of having given him a kick.

During this time crowds were penetrating into the dungeons, examining with terror the old instruments of torture, the old fantastic engines of war, and iron corslets (had Louis XVI. abolished the use of them also in abolishing torture ?) and setting free the seven prisoners who were still shut up in the fortress. M. de Solages, who had been imprisoned, in 1782, at the request of his father, in consequence of his extravagance in money matters, had not received a single letter from his family or friends for seven years. He was ignorant of everything that had happened in France since his arrest ; he did not know that his father was dead ; that M. Lenoir was no longer Lieutenant of Police, and that the king had assembled the States General at Versailles. ‘ Having asked his jailer,’ says the ‘ Moniteur,’ ‘ what was the cause of the shots which he heard from his room, he was told that the people had revolted in consequence of the high price of bread. M. de Solages soon saw that it was not a revolt, but, in truth, as the king was told at the time, a *revolution*.

Another prisoner, Tavernier, the natural son of Paris Duverney, had been immured in the Bastille since August the 4th, 1759. He began to believe, after those thirty years, that ‘ there existed on earth no other human beings beside his jailers.’ A third, of the name of Whyte, appeared in the light of day without any one’s knowing whence he came ; or indeed who he was. He had been transferred one day from Vincennes to the Bastille. How many years had he been there? Nobody knew, and he, having become insane, could give no information respecting his previous life. He looked at the captors of the Bastille without seeing them ; he heard them speak without understanding their words.   Unheeding, the madman was borne through the rejoicing city.   He exchanged his prison only for a cell ; after a few days they shut him up at Charenton.

That day cost the life of ninety-eight of the as-sailants ; eighty-three were killed on the spot, fifteen died of their wounds ; seventy-three were wounded or maimed.   ' The besieged,' says the ' Moniteur,' ' lost one man only during the fight, four officers and four soldiers were hanged, or otherwise killed after the action.'

Two days later, 16th July, the Permanent Com-mittee of the Hôtel de Ville decreed that the Bastille should be pulled down *without loss of time, and even to its foundations,* under the direction of two architects. We learn from the memoirs of Bailly that the General Assembly of Electors approved and confirmed this decree, which was proclaimed by the city trumpets, in the courtyard of the Hotel, in the name of the General Commandant, Lafayette.   A certain individual named Palloy, who awarded to himself the appellation of ' Palloy the Patriot,' and whose muse did homage to all governments in turn,[1] made small models of the Bastille out of the stones of the demolished fortress, forged swords of the prisoners' chains, and made frames for pictures, representing the doings of July the 14th, of the leaden pipes.   A year later, on the site of the old citadel, an inscription, with an ironical ring in its gaiety, announced, ' Dancing here.'

It was not only a strong stone building which the Parisians had destroyed ; it was the Past which they had utterly overthrown.   The material facts of July

---

[1] Among his republished papers are verses addressed to Napoleon I. and Louis XVIII.

the 14th were of considerable importance; but the moral achievement, which those who endeavour to obscure the bearing of the contest do not recognise, was immense. Everything represented by the lofty towers of the Bastille, which was a deed of arbitrary power, and of evil memory,—*lettres de cachet*, the violation of personal freedom, the perpetual menace to public liberties, all the old abuses signified by that colossal petrified form, had suddenly crumbled into ruin. The honours of the strife vanished before such an unhoped-for reality, so 'inconceivable,' as Camille Desmoulins said, was the meaning of those words : *The Bastille is taken.* .

The nation had proved its strength ; thenceforth, it might hope that its right would not be contested. The next day, Louis XVI. went, according to the advice of the Duc de Liancourt, to the National Assembly, accompanied only by his brothers, and without any escort. He addressed the deputies, 'standing and uncovered.' For the first time, the king, instead of speaking of *the States-General,* called the Assembly by its true name, that name which it holds in its own right, *the National Assembly.* 'Our deputies,' writes Desmoulins, 'brought him back in triumph to the château. They assert that he wept profusely. He returned on foot without any other guard than the deputies who · escorted him.' The deputies mingled together, without distinction of orders, and formed a living rampart which protected him against the swarming crowd. How was it that Louis XVI. did not comprehend, that day, that his best, his sole support consisted in this gathering of men, who only asked him for the freedom of their country ? But, no. On the evening of the terrible day of the taking of the Bastille, Louis XVI. con-

tented himself with writing in the Journal, to which
he confided his daily impressions, the strange, incredible, impossible word, *Nothing!*[1] It is inscribed
under the date 14th July. Nothing! when everything
had begun!

During those tumultuous days, Camille Desmoulins
was, like Paris, in a fever. He had given the signal
for the loosing of the tempest, he had been seen,
marching alongside of Turgot, with a drawn sword, joining the popular triumph ; and he was on the breach of
the Bastille by the side of the men who hoisted the
colours of the French Guard. In his letters we find
the dash and spirit of those burning days. While the
Comte d'Artois and his two sons, Prince de Condé,
the Duc de Bourbon, the Duc d'Enghien, Prince de
Conti, the Duc Jules de Polignac and his wife, the
Princes de Lambesc and de Vaudemont, the old Maréchal de Broglie, the Duc de la Vauguyon, Baron de
Breteuil, and others, forsook the king, and the
emigration dated from the 16th of July, the nation
felt sure of itself; and it might have been said of the
Bastille, delivered up to demolition, as Göthe said of
Valmy, 'From this place and this day dates a new
era in the history of the world.'

Camille relates that, in the evening, the patrol of
militia and French guards, to which he was attached,
met a detachment of hussars coming in at the Porte St.
Jacques a little before midnight. '*Who goes there?*'
cried the gendarme who commanded the patrol. The
officer of hussars answered, '*France! The French
Nation.*'

France! It had just been born! The new France

---

[1] See the publication of the King's 'Journal,' by M. Nicolardot.

in love with liberty, intoxicated with hope, demanding her regeneration from the democracy. France ! That which, only the day before, was incarnate in the king, and which, henceforth, was to be composed of the entire nation, assembled under the tricoloured flag, had been born amid the roar of battle, and was already redolent of gunpowder.

CHAPTER II.

I.

ON the twelfth of July 1789, Camille Desmoulins may be said to have entered into history, never again to disappear from its records. Thenceforth, he belonged, body and soul, to the triumphant Revolution. Thenceforth, until April 1794, he was to be the most brilliant and personal of journalists ; and to reflect all the thoughts, hopes, and fantasies of the multitude through his nervous, feminine, easily excited temperament, readily carried away to every excess, but capable, nevertheless, of the 'second thoughts' which, in spite of the too famous saying, are not always the worst, and also by his passionate eloquence and irresistible wit. Day after day, he was to be the registrar of all the results of the new and prodigious activity ; the chronicler, in his style of exquisite irony, of all that was to be born and to die during those volcanic years. The day after the taking of the Bastille, Camille published ' La France

Libre,’ which he had written in the months of May and
June 1789. The opposition of his publisher only had
prevented the pamphlet from appearing, as we have
already seen ; and it is highly unjust to accuse Camille,
as M. Ed. Fleury accuses him, of having ‘profited by
the moment’ to publish a book which would have been
courageous the day before, but which needed no courage the day after. Once for all, let us render to
Momoro what is due to Momoro.

‘La France Libre,’ that patriotic work, as Desmoulins calls it, made a great noise, notwithstanding the
delay. Everyone read it; it was a clever and well-
informed criticism upon the past ; it was full of the
spirit of combat, and of aspiration towards the future.
The politicians of the Palais-Royal applauded it, just
as they had applauded the burning words of the enthusiastic young writer a few days before. Mirabeau, to
whom the new pamphlet owed some of its inspiration,
took the little work under his protection, which it well
deserved. In these pages the first cry of liberty found
utterance. It was, to quote a saying of M. Louis
Combes, like the ‘song of the Gallic lark,’ saluting
the dawn of freedom. So brisk and attractive was its
tone that Camille was speedily attacked by many who
were alarmed by his juvenile daring and impetuosity.
Not only people like Malouet, for example, or Mallot
du Pan (whom Camille afterwards called *Mallot
pendu*—a sorry joke), who desired to transform, to
reform, but not to overthrow the monarchy ; but,
even the most vehement royalists flung themselves
on the book, being unable to get at the author. Some
monks pillaged the shop of a bookseller at Oléron,
who was guilty of offering ‘ La France Libre ’ for sale.
A row ensued, and the unlucky bookseller was ‘ lamed

for the rest of his life.'[1] The Parliament of Toulouse went even further; it censured Camille's pamphlet and condemned it to be burned by the common executioner. Camille revenged himself by dedicating his second work, the 'Discours de la Lanterne,' to 'Nos seigneurs du parlement du Toulouse,' adding : 'May my dear Lanterne obtain the same favour at your hands. I doubt not that this younger bantling will have as much good fortune as the elder; but I beg of you not to sow jealousy in my family.'

'La France Libre' certainly did not deserve the condemnation of the Parliament of Toulouse; and Pascal would, no doubt, have said that the anger of the monks of Oléron was not a reason. In this little work, Camille, analysing the different questions which were under consideration during the first part of the year 1789, discussed in their turn 'deliberation by head and by order,' placed the rights of the nation and those of the nobility in opposition to each other with rare talent and surprising readiness of style; made war upon the clergy as a mere political body; and did this with erudition and wit worthy of the author of the 'Lettres Provinciales' himself; then after having shown that a democracy is not incompatible with nobility of a certain kind, *i.e.*, that of personal worth, not of rank, he passed in review the long list of the kings, with studied severity, indeed, but not always without truth, drawing with a powerful pen a picture of what is often called 'the good old time.' This satirical picture has sometimes been compared with the worthless book of Lavicomterie, 'Les crimes des rois de France;' but the style of Camille, his wit, his dash, and his irony are very different. They are keen, caustic, and telling.

[1] Ed. Fleury, 'Camille Desmoulins et Boch Marcandier.'

The most characteristic chapter of 'La France Libre,' that which defines its sense and its aim, is the sixth, in which Desmoulins asks : '*What constitution is best suited for France?*' 'I am prepared for the clamour which this paragraph will excite,' he says. In fact, after having framed an indictment against kings, he concludes, quoting Diocletian, against royalty itself. 'How can people have placed their hopes in one single man?' he asks. This was proclaiming, by implication, that the constitution which Desmoulins desired and demanded for France was a republican constitution. 'The nation shall govern itself after the example of America, after the example of Greece. This is the only government fit for men, for Frenchmen, and for the Frenchmen of this age.' 'What parity is there between a king and a nation?' he adds. 'Put Louis XVI. on one side, and on the other the National Assembly. On which side are experience and wisdom to be found?' As for the Republic itself, Desmoulins would have it *one*, as it was to be proclaimed afterwards : 'Why should we wish to be Bretons, Bearnais, Flemings? Could there be under heaven a finer name than that of Frenchmen? To that famous name ought all to sacrifice our own.'

Like all the men of that epoch, Camille was essentially a *patriot*. Under Louis XIV., Saint Simon only used that word ; in 1789, every one gloried in it. But everybody was not republican. On this point Camille was a precursor ; and he, perhaps, was, of all the writers, the first to demand the advent of the Republic. Yet no, I am mistaken. The Comte d'Entraigues, in his ' Mémoires sur les Etats-Généraux ; leurs droits, et la manière de les convoquer,' written in 1788, says : 'It was, doubtless, in order to give a

F

country, worthy of them, to the most heroic virtues, that
Heaven willed that Republics should exist; and, perhaps, it is in order to punish the ambition of men that
Heaven permits the rise of great empires, kings, and
masters.'   D'Entraigues had preceded Camille ; but
his pamphlet was speedily forgotten. 'La France
Libre,' on the contrary, literally set fire to the powder.
It was thus that Camille took credit to himself for
having been first, among the first, to demand a republican constitution.

'On July 12, 1789,' he writes in his 'Fragment de
l'Histoire secrète de la Révolution' (page 8), 'there
were, perhaps, not ten republicans in Paris, and what
covers the *vieux Cordeliers* with glory is, that they
commenced such an enterprise as the Republic with
such small means.'

Then he adds a note :—

'Our republicans were for the most part youths,
who, having been fed on Cicero at school, had there conceived a passion for liberty.   We were educated in
the schools of Rome and Athens, and in the pride of
the Republic, to live in the subjection of monarchy,
and under the rule of Claudius and Vitellius.   What
an insensate government to imagine that we could
be inspired with a passionate admiration for the
fathers of those countries, for the Capitol, without
a corresponding horror of the men-eaters of Versailles ; that we could admire the past without
.condemning the present, *ulteriora mirari, præsentia
secuturos !* '

It was the famous sixth chapter of 'La France
Libre' which let loose the crowd of royalist writers
upon Camille. The Vicomte de Mirabeau, *Mirabeau-
Tonneau*, replied fiercely to him, and the future author

of 'Les Révolutions de France et de Brabant' afterwards made him pay dearly for the answer.[1]

Camille, who was in his element in noise and stir,
and enchanted with his success, was intoxicated with
his dawning popularity, and the joyous ardour which
animated the nation. His letters to his father are full
of enthusiasm and excitement.

'You cannot form an idea,' he writes, 'of the joy
which our regeneration causes me. Liberty must be
a grand thing, since Cato tore out his entrails rather
than have a master.'

Then the young man, who, at least, cannot be reproached with reticence, adds frankly :—

'But, alas! I wish earnestly to regenerate myself,
and I find still the same weaknesses in myself—must I

---

[1] In evidence of this we find the following verses, in which Camille
attacks the two Mirabeaus at the same time :—

La Question difficile à résoudre.

'Mes amis, des deux Mirabeau,
Ou du pendard ou de l'ivrogne,
Décidez quel est le plus beau
Et lequel a moins de vergogne :
Le colonel, brave à trois poils,
Surpasse, d'estoc et de taille,
Le vieux preux de langue d'oils
Et ceux du quai de la Ferraille.
On admire dans le combat·
Ce Laridon et ce Paillasse ;
Coclès, aux portes du sabbat,
Brave lui-même la populace,
Et presente sa large face
Aux pistolets comme aux crachats.
Mais pour son frère Barabas,
Celui-là n'est rien moins que brave ;
Bien qu'aidé d'un manche à balai,
Sans cesse il rosse son valet,
Presentez-lui le pistolet,
De rouge comme une *betterave*
Il devient plus blanc qu'un navet.'

say, the same vices? At least, lack of love for my
father is not one of them.'

No, indeed; but, among these vices we are forced to
recognise a dangerous one, vanity. Camille, who was
greedy for fame, contented himself too easily with a
second-rate renown. Notwithstanding the ironical
and aggressive style of 'La France Libre,' it was
written for educated men and thinkers; but before
long we shall find him writing his 'Discours de la
Lanterne' for that section of the public which confers
a flashy popularity, but not a solid reputation founded
on respect.

What a pamphlet that was, notwithstanding!
What marvellous astuteness and vigour were displayed
in the 'Discours de la Lanterne aux Parisiens,' which
forms the antithesis of the 'Vieux Cordelier' among
the works of Camille Desmoulins. The 'Discours'
reveals to us a Camille whose laughter is terrible; and
it was, indeed, a sinister notion to place his work
under the invocation of that 'lanterne' on which
a white-haired man, one of the *invalides*, who had
acted as a spy of M. de Launey, and, three months
afterwards, Foullon and François, the baker, had been
hanged. This 'lanterne' was an iron pole without
a lamp, which projected at the corner of the Place de
Grève and the Rue de la Vannerie, over the front of a
grocer's shop; and thither the howling mob dragged
those whom they were resolved to hang. The
terrible cry—*A la lanterne*—was raised also beneath a
sign bearing these words: *au coin du Roi.* There is
irony in most human things. It was this lamp-pole,
this iron rod, this street-lamp which Camille Desmoulins made famous; to it he gave the first place in
his pamphlet, which he further adorned with an

epigraph taken from St. Matthew : *Qui malè agit odit lucem :* or, as he translated it : ' Rogues object to the lamp-post.'

Never was there, in fact, anything more tragical than this pamphlet, which, in later days, Camille Desmoulins was bitterly and vainly to repent, and which procured for him the title (unhappily he sought it) of *procureur-général de la lanterne*. But also, never was there anything more eloquent. Its wit, even while it seems ill-employed in deadly personalities, dazzles us.[1]

---

[1] Camille Desmoulins had already sounded this aggressive note, in the following passage of 'La France Libre' :—

' It was reserved for our days to behold the return of liberty among the French. Yes, she has already been brought back to us ; she has not yet a temple for the States General, like that of Delphos, in Greece, for the assembly of the Amphictyons ; or that of Concord, in Rome, for the assembly of the Senate ; but she is already adored in tones louder than a whisper, and the worship of her is public. For forty years philosophy has been undermining the foundations of despotism in all their parts ; and, as Rome before Cæsar was already enslaved by its vices, so France before Necker was already enfranchised by its intelligence.

' From Paris and Lyons, from Rouen and Bordeaux, from Calais and Marseilles, from one end of France to the other, the same universal cry comes to our ears. With what pleasure all good citizens scan the *cahiers* of the provinces ! With what rage must the perusal of them fill the breasts of our oppressors ! 1 thank, thee, O Heaven, that thou hast decreed my birth before the end of this century. 1 shall behold the erection of that bronze pillar which the Paris *cahier* demands, that pillar on which our rights and the history of the Revolution shall be inscribed ; and I will teach my children to read in this citizen's cate-chism. Everywhere the nation has uttered the same aspiration. All desire to be free. Yes, my dear fellow-citizens, we shall all be free ; who shall prevent us ? Will the provinces of the North demand other things than the South? are the districts of election in opposition to the dis-tricts of states, so that we should have to fear a schism and a civil war ?

' No, there will be no civil war. We are the strongest, we are the most numerous. Look at the capital—that hot-bed of corruption, where the monarchy, the born enemy of morality, seeks only to deprave us, to enervate the national character, to degrade us by multiplying the snares of seduction for youth, by creating facilities for debauch and besieging us with prostitutes—the capital itself contains more than thirty thousand

The erudite writer multiplies quotations, com-
parisons, and anecdotes with singular felicity.   The
pamphlet is a model of aggressive dexterity.   But what
a war !   In vain does Camille say, making the *lanterne* speak for him : ' Not that I like justice to be
too expeditious ; you know that I gave signs of discontent on the occasion of the ascent of Foullon and
Bertier ; that I broke the fatal loop twice ;' the truth is,
that he urged vigorous measures.   He denounces
people, he, who shall afterwards stigmatise in-
formers so ruthlessly !   A year later, we find him con-
gratulating himself upon having ' resigned his functions
as *procureur-général de la lanterne*;' and, referring to
the fury of the crowd of self-made dealers in justice,
he says, 'It is a great evil that the people should
become familiar with games of this kind.'   He makes
this reply to Marat (in his ' Révolutions de France et
de Brabant'), and adds : ' Executions by the people
are atrocious, now that they send the halter about with

men who are ready to bid adieu to all its pleasures and join the sacred
cohorts of our country at the first signal, so soon as liberty shall have
raised her standard in one province, and rallied its good citizens around
it.   Paris, like the rest of France, calls aloud for liberty.   The infamous
police, that monster with ten thousand heads, seems at last to be
paralysed in all its limbs.   Its eyes no longer see, its ears no longer hear.
The patriots only raise their voices.   The enemies of the public welfare
keep silence, or, if they dare to speak, they are instantly punished for
their felony or their treason.   They are compelled to sue for pardon on
their knees.   Linguet, who had the impudence to steal in among the
deputies, is hunted out by them ; Maury is driven away by his host ;
Desprémesnil is hissed even by his lackeys ; the Keeper of the Seals is
harried and covered with contumely, even in the midst of his guards ;
the Archbishop of Paris is pelted with stones ; Condé, Conti, D'Artois,
are publicly devoted to the infernal gods.   Patriotism spreads, day by
day, with the devouring rapidity of a great conflagration.   The young
take fire ; old men cease, for the first time, to regret the past ; they blush
for it.   The people bind themselves by oaths in a solemn engagement to
die for their country.'

as much facility as the Sultan sends the bowstring. Marat, you are getting us into serious trouble.' His remorse was to follow quickly; but that, for even one day, Camille Desmoulins should have filled the 'great office' of *procureur* to the lamp-post is a terrible fact, and, at a later period, he was destined to shed bitter tears over those pages which no tears can ever efface.

On the other hand, let us hasten to point out that there are other things in this 'Discours de la Lanterne' than personalities and denunciations; there is true patriotism, and thoroughly French fervour. He makes known the Republic (which he had presented to the world in 'La France Libre'), such as he would have it to be; elegant, refined, cultivated, accessible; such as the *Mondain* of Voltaire might have conceived it, and as far removed from the oppression of despotism, as from the icy austerity and the ferocious rule of a Jacobin Republic. He desires *fêtes* and pleasures, the free repasts of the antique cities, a sort of immense federation and mutual embrace; a Republic where kisses shall sound louder than cries of hate; a fraternal Republic, all love and pleasure. Before the eyes of this modern Gaul floated the vision of Athens. 'What consoled me for not being able to make my readers laugh as much as Molière did,' he says somewhere, 'is that Molière was sad. I am not so taciturn and melancholy.' Then he demands a little gaiety from the State. 'I had dreamed,' said he, in later days, '*of a Republic in which everyone would have loved.*' Let us retain this saying; it was, in truth, his last will and testament.

Desmoulins, in fact, when we look closely into his mind at that time, was by no means so well satisfied with the 'Discours de la Lanterne' as he had been with 'La France Libre.' A scholar's secret instinct warned him that he had, so to speak, forced the 'note,' and shot beyond his aim. He had published this anonymous pamphlet, in the first instance, because he was afraid of 'declining in opinion.' The pamphlet having been sold out, he hesitates for a moment about issuing a second edition, for 'we are tired of all these writings.' How easily we recognise, in this hesitation and discontent, the ill-balanced man, of febrile temperament, who wrote to his father: 'At one moment I think life a delicious thing, and the moment after it seems almost insupportable; and this happens to me ten times a day.' Such natures are dangerous to themselves and to others, when they are engaged in the struggles of a revolution. They are made for the free existence of men of letters, for a life in which their very hesitations serve to put new faces upon their talent, and act upon them daily like whip and spur.

II.

AT this epoch in his life (September, 1789), Camille Desmoulins was not happy either morally or materially. He lodged at the *Hôtel de Pologne*, opposite the *Hôtel de Nivernais;* he was in needy circumstances, and more than once we find him asking assistance from his good parents at Guise. 'You will oblige me by sending me some shirts and two pairs of sheets, as soon as possible,' he writes on September 20. He is tired of living in these little Parisian hotels. 'I hope to have a house of my own by Saint-Remy's day.' —'Send me six louis,' he writes soon after to his father. No doubt his first pamphlets brought him very little money; but he at least won fame by them. 'I have made myself a name, and I begin to hear it said, " There is a pamphlet out by Desmoulins," not any longer, " by an author called Desmoulins ; " and then, " Desmoulins has just been defending the Marquis de Saint-Huruge." [1]   This 'name' which he has made for himself evidently consoles Desmoulins for his poverty. Now, he hardly regrets that his father, who would not accept the mandate of a deputy, did not at least lend his influence to the election of his son.

'You made a blunder in policy,' wrote Camille to him, ' when last year you would not come to Laon and recommmend me to the person who could have had me nominated. But I can afford to laugh at them now. I have written my name on the history of the Revolution, in larger letters than those of all our deputies from Picardy.'

Nevertheless, he refers more than once again to this sort of abdication on his father's part ; he cannot understand the love of calm which satisfied the hard-working man.[2] ' You lack activity,' he says ; ' you remain in your study ; and, in democracies, one must show oneself.'   M. Desmoulins must, many a time, have smiled sadly on perusing these letters ; for his head was by no means turned by the sudden fame of

---

[1] Victor-Amédée, Marquis de Saint-Huruge, the popular agitator, had just been arrested, and taken to the Châtelet. Desmoulins defended him (September 1789) in a pamphlet entitled ' Réclamation en faveur du Marquis de Saint-Huruge,' which has now lost much of its interest. ' I will not say in his defence,' wrote Camille, ' that he is a gentleman, and the godson of the king of Sardinia ; I will say, he is a French citizen.' The marquis, who was born at Macon in 1750, died, forgotten, in 1810, after having been one of the most fiery of the mob-orators.

[2] The enemies of Camille have tried to make out that he hated his father. ' His first case,' says the Leipzig biography, ' was against his father, *who had refused to make him an allowance.*' ' You are on your way to the scaffold,' replied M. Desmoulins. All the letters from the father to his son triumphantly refute these infamous calumnies.

his son. On the contrary, he pursued his slow and modest task, at Guise, more resolutely than ever.

During this time, Camille, having made himself a name, was making friends. The author of the ' Tableau de Paris,' introduced him at several houses. Mirabeau invited him to his house at Versailles ; and thence, where he enjoyed himself, Camille wrote, gaily :—

' I feel myself corrupted by his table, which is too profuse and too dainty. His Bordeaux wine and Maraschino have merits which I vainly endeavour to disguise from myself; and I find it very difficult to resume my republican austerity, and to detest the aristocrats whose crime is to set store by these excellent dinners.'

Desmoulins was evidently, for the time, under the inspiration of Mirabeau, just as, at a later period, he was under that of Danton. Weak natures like his need stronger for counsel, as the ivy needs a support for growth.

Although he was more or less pleased with his growing renown, Camille was troubled and discontent at his heart. He was always preoccupied about 'what they would say ' in his native town, and the accounts of him which might reach his parents. He writes to his father as follows :—

' If you hear any evil said of me, console yourself by recalling the testimony which has been borne to me by MM. de Mirabeau, Targot, M. de Robespierre, Gleizal, and more than two hundred deputies. Reflect that a great part of the capital numbers me among the chief authors of the Revolution. Many even go so far as to say that I am its sole author.'

Here, Camille goes too far. But his self-love had

something to depress it more than a little when the guest of Mirabeau, on returning to Paris, was obliged to remember that in all the great city, he had no home except a room in a third-rate inn. *And I am thirty years old!* he says, with a sort of frightened bitterness Thirty years; the first step towards decisive maturity; the age at which the smile becomes less confident upon the contracted lips; the hour at which one sees obstacles uprising on every side where all lay smooth at twenty; the age at which having hitherto counted one's friends only, one begins to reckon one's rivals. Camille was thirty years old, and still vegetating! We must do him the justice to admit that as soon as this thought assailed him, he made a violent effort to stifle it; for he was ardent, inspired, earnest, and full of the love of his work. He resolved that he would not be content with a few pages printed in pamphlet form; he desired to found one of those personal journals of which so many existed at the time; and from the month of November 1789, he set himself firmly to accomplish this project. The first number of the 'Révolutions de France et de Brabant' appeared on November 28. Desmoulins' journal was destined to last until July 1792 (No. 86), when Camille, who was in danger in consequence of the affair of the Champ de Mars, sent in, as he said, his *resignation as a journalist,* to La Fayette.

Camille Desmoulins followed the prevailing fashion by borrowing the title of *Révolutions* from the journals already in favour, and he added the name of Brabant to that of France, because Brabant had rebelled so gallantly against the Empire.[1] This

---

[1] He afterwards struck out the name of Brabant, declaring that he gave up *a people stupid enough to kiss Bender's boots.*

journal is incisive, and sparkling, and, though often the most cruel, yet always the most inspired monument of the French Revolution.   It consisted of a weekly pamphlet, in a grey paper cover, and was adorned with an engraving, generally a caricature, for which Garnéry, the publisher, was responsible.   Camille dwells upon this detail.   He frequently repeated, ' I protest against the engravings placed at the head of my sheets.   The Assembly has not abolished every kind of servitude.'

It is much to be regretted, apart from political considerations, that no publisher has yet ventured to reprint those ' Révolutions de France et de Brabant ' in their integrity, for they form a masterpiece of language and polemic, a repertory of knowledge, and a marvel of wit.   I do not know, I will not say in journalistic literature only, but in the entire literature of our country, a pamphlet more brilliant, more varied, one in which sarcasm, passion, wit, emotion, anger and irony have so much place, and succeed each other so rapidly, ever satisfying and ever new.   We may say of Camille, in respect of his pamphlets, what Suetonius says of the soldiers of Julius Cæsar, ' They knew how to fight, perfumed though they were, *etiam unguentati pugnare.*'   With what unparalleled vigour he pursues his enemies and pitilessly riddles them with the barbed arrows of his pen.   He was thoroughly secured by the sound classicism of his education, and he called to his aid all the resources of that antiquity which was his familiar source of argument and illustration.[1]

I have in my possession a manuscript book full of curious quotations, collected by Camille, in the course

---

[1] Camille was no pedant, though he draws at every page on the resources of antiquity. In one of his writings he finds the idea of *pro-*

of his reading, classed according to their subjects, and to which he evidently referred in his polemics.

'The universe and all its follies,' he had said, 'shall be included in the jurisdiction of this hypercritical journal.' According to Mangourit, he was about to sound *the second drum-tap*. A Journalist! It was not long since 'that unfortunate gazetteer of Holland,' as 'La France Libre' called him, had been shut up in the 'cage' at Mont St. Michel. But a new era had commenced, and speech was free!

During the first months of the publication of the 'Révolutions de France et de Brabant,' which had a rapid success, Camille Desmoulins did the whole of the work unassisted; but in July 1790, he allowed a portion of it to devolve upon Stanislas Fréron, his friend, who was afterwards his nominal collaborator in the 'Tribune des Patriotes' and his colleague at the National Convocation.

Fréron, who was a man of quick intelligence, was the son of Fréron, the critic, who was so severely castigated by Voltaire, and exactly calculated to 'double' Camille Desmoulins, as he was said to do. He was a cultivated and humorous writer; he read and translated Petrarch. Arnault said of him that he was 'neither spiteful nor ambitious.' The following deed of agreement between him, Camille, and Laffrey, the publisher, will give a strange idea of the prices paid to journalists at that time, and of their relations with book-

---

gress indicated in the inscriptions, or rather in the songs and choruses, of Lacedemonian *fêtes*, of which Plutarch speaks :—

LES VIEILLARDS.	LES ENFANTS.
Nous avons été jadis	Et nous bientôt le serons,
Jeunes, vaillants et hardis,	*Qui tous vous surpasserons.*

'Révolutions de France et de Brabant,' No. 35, vol. iii. p. 515.

sellers. It appears in print for the first time in these pages :—

We, the undersigned, Camille Desmoulins and Stanislas Fréron, the former living in the Rue du Théâtre Français, the latter in the Rue de la Lune, Porte St. Denys, of the one part ; and Jean-Jacques Laffrey, living in the Rue du Théâtre Français, of the other part, have agreed as follows :—

1. I, Camille Desmoulins, engage to delegate to Stanislas Fréron the sum of three thousand livres, out of the sum of ten thousand livres, which Jean-Jacques Laffrey has bound himself, by a bond between us, to pay me annually as the price of the editing of my journal, entitled ‘ Révolutions de France et de Brabant,’ of three printed sheets, under the express condition that the said Stanislas Fréron shall furnish one sheet and a half to each number, and that during the whole term of my agreement with the said Laffrey.

2. I, Stanislas Fréron, engage to furnish for each number of the said journal of the ‘ Révolutions de France et de Brabant,’ composed of three sheets, one sheet and a half, under the direction of the said Camille Desmoulins, with the understanding that this sheet and a half shall form one-half of the three sheets of which each number is composed. I engage to deliver a portion of the copy of this said sheet and a half on the Wednesday of each week, and the rest during the day on Thursday, and this counting inclusively from the thirty-third number until the close of the agreement between Camille Desmoulins and Jean-Jacques Laffrey.

3. I, Jean-Jacques Laffrey, accept the delegation made by Camille Desmoulins of the sum of three thousand livres, payable, in equal payments, at the issue of each number, to Stanislas Fréron, to the clauses and conditions herein-under ; and I engage, besides, to pay to the said Stanislas Fréron the sum of one thousand livres, also payable in equal payments, on the publication of each number, which thousand livres shall be over and above the said salary of three thousand livres on condition that the said Stanislas Fréron shall furnish to the said journal an additional sheet per week which shall be devoted to news—to begin from the thirty-ninth number, which commences the approaching quarter.

ˈ And I, Stanislas Fréron, engage to furnish, at the stipulated periods, the said sheet over and above, in consideration
of the sum of one thousand livres, in addition to the three
thousand livres delegated by Camille Desmoulins.

Done, in triplicate, between us, at Paris, July 4, 1790.

(Signed)   STANISLAS FRERON.

Approved the above   (Signed)   LAFFREY,
C. DESMOULINS.

The 'Révolutions de France et de Brabant,' had
existed for hardly a year, and, as we see, Camille had
already ceased to be a needy man. 'My first number
is considered perfect,' he writes to his father, in
November '89, 'but shall I be able to keep up to this
mark ?' He did keep up to it, bravely.

This journal is the best known and the most
entirely personal of Camille's works. In it his
sarcasm, his wit, his elegance, and his ardour are most
brilliantly and easily displayed. In it, let us hasten to
say, his talent is most formidable, and, too often, most
cruel. He sharpens the edge of his wit until it cuts
like a steel blade wrought by an artist's hand, delicate
as jeweller's work, but which pierces the heart of an
enemy only the more quickly for that. A journalist in
his soul, impelled by the imperious necessity which
drives men of that particular temperament to fling
their red-hot ideas on paper, and send sheets on which
the ink is not yet dry to the printers, Camille Desmou-
lin's programme was the eternal 'Quid novi ?' of the
gazetteers. 'Quid novi ?' This is the epigraph of his
prospectus. He sought for novelty, for 'actuality' as
we now call it, everywhere ; at the Assembly, in Paris,
at Versailles, at the popular meetings, at literary gather-
ings, and in the streets. His journal is the living
chronicle of the doings of Paris in those stormy days.

It is, in truth, in the ' Révolutions de France et de Brabant' that posterity finds the most vivid picture of the troublous time between November 28, 1789, and July 1792. The collection formed by those eighty-six numbers is unique in the history of Journalism ; they are in reality a succession of pamphlets, in which noisy enthusiasm, anger, and laughter alternate, with felicity of expression, grace of form, boundless audacity of tone ; a series of satires, harangues, epigrams, personalities, jests, now resembling the invective of hatred, again like the trumpet-blare saluting liberty ; brilliant and incisive pages, by turns witty and fierce, the Menippean Satire of the French Revolution. They have the youth, the fire, the dash, the joyous readiness, and the gaiety of the Gallic nation, acidulated sometimes by a more bitter laughter ; Lucian and Aristophanes could not have invented raillery more cutting than that of Desmoulins.[1] His arrows have barbed points which wound and bury themselves far beneath the surface. Camille is an implacable adversary. This Athenian Picard had yet to learn the supreme virtue, pity.

He amuses himself with everything, with the dawn of enfranchisement which seems rising over the world. He 'drinks in punch the health of the English who drink the health of France in wine.' He cheers the patriots of Brabant, who have risen against Joseph II.— perhaps, to give his gazette a legitimate right to its title :—' Courage, men of Brabant,' he says to them ; ' remember that the French behold you.' Every week men and things pass under review in his pamphlet, enriched, or, as I think, weighted by an engraving

---

[1] A portrait of Desmoulins, in verse, by M. Emanuel des Essarts, a poet of rare merit, who has closely studied the revolutionary epoch, will be found in the Appendix.

against which Camille protests repeatedly.   He vigorously attacks courtiers who still retain influence, and
abuses which are not yet uprooted.[1]   In his pages the
act of accusation against the old Monarchy is swollen
to portentous dimensions.

Here is an example :—

'Let us see to what an extent they have pushed the art
of inventing pensions,' says Desmoulins.   'The incomparable
Pierre Lenoir created pensions for himself on oils and
tallows, on sand and *cloacina*.   Associations of swindlers,
every kind of vice, and every sort of filth, were tributary to
our Lieutenant of Police, who, in virtue of his position, ought
to have been *magister morum*, the guardian of the public
morals.   At length, he contrived to put the moon under
contribution, and assigned to one of his mistresses a pension,
known under the name of *pension of the moon*.   I know of
one minister who assigned to his mistress a pension of 12,000
livres, raised on the contract for the bread supplied to the
convicts at the galleys, which she enjoys to this day.'   Again :
'In the list of pensions I see that four are granted to a
German prince, the first and second for his services as a
colonel, the third and fourth for his services as a non-colonel.
Total of the German prince's pensions ; 48,000 livres.'

Camille allows nothing to pass, neither folly, nor
time-serving.   He exposes everything of the kind
with extraordinary skill and point.   M. de Boufflers
makes a speech before the king and queen in which he
vaunts the 'almost divine grace' of Marie Antoinette :—

[1] 'I protest,' he says in No. 17, 'against the woodcut at the head of
my last number.   I have already stated that I do not meddle with the
frontispiece and the figures, except in three or four instances when I gave
the idea. But I owe it none the less to my character and to my principles to
declare that I am not an accomplice in the insolent outrage inflicted on
the assembled nation by the plate in No. 16. It is a crime of *lèse-nation* on
the part of the engraver, and I denounce him to the Châtelet for having
represented the king with his hat on his head in the presence of the
National Assembly, during the sitting of February 4.'—'Révolutions de
France et de Brabant.'

'Boileau,' writes Camille Desmoulins, 'said to Louis XIV., "L'Univers sous ton règne a-t-il des malheureux?" but he belonged to the French Academy! A far more surprising fact is that the Chancellor de l'Hôpital, in his poem on the States General, said to Francis II., "Has there ever existed a gentler or more indulgent woman than his (the king's) respectable mother (Catherine de Médicis)?" *All kings and queens are, like the unfortunate Francis II., poisoned through the ear.*'.

The 'détestables flatteurs' of Racine is not more eloquent than these two lines written by Camille against courtiers.

When Desmoulins is discussing a projected law or a political doctrine we can trace the legist in him, and his eloquence is equalled by his knowledge. When the Assembly talks about the 'silver marc, and qualification,' which it proposes to exact from eligible citizens, he says :—' Then Jean-Jacques Rousseau, Corneille, Mably, would not have been eligible.' 'Priests of a proletarian God,' he adds, addressing himself more particularly to the deputies of the clergy, 'respect that poverty which He has ennobled.' Courageous utterances like these are not rare in the numbers of Desmoulins' Journal, but his personality pleases us better when he delivers battle to some enemy, direct, and face to face. The Abbé Maury, the Vicomte de Mirabeau (known as Mirabeau-Tonneau), and the queen furnished his arrows with unfailing targets. No doubt the hour came when he regretted that he had attacked a woman; for the wheel of persecution, turning, like that of fortune, struck in her turn the woman whom he loved; but we may be quite certain he never regretted the epigrams that he darted at Mirabeau 'the tun,' or at Maury.

'Duclos,' writes Desmoulins, 'has said in his "Caractères:"
"There are societies in which parts are distributed just as they
are distributed on the stage ; one man is cynical, another
grave ; one is good-natured, another caustic ; one melancholy,
another given to laughter; one a philosopher, another a
scamp ; a third plays the buffoon who at first thought
to take a leading part, but found the buskin bespoken."
Now this latter is exactly the case of our Vicomte de Mirabeau ; his brother has left him nothing but the sock.'

This is one of the mildest of the continual attacks
made on the brother of the great orator whom
also Camille praised and assailed by turns. The
Vicomte de Mirabeau was the butt of Desmoulins'
fiercest jests. While he praises 'M. de Robespierre, his dear school friend, the ornament of the
Northern Deputation,' he heaps ridicule on Mirabeau-
Tonneau, not only in words, but by the illustrations
of his journal. He did not indeed execute them
himself, but the caricature emphasising the pamphlet
is a terrible weapon against one's enemies. The
graver aided the pen in its spiteful, indeed more than
that, its murderous work.

Camille did more cruel things even than those ; and
when, in after days, in his prison, he was forced to remember writings which he then admitted to have been
too numerous, doubtless he bethought himself of the
pages in which he contrived, by I don't know what
sophistry, to justify the murder of Favras. Favras had
been 'judged, and legally condemned by thirty-eight
judges.'

'Out of these thirty-eight votes,' says Camille, 'thirty-two
were for death. When we remember that one Adrien, a
labouring man, was tried, condemned, and hanged within the
space of twenty-four hours for having carried a seditious note
to different houses, though he did not know how to read, it

seems strange that there should be persons found to protest against the condemnation of Favras, who was convicted upon a multitude of much graver accusations. So difficult is it to uproot certain aristocratic prejudices, such as the belief in a difference of specific gravity between a labourer and a marquis, in the scales of justice!'[1]

True, but is that a reason for writing as follows?—

'I will not accuse the people's joy at this execution of being barbarous. What! because such was the good pleasure of the prince, an army of a hundred thousand Frenchmen went to shoot, disembowel, and put to the sword Englishmen and Hanoverians, as foolish as themselves, and who knew no more than they did why they were murdering each other on the open field by thousands! It did not come into any-body's head to tax those soldiers with cruelty, who, in cold blood, drove their bayonets into the breasts of the men opposite to them, whom they did not know, and who had not done them any harm; and shall I listen to accu-sations of barbarity against a people who rejoice that human justice sometimes acts in the place of divine vengeance!'[2]

---

[1] 'Révolutions de France et de Brabant,' vol. ii. p. 7.

[2] 'Not the people, but the despot is the tiger. There has never been a people-Caligula, or a people-Nero, if I may speak thus. Without quoting these monsters, let anyone show me a people who has kept its enemy in an iron cage for eleven years, as Louis XI. kept Cardinal de la Balue, and Louis XIV. kept the Dutch gazetteer; let anyone show me a people who had Bastilles, or ordered a massacre of St. Bartholomew, or, like so many tyrants, condemned men to death for insulting them by libels. On the criminal code the character of the government is impressed; let us look at the cruelty of punishments under monarchy. In monarch-ruled countries, we find the wheel, the stake, the burning steel, we have angels tortured, impaled, and sawn asunder. The people gave henbane to drink at Athens; they flung from the Tarpeian rock at Rome; or they stoned to death among the Jews; but when the people cried, "Crucify, crucify," it was because the Roman prætors had corrupted them by introducing the punishment of the cross, invented by the aristocracy for slaves. It is, then, an absurd calumny to call the people tigers. The people are gentle when they are the masters, and how should they not be compassionate? They suffer too much to be aught but tender-hearted; it is rather against their compassion that they ought to be warned than against their severity.'—No. 15, p. 88.

'We should have been lost,' he adds, 'if the people could have witnessed the punishment of such men as De Launey, Berthier, and Favras, unmoved. As for me, notwithstanding the cries of fury uttered by the aristocrats against what Barnave said [1]—Barnave who is as eloquent as an orator as he is excellent as a citizen—I will repeat with him : Was Brutus a barbarian when, showing the people the poniard which still reeked with the blood of his benefactor, he congratulated himself upon having delivered his country ? Was Cicero a barbarian when, after he had had Lentulus and Cethegus strangled, he clasped Cato's hand and proceeded to his place in the Senate with ill-dissembled joy, saying, *They have lived ?* Was Aristogeiton a barbarian when he said, with such elation, of Hipparchus, *Tyrant, would that all thy slaves were dead ; but at least I shall have caused the death of thy best friends !* '

Accursed be antiquity if it inspires us only with the ideal of an extrahuman virtue ! The classical reminiscences of Camille led him astray. To this tirade he added a final touch, alleging that the firmness with which Favras died was all pretence and parade ; he ventured to write that it was 'that of a gladiator, who, being mortally wounded, strives to fall with decency and dignity.'

Well, and is it not something to know how to die ? One day Camille will learn that it is so. It is not easy to fall 'with decency and dignity.'

How infinitely preferable to these sanguinary pages are those enthusiastic ones in which Desmoulins

---

[1] 'The blood that is flowing, is it then so pure ?' When Barnave was on his way to execution, a royalist, who saw him pass by, flung these same words at him.

relates his entry into the '*district of the Cordeliers,*' of which he said that ' even if the seven sages of Greece had been members of it, logic could not have been sounder there.'

' Since I came to dwell in this land of liberty,' he says, ' I have longed to take possession of my title as an honourable member of the illustrious district. Therefore, I went one day lately to take my civic oath and salute the fathers of the country, my neighbours. With what pleasure I inscribed my name, not on those useless baptismal registers which could not defend us from despotism, royal, sacerdotal, magisterial, or feudal ; and from which Ministers and Pierre Lenoir, lawyers and harlots, efface you so readily, leaving no trace of your existence ; but upon the tablets of my tribe, upon the register of Pierre Duplain, upon this true book of life, the faithful and incorruptible depository of all those names, and which will give an account of them to the ever-watchful district.'

' I cannot but yield,' he adds, ' to a religious sentiment ; I could believe myself to have been born again.'[1]

When the ceremony, which was very simple and agitating only to a novice, was terminated, Camille writes :

' I was about to retire thanking God, if not, like Pangloss, for being in the best of all possible worlds, at least for being in the best of all possible districts,

---

[1] Camille Desmoulins, although not mentioned by M. E. Rebold, in his ' Histoire Générale de la Franc-Maçonnerie,' among famous masons, was a freemason, like Voltaire, Helvetius, D'Alembert, Gustavus III. of Sweden, Boucher, Champfort, Parny, Delille, Lalande, Joseph Buonaparte the future king of Spain, Eugène de Beauharnais, Bernadotte, Augereau, Fichte, Condorcet, Masséna, Oudinot, &c. In the eighteenth century freemasonry was powerful ; since then it has lost its influence. I have in my possession the Rosicrucian decoration (a little triangular ornament, with a pelican tearing its breast, in the middle) which Desmoulins wore at all the ceremonies of his lodge. This historical curiosity came into my hands through those of M. Armingaud, who had it from his father-in-law, to whom it was given by Horace Desmoulins, the son of Camille. It is, therefore, perfectly authentic.

when the sentinel called the doorkeeper, and the door-keeper announced to the President that a young lady positively insisted on coming into the hall.

'This was the celebrated Mademoiselle Théroigne, who demanded permission to speak, and to propose a motion?'

A strange one it must be admitted. Théroigne was simply about to propose that a Temple to the National Assembly should be constructed.

'It is the Queen of Sheba come to visit the Solomon of the districts,' cried Desmoulins, quite dazzled by the strange beauty of this woman, who has been alleged, by some writers, to have become his mistress.

Anne Terwagne, 'the fair Liégeoise,' whom the Court Journal, 'Le Petit Gauthier,' confounded with Madame de Staël (perhaps to please the Queen, who hated Necker's daughter to the point of refusing to owe her safety to her, as Malouet tells us), was at that time hardly twenty years old. She was rather one of the 'un-classed' and artist world than a courtesan; her seducer, a German baron, had basely abandoned her, and she rushed into extravagance and violence, in the bitter-ness and grief caused by his desertion. Calling herself Théroigne de Méricourt, or, rather, de Marcourt (Luxembourg), she attracted some of the deputies to the National Assembly to the hôtel de Grenoble in the Rue du Bouloi, where she lodged; and, like the Greek courtesans, who, following the example of Aspasia, surrounded themselves with philosophers, she sought her associates among thinkers and politicians armed for the strife.

'Her principles are those of the Portico,' said Champcenetz, alluding to her in his 'Actes des Apô-tres;' but she would not object to those of the 'Arcades.'

The defenders of the throne respected women as
little as its enemies; the allusion to the 'Arcades'
was aimed at the Palais-Royal and the women who
frequented it.   Nor was this all.   The 'Apôtres'
invented a marriage between Théroigne and Populus,[1]
stigmatised the poor girl, insulted her through her past
life, her present life, her unhappy love, even her personal appearance.   In every way they harassed the
unfortunate creature, who was afterwards, on the 10th
of August, to exhibit herself, astride upon a cannon,
as the Fury of the civil war, and ultimately to be driven
quite mad by the cowardly treatment inflicted upon her
by the 'Muscadins,' who had her flogged upon the
terrace of the Feuillants.

I have mentioned the 'Actes des Apôtres' as the
most overt enemy of Camille Desmoulins.   It was a
laboratory of royalist calumnies and abuse.   The
'Révolutions de France et de Brabant' may be reproached for its cruelty, but let us consider the vileness
of Peltier's journal.   It was at Gattey's, in the Palais-
Royal that Peltier first published the paper which, as
is evident from its nominal title, was intended to turn
the acts of 'the Apostles of liberty' into ridicule.   All
the contributors to this aggressive publication are not
known; they were, if its own statement be believed,
forty-five.   More than once they dub themselves the
forty-five apostles.   Camille calls them 'disciples of
Jérome Vadé.'   Their boudoir pleasantries have a
flavour of the fish market about them.   'The "Actes
des Apôtres,"' said Camille, 'form the highest eulogium
on the tolerance of the National Assembly, just as
the blasphemies of Atheists form the highest eulogium

---

[1] See the monograph of M. Marcellin Pellet, 'Les Actes des Apôtres'
(1789-1791), vol. i.   1873.

on the clemency of the Supreme Being' (' Révolutions de France et de Brabant,' No. 17, p. 148). Learned Voltairians, angry nobles, unfrocked abbés, idle *beaux esprits*, Rivarol, Champcenetz, Suleau, Bergasse, Montlosier, the Comte de Lauraguais, the Abbé de la Bintinaie, Canon Turménie, and many others, had banded themselves together to make a war of little epigrams and big calumnies against the new-born Revolution. To read them is like being present at a farewell orgie of the departing age. Licentious verse diverges into virulent attack; libertine song shows its teeth in an attempted smile. Smart wit turns to gall, jests are steeped in venom. The good taste of the quiddities of old times is replaced by a blind rage which deprives these enemies of the new epoch of all their graces of style.

Here and there, however, a man of true wit lets fall a perfumed and acid drop into the deluge of heavy insolence. More than once in these pages we find the mark of Rivarol's talons. While the celebration of the Fête of the Federation was going on in the Champ de Mars, it rained heavily; and the following lines appeared in the 'Actes des Apôtres :

> ' Toujours de l'eau ! quel temps maudit !
> Disait, au Champ de Mars, Damis le démocrate.
> C'est fait exprès, je l'avais bien prédit,
> Que le Père Eternel était aristocrate.'

These Apostles were defenders of the Altar, as well as of the Throne, after the fashion of men who combine impiety with gallantry. Their god was, in fact, Voltaire, who could have done very well without their worship. They were by way of being champions of royalty, and they accustomed the nation to disrespect for the National Assembly which then represented France. The sound of the President's bell inspired them with such verses as this :

> ' Encor ce bruit original
> " *Gredin, Gredin !* " dont toute l'Assemblée
> A comme moi, la cervelle fêlĕe ;
> Que dit-il donc ?   C'est l'appel nominal ! '

' Liberty, gaiety, royal democracy,' wrote they upon their programme. They might have added ' Licence and abuse.' Upon the organisation of the new tribunals, Robespierre is nominated to a judgeship at Marseilles, and they write :—

> ' Juger vaut mieux qu'être pendu,
> Je le crois bien, mon bon apôtre,
> Mais différé n'est pas perdu,
> Et l'un n'empêchera pas l'autre.'

Mirabeau, whom they call a ' magnificent scoundrel,' is not spared.

> ' De forfaits, de crapule, exécrable assemblage,
> L'enfer, qui le vomit pour l'horreur de notre âge,
> Aurait comblé nos maux, si de sa lâcheté
> L'excès n'était égal à sa férocité.'

This was the prevailing tone. And we are astonished at Camille's occasional violence ! The servitors of royalty gave the pitch-note.

In the royalist pamphlets, such attacks upon Camille as the following were to be found :—

' The journalists have bread now, since honest folks lack it. The scribbler Desmoulins, who formerly slept on a bed of straw, now sleeps on one hung with blue damask. Formerly he fared like Strabo's valet, dining on fruit, onions and a bottle of water ; but now he eats at Méot's, at nine francs a head.'—' Petit Dictionnaire des Grands Hommes et des

Grandes Choses qui ont rapport à la Révolution,' composed by a Society of Aristocrats, 1791. [1]

Was there not even some talk of *imposing silence* on him? Did not Suleau[2] throw in his teeth the 'shamelessness which well becomes liberty?' More and more low and stupid became the abuse which was heaped upon him. Everyone knows the dull, oft-quoted jest which dubbed Camille, *l'ânon des moulins.* It must have made him smile pityingly; but, perhaps, it also enraged the editor of the 'Révolutions de France et de Brabant.'

> ' Aux moulins de Montmartre est un petit ânon,
> Sans force encor, mais aussi traître,
> Aussi têtu qu'un âne pourrait être ;
> En un mot, la terreur des enfants du canton.
> Sa manie est de toujours braire ;
> Mais quand le bruit qu'il fait étourdit les voisins,
> Cent coups de bâton dans les reins
> Le font cesser ; c'est de cette manière
> Qu'on impose silence à *l'ânon des moulins.*'

Not by blows, but by elegant epigrams did Desmoulins reply to these vulgar attacks. The mere lawyer gave lessons in politeness and in fence with words to these frantic 'gentlemen.' He laughed at their clumsy wit, and though he condescended too often to imitate their misplaced buffoonery (he called Fontanes, *Font âne,* and Mallet du Pan, *Mallet Pendu*), he rallies them for

---

[1] At a later date I find in the 'Journal Français' the following ' will' of Count Journiac Saint-Médard : ' I bequeathe to Camille, *a bottled viper* ; to Billaud, the first crop of my hay ; to Anarchasis Clootz, a conjuror's box and balls ; to Danton, a wren of the smallest species, stuffed with the greatest care.'

[2] 'Who does not know the famous Suleau, who, like Robespierre, comes from the College of Louis-le-Grand, but has profited far better by the lessons of Royou, his teacher, so that he has become the Don Quixote of the aristocracy, and, as he informs us, he is called *the knight of difficulty* ?'—' Révolutions de France et de Brabant,' No. 68.

the most part with a charming tone of superiority.
For instance, when he speaks of Rivarol, and Peltier.[1]
The latter, indeed, was completely crushed by Camille's
deadly pleasantries.   Here is a passage about Peltier.
'A district having invested the printing-office of M.
Didot has seized a great number of copies of the "Actes
des Apôtres."   M. Didot sent back to M. Manuel the
manuscript signed *Peltier*.   The apostle immediately
repaired to M. Manuel's presence, invoked the indefi-
nite liberty of the press, and perorated in these words :
"What will the Queen say if she has not the number
to-morrow morning ?"   Happy Peltier !   It was not,
then, enough for thee that a charming Greek, who had
held in her hands the urn of Achilles, came express to
the banks of the Seine, but the wife of the King must
look for the reading of thy productions as for the
morning dew !   I am no longer astonished at thy marvellous riddles, at thine inexhaustible gaiety and those
divine fictions of the child-bed of Target and the loves
of M. Populus !'[2]

[1] Camille sometimes rhymed his epigrams; for example, he writes
about D'Esprémesnil—(the language is very curious) :—

> ' Il aimait fort le bien *public* :
> En lui c'était vraiment un *tic*,
> Et seul n'entendait mieux le *chic*.'

On the branding of Madame de la Motte :—

> ' Maintenant peut-on douter
> Que des Valois la Motte soit la fille ?
> Un arrêt lui fait porter
> Les armes de sa famille !'

Calonne also, whom in ' La France Libre' he called 'ô mon cher
Calonne,' comes in for his share of raillery :—

> ' Calonne a beau faire la chattemite,
> Puis-je croire à la poule au pot,
> Lorsque pour payer son impôt
> Il me fait vendre la marmite ?'

[2] No. 22, p. 417.

Bergasse is the most hardly dealt with of all, and No. 23 of the ' Révolutions de France et de Brabant' is a masterpiece of keen raillery. It relates to Bergasse and to Guillaume Kornmann ; and Camille affects the lyrical style in order to mock more effectually at Bergasse, in love with Kornmann. He represents Bergasse as gone mad for love :—

'Now,' he says, 'Bergasse, a second Narcissus, loves no one but himself. Not, however, like the young shepherd, who, bending over a fountain, contemplated his image in the mirror of the waters, does he indulge his passion ; but in his arm-chair, under the shade of an acacia, he reads, without ceasing, his projects of laws ; there he admires the beauty of his genius, there he worships himself, and falls into prolonged ecstasies.'

In this there is finished and exquisite humour ; infinitely preferable, even from the point of view of the quarrel in which he was engaged and of its final result, to the pages in which Desmoulins boasts of being *procureur-général de la lanterne.*[1]

One of the most reprehensible errors of Camille was the idea of making an individual the justice-dealer, and substituting the mob for the law. The famous cobbler of Messina, the anonymous executioner of the ' perverse,' was an ideal in Camille's eyes. According to this notion, he would have accepted a Republic superintended by free-judges. Could such a state of things be even imagined, much less desired ? And yet Camille writes :—

---

[1] 'Révolutions de France et de Brabant,' No. 24.—Desmoulins had said of Bergasse that he received from the king's party eighteen livres a-day. 'What an impudent scoundrel !' exclaimed Bergasse. Camille retorted by printing in his journal, 'We must let Bergasse off the lamp-post, because he is a fool.' The unhappy Camille was playing with death, as a child plays with a sword.

'This much-calumniated people is moved by principles of equity ; it has wholesome notions in this respect, and nothing angers it so much as injustice. Let us remember the cobbler of Messina ! He was born with an intense love of order and justice, and, rendered indignant by monopolies, tricks, public robberies, and the impunity of the guilty, he set to work, without any more ado, to purge society of the criminals. He asked for none of the ordinary formalities which accompany the punishment of evil deeds. His vigilant eye spied out every crime ; and, after a trial with closed doors, he added the duties of the executioner to those of the prosecutor and the judge. He purchased a short arquebuse, which he carried hidden under his cloak (perhaps there were no lamp-posts at Messina in his time) ; and when the malefactors walked abroad in unfrequented ways, or, in pursuit of their criminal business, prolonged their nocturnal expeditions, this friend of order tracked them and shot them down fairly, with five or six bullets in their bodies. After such an exploit he quietly went his way, without ever touching a corpse, and regained his home with the satisfaction of a man who had just killed a wolf or a mad dog.' [1]

Camille's masterpiece, the most remarkable number of the ' Révolutions de France et de Brabant,' is No. 34, in which he thus describes the Fête of the Federation, on the morning of the taking of the Bastille (July 14, 1790) ; a fête which he had hailed as ' the Pasch ' a month before, in No. 30, page 285 :—
' This is the day of release from the servitude of Egypt, and of the passage of the Red Sea. This is the first day of the first year of Liberty. This is the day which the Prophet Ezekiel predicted, the day of destiny, the great *feast of lanterns*.' One turns gladly from the fresh stroke of cruelty which terminates his biblical enumeration to the evidence of the pro-

---

[1] ' Révolutions de France et de Brabant,' No. 27, p. 21.

foundly artistic nature of Camille, which we find in the emotion with which he writes about the music which is to usher in the festival :—

'I dearly love that idea for the opening of the fête. I remember, the first time that I followed the crowd, which took me that day to the Tuileries, with what pleasure I listened to the serenade, which was still given in honour of the king. I was far off from the lights, and the sky was dark with clouds. Alone in the crowd, and a hundred leagues away from it in the isolation of my spirit, I closed my eyes that I might hear the better, and awaited the first scrape of the bow.'

After the fête was over, Camille retraced all its incidents with such enthusiasm that, even now, when eighty-four years have passed away, we cannot read his words without a thrill of retrospective excitement. What happy dreams were those of the early days of the French Revolution! What hours of hope, during which men believed that Liberty had really been won! What bursts of patriotic gladness, the joyous intoxication of a people who did not foresee the trials and misfortunes to come!

National guards from the Departments swarmed into Paris. Platforms for the patriots were in course of construction in the Champ de Mars, when it was rumoured abroad that fifteen thousand workmen were not sufficient to finish the work in time. A simultaneous impulse moved the entire population at the report; and Camille shows us how in the Champ de Mars there was 'an ant-hill of a hundred and fifty thousand workmen, trundling wheelbarrows and digging the ground in a workshop forty thousand yards in width, and whose length went clean beyond sight.'

'Every district, every corporation, every family was

represented there; drums were beating, bands were playing, women and children came on three abreast, with spades upon their shoulders, singing the new song, 'Ça ira.' Old men and old women aided in erecting the altar of the country, of the civic oath, of the oath of liberty and equality! We learn how Saint-Just, while trundling his wheelbarrow, met Madame du Barry with a spade in her hand. Whether this be a true incident or a fable, it shews us the enthusiasm of Paris, that enthusiasm which animates the ardent, eloquent, febrile pages of Desmoulins. 'A patriot tears the barrow from the hands of a languid abbé and pitches the earth on the dust-heap.' The pensioners of the Hôtel des Invalides come to the scene of general activity; peasants flock thither, headed by Mayors begirt with their scarves; a man with broken ribs is hoisted on the shoulders of an old invalid of the time of Louis XIV., who works away, notwithstanding his wooden leg. Collegians, school-boys, the whole Montagne-Ste-Geneviève, students of the Academy of Painting, of the Veterinary School, the flower of Auvergne (the water-carriers), market porters, 'who are as good as the strong men of Israel,' printers,—those of M. Prudhomme decorated with the cover of 'Les Révolutions de Paris,'—charcoal-burners, *Chartreux*, headed by M. Gerle, who had quitted their living sepulchres, and were asking in bewilderment, 'What is this psalm, "Ça ira"?' thither they came, full of enthusiasm; and Camille, in depicting them, seems to have dipped his pen in sunshine. The women laughed and danced around the bewildered monks. Swiss guards, French guards, women from the markets, and even court-ladies were there. The king came, and they applauded him.

La Fayette came and they applauded him more loudly than the king. All was confidence and fraternity during those blissful hours. Not a theft took place. A young man left his two watches on the ground while he was working. A generous citizen wheeled a barrow laden with a barrel of wine, and gave the grateful drink gratis to the patriotic labourers. A marquise removed her glove to shake hands with a coalporter. The whole scene was like an immense ball. Camille described it as a stage *ballet*, the scene being ' The Reunion of the Orders.' Eleven hundred Bretons had come from Brittany, on foot, carrying their arms. Numerous inscriptions drew attention to the object of this fête, and the dream of the people.

'Les mortels sont égaux. Ce n'est pas la naissance,
C'est la seule vertu qui fait la différence.'

'La loi dans tout Etat doit être universelle.'

Delicate hands wielded the pickaxe, young girls coveted callosities which should testify to their patriotism. 'Ah,' cries Camille, 'at least let not the hard leather strap of the truck hurt the delicate breasts of that young girl. Let it not hinder those two faithful witnesses from deposing to the secret desire of her heart !' I know not why, but it seems to me that in this exclamation, uttered in the style of the time, Camille refers to Lucile, when he caught sight of Mademoiselle Duplessis, whom he loved, among the zealous workers.

In No. 36, Camille continues to describe this fête in the same felicitous and brilliant style.

A great number of citizens had passed the night on the Champ de Mars. Others had been up and stirring since five o'clock.　Camille describes the icy wind and the intermittent rain which blew and beat upon half a million of men.　Nevertheless, in the teeth of the wind and under the lash of the rain, the Auvergnats danced their *bourrée*, and the Provençaux their *farandoles*. Immense rings of dancers were formed.　'Look at those Frenchmen dancing while the rain is falling in torrents,' said the foreigners.　After the taking of the civic oath, came beating of drums, firing of guns, waving of swords, shouts of triumph, hats tossed in the air, the unfurling of eighty-three white banners, and of the oriflammes and flags of sixty districts.　All this is marvellously described by Desmoulins.　One unanimous cry issued from the lips of six hundred thousand persons :—'France is free!　We swear it!' Fathers held up the hands of their children.　An old man from the faubourg Saint Honoré, who had been bed-ridden for two years, had himself carried to the altar of the country.　A banquet for twenty-two thousand people was served in the gardens of the Château de la Muette ; and as there were only five or six thousand guests (all in uniform), the remainder of the dishes were distributed to the poor.　The trees were hung with lamps.　One orchestra served for ten country dances at once.　The site of the Bastille was turned into an artificial wood, in which large trees were lighted up, and adorned with pikes and Phrygian caps, and with the famous inscription, *Dancing here!*

At Nôtre Dame, on the thirteenth, six hundred musicians had played the ' Prise de la Bastille,' 'Words by King David, music by M. Désaugiers.'　The corn-market was brilliantly illuminated.　The Champs Elysées were lighted up with candles.　At ten o'clock on the morning of Wednesday, July 14, the widows and orphans of the conquerors of the Bastille listened to a eulogium upon their dead. The festival of French liberty was also celebrated in London. At the Crown and Anchor tavern, in the Strand, the Whig Club, consisting of six hundred and fifty-two persons, presided over by Lord Stanhope, drank to 'The liberty of the world.' A servant got up on the table with a fragment of stone from the Bastille in his hand and proposed the following toast : ' To the extinction of all jealousy between France and England, and may they seek only to defend peace and liberty !'

Dr. Price demanded the foundation of a League of Peace ; the first idea of the Utopia of to-day which will, perhaps, be the reality of to-morrow.

In these descriptions, written by Desmoulins, we find the already famous name of Danton ; who had protested, at the special fête of the Cordeliers, at Vaux Hall, against official toasts. He would not drink any health but that of the Country.

These few quotations give a very imperfect notion of the inexhaustible store of ideas, facts, and happy turns of style, called ' Les Révolutions de France et de Brabant,' in which the men who made the Revolution defile before us ; from Robespierre, 'my dear schoolfellow, and the ornament of the Northern Deputation,' as Camille calls him, to Davoust, 'a young officer, and good patriot.' On one page is the announcement of the ' *Organt* ' of Saint-Just, on another a letter from Marat, or De Merlin (of Douai), or from Linguet, calling Desmoulins his ' dear brother in arms.' ' Your country prides itself upon you,' writes Saint-Just,—who was also from Picardy,—and then he adds :—' Glory, peace, and patriotic passion.' 'I am democratically your friend,' says Stanislas Fréron. Lafayette, Rewbell, Manuel (the future *procureur* of the Commune of Paris), write to him. Mirabeau overwhelms him with compliments, until the day comes when in speaking of him he shall call him '*that poor Camille.*' 'Well, poor Camille, has your head come right again! We have sulked with you, but we forgive you.' (Letter from Mirabeau, May 2, 1790.) 'Adieu, *good boy*, you deserve to be loved, notwithstanding your fiery flights.' I may observe, by the way, that, almost at the same time (August 16, 1790), Marat addresses Camille very much in the same tone. *Cassandre-Marat* writes in 'L'Ami du Peuple,'—'Notwithstanding all your cleverness, my dear Camille, you are a complete novice in politics. Perhaps that amiable gaiety which is the fundamental trait of your character, and which shows itself in your treatment of the gravest subjects, opposes itself to serious reflection; but you are vacillating in your judgments; you seem to have neither plan nor aim.' 'L'Ami du Peuple' and the son of 'the friend of men' are equally severe.

'Good boy! Poor Camille!' Perhaps it was a word of this kind which alienated Camille from Mirabeau, whom, after having praised him as the marvellous man who, for a moment, bore the Revolution and its fortunes on his own shoulders, he afterwards overwhelmed with satire. Praise and censure were alike unmeasured. Camille was not destined long to remain the friend of Mirabeau, of whom De la Marck said justly: 'He carried with him to the tomb the consolation of having had many friends.'

'I have often varied,' said Camille, afterwards, 'because there are so few men who are consistent; but,

as I have said, it is not the weathercock which turns, it
is the wind !'

Nevertheless, the weathercock is very severe upon
the wind. No. 72 of the ' Révolutions' is violent and
bitter against a man of whom Lafayette said : ' Mirabeau never got himself paid except in the sense of his
opinions,' and Rivarol, more ill-naturedly : ' The Court
reckoned little upon a man with whom one always had
to reckon ;' a man of whom Camille had written :—

' Death, which knits up again every attachment, brought
me back to his house before it entered there, as indeed any
peril of his would have brought me back ; and it was not my
fault if his servants did not tell him how much I grieved for
his illness. But I could do no more than write my name at
his door. I had preferred my love for truth to the friendship
of Mirabeau.

' Mirabeau ! the patriot, the tribune of the people, the
father of the Constitution, the friend of the negroes, he who
exercises the only dictatorship to which a free people submits,
—that of speech ; and before whom it seems to me that the
fasces of eloquence and the twenty-four axes of Demosthenes
are carried.'

Afterwards he regrets that he did not witness Mirabeau's death. Herein is the secret of his heart. His
admiration of the man exists always, in spite of everything, although, for example, he writes that Mirabeau,.
in common with Buffon, indulged in the puerility of
having himself called ' Monsieur le Comte.' He even
adds, ' Mirabeau made ample use of the free leave
which the dying have, to sound their own praises :
" Hold my head up," said he to his servant, at a critical
moment; " you will never hold another like it." ' Is not
this somewhat like the dying utterance of Danton ;
that Danton who was a kind of *bourgeois* Mirabeau,
equally powerful, but neither dissolute, nor venal ?

Camille, who ought not to have added anything to Marat's sufficiently insulting saying, 'Mirabeau was a patriot one day, and he is dead,' collects all the current rumours about the death. Some protested that Mirabeau had been poisoned : Cabanis asserts that 'he died, suffocated with truffles, and scorched with côte-rôtie.'

'He said to me one day,' continues Desmoulins, '"I hold the proof that the Lameths employed M. La Croix to write 'The Great Treason of Mirabeau,' and I have in my desk the warrant of arrest which I procured against M. La Croix ; but I made no use of it, because I believed that not only liberty, but licence of the press was, at that time, necessary." "It would have been better," said Danton, "not to have applied for a warrant for the arrest of M. La Croix."'

In giving an account of the funeral procession, Desmoulins cannot refrain from acknowledging that all Paris was deeply affected by the death of Mirabeau.

'In the Rue Louis-le-Grand, a man at a window cried out, as we passed, "There go the thirty-three." We might have replied, "Say, rather, the thirty-three thousand!"' In fact, the procession of the Jacobins numbered no less than that.

'In his life-time,' he adds, 'I called Mirabeau, the Great Mirabeau, Demosthenes Mirabeau, Mirabeau the Thunderer, Hercules Mirabeau, Saint Mirabeau. Such hyperbole was allowable then. I knew that he loved fame ; more than once he has sent his secretary to me, from a distance of two leagues, to entreat me to efface a page in my paper, for he dreaded its censure. I had only praise to set against the gold by which the despots sought to attract him !'

He afterwards attacks the dead Mirabeau, a fallen victim, with terrible bitterness.

' Mirabeau was eloquent,' he says, ' but he reigned in the tribune rather by his talent as an actor than by the power of his mind.'

Camille, who was afterwards to be reproached with his own friendship for Dillon, actually upbraids. Mirabeau with his ubiquity :—' Breakfasting with the Jacobins, dining with 89, and supping with La Marck and the Monarchists. Where he slept it is not for me to tell.' This question of Mirabeau's dinners turns up very often under Camille's pen. Had he forgotten the pleasure with which he dined at Mirabeau's house, and tasted his maraschino ? ' Mirabeau,' he says, in his No. 67, ' sups at Velloni's, the Italian restaurant, Place des Victoires, with the former Bishop of Autun.' The very things with which Desmoulins reproaches others form the subject of reproach against himself afterwards.

' I am taunted,' he said, at a later date, ' with having dined recently with some of the great props of the royalist aristocracy. The harm is not in dining with these gentlemen, but in holding their opinions. I thought that I was quite equal to a doctor of the Sorbonne to whom it was permitted to read forbidden books, and that I might even dine with authors on the Index.'

Did Desmoulins at least repent of having denounced Mirabeau because he supped with M. de la Marck ? Not so : in No. 73 of the ' Révolutions de France et de Brabant,' he continues his fierce attack.

Camille relates how, after the decree on peace and war had been passed, he met Mirabeau as he came out of the Assembly, in the cloister of the Feuillants, and said to him, ' You have sold yourself for a hundred thousand crowns.' Mirabeau smiled, took him by the arm, led him to the Rue de l'Échelle, and said amiably,

'Come and dine.' This was his only attempt at justifying himself. Then he goes on to compute the fortune of Mirabeau, whose father died insolvent :—

'Some months before the opening of the States General,' says Camille, 'he pawned a neckcloth-buckle at the Mont de Piété, and two years later he bequeathed by his will :—

To a child who was dear to him .	24,000 livres	
To his secretary	24,000 „	
To his physician	24,000 „	
To each of the Demoiselles du Saillant	2,800 „	*per ann.*
To each of his other nieces . .	600 „	„
To M. de la Marck, his library, for which he paid . . .	200,000 livres	

He also remits the whole of Madame de Jay's debts to him.'

Camille again dwells on 'the pomp of Lucullus,' the banquets which the great orator gave to his section, at a cost of fifteen thousand livres ; and, roused to irritation, even to violence, oblivious of the Count's dinners and his maraschino, he exclaims :—

. 'Go then, O corrupt nation, O stupid people, and prostrate yourself before the tomb of this honest man, the Mercury of his age, and the god of orators, liars and thieves !'

Camille afterwards tried to explain his variation of opinion respecting Mirabeau, in a letter to Brissot :—

'Mirabeau,' he says, 'made me live with him under the same roof at Versailles. He flattered me by his esteem, he touched me by his friendship, he mastered me by his genius and his great qualities. I loved him to idolatry ; his friends knew how much he dreaded my censure, which was read by Marseilles, and which will be read by posterity. It is well known that, more than once, he sent his secretary from a distance of two leagues to entreat me to withdraw a page of what I had written; to make this sacrifice to friendship, to his great past services, and to the hope of those in the future. Say then, whether I sold myself to Mirabeau! I did not know that traitors, immensely inferior to him in talent, and but recently listened to from the tribune, were about to lead us to the ruin of our liberty far more treacherously than he; and that they would force me to implore pardon from his great shade, and daily to mourn the loss to France of her resources in his genius, and the loss to liberty of his love of glory.'

Notwithstanding all that he had previously said, and all that he had written, even in the presence of the corpse of a man who desired—they are Mirabeau's own words—'*Order*, but not the *old Order*,' we feel that Camille had really loved Mirabeau. Yes! though he boasted, in the 'Révolutions de France et de Brabant,' that he had gazed with dry eyes on the superb brow of the great dead, wrapped in his shroud! Alas! the saying of the mighty orator was terribly true! That saying was destined to be repeated by posterity concerning this man whose talents were so great, but whose weakness was greater, whose sensibility made him deplore his fits of murderous invective quickly, indeed, but too late; and for all future time Desmoulins was to be, as he had been for Mirabeau—*That poor Camille!*

III.

The picture of Camille Desmoulins as a journalist would not be complete without a sketch of the polemics in which he engaged. The *Anon des Moulins*, to use the attic language of the Apôtres, was one of the

best-abused, most calumniated, and oftenest threatened
of the journalists of the Revolution.   Now, he is accused of having disguised himself in female attire and
joined the concourse of the Mænads, as Carlyle calls
them, who flocked down to Versailles in the train of
Maillart; again, he is overwhelmed with charges of
the basest venality and corruption.   Money, as history
now knows, never soiled the hands of either Desmoulins or Danton.   ' I congratulate myself hourly,' Camille
wrote to his father (7th July 1793), ' on having come out
of the Convocation and the Revolution as I went into
them, without having increased my patrimony.   No
one can ever accuse me of having used the Revolution as a speculation.'

The attacks upon Camille only embittered the tone
of his writings.   He continued to ridicule his adversaries, and the wounds inflicted by his caustic humour
were very severe.   How furious he must have made
the men whom he mocked !—for instance, the Vicomte
de Mirabeau, whom he reproaches for a ' Vaugirard
kind of gaiety ; ' and whose portrait he draws as follows,
from a caricature :—

' He is easily recognised by his double epaulettes, with
their fringe of sausages, and his sleeves formed of wine-
pitchers.   His breeches are two little barrels, and his legs are
clothed in Champagne bottles turned upside down ; the
tumbling, foaming wine as it spills form the feet, which are
more like those of a faun than of a man.   In short, lest anyone should fail to recognise him, there is an inscription on
the barrel on the right, V. D. M.—*Vin de Malvoisie,* or *Vicomte
de Mirabeau.*'

Mirabeau-Tonneau was not the only victim of
Camille's ridicule.   He mocked at the *eight hundred
farms* of the Abbé Maury, whom he sometimes calls

l'abbé Maudit ; he satirised Malouet, Cazalès, and then, pausing in the attack, he says, with terrible irony :—

'But I am very wrong to complain of you, gentlemen, of Monsieur Cazalès, of Mirabeau the younger, of Maury and of Malouet. What would become of my journal if you should agree among yourselves to turn honest, or if you should set out with D'Esprémesnil to rebuild your turreted castles, with right of venery and dovecot, on the banks of the Scioto ? I shudder to think of it. We should be ruined, my publisher and I !'

It is easy to imagine what an outcry was raised about these utterances of Camille. One day, as we are told by Regnault de Saint-Jean d'Angèly, a certain person named Bonne-Carrère threatened, in the tribune at the Jacobins, to inflict five hundred blows with a cane upon Desmoulins. On another occasion the Spanish Ambassador, Count Fernand Nunez, complained to M. de Montmorin of the audacity of Camille. M. de Montmorin could do nothing in the matter. At length Malouet, tired of such reiterated abuse, declared that he would speak from the tribune, of the 'Révolutions de France et de Brabant.'

But Camille held his ground. 'I will not have it said,' he declared, 'that a Picard has yielded to an Auvergnat ;—I shall go on with my journal.'

During the sitting of the 31st July, 1790, Malouet denounced Camille. 'It is not,' he said, 'a private injury which I wish to avenge. After a whole year of silence and contempt, I come here as the avenger of a public crime.' 'Go on, Malouet!' writes Camille, 'that's the way to pay your court to the king's wife!'

'It was expected,' he adds, 'that Malouet was

going to justify his tirade by reading aloud the passages he had denounced. But, not so ; after he had abused Desmoulins, he read Marat.'

On the motion of Malouet, the Assembly decreed that the *procureur du roi* to the Châtelet should be instructed to prosecute these incendiary productions as acts of *lèse-nation.* Two days afterwards, 2nd August, an address by Camille, in which he complained that his denouncer had not read the implicated number of the Journal, was read to the Assembly. 'The question is about my complaint,' said Malouet; 'is Camille Desmoulins innocent ? Then let him justify himself. Is he guilty ? Then I will be his accuser and that of all who shall defend him. Let him justify himself, if he dares !' 'I was choking at all these replies,' writes Camille, who was present at the sitting. 'The violence of my feelings was such that if I had been dumb, I believe I should have found a tongue like the son of Crœsus at the taking of Sardis.'

He rose, and replied to the defiance of Malouet.

'Yes, I do dare,' he cried.

Then arose an indescribable uproar.

'Arrest him, arrest him !' shouted the representatives; and for a moment Camille thought he should be brought to the bar. 'I was quite flattered at the notion of appearing at the bar,' he says, 'and glad I had on my very best shirt for the occasion.' . But he was really glad to escape. He says, 'The bailiffs, who were on the look out for a half-starved author, let *me* pass.' During this time Robespierre had ascended the tribune and was defending Camille, whose arrest he succeeded in preventing.

'My dear Robespierre did not forsake me at that moment.' adds Desmoulins, when he relates the circumstances. In the 'Portefeuille de Camille' (published by the elder M. Matton), there is a letter from an individual, unnamed, who was very near being arrested in place of Desmoulins. But for Robespierre's harangue, there is no doubt that Camille would have had to pay dearly for his explanation. The skill of his friend Maximilian saved him.

Our space would not suffice to record all the discussions and prosecutions into which the licence of his pen plunged Camille. 'There is,' said he, 'an excess of good sense and of wisdom which one ought to avoid.' The truth is that he avoided it too successfully. We should digress too widely were we to relate, in detail, the strife between the author of the 'Révolutions de France et de Brabant' and the enemies whom he made for himself. Such is, however, the fate of every journalist. It is impossible, as was said by a journalist of that time, to beat a dog and keep it from howling. Mounier had protested, as strongly as Malouet, against what he called the *infamous libels* of Camille. On another occasion Desmoulins, in speaking of a 'Crillon committee,' called M. de Crillon a 'doubtful citizen.' M. de Crillon immediately demanded one hundred thousand livres damages, or a retraction. 'I retract,' replied Camille, 'but I ask M. de Crillon where is that freedom of the press which M. de Crillon himself caused to be decreed?' Desmoulins had said that M. Talon, civil lieutenant at the Châtelet, was 'bought;' that he had been offered a post in the Municipality. (See Révolutions, No. 29.) Talon applied to have him arrested, and Desmoulins learned afterwards from Mirabeau that La Fayette had prevented this being done. Antoine Talon then indicted him for calumny. He demanded ten livres as damages, to be given to the poor.   Camille replies ; 'Wait, Antoine Talon, I shall be with you in á moment!'   Already we find in the 'Révolutions de France et de Brabant' the famous style, the celebrated menace, the cry : 'Wait, Hebert!' of the ' *Vieux Cordelier.*'   Desmoulins was condemned by default at the Châtelet.

After Talon, it is the turn of Bergasse to be accused by Camille of being 'bought.'   ' He gets eighteen livres a day,' said Desmoulins.   Bergasse was furiously angry : 'What an impudent scoundrel!' said he.   Camille, ironical and implacable, shrugged his shoulders, and remarked : ' Bergasse must be let off the lamp-post because he is mad !'   No doubt it was Mirabeau who excited Camille's animosity against this personage, from jealousy of the favour in which so commonplace an individual was held at court.   Bergasse was much more in his place at Mesmer's *baquet* than at the head of a political movement.   Nor was this the only instance in which Mirabeau supplied Camille with a target for his arrows.

From the list of the squabbles of Camille with his contemporaries we must not omit the writ which was served upon the author of the ' Révolutions de France et de Brabant,' jointly with Gorsas (see Appendix), and the suit brought against him by M. and Madame de Carondelet, whom he accused of bigamy, on information which he received from two persons, named respectively, Macdonagh and Ruttledge.   This was a strange and romantic affair.   Macdonagh, an Irishman, claimed Rose Plunkett, who had become Marquise de Carondelet, as his wife.   Camille published this person's claim in his journal, and the matter caused a great sensation.   The proceedings in this strange business, which resembles fiction rather than fact, are very voluminous. They are all to be found in the 'Archives Nationales.'

Camille had another action brought against him; this time, it was for having called Sanson 'the executioner' (*bourreau*).

' I call a *cat* a *cat*, and Sanson the *executioner*,' was his laughing comment upon the charge.

' Notwithstanding the prodigious gaiety of the singing aristocrats,' he wrote, ' I doubt whether they make the weeping aristocrats laugh. I am assured that their journal is a facetious collection of the verses which "the Round Table" of aristocrats used to sing at their suppers at the house of the Paris executioner.'

Hence the proceedings at the suit of Sanson.

The following is the text of the citation of the 'executioner of criminal judgments' :—

'Year 1790, January 15, in the forenoon, at the requisition of Ch. H. Sanson, executor of criminal judgments, residing in Paris in the Rue Neuve Saint Jean, in the parish of Saint Laurent, Louis-Philippe Thevénin-Durozay summons Camille Desmoulins, residing at No. 42 in the Rue de Tournon, to appear on Saturday (to-morrow) at ten A.M. with the sieur Garnery, bookseller, at the tribunal of police sitting at the Hôtel de Ville, Paris, and to pay 3,000 livres damages, to be expended in bread for the poor of the parish of Saint Laurent, and to make reparation of honour.

' 3,000 copies of the sentence shall be posted.'

Camille replied :

'You are an ingrate, Monsieur Sanson. I had believed that your interior consciousness of the baseness of your employment prevented you from raising your eyes or daring to write to a citizen, even to thank him; for you owe me thanks for having called you in my prospectus the *representative of the executive power*. I shall not stoop to measure

myself against Sanson, but I am going to teach the executioner (M. le bourreau) what he ought to think of his office.'

The gloomy logic of that terrible time was destined to bring the head of the satirist, one dreadful day,
under the blade of the *representative of the executive
power.* It would even appear that Desmoulins had a
sort of foreknowledge that so it must be, when he wrote,
early in those years of strife : ' I could die with honour
by the hand of Sanson, but to die by the hand of a
hired assassin would be to perish of the bite of a taran-
tula.' What assassin threatened Camille ? Doubtless,
more than one. The gentlemen partisans of the court
had, at one time, sworn to rid the monarchy of its most
dreaded adversaries, the Barnaves of the Parliament,
the Desmoulins of the Press. Charles Lameth's duel
with M. de Castries had exasperated Paris. A private
association was formed for the purpose of protecting
the patriots against assassins, and its skilful swordsmen
were called *spadassinicides.* ' I have taken an oath
to defend all the deputies against their enemies,' wrote
a certain M. Boyer to Prudhomme ; and he did actually
beat off a bully, named Sainte-Luce, who had placed
himself at the head of fifty *spadassinicides.* He made
his address known ; it was in the Passage du Bois
de Boulogne, Faubourg St. Denis. In truth, the
patriots had need of being defended. A national
guard said aloud, after the incident of Malouet's charge
against Desmoulins from the tribune : ' If I meet
Desmoulins I will cut his head open with my sword !'
' That man,' wrote Camille, ' evidently does not like a
joke.'

This swaggerer was worthy to be coupled with
Bonne - Carrère, who had just before threatened

Desmoulins with 'five hundred blows of a cane or a stick.' The cudgel was, it appears, an argument in the eighteenth century. Voltaire himself knew something about that.

One day at the Palais-Royal, Camille tells us, he and Danton narrowly escaped being killed by some six-feet high supporters of *Washington pot au feu* (La Fayette). Carra had just before been struck by Parisot, the aide-de-camp.

After these royalists came the actors to pick a quarrel with Camille. He had ridiculed rather broadly one Naudet, a captain of grenadiers in the National Guard, and a fat actor called Dessessarts, a sapper in the same battalion with Naudet.

The formidable bulk of Dessessarts was proverbial, and Camille made fun of it. Denis Dechanet, who called himself Dessessarts, was born at Langres, in 1738, and died at Baréges, in October 1793. He it was who had procured the suspension of the 'Année Littéraire' (Fréron's) for a year, and tried to get the critic imprisoned in For-l'Evêque, because Fréron had said: 'If the rôle of the Marquis de Ranneville has not succeeded, it is not the fault of the author, but of the *fat ventriloquist* who has so cruelly misrepresented it. This M. Dessessarts is really worth seeing when he makes up his mind to act badly, or to give vent to his hatred against men of letters; then he leaves nothing to be desired!' Dessessarts was a regular begging-actor; and had been constantly in the habit of receiving 'gratifications' from the Duc de Villequer under the old order of things. The actors, of course, regretted the cessation of these 'gratifications.' Hence their attachment to the old *régime.* Michelét has remarked, in his 'History of the French Revolu-

I

tion' (vol. 3, and elsewhere), that 'the hairdressers were essentially counter-revolutionary;'—and he explains why :—because those who live by luxury care little for liberty. I find in the 'Rapport' of Camus, Bancal, Quinette, Lamarque (nivose, year iv. page 56), —'There were people of all sorts : priests, monks, emigrants, women of the town, and hairdressers.'

Without implying any slight to their profession by the remark, we may also say of the actors,—and in particular of Dessessarts,—that they missed the perquisites of the old *régime.*

No. 42 of the 'Revolutions of France and of Brabant' contained the following announcement :—

Important notice to pregnant women.—A letter has reached us, signed Parochel, accoucheur, which informs us that a woman has given birth to an elephant, in consequence of the shock which she experienced from the apparition of the sieur Dessessarts at the moment when he emerges from under the table in the fourth act of 'Tartuffe.' The actors of the Comédie Française are requested to warn the public of the days on which the sieur Dessessarts is to act, by posters printed in the largest type.

Parochel immediately protested, declaring the letter to be false. Dessessarts grew angry, and Desmoulins refused his challenge.[1] 'I should have to pass my

---

[1] M. Desmoulins, author of 'The Revolutions of France and Brabant,' was dining a few days ago at the restaurant kept by the *Suisse* of the Luxembourg. Messieurs Naudet and Dessessarts, of the Comédie Française, were also dining in the same room. They began to abuse Desmoulins violently, and Dessessarts came towards him, with clenched fists, and offered him a challenge. 'It will be,' said M. Desmoulins, 'by continuing to harass the black party and the ministerialists that I shall avenge myself. I might pass my life at the Bois de Boulogne, if I had to give satisfaction to every one who takes offence at my plain speaking. Let them accuse me of cowardice if they like.'—*Anecdotes curieuses et plaisantes relatives à la Révolution de France* ; Paris, 1791.

whole life in the *Bois de Boulogne*,' said he, 'if I were obliged to give satisfaction to everybody who takes offence at my plain speaking. Have patience ! . . . . I fear the time is not far off when we shall have opportunities of dying more usefully and gloriously.' Loustallot says : ' M. Desmoulins merits all honour and praise in this affair, and the two cut-throats a proportionate measure of contempt. . . . If the prejudice in favour of duelling survives the feudal system, true liberty will never exist. The best citizen, the most honest man will always be the slave of the first vagabond, the first hired ruffian who may be let loose upon him.' Talma afterwards interfered to induce Desmoulins to forgive Dessessarts.

On another occasion, when Camille was coming out of Vandefleury's reading-rooms in the Palais Royal with, as he said, ' my *veni mecum* (a stout cane, and pistols, our *veto* '), a shopman followed him, holding in his hand No. 74 of ' Les Révolutions,' came up with him, struck him in the face with the newspaper, and announced that he would like to cut his throat. ' I might have blown your brains out,' said Camille coolly, showing the man the pistols which he always carried, and then contented himself with administering a caning to his assailant. A crowd gathered round and threatened him, while only one national guard from Isère, and a journalist out of the reading-rooms came to his aid. The Marquis de Saint-Huruge, for whom he had pleaded so warmly, sat there quietly reading a newspaper and took no notice. ' For two years past,' says Camille, ' I have been walking through a forest.' And, in No. 34 :—

I begin to doubt whether I ought to sharpen so many daggers to be used against myself, in order to enlighten ungrateful *fédérés*, who proposed, at the Palais Royal in my own hearing, that I should be hanged. I begin to doubt whether a journalist, who has not been placed on guard by the people, but is a self-constituted sentinel, is obliged by his conscience to lead the wandering and underground life of M. Marat. It is all very well to jump into the gulf, like Curtius, when one believes that one's death will save one's country. Jesus of Nazareth went to His Cross because He was certain of effecting the redemption of the human race : nevertheless He sweated blood at the approach of M. Sanson.

These doubts avail nothing. Camille will persevere in his career as a *volunteer journalist*, as he called himself. He will brave abuses and allow calumny to pass unnoticed. Mud does not stain, it only soils the hands which throw it. When Camille was attacked and ridiculed, he always employed a correct and literary style. But the journalists who abused and insulted him, condescended to language of the lowest description, and deserved the contempt with which he wrote of them :—

As for me, when I see many of my *confrères* doing the business of journalists in the style in which Pradon did the business of Corneille, labouring hard to turn me into ridicule, and thus undermine the little credit which my sincerity and patriotism have won for me, I congratulate myself on the fact that the funds of the civil list supply the payment for all these bad jokes, to my injury. The money might be employed in a way much more dangerous to liberty.

In spite of all this well-founded contempt, however, Camille Desmoulins must have reflected bitterly enough upon the risks which he was incurring, and the danger in the atmosphere around him. In a letter to his father we find the following words, which we retain as the cry of the soul of the man who is hereafter to

brave death for the writing of the 'Vieux Cordelier:'
'How many men are there who sell their lives to
kings for a few sous! Shall I do nothing for the love
of my country, of truth, and of justice? I apply to
myself Achilles' words :

'"*Patroclus is dead who was worth far more
than I.*"'[1]

[1] For certain curious documents connected with the quarrel between
Desmoulins and Dessessarts, and also for further samples of the personalities in which Camille indulged at this time, see Appendix.

CHAPTER III.

WHEN Desmoulins wrote to his father that his mind was troubled, a real cause for his hesitation and distress existed. He was suffering from an unhappy attachment which made him wretched and dissatisfied with life. His path had been crossed by a woman to whom he had by degrees surrendered his whole heart. He loved her with deep affection and tenderness. Lucile Duplessis (she frequently wrote her name *Lucille*) became (with Liberty) the supreme passion of Camille's existence, and—so powerful is sentiment in the judgments of history—it is to her seductive image that he owes a great part of the sympathy which is still felt for him. Is it that posterity loves those who in their lifetime have made themselves beloved?

In the memory of men the romance of the life of Camille Desmoulins fills a larger place than its history.

That romance was a long and troubled one. Many obstacles beset the course of that true love. Camille had seen Lucile grow from girlhood—she was eighteen—into womanhood, and had come to love her with an irresistible passion. How had this love sprung up? He had long regarded her as a child, and one day he perceived that she was a woman, and that he loved her. The Leipsic 'Biography,' whose inaccuracies I have frequently detected, pretends that Camille was in strict alliance with the Duke of Orleans, that he went frequently to Mousseaux (Monceaux), and that he wished to marry Pamela, the pupil of Madame de Genlis.[1] I do not believe a word of this. It is true that Camille was attracted for a short time by his cousin Mademoiselle Flora Godart, who after-

---

[1] Camille did, in fact, go to the Duke's *fêtes* at Monceaux, and no doubt gave loose to all his enthusiasm in the beautiful park, where since then Lamartine's genius makes *Raphael* wander. Robespierre was invited to these *fêtes*, but he replied, ' No, I stay at home. *Tisane* of Champagne is the poison of liberty.' With respect to Camille's affection for the Duke of Orleans, we find in No. 49 of the 'Révolutions de France et Brabant' an apostrophe to this effect: ' Dear Philippe ! lofty and republican soul !' (p. 441). See also the defence of the conduct of the Duke of Orleans on October 5 and 6, of which Camille said, ' *These are the happiest days of France.*' ' On July 14,' he adds, ' the people took only the Bastille ; but on October 5 they took the king and his wife.' The son of the Duke of Orleans, the Duke de Chartres (afterwards a soldier at Valmy, and king of the French under the name of Louis Philippe I.), having visited the patients of the Hôtel Dieu, during an epidemic, Camille Desmoulins spoke of the self-devotion of *that excellent Jacobin, M. de Chartres.* Certain biographers have not hesitated to state that on Camille's marriage the Duke of Orleans presented the young couple with the furniture of their apartment. It is hardly necessary to remark that the assertion is entirely unfounded.

wards married M. Tarrieux de Tailland.   He did
court her, perhaps ; and there is a story that his cousin
watched for his passing in the tumbril on his way to
the scaffold, that she might interchange a last look with
him.   But it is certain, and beyond all question, that
Lucile was the only love of Camille.

They met at the Luxembourg, in the shady garden-
alleys of the palace of Marie de Medicis, which, in the
irony of coincidences, was afterwards to be Camille's
prison.   He was a student, greedy of fame; she, a
child quite ignorant of life, when they saw each other
first, and made acquaintance under the eye of Lucile's
mother, Madame Duplessis.   No doubt a certain
sympathy sprang up in the mind of Madame Duplessis
for the ardent young man who went about confiding
his dreams to all comers, and whom the Revolution
had made famous, since July 1789.   Madame Duplessis
knew Desmoulins ; he had met the mother and her
young daughter long before the taking of the Bastille ;
but the light of renown which now shone upon him
was not likely to injure him with the elder lady.   The
adventure at the Palais Royal, the distribution of
green leaves, typical of hope, had a romantic air about
it eminently calculated to charm the fancy of a woman.
As for Lucile, she was probably captivated rather by
the sudden fame which he had acquired than by the
indisputably great charm of Camille Desmoulins
himself.   The girl was of a fanciful and romantic
temperament, full of the vague suffering which, although
unreal, is deep seated and tormenting.   The whole
of society at a later epoch was destined to feel the
pain which a few exceptional natures were then under-
going, distrust of themselves, the melancholy and dis-
quietude of youth, and instinctive hatred of a world

which attracts by its seductions, but repels by its base-ness. Rousseau, the sickly and unwholesome Rousseau, falsest and most deceitful of minds, had already spread abroad that interior' sadness and causeless discontent which a few years later was to be the disease of René.[1] Rousseau, who probably did not feel the griefs which he made others experience, had already acted strongly upon society. Lucile Duplessis was one of his victims.

In person, Lucile was of small stature, and very graceful; her beautiful fair hair fell around a smiling, childish face, one which Greuze might have painted. She did not exhibit, in appearance or manner, any of the vague disquiet which reveals itself in the pages of her journal. The sketch made at a later date by the person who afterwards became Marshal Brune does not give us any true idea of the irresistible grace of this woman, who was indeed an heroic child. I have only preserved this remembrance because' it is, in a double sense, as relating to the artist and the subject, a historical document. But Lucile was far otherwise charming and attractive. The venerable Moreau de Jonnès (of the Institute), who was present at the most terrible scenes of the Revolution, on June 30 and on August 10, whose testimony I have already invoked, and who honoured me with his friendship, once described to me a sitting of the Cordeliers at which Camille and Lucile Desmoulins were present. He witnessed their entry; they came in smiling, radiant with youth and happiness. He said of Lucile: ' She was an adorable little *blonde*.'

Had she loved the young man ever since he had begun to adore her ? Not so ; but he had come at the

---

[1] The hero of Chateaubriand's most famous romance.

hour I have described, the hour in which the young girl felt the strong need of loving, which was, I imagine, intensified by the political and social atmosphere of the time.

If we are to believe the evidence of his enemies, Camille was not handsome.   A writer who is ready to defame him either morally or physically says :—

He had a bilious complexion, like Robespierre's, a hard and sinister eye, more like that of the osprey than that of the eagle.   I saw him often, and he never seemed to me better looking than at first.   I know there were some who tried to make him out a handsome fellow, but either they were flatterers, or they had never seen him.[1]

A few lines found in a book belonging to M. de Saint-Beuve's library, and attributed to the father of the illustrious critic, state that 'Desmoulins had a *disagreeable exterior.*'   'I am not a handsome fellow, it must be allowed,' wrote Camille himself to Arthur Dillon.[2]

To the evidence of these two men we have to oppose that of a woman.   'He was ugly,' says the author of a very curious pamphlet on the Sainte-Amaranthe family, speaking of Camille ; 'but with that intellectual ugliness *which pleases.*'   In fact the mouth is sarcastic, the lips are stretched like a bow bent to let the arrow fly, the smile is sneering, not pensive like the smile of

[1] 'Souvenirs de la Terreur,' vol. i. p. 51.   'He was atrociously ugly,' says the calumnious Leipsic 'Biography ;' 'his complexion was very dark, and there was something sinister in his look.'

[2] A remarkable writer, M. Ed. Schérer, made this mistake in his article on 'La Bibliothèque de Sainte-Beuve,' and I followed his example in my compilation of 'Œuvres de Camille Desmoulins' (Charpentier's edition, vol. i. p. 48).   These lines are taken from the 'Histoire de la Conjuration de Maximilien Robespierre,' by Montjoie (Paris, 1801 : vol. ii. p. 21).   Georges Duval and Montjoie are worthy of each other. *Arcades ambo.*

Erasmus, but satirical like that of Sterne, a Voltairian smile. In the face there is something demonlike, an infernal wit, which is the *beauté du diable* of a man. The forehead is beautiful, broad and well moulded, the black burning eyes sparkle. Such is Camille in most of the well known portraits, especially in that which was done by Boze at the Conciergerie, and in the miniature in my possession, which has been engraved for the frontispiece of the present volume.[1]

Camille was witty and very capable of pleasing; the sort of man to be loved by Lucile. She was of a romantic nature. She loved solitude. In the busy world of Paris, this young girl, sixteen or eighteen years old, eagerly sought, not the crowd, but the bitter-sweet of her own thoughts and dreams. She had no other confidant than the little copybook of rough

---

[1] I have seen a still more curious portrait of Camille Desmoulins as a young lawyer, on the eve of the event of the Palais Royal, and of the 14th of July; the Camille of the early days of his meetings with Lucile. The countenance is bright, intelligent, but not satirical, that of the young man of twenty, not the pamphleteer of thirty. This miniature, which is unique, and was shown to me by M. Louis Ulbach, belonged to the famous collection of M. Walferdin, the fortunate possessor of many unpublished writings by Diderot, and the editor of some others. M. Walferdin gave this miniature to M. Emanuel Arago, when he learned that Camille was a cousin of the deputy's maternal grandmother.

In this picture Camille Desmoulins is still a youth; around his almost childish face hangs his powdered hair. In after days Camille wore his long black hair falling almost to his shoulders. Two manuscript inscriptions, still quite legible, are to be found behind the original miniature, now the property of M. Arago. The first is simply the name:

'Camille Desmoulins.'

The second is rather an odd one. It runs thus :—
'Sold by the mother of a mistress of Camille Desmoulins, Madame Montbarne, residing in the Rue Sainte-Anne, 75.'

The words—*the mother of a mistress*—are ample proof, when we are acquainted with the married life of Camille and Lucile, that the date of the portrait is prior to their marriage. I have not reproduced this portrait in the present work, thinking that an engraving by Rajon, from a miniature in my own possession, would be more satisfactory.

paper—now yellow with time—in which she wrote
down her thoughts, in the night, in her own little room,
when she was alone, out of sight of her father and
mother, and of her sister Adèle, whom Robespierre
wanted to marry. I fancy I can see her, afraid of
being surprised, writing in her bed, the book on her
knees, with a flickering light by her side ; listening in
the dread of interruption, and expressing the profound
pleasure which one derives from self-study, from self-
abandonment, while she confides her sighs to the paper
before her, as she might breathe them on the wind ;
scribbling with a rapid pen those pages to which, more
than eighty years afterwards, history will turn, and
therein probe the secrets of her girlish heart.

I have said she loved solitude. Like Rousseau,
she has a horror of men. At seventeen! She cares
for the Luxembourg only when it is deserted during the
week, or in the evening when the night is falling :

'Ladies will come there every Sunday,' she writes, 'and I
shall not be able to come and muse in the groves. They will
be no longer solitary ; I will fly from that noisy mirth often
so opposed to the situation in which the heart finds itself.
I feel that I am born to live far from men. Alas! the
more I examine them, the more I seek to understand them,
the more I see that one ought to flee from them. There is
no cordiality, no sincerity among them. I live like an
animal, I no longer exist. . . . I have nothing but material
life. Last evening I feared that I should faint. I am in my
bed. A light and an extinguisher are on my bed. If I hear
a noise I will put out the light.'

There is pain in this, smarting pain. Certain
natures are as much hurt and frightened by apprehension of what life may mean as others are by the experience of life itself. Lucile hates men. Why ? No
doubt because she does not love one particular man.

'I do not love,' she says, with a sort of terror. 'When shall I love? They say that everybody must love. Shall I love when I am twenty-four? . . . . I am marble. Ah, what a strange thing is life!'

I am marble! The poor child frets because she does not love at a time when she knows nothing more of life than that she is adored by her father, by her loving sister, by the mother who *spoils her*, as we are now ready to say. She finds her consolation in nature, in trees, in 'the majestic lime tree which Lucile visits in the evening when, seeking repose, she waits for the coming night under its cool shade.' Imaginary griefs, sufferings which I venture to call literary, and which have been endured by all those who have read a great deal before they have seen much ; but real and deep suffering to which Lucile gives words, sometimes in misanthropical maledictions, sometimes in prayers.

The most ardent, the strangest, the least ordinary of prayers is the following meditation, which Lucile wrote, as she says herself, on June 6, 1789, at seven o'clock in the evening, in her bed, by the light of a candle. She calls this page her *Prayer to God.* The faith of a woman who has read Pascal is mingled in it with the doubts of a mind which has studied Fontenelle :—

PRAYER TO GOD.

Being of beings, indefinable Being! Thou whom all the earth adore. Thou my sole consolation. Mighty God, receive the offering of a heart which loves none but Thee; enlighten my soul, teach me to know Thee. Alas, what mortal has that happiness? Teach me to know error so that I may not fall into the frightful abyss which surrounds it. O my God! Why dost Thou abandon Thy creatures? Look upon them with a favouring eye. Alas! what can I do, I, a weak mortal? Dost Thou hear my voice in the immensity which Thou fillest? Can it penetrate even to Thee? Pardon this doubt; it is the only one which has come out of my heart. Celestial Being, enlighten my spirit!

I hate the world. Is this wrong? Why dost Thou suffer it to be so wicked? Canst Thou leave imperfect Thy fairest work? O my God! when shall I fly to Thy bosom? When shall I lift up my humble eyelids, and behold Thee? When may I, while contemplating Thy glory, fall at Thy feet, water them with my tears, and ask of Thee that pardon which Thou shalt have granted already? I am filled with Thee; I think of Thee without ceasing. Art Thou a spirit? Art Thou a flame? Ah, let that flame appear and consume me! Come to me, and nevermore leave me. Thou seest my mind goes astray. . . . How do I know what I am? My God, I know not what spring makes me act. Is it a portion of Thee? Oh, no, then I should be perfect. Every day I ask what Thou art. Everybody tells me, and nobody knows. What is the sun? It is fire. Alas! I know that, but what *is* fire? Nobody knows anything about it. I adore Thee without understanding Thee; I pray to Thee without knowing Thee; Thou art in my heart; I feel and cannot divine Thee. Thou art the secret of nature, and that secret is one which cannot be discovered.

To Thee I can speak. Thou art above that which man calls offence. Open the eyes of the universe. My God! we are all blind. Make us to see the pure light which surrounds Thee. Work another miracle. Make Thyself known. But no; in vain I implore Thee. I am not worthy of Thy benefits. Must we then crawl for ever?

Where shall we find that happiness which we are all seeking? Man grows dazzled, and when he forgets himself he thinks he is happy. No, there is no happiness upon the earth; it is only a chimera. When the world shall no longer exist. . . . But can it be annihilated? They say that there will be nothing any more! Nothing! what a picture! What! Nothing! I lose myself in the thought. The sun to lose its brightness, to shine no more! What will become of it? How will it set about becoming nothing?

My God, Thy power is very great ; it is to Thee that I must leave everything. I must then just love Thee, serve Thee, and keep silence.[1]

I have alluded to Fontenelle, but in truth the ring of the eighteenth century is not in these accents. They are the cries of a soul which thirsts for faith and love, the divine ecstasy of the solitary's prayers, or rather, they are the aspirations which are inspired by the catechetical teaching of the Church ; a step further, and such a soul, fearful of the world, and shrinking into itself like a sensitive plant, on the very threshold of life, would seek the shelter of the cloister. The 'nothing' uttered by this young girl of the eighteenth century might easily melt away in one of those ecstatic passions, like Saint Theresa's, in which the love of the divine springs forth like a torrent under the terror of the love of the human.

In Lucile's case, however, this phase of mingled doubt and religiosity had only a brief duration. She was a woman, and a woman of her time. She was about to love. These ecstatic reflections were speedily to give place to humbler thoughts, with a nearer object. All the pages of Lucile's journal do not boast the eloquence of this *Prayer to God*, which reminds us of a fragment of 'Young's Night Thoughts,' a book which Camille took with him into his prison. Lucile was destined to partake of the spirit of her time, of an age which was fascinated by naturalism, by a sort of floral sentimentality, of botanical sensibility, if I may use such a phrase. Everybody was thinking just then of Rousseau's periwinkle ; everybody wanted to have a periwinkle of his or her own. A little later and Robespierre will smell a bunch of flowers on his way to

[1] Copied from the original by M. Matton, the elder (of Vervins).

the Committee of General Safety.   More than one of
the condemned will mount the scaffold holding a rose
between their lips.   This time of moral tempest did
not hinder the blossoming of the lilac.

The *Prayer to God* takes us out of the eighteenth
century; but Lucile's *Violet*, whose sufferings she
relates in the following page, brings us back to it, and
to its mock eclogues :

THE VIOLET.

It was the first day of spring, and I walked out, descending
into a valley filled with willows, which, alas! were not yet
green.   I turned away my eyes from the sight of those
melancholy trees denuded of their leaves, and thought only
of seeking amid the fresh-springing grass for the first flower of
the fairest season.   I walked a long time without finding
anything, but at length, as far off as my sight could reach, I
perceived a violet, one single violet!   Oh, how beautiful it
was!   I flew to the spot, and was about to gather it, when,
(what was my surprise!) the humble flower stirred, and
seemed to endeavour to extricate itself from beneath my
fingers!   Fearing to deceive myself, I stretched out my hand.
Then a voice, as sweet as its perfume, made itself heard,
'What dost thou, Lucile,' it said to me ; 'why wouldst thou
tear me from the earth ?   Alas! suffer me to live yet awhile ;
no one here treads me underfoot ; thou wilt soon find thousands
more beautiful than I ; in a bouquet I should be lost, mixed
up with others, and I should add nothing to its size ; let me
end my days here.'   Touched by such affecting language,
'Fear nothing, gentle flower,' I replied, 'I would never be
so cruel as to destroy thee ; let me only inhale thy breath.'
Then she lifted her odorous head, and her leaves unfolded
themselves.   Moved to tears, I allowed one to fall into her
calix.   She said to me : 'Thy tears recruit my strength; I
shall live longer than my fellows.'   Then said I, 'I will come
every day and moisten thy leaves with sweet pure water.'
'Come,' she replied, 'but come always alone.'   I promised

her this, and every day I went to tend her, and to inhale her delicious perfume. Alas! I shall never see my friend again! My charming violet—one evening—in vain I sustained her bending stem, in vain slightly sprinkled her with water drops to revive her; her last hour had come. I shall visit that valley no more, but I shall ever think of my sweet violet.[1]

The editor of 'Madame Roland's Letters,' M. Dauban, who quotes certain portions of Lucile's journal (among others a pastoral story called 'La Volière,' —the Aviary), makes the following comment upon them :—'Lucile Desmoulins is not a woman of the Revolution as the great Madame Roland is.' Nevertheless, in his collection of the 'Letters of Madame Roland,' he has published a production which may fairly be compared to these *Reliquiæ* of Lucile, a page written by the pen of the then Mademoiselle Phlipon, and extracted from 'Mes Loisirs:' 'I repaired to the foot of the hill, the place was wild and solitary,' &c. (See Appendix to the 'Lettres de Mademoiselle Phlipon,' page 481.) There is little difference between the letters of Mademoiselle Phlipon and those of Mademoiselle Duplessis. Their extravagance is similar; and in both we find the same truth-seeking, through all the suggestions of doubt, pursued with the same vivacity and the same passion. There was one point in common between those two women; a sort of philosophical enthusiasm, which found utterance by Lucile in a prayer to God, and by Manon in a dithyramb in honour of Diderot as 'the new Prometheus.'

Other writings of Lucile's—extracts from her journals and scribbling-books, both as a girl and a wife— enable us to see more deeply into her mind. Baron de Girardot, formerly Secretary-General to the Pre-

---

[1] Hitherto unpublished. Communicated by M. de Lescure.

fecture of Nantes, has preserved and shown to a few persons a scrap-book which belonged to Lucile, and which contains extracts from poems, songs, sonnets, and thoughts. This is a precious relic, full of deep personal interest.

It is only a small copybook, with a red cardboard cover; and it consists of twenty-two leaves of thick, rough, yellow paper, only thirteen being written over in Lucile's hand. It contains verses composed in honour of Mademoiselle Duplessis, or copied by her from the different collections in vogue at the time. Baron de Girardot, to whom the little volume belonged, wrote the following words on the first page :—

'Written by the hand of Lucile Duplessis, wife of Camille Desmoulins. This book was given to me in Paris, by Lucile's sister, in 1834.

'B. DE GIRARDOT.'

The book is at present the property of M. de Lescure, who kindly permitted me to see it. I have held it in my hands, turned over and perused the pages which enable me to divine, or to read, the thoughts of Lucile, on the eve and on the morrow of her marriage. When she began to note down the verses which struck or pleased her, she was evidently already attracted by Camille. This love was crossed, for her father had seen the growing passion of Camille for his daughter with dislike. M. Duplessis, the son of a humble village blacksmith, was a man of a practical turn of mind, who had risen, thanks to patient and constant industry and effort, to the position of first clerk in the office of the General Control of Finance ; and he loved money with all the intensity which comes of knowing what it costs to gain. He could pass for being wealthy, though he was not so ; and being much disinclined to adventure of any kind, he would rather have given his daughter to a man who was not a newspaper writer. Camille's future, notwithstanding his recognised talent and his growing renown, seemed very uncertain in the prudent eyes of M. Duplessis. He was a Liberal, as was afterwards said, but not a Revolutionist; and he was alarmed by the militant attitude and provocative style of the 'Révolutions de France et de Brabant.' Though Camille Desmoulins had made a conquest of the mother, he merely frightened the father. As for Lucile, she loved him, and in that all is said. The *marble*, to which she had recently likened herself, had come to life. She who, as the faithful and passionately-loving wife of Camille, shall afterwards write down this line in her scrap-book, a line which corresponds with the single thought of her life,

'Write upon my tomb :—She loved,'

was fascinated by the impetuous young man, who was always eloquent, even in private conversation, and whose great black eyes darted flames. M. Duplessis, like a practical man of business, would not listen to sentimental arguments at first, when Camille spoke to him about his projects and timidly hinted at his hopes, but met him with a decided refusal. The lover went away; Madame Duplessis mourned; Lucile despaired. We find utterances of profound sadness, true grief of the heart, in the collection of verses which Mademoiselle Duplessis copied into her little red book; tender, sorrowful, loving verses, all of them, which sing the sorrows of lovers severed by the parental will. Lucile learns them by heart; she copies and re-copies them.

K 2

Sylvain Maréchal, who called himself 'Sylvain the Shepherd,' had set the sufferings of persecuted lovers to rhyme which depicted the torments of Lucile ; and she transcribed them, with mournful pleasure, in her red book, where they figure under the title which Maréchal gave them, as ' Romance historique.'

We have the story of Sylvandre, 'born in indigence' and tending the flocks of a 'proud labourer,' who refuses him the hand of his daughter, Nice. The unhappy Sylvandre allows himself to perish of hunger in his 'obscure hut.' Discovered by the barking of his 'faithful dog,' his corpse strikes the wretched Nice with despair. She weeps ; she laments ; and then, summoning all her courage, she dies beside her Sylvandre.

All the childishly elegiac poetry of the time is to be traced in these extracts, read and re-read by Lucile, with innocent, sincere, deep sentiment and pain.

Again, we have the 'Contrat de mariage par devant Nature,' in which the influence of Rousseau is plainly discernible. The young Hylas loves the young Hélène, but their families are divided by a mutual hate, and the young couple are separated as hopelessly as Romeo and Juliet. Shall they, too, die ? No ; they fly 'with a light foot' to a wild region, 'where hearts are free to pledge themselves,' and far different from Nice and Sylvandre, previously sung by 'Sylvain the Shepherd'——

> ' Là sans prêtres et sans notaire,
> Sur un autel de gazon frais,
> Au milieu d'un bois solitaire,
> Ils s'unissent à peu de frais.'

Sylvain Maréchal, the friend of Lucile, who afterwards published a curious scheme for a law to be entitled, ' A Prohibition to teach women to read,'——of which one hundred copies only were published at Lille in 1841,—adds a conclusion and a counsel to this tale :

> ' Leurs travaux et leur industrie
> Embellissent ces lieux déserts.
> Ils oublièrent leur patrie
> Et furent pour eux l'univers.
> Vous qu'on persécute à la ville,
> Jeunes cœurs, accourez près d'eux.
> Leur toit de chaume sert d'asile
> A tous les amans malheureux.'

This production is signed ' Sylvain the Shepherd,' and dated September 1787. Camille was then twenty-seven years old, and Lucile seventeen. The young people were already deeply in love ; and they persisted in their clandestine attachment, although they met only under favour of the motherly weakness of Madame Duplessis, until 1790, when at length M. Duplessis yielded to the advice of his wife and the tears of his daughter. Three years of repressed, but ever-growing affection, of concerted meetings under the great trees of the Luxembourg, of stolen glances, of hastily exchanged thoughts ; three years of love, chaste, profound, and faithful ! The mother, touched and won over; as we have seen, to the cause of the young pair, watched over this reciprocal love of the two hearts in whose truth she believed. Nevertheless, that Lucile made a mystery of it is proved by the following note which she wrote, but did not send to Camille, and which shows us the girl's whole soul, in all its passionate purity :—

' Oh ! thou who art in the depths of my heart, thou whom I dare not love, or rather, whom I dare not say that I love ; thou believest me insensible ! Oh, cruel one, dost thou judge me after thine own heart ? and could that heart attach itself to a being without feeling ?

Ah well, yes—it is better that I suffer, it is better that you should forget me. O God! Judge by that of my courage—which of us two has the most to suffer! I dare not confess to myself what I feel for thee; I strive only to hide it from my own knowledge. Thou sufferest, sayest thou? Oh, I suffer more; thine image is incessantly present to my mind; it never quits me. I look for thy faults, I find them, and I love them. Tell me then why does all this strife exist? Why do I love to make a mystery of it even to my mother? I wish that she should know it, that she should divine it, but I would not tell it to her myself.' (See the *fac-simile* of this letter.)

How charming is this confession! How tender, and passionate! Can anything be more exquisite than that sentence?—' I look for thy faults, I find them, and I love them.' All the devotion of a woman who loves and kneels to the beloved one is in those simple words of touching, innate poetry. Did Camille ever read this letter, in which Lucile poured out all her ardent soul? It is at least certain that while he reproached Lucile with *insensibility*, he knew that he was loved; for the nervous, eager young man, so readily discouraged, who passed so rapidly from extreme enthusiasm to utter dejection, never lost courage in this respect, but remained unshaken in the strength of his constancy, unchanged in the fervour of his passion, during the years which elapsed ere M. Duplessis could be induced to listen to his suit.

What a joyful, what an intoxicating hour it was for Camille, when in December, 1790, M. Duplessis consented to receive him as his son-in-law. He announces this unhoped-for happiness to his parents in a letter full of youthful exultation.

'To-day, this 11th December, I have at length reached the summit of my wishes. I have been kept waiting for happiness for a very long time, but it has come at last, and I am as happy as one can be on this earth. That charming Lucile, of whom I have told you so much, with whom I have been in love for eight years, has at last been given to me by her parents, and does not refuse me herself. Just now her mother came, weeping for joy, to tell me this good news. Inequality of fortune—for M. Duplessis has 20,000 francs a year—has hitherto hindered my happiness; the father being tempted by the brilliant offers which he received. He has rejected a suitor who pleaded his cause backed by 100,000 francs; Lucile had no trouble about refusing him, as she had already said "no" to 25,000 francs a year. You will know her at once by this trait of character alone. *Only a moment after her mother had given her to me, she led me to Lucile's chamber, and I threw myself at her feet. Surprised to hear her laugh, I raised my eyes to hers; they were in no better condition than my own. She was all tears; she was crying abundantly at that very moment, and yet she was also laughing. Never have I seen so enchanting a spectacle,* and I could not have imagined that nature and sensibility could combine those two contrasts to such an extent. Her father told me he would only defer our marriage in order to give me the hundred thousand francs which he had promised to his daughter, and that I might go with him to the notary's as soon as I pleased. I answered: "You are a capitalist, you have been handling money all your life; I would rather have nothing to do with the contract. So much money would only embarrass me. You love your daughter too well for me to make any stipulation for her. You ask nothing from me; pray frame the contract as you please." He gives me, in addition, one half of his plate, which amounts to ten thousand francs.'

Camille, just as if he had foreseen that a day would come when, in order to push him more promptly to the scaffold, his enemies would accuse him of having *married a rich woman*, enjoins his parents afterwards

' not to talk much about all this,' and entreats them ' to send their consent by return of post.' Then, with a somewhat misplaced affectation he adds :—

' I am now in a position to be able to help you, and that forms a great part of my joy : my mistress, my wife, your daughter, and all the family embrace you.'

Camille was quite wild with joy. He awaited the paternal consent with feverish impatience. Three times he wrote and demanded it ; on the 18th and 20th December, he implored his father not to oppose a formal *veto* to this marriage.

' My dearest Father,—How has it happened that on receiving my last letter, countersigned by the Keeper of the Seals, you did not send Charles, the notary, to convey to me your consent and that of my good mother, drawn up in proper legal form ? Your slowness has retarded my marriage for a week. Pray remember that I am counting the minutes, and do not prolong your suspensory veto. This marriage will make my fortune and yours, and secure my happiness ; therefore hasten to send me your consent, and do not grieve me any longer.

' C. DESMOULINS.

' Your son so advantageously married, and yourself appointed *commissaire du roi* —it seems to me that you have much reason to rejoice.' [1]

But Camille in his excitement had forgotten to furnish his father with the Christian and surnames of his future wife and her parents. M. Desmoulins writes in his turn to his son :—

' Guise : December 15, 1790, 9 P.M.

' I have this moment received your letter, but too late to have the consent of your mother and myself put into correct form before the post closes for to-day, even if you had not

---

[1] Communicated to me by M. de Lescure, and hitherto unpublished. The *fac-simile* of this autograph is given.

a Monsieur

Monsieur Desmoulins

homme de loi

a Guise

forgotten to give me the names of your betrothed and of her father and mother. But while I am waiting for this indispensable information, which you can send me by return of post, believe fully that we all share your happiness, your satisfaction, your delight. Assure the charming family to which you seem to have clung for all your happiness for eight years past, that if you win her who has been the object of all your wishes, Mademoiselle Lucile, your welfare will always constitute ours. I have only a moment to catch this post, and to repeat that I am your best friend.

(Signed)   'DESMOULINS.

'All the family embrace you and present their homage to that of M. Duplessis.

'Continue to use your good offices on my behalf with the Keeper of the Seals.'

(This letter has been hitherto unpublished.)

This delay was not the only tribulation which befel Camille respecting his marriage. The event was fixed for the 29th of December, and a dispensation must be had, to enable the young couple to be married in Advent. Camille went to the Grand-Vicar of the Archbishop of Paris, M. de Floriac, who reproached him with the burning of a château and the loss of an income of 20,000 livres, and refused the dispensation. Vainly did some of the deputies interfere and entreat. At length, after sundry ineffectual efforts, a dispensation was obtained by the venerable Abbé Bérardier, the principal of the Louis-le-Grand College. Bérardier loved his old pupil, he never forgot the once dreamy school-boy, and every year Camille went to congratulate him on his birthday. Bérardier was anxious to marry the young couple, and M. de Pancemont, the curé of St. Sulpice, consented to 'assist' only on the occasion. The preliminary interview between M. de Pancemont and Camille, when he arrived at St. Sulpice accom-

panied by a notary, is worth relating.   It is no less
than a moral duel between the Voltairian and the
priest.   The curé preserves an attitude which is polite
but not supplicatory, and the free-thinker holds out his
neck for the yoke, whose weight the priest—a priest
never abdicates—takes no pains to lighten.   The first
question put by M. de Pancemont is the following:

'Are you a Catholic?'—

'Why do you ask me?'

'Because if you be not, I cannot confer upon you a
Sacrament of the Catholic religion.'

'Well then, yes, I am a Catholic.'

'I cannot believe a man who has said in one of his
Numbers that the religion of Mahomet is quite as much
proven to his mind as the religion of Jesus Christ.'

'You read my Numbers then?'

'Sometimes.'

'And you will not marry me, Monsieur le Curé.'

'No, Sir, I cannot do so, unless you make a public profession of faith in the Catholic religion.'

'Then I must have recourse to the Ecclesiastical Committee,' replied Camille.

The conversation, taken down by the notary, was then
reported to the Committee.

Afterwards Camille returned to the curé with a written
'opinion' of Mirabeau's, in which the latter maintained:
'That the only evidence of belief is the external profession of
faith, and that marriage cannot be refused to the person who
demands it, since he has stated that he is a Catholic.'

'Since when has Mirabeau been a father of the Church?'
was the curé's quiet comment upon this.

Camille could not restrain his laughter at this question.

'Ha! ha! Mirabeau a father of the Church! I will tell
him that; he will be amused!'

'But,' continued the curé of St. Sulpice, 'the opinion
itself condemns you, if you are to be judged by your external
profession of faith, because that profession is in print.   Before
I marry you, I must exact a retractation.'

'I do not intend to write any more Numbers before my marriage.'

'You must make the retractation afterwards.'

'I promise you that I will do so,' said Camille. (He never fulfilled that promise.)

'I also exact from you,' added M. de Pancemont, 'that you fulfil all the duties prescribed by the Church to those about to marry, and that you make your confession.'

'To yourself, M. le Curé?'[1]

And Camille Desmoulins did so. His love for Lucile was strong enough to induce the pamphleteer to bend his proud head. But how quickly he raised it, and how angrily! To the priest, inflexible in his ministry, was opposed an enemy eager and fierce in fight. The marriage was celebrated at Saint Sulpice, on the 29th of December. Among the witnesses Pétion and Robespierre figure. Mirabeau was not there, though he had promised to be present. The Abbé Bérardier addressed a touching exhortation to the bride and bridegroom, and Camille's eyes filled with tears. 'Cry, if you want to cry!' said Robespierre to him. In later days, Saint-Just, and even Robespierre himself, reproached Camille for those ready tears.

The following is the form in which the marriage of Camille and Lucile is registered :—

[1] These details are taken from 'L'examen critique des dictionnaires historiques,' by M. Barbier, who copied them from a pamphlet entitled, 'Histoire des événements arrivés sur la paroisse Saint Sulpice pendant la Révolution :' Paris ; Crapart's printing-office, 1792 ; pp. 23, 24, 25. Afterwards, when, *à propos* of the civic oath imposed upon the priests, M. de Pancefort said that 'hell had filled the breast of the nation,' Camille wrote : 'Oh, monsieur le curé, you who are a clever man !' and in his "Révolutions,' No. 60, he added, 'I am sorry the curé of Saint Sulpice, who had won my affections, should have caused so great a scandal. It is quite true that he said to me (I quote his words) : "Formerly it was the king who had the power, now it is the nation. St. Paul teaches us that we ought to obey the powers that be ; therefore I shall obey."'

On the 29th of December, 1790, was celebrated the marriage of Lucile Simplice Camille Benoît Desmoulins, barrister, aged thirty years, son of Jean Benoist Nicolas Desmoulins, lieutenant-general to the bailiwick of Guise, and of Marie Magdeleine Godard, consenting parties, with Anne Lucile Philippe Laridon Duplessis, aged twenty years, daughter of Claude Etienne Laridon Duplessis, pensionary of the King, and of Anne Françoise Marie Boisdeveix, present and consenting, both parties being of this parish, the husband having resided for six years in the Rue du Théâtre Français, the wife having resided for six years with her parents here present.

Jérôme Pétion, Deputy to the National Assembly, Rue Neuve des Mathurins ; Charles Alexis Brulard, Deputy to the National Assembly, Rue Neuve des Mathurins ; Maximilien Marie Isidore Robespierre, Deputy to the National Assembly, Rue Saintonge, parish of Saint Louis-en-l'Ile (*sic*).

(Signed)   CAMILLE DESMOULINS,
LARIDON DUPLESSIS (the wife),
LARIDON DUPLESSIS,
BOISDEVEIX,
PÉTION,
BRULARD,
ROBESPIERRE,   •
MERCIER,
J. N. BRISSOT (Deputy to the National Assembly),
GUEUDEVILLE (Vicar at St. Sulpice.)

This extract is made from the Register of the parish of Saint Sulpice. The Abbé Bérardier and the Curé Pancemont did not sign.

When we read this document, in which the names of friends who within three short years are to become deadly enemies are found side by side, we cannot escape from bitter reflections and mournful associations. Here is the signature of Brissot, who denounced Camille, and the signature of Robespierre, who suffered his friend to mount the scaffold. Cruel times were those, when the kiss of to-day became a bite to-morrow.

Bloody were the fatalities of those mortal struggles. Friend slays friend. Here, in 1790, Brissot clasps Camille's hand, and wishes him joy; and in 1793, Camille will invent a deadly neologism against him, the verb *brissoter*, which shall signify *to steal*. Robespierre shall draft for Saint-Just a deadly 'note' in which Camille shall be portrayed as a dupe and an accomplice by turns. But who foresees such an ending to the bright story of the bridal day? What trusting smiles bedeck the faces of all present, when Camille, who is thirty years old, leads the fair Lucile, who is hardly twenty, to the altar! In his right hand he holds the left hand of his bride; as they approach the draped shrine, the well-known and beloved voice of the abbé Bérardier evokes the memories of his childhood while it defines the duties of his manhood. Transported with happiness, his heart swelling with hope, Camille weeps happy tears, too soon to be followed by tears of blood.

II.

Those were blessed hours for the young couple, and days full of the profound joy, the bliss, at once sober and intoxicating, of great happiness. They installed themselves in the same house with Danton, in the Cour du Commerce. Friendly letters, full of compliments and kind wishes, poured in upon them. Luce de Lancival, afterwards the author of 'Mucius Scævola,' 'Archibal' and 'Fernandez,' tragedies full of icy patriotism, which, however, Napoleon called 'capital head-quarters' plays,' wrote to Desmoulins as follows:—

'Faithful to the country, faithful to love, faithful to friendship, you deserve to be the happiest of men. You now have in addition to your pen another infallible means of winning partisans for the Revolution ; if you are acquainted with any bad citizens, present your wife to them ; not one of them but will imitate your patriotism on seeing it so well rewarded.'

Subscribers to the ' Révolutions de France et de Brabant' sent verses to Camille, and might have said, like Lancival :—

'A cent rivaux, ardents à la lui disputer,
Camille enlève enfin cette femme accomplie
Que je venais lui souhaiter ! '

The ' Berger Sylvain' made his appearance again, and re-strung his little rhymes in honour of the newly-wedded pair.   But at the same time hatred sharpened afresh its weapons of calumny ; falsehood spat out its coarsest insults ; the royalist pamphleteers and newspaper men invented the infamous scandal, injurious alike to an honest man and an honest woman, that Camille's wife was the bastard daughter of the Abbé Terray.   ' He even wished to marry her at the altar of the country, on the Champ de Mars,' writes one of these libellers, ' but the rain interfered and forced him to marry her in the Church.'   ' Utter nonsense,' writes Desmoulins to his father (January 3, 1791). ' Madame Duplessis never saw the Abbé Terray ; her husband was not appointed to the head-clerkship of the General Control until after his death, and it was under M. de Clugny, not the Abbé Terray, that he was at the Treasury.'   Camille was strongly disposed to sue the ' Journal de la Cour et de la Ville' for damages for the publication of these rascally falsehoods, but his father and the Duplessis family dissuaded him, advising him to treat such calumnies with contempt.   ' What signifies the venom and the spite of the tale-bearers of the day, and their ephemeral calumny ? ' writes M.

Desmoulins from his quiet provincial home. Might not Camille, on this occasion at least, have reflected on the deep and painful wounds which may be inflicted by the press ?

He, at least, if he thrust in the dart, sharpened, but did not poison it ! But what odious falsehood was there in the pamphlets aimed against him ! Peltier, in the ' Actes des Apôtres,' meanly lent himself to the reproduction of them in his ' Paris pendant l'année 1795 ; ' and even his pages are moderate by the side of those which accuse Camille of 'having lived on alms until his marriage with a bastard, and that bastard the daughter of that Abbé Terray who boasted of picking people's pockets so cleverly.'[1]

'Camille Desmoulins,' says Peltier, ' had married a bastard of the Abbé Terray's. This marriage brought him an income of 6,000 livres. The following anecdote is known to very few people, but it is worth being recorded for posterity, as an example of the harmony which exists between the principles and the conduct of certain innovators.

'Camille Desmoulins wished to be married, not according to the forms prescribed by the new régime, but according to the Roman rite ; that is to say, not by municipal officers, but by a Catholic priest. What is still more surprising is that *he would not have a Constitutional priest ; he wished for, and sought for, a non-juring priest, and found one.* It was Bérardier, the former principal of the College of Louis-le-Grand, and a member of the Constituent Assembly, who gave the nuptial benediction tò Camille Desmoulins and his wife. Bérardier died of phthisis, in April, 1794 ; there is, therefore, no reason why the public should not be informed that it was he who celebrated this marriage.

'Such orthodoxy on the part of Camille Desmoulins is certainly very extraordinary, but our surprise is raised to its greatest height when we find that he was aided and abetted

---

[1] See Appendix for note on the Abbé Terray.

in this act of religion by Robespierre and Saint-Just, who were perfectly well aware that Bérardier had not taken either the Constitutional oath or that of equality.

'This anecdote is quite authentic. I may add that during the whole course of Robespierre's fury against the priests, jurors and non-jurors, Bérardier was never molested, and that he died peacefully in his bed. Why was that respected in him which was execrated in others? This is one of the unaccountable contradictions which prove that Robespierre and his party governed, not by principles, but by caprice, the most fatal of all methods of government for the people.'

Rêtif de la Bretonne, one of the eccentric chroniclers of that time, gives some calumnious details of the domestic life of Camille Duplessis and his wife; and draws a portrait of Lucile in the last volume of 'L'année des Dames nationales, ou le Calendrier des Citoyennes' (vol xii. Decr. page 3821).

'*The young Duplessis, wife of Camille Desmoulins.*—We conclude this *hors d'œuvre* by the most-to-be-pitied woman of all those whose lives were taken. The young Duplessis was not born in wedlock; but the citizen Duplessis, having married her mother, adopted her. Camille Desmoulins was intimate in their house, as were Mercier, De Langle, and several others. Camille fell in love with the little Duplessis while she was still a child. Unfortunately, the citizen Duplessis had fallen into a state of apathy which almost amounted to imbecility, and Camille had only to win over the mother, who was still pretty, and almost without education. For seven years he persecuted this mother, until at length he obtained from her one of the handsomest girls in Paris, with a good fortune. We have seen the young Duplessis at the *Italiens*, and were dazzled by her beauty. Camille, who was wild almost to madness, and excessively headstrong, gained with the help of Mercier the hand of the unfortunate young girl, whom he was to lead to the scaffold before she was twenty-three; for it is certain that, had she had any other husband, the young Duplessis would never have dreamed of receiving and giving money to procure the assassination of members of the revolutionary tribunal. It is said that a most worthy man became attached to the handsome young Duplessis, but that he would not have a madman like Camille for a rival. Among his acquaintance was an old man of ninety, with a mortal disease which made his death within a month or two certain. He proposed this old man as a son-in-law to Duplessis, whom he gave to understand that, although he could not marry his adopted daughter, there would be no difficulty about his wedding the widow of an eminently respectable person. Duplessis appreciated the force of this argument, and proposed the marriage to his wife. But the latter felt some misgiving about the transaction, and consulted one of her friends, who was, unfortunately, still more friendly to Camille. The news drove Camille frantic; he contrived to speak to his mistress, and to persuade her that a scheme was on foot for delivering her up to the most odious and disgusting of old men. He gave her a false version of the devices which were to be practised, but one which approached the truth. The young Duplessis believed herself to be sufficiently forearmed by the forewarning of her lover, and when her mother, persuaded of the sincerity of the worthy man who had made the proposal, wished to present him to her daughter, with the preamble which had been agreed upon, the girl threw herself at her feet in a transport of despair, and declared that she would prefer death to the fulfilment of such deceitful and perfidious plans; also, that her consent would be the death-warrant of her beloved Camille. Her mother, who loved her dearly, was so weak as to yield, and in a moment of enthusiasm, persuaded by the ardent Desmoulins, she consented to her daughter's marriage with him. The marriage was celebrated. . . .

'Camille was not slow to weary of his handsome wife. He flung himself into great affairs and into low intrigues. He ceased to be loved.

'O daughters! beware whom you wed! O mothers! watch over your daughters, and learn on their behalf those things which they cannot learn for themselves!'

It is not true that Camille speedily wearied of her

whom he loved. We shall find him, later, talking about his wife to Mesdames Sainte-Amaranthe, in the tone of a man for whom temptation does not exist. As for Lucile, she has purchased dearly enough the right to bequeath her love as an example to the world. Let us leave the calumniators in the muddy ditch into which they ought to have been carted, and endeavour to gain a correct notion of the mind and the character of the young wife of Camille Desmoulins.

Here again the red copybook will serve us for a guide. We have traced Lucile in its pages through the disquietudes of an ignorant young girl, and the sorrows of a loving one, separated from the object of her affections. We now find her as a wife, his beloved, devoted, and charming companion. In love with Camille, enthusiastic about all his ideas, carried away by his passionate politics, she shared his feverish existence, his hopes and his dreams, and afterwards she shared his perils. They loved one another, not only in their homely fireside happiness, in the sweet intimacy of two beings united by pro- found sympathy, but in that external life, in that rest- less agitated existence which pleased Lucile, and which Desmoulins had created for himself. We shall see her, on August 10, shuddering at the idea of the danger to which he may be exposed. More than once we shall find him laying his burning head on Lucile's knees to still the throbbing of his temples, after a terrible meeting or the Convention or the Jacobins. We shall see Lucile intoxicated by this perilous life, and full of pride in it, urging Camille onwards. The secret of her thoughts is written in the little book preserved by her sister. I shall not give you the whole of the collection of the verses in which, under a thin mythological disguise—

the fashion of the period—all the sufferings, all the tenderness of the young soul are depicted. Several of these pieces have no other interest than that of a retrospective curiosity; and the 'Chanson du Saule,' or the 'Chanson de la Rose,' 'after a sketch by M. Fragonard,' says Lucile, would add little that is characteristic to this feminine physiognomy, which was full of charm and winningness that turned, when the time came, to resolute energy.

There are, however, some other poems, 'romances' as they were then called, like the following, in which it seems to me we may trace the love story of Camille and Lucile, poeticised and dramatised no doubt, but still real, and reflecting the truth.

The following extract from Lucile's 'Red Book' is simply called,

ROMANCE.

Sur la pente de la colline
Qui borne d'ici l'horizon,
Distinguez-vous cette chaumine,
Qu'accompagne un petit donjon ?
Là, dans la paix et le silence,
Là, deux amans, enfin époux,
De leur tendre persévérance
Savourent les fruits les plus doux.

L'histoire en est des plus touchantes.
Vous qui gémissez sous la loi
Des durs parents, jeunes amantes,
Approchez-vous, écoutez-moi.
Courageuse autant que fidèle,
Cécile aussi que son amant
Peuvent vous servir de modèles
Pour un semblable événement.

De la nature et de sa mère
Cécile élève seulement

Possédait une âme trop fière
Pour prendre d'autre enseignement.
Mais un jeune homme bon et sage
Sut lui plaire sans beaucoup d'art.
Heureux Alain ! ce fut l'ouvrage
D'un seul moment, d'un seul regard.

Un autre que lui de Cécile
Poursuivait ardemment le cœur,
Dans l'art d'écrire maître habile,
Profond politique, orateur,
Il savait tout—hors l'art de plaire :
Novice encore en fait d'amour,
Colmat n'avait pu que du père
Obtenir un tendre retour.

Mais Colmat, l'âme satisfaite
Du consentement paternel,
Croit sa félicité parfaite,
Et déjà pense être à l'autel.
Déjà, dans sa vaste demeure
Le lit nuptial, à grand frais,
S'élève ; il n'attend plus que l'heure
De se voir heureux pour jamais.

Le père enfin dit à Cécile :
' Je ne vous donne qu'un moment,
Tout subterfuge est inutile,
Optez ! Colmat ou le couvent !'
'— Une union mal assortie
Plus qu'un cloître me ferait mal,
Et mieux vaut sortir de la vie
Que d'y traîner un joug fatal !'

Cécile au couvent est menée,
On l'y reçoit à bras ouverts :
Un peu d'or hâte la journée
Qui doit en priver l'univers.
Alain sait tout.   Cécile en larmes
S'est concertée avec Alain,

Et l'amour prépare les armes
Pour combattre un père inhumain.

Le temple s'ouvre et la victime
S'avance, mais d'un pas tardif ;
Alain la suit des yeux, l'anime,
Et n'attend qu'un regard furtif.
' Ma fille,' dit alors le prêtre,
' Que venez-vous chercher ici ? ·
Venez-vous à Dieu vous soumettre ?
Que demandez-vous ? '—' Un mari ! '

A ce mot, malgré la présence
Et de Colmat et des parents,
Ardent et fier, Alain s'élance ;
Cécile est dans ses bras tremblants.
Puis sans sortir de cet asile
L'un l'autre se donnant la main,
Dieu reçoit le vœu de Cécile,
Dieu reçoit le serment d'Alain.

Toutes les nonnes douairières
Prirent la fuite de dépit ;
Le prêtre changea de prières,
Le père enfin y consentit.
Les deux époux, dès le soir même
De ce beau jour tant orageux,
Goûtèrent le bonheur suprême
Dans leur foyer, simple comme eux.

By whom is this story, which combines the jesting
impertinence of the incredulous eighteenth century
with such simple sentimentality, written ? Is it by
Sylvain Maréchal, like ' Le Trésor,' or ' Le Contrat de
Mariage devant la Nature '—those queer ' historical
romances '? Is it by Camille Desmoulins himself ? We
do not know. We know only that, if Camille Desmoulins
had not to carry off his bride from the cold constraint
of a cloister, he did carry her off to Bourg-la-Reine

for awhile, where Madame Duplessis placed a house which she owned at the disposal of the bridal pair.

Was it over the threshold of this country house, or on the door of their apartment in the Cour du Commerce, that Maréchal or Fréron—at all events, a friend of Camille—wrote up these lines, which Lucile copied into her ' Red Book ' ?

> ' Qui que tu sois, quand tu serois l'Amour,
> Garde-toi de troubler la paix de cet asile ;
> Respecte ce riant séjour
> De l'innocence et de Lucile.'

It matters little : in all her thoughts we find the young wife's absorbing love. She takes delight in surrounding herself with everything that speaks to her most eloquently of this love; she abandons herself completely to Camille, the man whom she has pre-ferred, chosen, the only man whom she will ever love. Lucile will be a busy zealous mother, a resolute valiant woman. This young girl, who looks like a painting by Greuze, will develope the energies of the wife of Poetus by and bye; meanwhile she is the adored mistress of her lover; and Camille, who idolized her before their marriage, now prostrates himself before her. When he writes to his father he appends to his signature these words : ' *The happiest of men, and who desires nothing more in the world.*'

III.

Camille deceived himself. He still desired fame, he still hankered after that deceptive popularity to which he had already sacrificed too much.

He had belonged, from its foundation, to the club of the Cordeliers, who were afterwards to look upon him as a lukewarm member, and to contribute to his destruction. The Cordeliers' club was held in the Rue de l'École de Médecine, opposite the Rue Haute-feuille, in the monks' refectory. These monks were, as everybody knows, democratic mystics who had taken the vow of poverty, communists in the religious garb.

Etienne Marcel had appeared there in the four-teenth century, and Danton made himself visible in the eighteenth. In the spot where the Musée Dupuytren now displays its horrors, the meetings of the club took place. Those walls have listened to the harangues of Marat, whose printing-press was hidden for a short time in the subterranean church of the convent. The Cordeliers' club was the offspring of the district, of which Camille said : ' If the Seven Wise Men of Greece themselves were members of it, I defy its logic to be more sound.' [1]

The meetings were at first held in the convent ; in 1792 they were transferred to the church of Saint-André des Arts—which no longer exists—but soon afterwards they were resumed at the place of their origin. In the interval they were held in the great hall of the Museum, in the Rue de la Dauphine, then Rue de Thionville. The club was genuinely popular ; any one who chose might enter, and the

---

[1] One of the deliberations of the district in which we find the name of *D'Anton*, in the ' Révolutions de France et de Brabant,' is as follows :— ' The district of the Cordeliers, indignant at the species of derision in which the Executive Power has thought fit to indulge by lodging the Legis-lative Power first in a hall of *Menus-plaisirs*, and afterwards in a riding-school, demands that the temple of Liberty shall be constructed on the site of the Bastille. It is a fine idea to build the Capitol there, as the Greeks formerly built the temple of Delphos on the place which had served the Python for his den.'

Commissioners for the drafting of the address : Paré, president, D'Anton, ex-president, Fabre d'Eglantine, vice-president, Camille Desmoulins and Dufourny de Villiers.

surging multitude sometimes excited the speaker in
the tribune almost to the point of madness. The
Jacobins have been likened to a grave, prudent,
casuistical seminary; the Cordeliers might have been
compared to a regiment always under arms. Street
revolution growled in that lair, while Parliamentary
revolution debated at the Jacobins. Danton, Desmoulins, Marat, Fréron, Hébert, Chaumette, Legendre,
Robert—he who hereafter drew up the petition of
the Champ de Mars, demanding the deposition of
Louis XVI.—Momoro, Anacharsis Clootz, Vincent,
Guzman, the *sans-culotte* Spanish Grandee—all these
belonged to the Cordeliers. A strange, turbulent, and
hostile assemblage, destined to send one another to
death. The Republic was born in this hothouse. The
device, 'Liberty, Fraternity, Equality,' was invented
by the Cordeliers (June 1791). August 10 found
its most energetic actors among them. Unhappily,
when the Revolution had sent the most illustrious of
the Cordeliers, including Danton and Desmoulins,
as deputies to the Convention in the name of Paris,
the influence of the club was given to the Hébertist
element, to the party of the Commune, to extreme
sansculottism. While the former members, the
'Vieux,' or old Cordeliers, became 'indulgents,' and
demanded clemency, those of the class to which Collot-
d'Herbois, Ronsin, Momoro, and Hébert belonged,
became ultra-revolutionists, and re-edited, both literally
and figuratively, *L'Ami du peuple* up to the moment
when the Committee of Public Safety subjected them
to that terrible 'purifying scrutiny' which established
the discipline of death among the Cordeliers.

But the hour of these terrible conflicts is yet
distant. Camille is fighting now only with the weapons

of speech and pen.[1]   His father is very apprehensive of the consequences of the militant turn which matters are taking, and of Camille's growing fame.   He writes to his son ('Rév. de Fr. et de Brab.,' No 7, p. 321) :—

'In the midst of the ruins which surround me, and which the National Assembly seem to have heaped together out of my existence (my office has become precarious, my syndicate escapes me before the legal term, the thread of my former life is cut, and all my associates are in a like case), I am consoled, and the ills of my position are much assuaged, by the hope that my son, with more modern and bolder principles, will be one of the first workmen to construct the ark which shall save himself and his brethren from the shipwreck of their common father.'

'They talk to me of your success,' adds this wise and honest man, ' and I am not insensible to it ; but I am more strongly affected by the dangers which you incur.'   Camille replies to this in the confident tone of a victor certain of himself :—

'So then, you no longer mock at my dreams, my republic, and my former predictions ; at all that *you have seen, what may be called seen, yes, seen with your own eyes.* You have passed your life in writing, in striving against minor oppressions.   That was attacking the branches ; we, thank heaven! have just cut down the tree.   Have no fear lest you should be

[1] In a pamphlet entitled 'A Description of the Civic Oath and Festival celebrated at the Bois de Boulogne, by the Society of the Jeu de Paume de Versailles, on June 20, 1789–1790,' I find the following mention of Camille :—

'A table of three hundred covers prepared by patriotic nymphs, covered with the simple fruits of nature, appealed agreeably to the senses.

'Danton proposed the first toast, then Menon, Santonax, Charles Lameth, Barnave, Laborde.

'M. de Robespierre proposed the health of the courageous writers who had risked so many dangers, and who still prove their valour by devoting themselves to the defence of the country.   During this motion a member pointed to Camille Desmoulins, who was vehemently applauded.' (An eight-page pamphlet, in 8vo ; Garnery, 17 Rue Serpente.)

crushed in its fall. That tree can fall only on the useless and the idle, not upon those who have deserved well of their country.'

Camille's father was then working at his ' Encyclopædia of Jurisprudence,' in eight octavo volumes, which had been commenced thirty years earlier.

' I am consoled on your account' (adds Camille), ' because there will always remain to you the recollection of a life passed in fighting against every kind of oppression under which our province laboured.'

Then he says, after alluding to the 'useless' toil of his father, 'already I have avenged you !' Avenged him upon whom ? Upon the *ci-devant* Duc de Guise, who had been so severe when fines had to be paid to him. What a singular difference between the temperaments and the dreams of the father and the son ! The father did not wish for revenge ; he simply aspired to greater prosperity.

Camille, then, continued to strive and fight, notwithstanding his love for Lucile, his joy in being beloved, his happiness in his home and in family life. Perhaps he remembered the lines, signed 'L. M.,' which he had inserted in No. 6 of the ' Révolutions :'—

> ' Tu dors, Camille, et Paris est esclave !
> D'autres tyrans usurpent le pouvoir,
> Que s'arrogeoient et Breteuil et le Noir !' [1]

Camille was fighting both in his journal and in the

---

[1] In this piece we find the often-quoted lines :—

> ' Quoi donc, Camille, ami de Robespierre,
> *De Chartres même honoré comme un frère !* '

The ' Nouvelle Biographie générale ' of Firmin Didot affirms that on the occasion of Camille's marriage, ' The Duke of Orleans had the apartment which the young couple were to occupy in the Rue de l'Odéon magnificently furnished at his expense.' This allegation is completely erroneous, and the biographer cannot have found anywhere a single proof of the fact which he states.

tribune. His polemics were, however, modified, and it was no longer against Malouet, but against Lafayette, that he aimed his heaviest blows. From 1790 Camille had attacked ' the white horse' and its rider, whom he called ' Blondinet ; ' but in September 1790, after the death of Loustallot, his attacks became more direct. ' This hypocrite,' Camille calls the General, ' who has the law always on his lips,' or ' this Tartuffe with two epaulettes.'

A striking contrast to Camille Desmoulins was presented by Loustallot, a militant journalist also, but full of attractive sensibility, ardently, truly republican of soul, young, brave and compassionate, *'pure from blood even in thought,'* says the author of ' Poems of the Revolution' when alluding to him. The two were pursuing the same ends, but with widely different arms : Camille Desmoulins with a finely-wrought weapon which he used sometimes poniard-fashion ; Loustallot with a plain sword, but of true temper and loyally wielded. The editor of the ' Révolutions de Paris,' founded by the bookseller, Prud'homme, was a publicist, aiming at clearness rather than at elegance, at conviction rather than brilliancy. He had not the Aristophanic force of Camille, but he had more serious-ness of mind. It is true that he addressed a different public. Camille spoke to the educated classes, Lous-tallot to the people. The two men were staunch friends, and when, on the news of the massacre of the Swiss at Nancy reaching Paris, Loustallot died of grief, in September 1790, in his twenty-eighth year, Camille Desmoulins delivered his funeral oration.[1] ' Loustallot

---

[1] The author of ' Pièces de la vie du fameux Loustallot, auteur des " Révolutions de Paris," sous le nom de Prud'homme,' calls Elysée Lou-stallot the *' brother demagogue '* of Camille, and adds that he had more

did not sign his articles,' said Camille ; ' he knew that by showing oneself but little one does much.' In another place he calls Loustallot 'the writer who has best served the Revolution.'

talent than Desmoulins. In allusion to the funeral panegyric of Loustallot by Camille, he says :—

'When the speaker had gone round the eternal circle in which he moves, he began again ; and wearied us all with the white horse of M. de Lafayette, the big stomach of Dessessarts, and the wife of the king, whom he will not call the queen. He runs after points, after so-called wit, and goes deeply into nothing, which is more convenient and less difficult. We are, however, far from supposing that M. Desmoulins cannot sometimes wield the formidable weapon of pleasantry and ridicule with skill and success. There are certain numbers of his journal in which plenty of wit and gaiety may be found, but these qualities do not suffice for a complete success. A journalist must be just, impartial, and not carried away by the turmoil of party strife.' The pamphleteer states that Loustallot killed himself by drinking ardent liquor. This is a complete calumny.

The following is a passage from Camille's oration at the Jacobins' club, relative to the dignity and character proper to a journalist :—

'Loustallot,' said Camille, 'always despised the enemies who were eager to defame him ; he could not understand the baseness of a crowd of journalists who, instead of calling all men to liberty and equality, and the man of talent to his task of maintaining them, do not hesitate to serve the aristocrats whom they despise, for the sake of a little money; and defame those writers whom they cannot but esteem, in order to please their masters. Such men as these debase literature and talent to the level of domestic servitude, and are, as far as they can be, like the Greek slaves and *beaux esprits* who abounded in Rome during the later days of the Republic, when artists, savants, and poets were, in the eyes of the stupid rich, only servants like cooks or lackeys. Loustallot knew that his life and his works formed a severe censure upon writers of this despicable kind.'

' Unfortunate friend of the Constitution,' said Legendre at the grave of Loustallot, 'go into the other world, since such is thy destiny. Grief for the massacre of so many of our brethren at Nancy has caused thy death. Go and tell them that at the mere name of Bailly patriotism shudders ; tell them that nothing remains unpunished by a free people ; tell them that sooner or later they shall be avenged.'

' Did anything more sublime come out of the mouth of Demosthenes himself?' asks Camille Desmoulins. But he puts it in another way in No. 44 : 'I have read nothing finer in Demosthenes and Cicero than the few words spoken by this master-butcher.'

Camille achieved an oratorical success by his speech on the occasion of the funeral of Loustallot, of whom his own fellow-countryman and friend, Saint-Jean d'Angely said, when he heard of his death, '*Ah! then, he has sucked his own pen!*' ' I have received,' said Camille, 'applause, whose vehemence is applicable only to the dead ; I have inherited from him the public goodwill.'

He added, in a terrible accent of menace : ' Yes, it is thou, Lafayette, who hast killed him.' The strife, destined to last long, had commenced.

Camille Desmoulins was still editing the ' Révolutions de France et de Brabant' when, on June 21, 1791, Louis XVI. attempted to fly and was arrested at Varennes by Drouot, the postmaster, who was afterwards the deputy to the Convention from Vendôme.

'On Tuesday, the 21st June,' says Camille, 'it became known that the king and all his family had fled. It was at eleven o'clock at night that the general *décampativos* of the male and female Capets took place, and it was not until nine o'clock in the morning that the news was known. Treason ! Perjury ! Barnave and Lafayette are abusing our confidence.' —' Révolutions,' No. 82.

His subsequent speculations on the way in which the attempt was made have a certain historical interest :—

'I was coming away from the Jacobins with Danton and some other patriots at eleven o'clock, and all the way we met with only one patrol. Paris seemed to be so completely deserted that I made the remark. One of us who had a letter in his pocket in which he was apprised that the king was to go away that night, went to have a look at the château, and saw M. de Lafayette entering the gates at eleven o'clock.'

The fury of Camille speedily reached such a height that he demanded the death of him whom he called the ' king-animal,' in a style entirely unworthy of him :—

'As,' he says, 'the king-animal is an aliquot portion of the human species, and as men have had the simplicity to make him an integral portion of the body politic, it is essential that he should be subjected to the laws of society, which have declared that any man who shall be taken with arms in his hand against the nation shall be punished with death ; and also to the laws of the human species, to the natural right which permits me to kill the enemy who attacks me. Now the king has aimed at the nation. It is true that he has missed fire, but it is the nation's turn now.'—P. 158.

In order to explain this fury we must endeavour to realise the effect which the flight of the king had produced. The terrified people, threatened by the Powers, believed that they had been given over to the foreigner ; the tocsin was rung, the National Guard was summoned, all the citizens armed themselves. In the clubs such motions as the following were made :—

' *M. le président*, if the traitors (Bailly and the Ministers) present themselves, I claim to speak. I consent that two scaffolds should be erected ; and I consent to perish on one of them, if I do not prove to these men that their heads ought to fall at the feet of the nation against which they have never ceased to conspire.'

At the Cordeliers, Danton accused Lafayette of having had sixty citizens arrested, and exclaimed :—

'You had sworn that the king should not go away, you had gone bail for him. Either of two things is true : you are a traitor who have sold your country, or you are stupid to have answered for a person for whom you cannot answer. In the more favourable case of the two you have proved your-self incapable of commanding us. I leave the tribune : I have said enough to show that, though I despise traitors, I do not fear assassins ! ' [1]

It was not only with the pen that Camille fought against the king.   He tells us himself that, on July 16, 1791, the popular societies having drafted a petition to

[1] Here are a few extracts from the 'Révolutions de France et de Brabant' relative to the flight of the king :—

'On what trifles do great events turn ! At Sainte-Ménéhould, the name of the place reminds our crowned Sancho Panza of the famous pigs' feet. It shall not be said that he changed horses at Sainte-Ménéhould without having eaten pettitoes on the classic spot.   He does not remember the proverb, *Plures occidit gula quam gladius.*   The delay about getting the pettitoes ready, and the too correct portrait of himself on an *assignat*, were fatal to him.   The postmaster recognised him.'

In No. 83 Camille goes too far—indeed to actual insult—but he gives some curious details :—

'When Louis XVI. re-entered his apartment in the Tuileries, he threw himself into an armchair, saying, " It's devilish hot !" and then, " That was a —— journey.   However, I had it in my head for a long time." Afterwards, looking towards the National Guards, who were present, he said, " I have done a foolish thing, I acknowledge. *But must not I have my follies like other people ?*   Come along !   Bring me a chicken !"   One of his valets came.   "Ah, there you are," said he, "and here I am."   They brought the chicken, and Louis XVI. ate and drank with an appetite which would have done honour to the king of Cockayne.'

Afterwards he says, in reference to the queen and her demeanour on her arrival :—

'She got out of the carriage in the attitude of a suppliant, and with a humiliated countenance ; but she walked up the staircase with her nose in the air, and quite unabashed.'   The truth is that Marie Antoinette re-entered the Tuileries with dignity.   Mirabeau was right when he said, 'There was only one man about the king—his wife.'   Some days later she wrote : ' I can say nothing to you about the state of my mind.   We exist, that is all.'

In No. 84 Camille complains that the Assembly has treated the king, now an ' accused person,' too well.   ' They ought not to have awaited his convenience, to have permitted a criminal to take a bath when the commissioners were coming, and waited in the ante-room until his bell rang for the National Assembly to be admitted, like bath attendants.   Did any one ever see judges writing their names in the lodge-keeper's book at a prison, by way of humbly asking the accused to favour them with an audience, and to name the hour ?   Such subservience never was heard of before.'—P. 241.

the National Assembly demanding the deposition of
Louis XVI., he was sent to the Municipality, as head
of the deputation, to inform them of this project. Paris
was in a ferment that day.   In the centre of the Place
Vendôme (soon to become the Place des Piques), an
orator who cried 'No more kings!' was loudly applauded ; and the popular excitement spreading, it was
soon not only the deposition of the king for which the
people clamoured, but the trial of Louis XVI. and
the arrest of Lafayette and Bailly.   On the following
day, July 17, the anniversary of the fête of the Federation was to be celebrated at the Champ de Mars.
On that day the red flag of martial law was displayed by
order of Lafayette, who led Bailly into using severe
measures.   There was some bloodshed.   The violent
harangues of the popular orators having provoked
some stone-throwing at the National Guard on the
part of the over-excited population (Fournier, an
American and a madman, presented his pistol at the
breast of Lafayette), the drums were beaten, and the
National Guard fired on the people.   The crowd who
had come thither to sign the petition upon the altar of
the country were shot down, and scattered, and they
fled wildly in every direction.   A man named Provart
killed himself in despair.[1]   Certain biographers have
asserted that Camille Desmoulins figured on that day
among the persons who incited the people to make
the disturbance ; others affirm, on the contrary, that,
instead of going to the Champ de Mars, Camille dined

[1] Decree of the Commune of Paris : 'That the petition of the
Champ de Mars of July 17, 1791, shall be placed under a glass case, and
that the bust of Provart, who killed himself on that day, declaring that
liberty was lost, shall be placed in the hall of the Communal House by
the side of that of Marat, assassinated July 13.'—'Répertoire,' vol. i.
p. 154.

in the country with Danton, Legendre, and Fréron. It is quite certain that on the same evening warrants were issued for the arrest of Danton and Camille. The newspaper-sellers were prohibited from crying their journals in the streets, and the red flag floated for a fortnight over the portal of the Hôtel de Ville.

The wrath of the National Guard against the petitioners was hot. Prud'homme relates in his ' Révolutions de Paris' (not in the ' Tribune des Patriotes,' as M. Ed. Fleury states), that he had a narrow escape of being assassinated, in place of Desmoulins, on the Pont Neuf. Fréron, who was trampled under foot, also on the Pont Neuf, was saved by the National Guards of his own section. Danton took refuge at the house of his father-in-law, at Fontenay-sous-Bois ; while Camille made his appearance on that very same evening at the Jacobins, where he thundered against Lafayette and Bailly, whom he called ' two arch-Tartuffes of civism.' He then promptly sought a place of safety, and concealed himself, not in a cellar like Marat, but in the house of some friend or relative. During this time the armed force charged with the duty of arresting Camille found nobody at the office of the ' Révolutions ' except Roch Marcandier, a fellow-townsman of Camille, who was acting as his secretary. This man, who was a hack journalist, afterwards published a number of infamous calumnies concerning Desmoulins, in his ' Histoire des hommes de proie.' On this occasion Marcandier, who was a hot-headed Guisard, made a futile resistance, fired a pistol upon the soldiers, and at length, beaten and exhausted, with his clothes torn into shreds, was dragged out of the house by them.

M

Camille Desmoulins published one more number of the 'Révolutions,' signed it with his title of 'Elector of the department of Paris,' dedicated it to Lafayette, 'the phœnix of alguazil-mayors,' and dated it from an imaginary land of liberty, where, he said, he was in exile, like Camillus, his patron. He charged Prud'-homme to supply five numbers of the 'Révolutions de Paris' to all the subscribers to the 'Révolutions de France et de Brabant,' in order to complete the three months due to them. Then, with the farewell words in which the born journalist speaks—' It costs me much to lay down my pen '—he retired for a while into oblivion and silence. The day was, however, to come when, fired with fresh ardour, he would again seize his pen and recommence the never-ending strife.

He loved that profession of journalism which is so vile in certain hands, but so noble in those of an honest man; that profession of which he said :—

At the present day journalists exercise ministerial functions. They denounce, they decree, they rule in unforeseen matters, they absolve or condemn. Every day they ascend the orator's tribune, and among them are stentorian voices which make themselves heard in the eighty-three departments. Places to hear these orators cost only two sous; journals rain down every morning like the manna from heaven; and fifty broadsheets enlighten the world each day, punctually as the sun.—' Rév.,' No. 17, p. 183.

For the present Camille was unheard from the 'orator's tribune,' and his sun, or rather his lantern, had ceased to give out light.

IV.

Was Camille happy during those hours of respite, waiting, and reflection ? He was at the height of his love-fever. Lucile was about to become a mother, and it may easily be imagined that one so eager for new sensations, emotions, and affections as Camille, would be full of joy at the idea of paternity. All the former trials of his life seem to have been forgotten, and I do not doubt that in his temporary retreat he found a shadow of that blissful 'Otaheite' which he dreamed of afterwards in his dungeon, when he allowed the secret of his temperament, and his soul, to escape in the words ' I was born to make verses.'

Such a man was not, however, likely to rest contented for any length of time with obscurity, and the quiet happiness which, though it was troubled by fear, he enjoyed. After September 9, 1791, Camille applied to the National Assembly to know whether he still preserved his functions and his title of Elector. The Assembly passed to the order of the day. A month later he presented himself at the Jacobin club, with a speech in his hand. The intention to prosecute him had been abandoned, and Camille re-appeared, not as an orator, but to read a paper containing his opinion upon the *political situation of the nation*, at the opening of the second session of the National Assembly. Camille considered that he was bound to reply by this lecture to his recent nomination as Secretary to the Society of Friends of the Constitution. ' I have regarded this choice as an invitation to break silence,' said he. Indeed, his pen must have been burning his fingers for three months past.

In this much-applauded production we still find the Desmoulins of old, aggressive and addicted to personalities. Bailly, Lafayette, Dandré, Chapelier, the Assembly itself, all are violently attacked, and Desmoulins exclaims :—

'We did not demand only that royalty should be extinguished, but that a tyranny worse than royalty should not be established in its place; for, I ask, when was any royal individual so inviolable that he would have ventured to treat his subjects as the citizens were treated at Nancy and on the Champ de Mars, without exposing himself to the tragic fate of a Nero or a Caligula ?'

This triumph of an evening, this violent reply to the warrant of arrest issued against him, was not sufficient for Camille. Once more he regretted his forsaken journal, his 'Révolutions de France et de Brabant,' —its title had been dishonestly used by another person who continued the publication. 'My journal was a power,' he said to his father; and added, alluding to his having suffered it to drop, 'that was a great folly of which I was guilty.' In the order of things intellectual there exists a special passion, which may be called the passion of journalism. Every man who has once tasted the pleasure of reading off his thoughts *printed while they are hot*, who has experienced the delight of speaking out of his closet to thousands of people, is eternally condemned to this ungrateful, crushing, feverish, exhausting task. Camille dreamed only of re-establishing a journal. He had a strong friendship for Fréron, his former colleague, induced by the business relations already described between them. This Fréron was he whom Lucile laughingly called ' The Rabbit,' and who in later days belonged to the reactionary party ; he who had insisted that Marie Antoinette should be dragged

through the streets of Paris, like Frédégonde, at the
tail of a stallion (June 1791); he, *the Saviour of the
South*, the Man of Toulon, whom Hébert ridiculed as
a dandy (Muscadin), and who afterwards turned Mar-
tainville into a collaborator, and made soldiers of ' *the
gilded youth.*' In those later days he called Camille
' *that clever, simple fellow.*'—(See ' Mémoire historique
sur la réaction royaliste et les massacres du Midi; '
par Fréron, ex-député. An IV. p. 38.)

In April 1792, Camille and Fréron, ' the people's
orator' and President of the Cordeliers, issued a prospectus of a new journal, destined to succeed the ' Révolutions de France et de Brabant,' and called ' La
Tribune des Patriotes.' This time Camille selected
one Pierre-Jacques Duplain, who also lived in the
Cour du Commerce, to print the journal. Notwithstanding the attractive promises of the prospectus, the
' Tribune des Patriotes' did not succeed. Only four
numbers were published. ' The making of books,'
Camille had said, ' is a business which one learns and
forgets like any other. Ask Mercier. But it is idleness
and want of practice which have pared my nails, and
I hope, my dear friends and brethren, that with a little
exercise they will soon be as long as your own.' The
nails, which did not scratch so deeply as they had
formerly done, had not much time to grow; by the end
of May 1791 the journal had ceased to exist. None
the less, however, it had had its influence upon the
crowd, and Desmoulins had recovered his position and
his authority.

He had also been brought into prominent notice by
a violent pamphlet against Brissot, his former friend,
who had been one of the witnesses to his marriage
contract. Brissot, who was a kind of Quaker, and

whose patriotism Camille had once said he 'envied,' had already alienated the affection of the author of 'La France libre,' when the editor of the 'Patriote Français' wrote of Desmoulins as a *'young man'* (Révolutions de Brabant,' May 1791).[1] Camille never forgave anybody who pretended to lecture or control him. This, even Marat, the redoubtable Marat himself, learned to his cost, when Desmoulins, though he did not wish to break absolutely with so terrible an adversary, said to him: 'After all, Marat, the Republic must be defended, not only with men, but with dogs!'

'Spite,' said Hérault de Séchelles in his 'Pensées' —'spite is a note of vain characters. This sentiment is the anger of vanity; it belongs to women and to feminine men; it breeds small and great atrocities.' Unhappily, Camille was subject to this weakness.

Since the cessation of his 'Révolutions,' Camille, who had also sustained considerable pecuniary losses in consequence of the depreciation of the value of bonds on the Hôtel de Ville, had resumed his profession. 'I return, after the Revolution, to the Bar,' he

---

[1] 'Camille Desmoulins to' Jean-Pierre Brissot, greeting. Hitherto I have not been attacked, except by honourable abuse. I am much indebted to you, Brissot, for having attacked me formally, and summoned me before the tribunal of opinion by three long, grave, sententious, and libellous letters. Polemics are my element; and accusation is the test of the citizen, and the touchstone of Patriotism. I could not perfectly esteem the man of whom no evil is said. When you said to me, *Young man, take and read,* all your readers must have perceived that you had a very great idea of yourself, and you are quite right to admire yourself so much. I think it is better to love oneself like Narcissus than to have no passion for anything, and I prefer Sterne to Horace, who preaches the happiness of the *nil admirari,* and who says, somewhere, if I don't mistake, "As for me, I have all my life been in love with one princess or another, and I hope I shall be so until my death."'—Fleury's Ed., vol. i. p. 235.

wrote to his father; and in his defence of the Society
of the Friends of the Constitution, at Marseilles,
against Dandré, the advocate pursues the personal
polemics of the publicist. In January 1792, he presented himself before the Correctional Police Court on
behalf of a woman named Beffroi, and a certain Di-
thurbide, a merchant, who were arrested, the one for
keeping a gambling-house in the Passage Radziville, the
other for being her accomplice. They were both condemned to six months' imprisonment, the woman at the
Salpétrière, the man at Bicêtre, notwithstanding their
appeals, offers of verification, &c. Desmoulins protested
against this arbitrary act in a half-jesting tone, defending
play, and pretending that 'in the forests of Gaul and
Germany our fathers (this is incontestable historic truth)
played at *trente-et-un* and even at *biribi* for their individual liberty.' He afterwards loudly protested, in
reference to the incarceration of his clients, against a
measure which confounded 'vices with crimes,' and 'the
gamester with the thief.'

This protest, published in a broadsheet, and pla-
carded, gave rise to the hatred which sprang up between
Camille and Brissot. The slightly puritanical austerity
of Brissot forbade him to allow the broadsheet of his
former friend to pass without a protest on his part. The
'Patriote Français' attacked the opinion of Desmoulins
as contrary to morals. 'This man,' cried Brissot, in
allusion to Camille, 'calls himself a patriot that he may
insult patriotism.' He accused him of having 'soiled
the walls with his scandalous apology for games of
chance.' Camille was keenly hurt and offended.
That feminine spite of which Hérault speaks took
possession of him, and he replied to Brissot's attack in
a stinging pamphlet. 'Jean-Pierre Brissot Unmasked'

struck Brissot de Warville in the face, like a sharp
stone from a sling. Camille had never been more
violent or more virulent. He called Brissot a rogue,
and quoted the Prophets against him : ' *Factus sum in
proverbium.*' He invented the verb *brissoter*, against
Brissot (copying Aristophanes in his quarrel with
Sophocles) ; he made a street boy say, 'On m'a
brissoté ma toupie.' He compared the man whom he
ironically called *the honest Brissot* with the wretched
Morande, who had signed the acknowledgment of his
own dishonour with his own hand. He reproached
Brissot—it reads oddly from Camille—with having
dared to declare himself a republican ' when the word
Republic frightened nine-tenths of the nation,' when
Robespierre, Carra, Loustallot, and Danton, had 'forbidden themselves to pronounce that word.'

Unhappily, this bitter pamphlet, full of hate, was
destined, before a year had elapsed, to have a terrible
and sinister result. After having written ' Jean-Pierre
Brissot Unmasked,' Desmoulins in 1793 published his
' Fragment of the Secret History of the Revolution,' in
which the ' Brissotins,' the Girondists, were attacked and
given up to the judgment which awaited them. These
two pamphlets are among the writings which one earnestly desires to blot out of the works of such a man.
These are among the pages which Desmoulins regretted so bitterly, when from his prison he turned a
mental glance back to his 'too numerous writings.'

When Camille was writing his ' Brissot Unmasked '
he was surrounded by pleas for gentleness, kindness,
and indulgence. But angry self-love pardons nothing ;
it is implacable. Camille was happy ; he might have
already adopted the mild tone of his later days.

His adored Lucile was about to give him a son. The sunshine of love and joy dwelt upon the little household. Camille and his wife lived at No. 1 in the Cour du Commerce, Saint-André des Arts, which had been built on the former site of a tennis-court, and they had for neighbours on the upper story, M. and Madame Danton. How often have Camille and Danton left the house together, arm in arm, to go to the Cordeliers' club, close by. In a letter written by Camille to his father, April 3, 1792, he says, speaking of Danton : 'A man who esteems me too much to extend to myself the hatred which he bears to my opinions.' Danton, strong, manly, threatening, but kindly, must indeed have more than once reprimanded the sarcastic Camille.

The neighbours visited each other frequently, although Camille was, at this period, under the influence of Robespierre rather than of Danton. Stanislas Fréron, *Fréron-Lapin*, came often to the Cour du Commerce, and Brune, the future Marshal of France, who was then a member of the Cordeliers' club. Brune was an educated man, and in 1788 had published a book called 'Voyage pittoresque et sentimental dans plusieurs Provinces Occidentales de France.' It was a medley of prose and verse, in which Sterne was mixed up with Chapelle and Bachaumont. He was working at this time at other literary tasks, and he quoted Horace just as Camille quoted Cicero. The friendly circle which was so soon to be broken up by death had other members. Madame Duplessis came to Lucile's house occasionally, accompanied by her second daughter Adèle, whom Robespierre had a passing fancy to marry. What laughter, what joys, what projects, what dreams

must that little dwelling have heard and seen! There
were many such quiet corners where the idyllic took
refuge from the angry crowd and the roar of cannon.
It has required the trials through which France has
recently passed to make us understand this aspect of
that terrible old time, to make us comprehend these
profound antitheses : kisses amid the discharge of
artillery ; smiles lighting up faces blanched with pain ;
lovers who go on loving throughout every kind of
disaster, like the swallows who make their nest in the
angles of walls which have been riddled with bomb-
shells.

These fierce beings loved each other. They
smiled in the midst of their cares and their terrors.
Camille tended his pregnant wife, and was impatient
for the birth of his son. He wrapped himself up in
the possession of his happiness. At this time his
father asked him if he could not purchase the small
patrimony at Guise, the house in which Camille and
his brothers and sisters were born. M. Desmoulins
was in needy circumstances, and he thought of selling
the house, which was already mortgaged. Camille
replied :—

'How can you suppose that at a moment when everything
is half as dear again as it used to be, I could buy a property worth 30,000 francs out of an income of 4,000 ? Your
house, the house in which I was born, is dear to me : no one
can understand better than I the pleasure with which Ulysses
beheld the smoke from Ithaca afar off ; but with 4,000 francs,
which at present represent only 2,000 livres, how could I give
30,000 for a house ?'

He pleads 'household expenses.' He has to think
of the cost of the 'layette.' A little while and there
will be a child to provide for.

Horace-Camille Desmoulins,—he who will remain
for ever, in the eyes of history, 'the little Horace,'
Camille's son, whom Robespierre danced so often on
his knees—was born July 6, 1792. On the 8th,
Camille presented him at the Municipality, followed by
Laurent Lecointre (of Versailles) and Antoine Merlin
(of Thionville), deputies to the National Assembly.
Horace Desmoulins figures in the first act of the
'civil estate' of the Municipality of Paris, as the first
child who was presented before the Altar of the
country. In 'La Presse,' of November 24, 1847, we
find : 'On July 8, 1792, year IV. of Liberty, Camille
demanded the formal statement of the civil estate of
his son, being desirous of sparing himself any future
reproach on his part for having bound him to religious
opinions which could not then have been his own.'
Shortly afterwards, Camille wrote to his father concerning the child : 'He was immediately put out to
nurse at l'Ile Adam (Seine-et-Oise), with the little
Danton.' No doubt Lucile was too delicate to nurse
him. She, worshipper of Rousseau as she had been,
would surely have acted on the instructions of the
author of 'Émile ;' but it is probable that Camille, who
was a disciple of Voltaire rather than of Jean-Jacques,
dissuaded his wife from suckling her child.

Camille had need of all the domestic happiness
which he enjoyed at this time to divert his mind from
the pecuniary anxieties under which he, as well as his
parents at Guise, was labouring. He was, in fact, on
the eve of losing a considerable portion of the dowry
of Lucile, which was placed, as it was called then, 'on
the King.' He was, besides, somewhat hampered by
the failure of his 'Tribune des Patriotes.' At the very
moment when he would fain have wielded a more

cutting weapon, a sharper pen, the caricaturists fell upon him, and his enemies did not lay down arms even before his domestic hearth. A royalist comic composition exhibited, in July 1792, what it called 'The Thaw.' This was the general cracking and break up of the new democratic world, while the terrified revolutionaries took to their heels and fled. Among the latter was a figure, hastily escaping, hampered with the weight of its lantern ; this, *Janot Desmoulins*, was Camille, 'wearing,' says M. Fleury, 'the cap of the Phrygian slaves.' No wonder the pamphleteer, reduced to silence, and without sufficient moral courage to oppose the spectacle of a quiet life in a happy home to such attacks, was furious ! With such a temperament as Camille's, he could not keep quiet during the crisis which France was then passing through, and in the face of the attacks which were made upon himself. The strife between the Monarchy and the Revolution had entered upon an implacable phase. The king, who had hesitated for some time, who had refused to yield to just demands lest he might be, as he said, constrained to endure heavy exactions, was finally following the deplorable counsels of those who urged him to reaction. The Revolution was served by hatred and the fear of liberty. ' It must be said plainly,' wrote M. de la Marche, a year before, to M. de Mercy-Argenteau, ' *the king is incapable of reigning.*' On March 11, 1792, Pellenc wrote to La Marck, ' They say that the king conducts himself in private like a man who is preparing for death.' The Court, in consternation at his resignation, which might lead to martyrdom, but could not lead to success, imagined that the popular movement could be suppressed by the Swiss Guard and the 'knights of the dagger,' and this, although June 20 had proved that the danger was great and the people were strong. When Paris was threatened with the closing of its clubs and the arrest of its orators, Paris rose. 'Persist, Sire!' wrote Lafayette from the camp at Maubeuge to Louis XVI. When Roland, who had been made Minister of the Interior some time previously, presented himself in a round hat and tied shoes, like Franklin's, the Master of the Ceremonies was scandalised, and, approaching Dumouriez, said, in an offended tone, 'Monsieur has no buckles in his shoes!' 'Ah, monsieur,' replied Dumouriez, with ironical calm, 'all is then lost!' Such was the state of things at Court, while the faubourgs were hardly to be restrained by Santerre—who followed, rather than directed, the popular movements—when the nation was irritated by Bertrand de Motteville's open favouring of 'the emigration,' and its knowledge that the king submitted to, but did not accept, Roland. Everywhere the Queen's saying, 'All this *tapage* will soon come to an end,' was repeated and commented on. To talk thus of *tapage* was to let it loose. Besides, the Court did more than talk; it acted. The king dismissed three members of his ministry, the three Girondists, 'factious, insolent persons,' he called them to Dumouriez. 'My patience is worn out,' said Louis.

The Girondists did not make any delay about their answer. 'Terror,' said Vergniaud, pointing to the Tuileries, 'has come out of that palace often enough; now let it re-enter it, in the name of the law.' Legendre, making himself the interpreter of Danton's great voice, exclaimed, in Santerre's hearing, 'It is to the Tuileries that we must go and demand the recall of the patriot ministers!' They went to the Tuileries. Those who repaired thither were called 'petitioners,' but they numbered 20,000 men. This armed crowd, headed by the colossal Marquis de Saint-Huruge, in the costume of a porter from the Halles, defiled through the Assembly, then speedily made their way into the Tuileries, where they invaded the apartments and spread themselves over them like the waves of a tumultuous sea. Wild, dishevelled women surrounded the Queen. Marie Antoinette, pale and unmoved, met their invectives with disdain. The king said, in his phlegmatic way, ' I am not afraid ; I have received the Sacraments.'

Some one had placed a red woollen cap on the head of the little Dauphin, as he stood closely pressed against his mother. Pétion, the Mayor of Paris, took it off, saying, ' This child is being stifled.' The king, who was suffering equally from the heat, put on the Phrygian cap. His faithful troops dared not move, lest the king should be hurt, and disorder turned into massacre. Isnard, Vergniaud, Merlin de Thionville, and finally, Pétion, at length set the king free. At eight in the evening the palace was vacated, and Louis XVI. indignantly flung down at his feet the red cap which he had worn until then.

The following passage from Camille's ' Réflexions sur le 20 Juin, 1792 ' (Baron de Girardot's Collection), which has been hitherto unpublished, gives us the exact tone of the revolutionary party at this time :—

' It is certain that all parties wished for an insurrection; but also that those among the Jacobins who have, hitherto, been least deceived in their political judgments upon men and events, were apprehensive of the results of that insurrection. We saw clearly that violence would only be profitable at Coblentz, or to Lafayette, or other ambitious persons, and would not serve the cause of liberty in the least. After I had applauded the petitioners in the Council-General of the Commune, when they came, five days in advance, to give notice to the Municipality that they proposed to celebrate the commemoration of the oath of the *Jeu de Paume* on June 20; after I had represented the procession of pikes which defiled before the National Assembly as a mere blessing of the flags, as a patriotic review, and very useful, in so far as it would have an imposing effect on the counter-revolutionists and the factions, and would restrain them by fear of the great number of the friends of the Constitution; after all this I made every possible effort at the Jacobins' to secure that this raising of the shields should not be anything more serious than a comminatory insurrection. Although I rarely demand my turn at the Jacobins', I spoke at three consecutive meetings on the following text: "Nothing is more likely to ruin the affairs of the Jacobins than a partial insurrection. The National Assembly, by its decree which ordered the publication of the address of the Marseillais in the eighty-three departments, had in reality decreed a general insurrection for July 14, and convened the Nation for that day on the Champ de Mars; that we must wait for that great armed National Assembly like our ancestors in their Champ de Mars or their Champ de Mai; that the Jacobins ought to profess more strongly than ever their attachment to the Constitution, because on the coarse mind of the multitude only words impress themselves; and since the word 'Constitution' has become, in the eighteenth century, as magical a rallying cry as the word 'Pope' was in the twelfth, they who shall defend the Constitution will naturally be the victors, and they who shall attack it the vanquished. The Constitution is like a great ditch on whose banks the two parties are ranged opposite to one another; the confederate royalists are more anxious to cross it than we are; but the first to do so will fall in and choke it up with dead men, thus forming a bridge for the other. It is easy to perceive that the noble, official, and wealthy classes—the

Coblentzists and the Feuillants, wanted to keep the two
Chambers for themselves; to instal themselves, so to speak,
in the salon, and relegate us, the people, to the antechamber;
but if the Jacobins have only sufficient good sense and self-
restraint to go on protesting incessantly that they did not
desire the Republic, but the Constitution, the whole Constitution, nothing but the Constitution, the two plenipotentiaries
for Coblentz and the Feuillants, the cousins Lafayette and
Bouillé, will be very shortly puzzled how to make the nation
ratify their secret treaty."

'This is the substance of what I said at the Jacobins, where
I especially recommended that the insurrection should be
calm, and that we should display a profound attachment to
the Constitution.   I pointed out that royalty was decaying
day by day, that the life of Louis XVI. was precious to the
Jacobins; that if he died we ought to have him stuffed, as
Mirabeau had said; and that the very best thing which could
happen would be that he should dismiss the Jacobin ministers
and send for others from Coblentz.'

Thus, it is evident that, in resisting the current
which had become national, Louis XVI. was playing
the game of his enemies.   He might have saved
everything by swimming with the tide.   But when, on
June 21, Pétion, in order to calm down the Parisian
effervescence, posted placards declaring that the law
forbade armed assemblies, and reproved every kind of
violence, and added, 'Remember that those peoples
are most free who are most obedient to the law,' the
king answered, no doubt boldly, but without tact, and
with utter ignorance of the situation, that nothing
should be obtained from him by violence, and ordered
an enquiry into the misdemeanours of the 20th.   One
more idle stroke of resistance, and it was too late.
The 20th of June might have been for the king the
flash of lightning which reveals the depth of a yawning
abyss;   but Louis XVI. saw nothing, he would see

nothing, and so the flash was simply that which pre-
cedes the thunder.

In this work, the history of a single individual, it
would be impossible to give the space which is due
to them to even the most important events of the
period. I do not pretend to relate the drama itself,
but only the parts which certain actors played in it.
Camille Desmoulins, Danton, Chabot, and Santerre
have been accused of having *prepared* the invasion
of the Tuileries and the insurrection of August 10, to
which the events of June 20 were only the prelude.
I repeat that the Court only, by a final laying down of
arms, could have prevented that catastrophe. But it
was not a formal kiss of peace which was requisite;
it was a genuine embrace, without reserve or double-
meaning; a general reconciliation in the face of the
enemy whose guns were threatening French soil.

Louis XVI. forgot that the spectre of the foreigner
was only too real and present to the inflamed imagination of the nation. He was trying to defend, one
after another, the prerogatives which were gone for
ever. Thus, on July 14, at the Fête of the Federation, he refused to set fire to the 'tree of feudality,'
because, he said, feudality no longer existed. Jean
Debry seized the torch and fired the tree. The King's
public refusal, his resistance in the face of the multitude, certainly displayed courage and determination, but
it must be admitted that it was not calculated to con-
ciliate the alienated feelings of the people.

At this time Camille had flung himself completely
into the stirring and feverish life of Paris. Lucile
was with Madame Duplessis at Bourg-la-Reine: he
writes to her as follows :—

N

'My good Lucile, don't cry, I beg, because you do not see your Monsieur "*Hon*"' (this was a nickname by which Lucile occasionally called Camille, who stammered a little, and used to begin his sentences with *hon, hon*). 'He is up to his neck in the Revolution. How delighted you would have been to see me to-day in the municipal cavalcade. This was the first time I played a part in public ; I was as proud as Don Quixote. Nevertheless, my good *Rouleau*, my Cachan hen, was sitting up behind me' (Rouleau was a pet name for Lucile, and 'Cachan hen' refers to a hen and her chickens which she and Camille had seen at Cachan). 'Don't love me so much, my dearest, if it gives you so much pain ! I dined at Robespierre's to-day, and talked ever so much about Rouleau, Rouleau, my poor Rouleau. Now I am finishing my speech, for I am told off to read it to the Municipality on Tuesday. The *rentiers* of the General Council are desperately frightened by a few words which I spoke yesterday in the tribune, and which were much applauded. This day I have consecrated to proclaiming the country in danger, mounted on my horse in the midst of three thousand National Guards and twenty pieces of cannon. To-morrow, I—(blank). I do not venture to talk to you about your baby, lest I should bring the tears into your eyes. It is eleven o'clock. I write so that you may have my letter to-morrow ; I am going to rest, but you will not lay your arm round my neck. I shall make haste with my speech, that I may fly to your arms. Adieu, my good angel, my Lolotte, mother of the little lizard. Kiss Daronne' (Madame Duplessis) 'and Horace for me.' (Copied from the original.)

Camille was not plotting in the dark, as has been said of him, any more than Danton and his friends. The hour had come when conspiracy ceased to exist; it was now open war. In the discourse which Camille had mentioned to Lucile, he was about to endeavour to tranquillise Paris respecting the consequences of such a crisis, to cheer up the class of small traders, of petty shopkeepers, of whom he said—and one cannot read his words without an aching heart—'they are more afraid of revolutionists than of Hulans!' The discourse is very eloquent, and when Desmoulins dreams of the 'agape' which shall unite 'us, disdainful bourgeois' and the people in fraternal bonds, the reader is carried away by the vision which was then, and still is, only a dream.

'If they dare to attack us,' he says, like a true Athenian of Paris, 'it is because we do not drink together! Well then, let us do to make liberty secure what Crassus did to make despotism secure. We cannot entertain the French people as Cæsar did, who entertained the Roman people at twenty-two thousand tables; or as Crassus did, who made a feast for the Roman people and afterwards gave to each citizen as much corn as he could use in three months. It seems that there is neither patriotism nor virtue except in poverty, or at least in moderate fortune. But let us spread tables before our doors, if, indeed, it be true that we believe in equality; let us entertain our equals for one day as the Romans entertained their slaves for a whole week; let us celebrate our deliverance from despotism and from the aristocracy, as the Jews celebrated their deliverance from Pharaoh; let us eat together before our doors the national roast mutton, even as they ate their paschal lamb. Come, respectable artizan, let thy hands, hardened by toil, meet mine, which have only held a pen, without contempt; come, let us drink together, let us embrace, and our enemies shall be overthrown!'

The conclusion of this harangue is more threatening, and smells of powder. August 10 is not far off.

'If the National Assembly,' concludes Desmoulins, 'does not believe that it can save the Constitution, let it declare in the words of the Constitution, and, *as was done among the Romans*' (these eternal classical recollections!), 'that it remits the charge to each of the citizens individually, and to them all collectively, by the decree *ut quisque reipublicæ consulat*. So soon as the tocsin is sounded let all the nation assemble ; let each man, as in Rome, be invested with the right to punish known conspirators with death ; and one single day of anarchy will do more for the security of liberty and the salvation of the country than four years of a National Assembly.'

Let me pause here for a moment to protest against this theory, whose only aim is to raise *coups-d'état* to the rank of government, and let me say that I hold such a doctrine to be fatal to the liberty, to the morality, and even to the life of nations.

We need not dwell upon this concluding phrase, and on the perpetual recurrence of the memories of old Rome which we find throughout Camille's writings, and which deprive him, and the greater number of his contemporaries, who were captivated, like himself, by antique tragedy, of the power of comprehending modern liberty which rests upon law. One thing is certain ; the much desired day was one of anarchy rather than of battle. From Wednesday, July 11, the country—dear invaded France, happier, however, than in 1814, 1815, and 1870, because she repulsed her invaders,—was declared to be in danger. ' Citizens, the Country is in danger !' were the terms of the decree of the Assembly. The army, which had not yet become the amalgam invented by Bouchotte —an amalgam which created the true French army— was already fighting bravely.

A column of the *émigrés*—voltigeurs of Condé's troops—finding themselves face to face with the former regiments of the king, which were now the regiments of the nation, shouted to the latter, ' Desert ! Desert ! brave men of the Dauphin's regiment !' But they were answered by a furious charge of the regiment with

During this time all Paris was reading the insolent manifesto of the Duke of Brunswick (it is preserved in the Archives and signed *Brunsvig*), in the streets, and at the clubs. People showed each other the threatening caricatures which the royalists concocted, feats of fancy representing the foreign powers 'making rabid deputies, and *Jacoquins* (Jacobins) dance the ballet of master Nicolas' turkeys.' The sections became troubled and threatening. Camille Desmoulins spoke loudly of the justice which was coming. Thirty thousand citizens of the section of Gravilliers—a boiling revolutionary caldron—and all those of the section of Mauconseil, proclaimed the deposition of Louis XVI. They were seconded by forty-six sections who declared that 'Louis the False' was no longer King of France. The unfortunate king saw that things were growing threatening indeed.

The duel was in fact imminent. The king collected around him all those who were still faithful to him, the last combatants of the expiring monarchy, his grenadiers of the Filles Saint-Thomas, and his Swiss Guard. He sent blue cards to his gentlemen, which meant 'Come!' He reckoned over and over again the number of devoted servants of whom he could dispose. Poor Louis! His last battle was lost in advance. The force of circumstances was against him.

One evening, in the twilight, when the storm was growling outside, and Louis and the Queen were sitting silent and thoughtful in the heavy, sulphurous atmosphere, a grand, terrifying, superb, unknown song burst upon their ears; a song which even the parodies of 1870 have failed to render ridiculous. The King was astounded, the Queen started and trembled. That which they heard then, they had never heard before. It was something indescribable and irresistible, a tremendous threat, the cry of a nation at bay, the trumpet blast of a people getting under arms, the rallying cry of liberty and deliverance, the triumphant neigh of the courser too long held in check, as he shakes off the hold of his master, the grand national refrain, the glorious song of free France ; it was the ' Marseillaise.'

The ' Marseillaise ' is the song of the revolution in arms, as the ' Chant du départ ' is its hymn of pomp and glory, and the 'Ça ira' is its threatening growl; the ' Marseillaise' is made for the frontier, the ' Chant du départ' for the Champ de Mars, and the ' Ça ira ' for the streets.

What must the Queen have felt when those fierce accents struck upon her ear ? No more, for her, was the sound of the clavecin to come through the pinewoods of Schoenbrunn ; no more was she to listen to the sweet Swiss air of ' Pauvre Jacques' at Trianon, to Rousseau's romance, ' Le Devin du village,' or the royalist hymns of Grétry. Instead of these came the military march music sung by the federates of Marseilles as they entered Paris, and thundered under the windows of the Tuileries, making the panes in the casements rattle :—

> Allons, enfants de la patrie,
> Le jour de gloire est arrivé !

The fierce, dauntless, terrible Marseillais—those men of Marseilles whom the '*spadassins*' of Count d'Aiglemont had sworn to put, one by one, to the sword—chanted their national song with clear metallic voices, full of pitiless resolution.

Antoinette felt that they were lost. And yet, incredible as it seems, it was the king and his adherents who commenced the attack. The body-guards insulted the deputies ; they threatened the deputies of the people. Those gentlemen, who, with the Count d'Hervilly at their head, were afterwards to fight and die so bravely, exposed royalty to its ultimate defeat by their sheer light-heartedness.

The rejection of the decree of accusation against Lafayette, who was accused of having designed to carry off the National Assembly, caused the general outbreak. On August 9, 1792, at midnight, the tocsin was rung. This was the signal. Paris rose *en masse* and marched on the Tuileries. The faubourgs were illuminated. Anxious and excited crowds gathered around the municipalities. The presidents of the sections, pale, resolute men, announced to the people that the hour had come when they must conquer or die.

The Parisian municipality entered the Hôtel de Ville, and assumed the direction of the battle. The serene and peaceful night was bright with stars. The profiles of the crowd showed sharply in the luminous shade of the streets. At the palace, the guards were drinking, and waiting. The victorious insurrectionists came upon heaps of bottles which these guards had emptied to the cry of 'Down with the Nation!' and 'Long live the King!' Louis, who knew now that his counsellors had been his ruin, was already thinking of seeking a refuge in the National Assembly. Too late, he comprehended that only the law could protect him. At eight o'clock he left his palace and took shelter in the reporters' box at the Assembly.

The people had already attacked the Carrousel, and

having been repulsed by the Swiss guards, they had returned in good order, dragging cannons with them. They did not falter under the cross-fire from the palace ; but they carried the Tuileries room by room, corridor after corridor. The staircases, the galleries, the chapel, all witnessed terrible fighting. The conquerors, now masters of the palace, flung the corpses of the Swiss guards out of the windows, and such as had contrived to escape from the building were massacred under the chestnut trees. They mustered round the small basin, and beat a retreat in good order. But the poor, brave fellows were killed, and they died intrepidly.

It is told that during this terrible struggle, a young man, wearing a threadbare coat, slight of figure and yellow of face, with contracted features and brilliant eyes, gazed at the Tuileries, which, it was said, that night, no one should enter ever more ; and then at the people, drunk with joy, who should never henceforth have a master.

That man was Napoleon Bonaparte.

'Is this,' he said to himself, '*the thawing of the nation ?*' (The words are his own.)

Then, turning his eyes on the Assembly, yonder, where Louis XVI. was quietly eating a roast chicken, while Vergniaud was talking about summoning a National Convention.

'Fool,' he muttered, 'hadn't you guns to sweep away the populace ?'[1]

The man who was to profit by the revolution and to succeed the Convention, then on the eve of its birth

---

[1] He had said on the previous evening to Pozzo di Borgo, that with two Swiss battalions and one hundred cavalry, he would undertake to give

at the Tuileries, was already lurking like a beast-tamer, behind the people, on August 10.

V.

What part had Camille and his friends been playing throughout that day? On this point we have the testimony of a unique document. It is an extract from the pocket-book of Lucile Desmoulins, dated December 12, in which she relates with poignant eloquence, in sentences which palpitate with terror, anguish, hope and love, all that she underwent during those dark hours. On Thursday, August 9, Lucile, who had returned from the country on the preceding day, wrote the following lines in her pocket-book; lines which contrast strongly in the truth of their emotion with the vague reveries of her girlish years:

'What will become of us? I can endure no more. Camille, O my poor Camille! what will become of you? I have no strength to breathe. This night, this fatal night! My God! if it be true that Thou hast any existence, save the men that are worthy of Thee. We want to be free. O God! the cost of it!'

Who can read without emotion the pages in which the young wife, still a prey to torments of apprehension, recalling the sufferings of the day before, lives them twice over in her vivid memory?

'I had come back from the country on August 8,' writes Lucile. 'The public mind was already in a ferment. An attempt had been made to assassinate Robespierre. On the 9th I had some of the Marseillais to dinner, and we amused ourselves pretty well. After dinner we all went to Danton's. The mother was crying; she looked very sad; the child had a bewildered look; Danton was resolute. As to me, I laughed like a madcap. They were afraid the affair would not take place. " How can anyone laugh like that ? " Madame Danton said over and over again. " Alas ! " I replied, " it is a sign that I shall shed many tears this evening." '

We can picture the young wife and mother nervously disguising her uneasiness under this affected gaiety, this convulsive laughter. By and bye, she goes down into the street, which is filled with people crying ' Long live the Nation ! ' and she is frightened. She hears the terrible tocsin, that uplifted voice of an alarmed city. Going back to Danton, she finds him agitated :

' Very soon,' she continues, ' I saw that they were all arming themselves. Camille, my dear Camille, came in with a gun.' (This time poor Lucile hid her face in her hands and wept.) ' However, as I did not want to show so much weakness, or to tell Camille out loud that I did not wish him to mix himself up with all this, I watched for a moment when I might speak to him without being overheard, and tell him all my fears. He reassured me by saying that he would not leave Danton. I have known since,' adds Lucile, with a certain conjugal pride and ill-disguised fear, ' *I have known since that he exposed himself to danger.*'

Fréron, who was determined to fight, asked nothing better than to die. ' I am weary of life,' he said. It happened strangely that, of all the group of men assembled there ready for the strife, he was to be the sole survivor. Twenty months later they were dead, and he was safe.

Danton, after he had snatched some brief rest, set off late in the night for the Hôtel de Ville. ' The tocsin of the Cordeliers rang,' says Lucile ; 'it rang for a long time. Alone, bathed in tears, on my knees by the window, my face hidden in my handkerchief, I listened to the sound of that fatal bell.' Madame Danton, also, was enduring similar pangs of distress

and terror. From time to time during the night mes-
sengers brought news to the two poor women. Sometimes the news was consoling, sometimes it was alarming,
but it was generally vague. Thus they learned, to their
great terror, that it was in contemplation at the 'Communal House' to march on the Tuileries. At one
o'clock Camille came in, and slept for a few minutes,
with his head on Lucile's shoulder. When day broke,
Madame Danton, who was restless, came down to
Lucile's rooms. Then Camille went to bed; Lucile
had a bed made up hastily in the salon for Madame
Danton, and the three tried to snatch a moment's
repose, the tocsin still ringing in their ears. But
Camille soon rose and went out again, and the two
women, left alone, endeavoured to eat their breakfast,
to read, to forget. All of a sudden Lucile cried out,
'They are firing guns!' Madame Danton listened,
caught the sound, turned pale, sank down, and fainted.
'I undressed her myself,' says Lucile; 'I was ready to
fall down, but the necessity for helping her gave me
strength. She came to herself.'

What life-likeness there is in this narrative of
Lucile's! The real truth is there indeed! Now a
neighbour goes by, shouting that all this is the fault of
Camille. Again, the baker shuts his door in Lucile's
face when the two women wish to pass through his
shop so as to get out of the Cour du Commerce. What
terrors, what anguish they endured! At length
Camille comes back. The people are victorious.
Camille had seen the head of Suleau, the journalist, fall.
'Suleau's head was cut off,' writes Lucile, 'and carried
about the streets. Camille told him, "You are going
to fight for the king to-morrow, then you will be
hanged!"' And his words have proved only too true.'

On the 11th, Camille and Lucile took the precaution of sleeping at the house of a friend named Robert, in the Rue de Tournon. 'The next day,' writes Lucile, 'when I went home, I learned that Danton was in the Ministry.'[1]

Camille, who had harangued and led the men of the faubourg on the 10th, became, as Danton said, Secretary-General to the Minister of Justice, *by the grace of the cannon.*

'If I had been conquered,' said Danton, proudly, at the National Assembly, 'I should have been criminal.' He triumphed. The section of the Quinze-Vingts declared that, like Gorsas, Prud'homme, and Carra, Desmoulins had deserved well of the country. Camille took up his position seriously from the commencement, and his first words were these: 'It remains for us to make France happy and flourishing as well as free. This is the task to which I am about to devote my energies.' And, in fact, he did occupy himself, together with Danton, in addressing a circular to the magistracy of France, to protest against abuses, and to organise justice. He thought of himself, and of the satisfaction of his vanity, only after he had concerned himself about the welfare of the nation. Nevertheless, he did not forget that the *Guisards* had formerly ridiculed his hopes, and in writing to his father he remarked that they would be filled with bitterness and envy at the news of what they would

---

[1] Lucile's letter is quoted by M. Beaumont-Vassy in his 'Mémoires Secrets du dix-neuvième Siécle.' It also contains the following striking details: 'All will be finished in a week. They are smashing the mirrors in the château, and have just brought us some sponges and brushes belonging to the Queen. They tread the plate under their feet, but do not take any of it. Oh, what a ferment!'

call his 'fortune.'   And then he gives expression to
the following reflection, inspired by that 'fortune :'

'It has but rendered me more than ever melancholy
and anxious, and made me feel more keenly all the
ills of my fellow-citizens, and the miseries of human
life.'

At last his heart beats.   We feel that pity is born
in the breast of the man who has entered, as he says,
'the palace of the Lamoignons and the Maupeons
through the breach in the palace of the Tuileries.'
A year later, on the recurrent 10th of August, tired of
this ephemeral power, grieved and heart-sick at the
spectacle of the public wounds, his dreams, his desires,
his hopes turned towards that little town of Guise.
He mocks it in 1792 : he will long for it in 1793.   And
then we shall hear him cry, 'Why can I not be as obscure as I am well known ?   *O ubi campi, Giusiâque !*
Where is the refuge, the cavern which might hide me
from every eye with my wife, my child, and my books ?'
He will long, as his father foretold, once more to behold
those blessed and peaceful banks of the Oise, and
the waters of the fountain of St. Martin la Bussertière,
and the beautiful alleys of the forest of Fay, 'which
are the work of our cousin Deviefville.'   Shall he ever
see them more ?   On September 15, 1792, he is appointed by the Executive Council to inspect Laon,
Soissons and Guise, and to decide whether the denunciations against the judges in each of these cities
merit consideration by the Minister of Justice ; and,
acting under the advice of his father, he will display
the qualities which are proper to that administration.
His father, whose affection is *jealous, like that
of lovers*, as he says, speaks to him in noble and
simple words.   The novel position of his son, far from

dazzling, alarms him. 'I should prefer to see you in peaceful possession of my places," he says, 'and first among the citizens of our natal town.' But, as accomplished facts must be accepted, M. Desmoulins sends his son wise counsel. 'Add to your acknowledged popularity,' he says, 'the spirit of integrity and moderation, which you will find frequent opportunities of developing; lay aside that of party, by which perhaps you have risen, but which will not maintain you in your high place. The uprightness which I know you to possess, and the moderation which I preach to you, will go far even in the most difficult post.' Too difficult, indeed. Oh! for the fields of Guise, the church-bells of the bygone childish days, and that mother *who shares all the feelings* of M. Desmoulins. After a year, how Camille regrets these things! How he thirsts to be with his parents once more!

Yes, within a year doubt and lassitude had entered into his soul, and Camille was about to burn more than one idol which he had hitherto worshipped, or, rather— the bloody gods o'erthrown—he was henceforth to pay true and fervent reverence only to those eternal deities, whose names are right, truth, humanity, pity, and justice.

CHAPTER IV.

I.

THE National Convention was the immediate result of August 10. To those who had long demanded it, this sovereign Convention represented an assembly concentrating all power, and exercising supreme dictatorship. The idea of it inspired Camus to say in open assembly, on June 1, 1790, 'We certainly have the power of changing our religion.' On Sunday, August 26, the primary assemblies met to nominate a number of electors equal to those who voted at the last elections ; on the following Sunday, September 2, these electors proceeded to the election of the deputies of the National Convention. 'The distinction between Frenchmen as *active* and *non-active* citizens, sanctioned by the Constitution of 1791, was suppressed, and the only conditions requisite for admission to the electoral assemblies were that the candidate should be a Frenchman, not under one-and-twenty, able to prove a year's domicile, and living upon ·his income or on the proceeds of his labour. Domestic servants only were excepted. In the same manner the various conditions of eligibility required by the Constitution of 1791, either for electors or for representatives, were declared inapplicable in the case of a National Convention; and every citizen, aged twenty-five, fulfilling the above conditions, could be chosen as an elector or elected as a deputy.'[1]

Camille was, quite naturally, pointed out to the choice of the electors. He was popular and beloved. One only thing could injure him—the very brilliance of his talents. It was to be feared that so sparkling a satirist would make a slightly frivolous legislator. It was necessary to ballot twice before Camille Desmoulins was proclaimed a deputy for Paris. His opponent was Kersaint. On Saturday, September 8, 1792, at the second vote, out of 677 voters—the absolute majority being 339 votes—Camille obtained 465 votes more than Kersaint. He was elected. He took his seat in that National Convention which numbered amongst its members (I do not give the condition in life of all the 749 members of the Assembly) 45 former constituents, 147 former legislators, 59 administrators of departments, 81 lawyers, 34 mayors, 28 presidents of districts, 14 bishops, 9 vicars-general, 7 parish priests, 26 justices of the peace, 5 professors, 21 doctors, 10 notaries, 5 merchants, 15 farmers, 2 apothecaries, 1 painter, 15 literary men, &c.

On Monday, September 20, under the presidency of Philippe Rühl, deputy of the Bas-Rhin, who was a dropsical octogenarian (he afterwards killed himself in *Prairial* year III. to escape the proscription) the National Convention met for the first time. What a

---

[1] It is interesting to recall these conditions at a time when the question of the indivisibility of universal suffrage is the primordial question. See in Didot's 'Complément de l'Encyclopédie moderne,' an excellent article by Edouard Carleron upon *Conventions nationales.*

first time! What a wonderful sight was this gathering, in the palace of the Tuileries, now a national edifice, of all that was most ardent, most generous, most terrible, and most patriotic in France; so many ideas, so many hopes, so many Utopian schemes, so much devotion to the country! The cannon of the invader was thundering in insulted France; rioters were swarming in the streets. Champagne was in Prussian hands; Longwy and Verdun had fallen; and the stones of the Abbaye were still red with the blood of the massacres of the 2nd of September. Nevertheless, Danton, Condorcet, Vergniaud, Saint-Just, Robespierre, Romme, Soubrany, Cambon, Robert Lindet, Rabaut, Lakanal, Carnot, Louvet, Guadet, Philippeaux, and many others accepted the difficult task of saving the shattered country; of securing liberty for France, liberty which is the happiness of nations, and independence which is their pride.

What ardent hopes were theirs, what mighty yearnings, what high courage rising to the formidable height of the circumstances! Camille Desmoulins has depicted in his 'Fragment de l'Histoire secrète de la Révolution' what I may call the psychological condition of the nation at this decisive moment.

'Those who have just been named deputies to the Convention,' he wrote, 'are indeed to be envied. Was there ever a more magnificent mission, a more splendid opportunity of glory? The heir of sixty-five despots, the Jupiter of kings, Louis XVI., the prisoner of the nation, and brought before the avenging sword of Justice! The ruins of palaces and castles, the fragments of the monarchy, for materials wherewith to build the Constitution; ninety thousand Prussians or Austrians arrested by seventeen thousand Frenchmen; the entire nation risen to its feet to exterminate them; Heaven the ally of our arms, and dysentery the auxiliary of our gunners; the king of Prussia, reduced to forty thousand effective men, pursued and surrounded by a victorious army of a hundred and ten thousand; Belgium, Savoy, England, Ireland, a great part of Germany, espousing the cause of liberty, and publicly wishing us success! Such was the state of things at the opening of the Convention.'

What tasks to accomplish! What a career of glory! To create the Republic; to revive the laws, the arts, commerce, industry; above all, 'to make the people!' *To make the people!* A grand saying of Camille's, which is, in itself, a programme, and which has yet to be carried out. Camille wished that Paris should be made 'less a department than a central town, common to all the citizens of those departments which are mingled in her, and of which her population is composed.[1] . . . This Paris,' he continues, 'which only subsisted by means of the monarchy, and which has made the Republic, must be supported, by being placed between the mouths of the Rhine and the mouths of the Rhône, and by having maritime commerce brought to her gates through a canal and a port.' And besides these:—'To avenge liberty and democracy upon their calumniators by the prosperity of France; by her laws, her arts, her commerce, her industry freed from its trammels and making a start which will astonish England—in one word, by the spectacle of public happiness. To restore the people—who, until our days, had been accounted as nothing: the people, whom Plato himself, in his imaginary Republic, had consigned to servitude; to their primitive rights, and to recall them to equality; such was the sublime

---

[1] Had he not already said, with respect to Paris, in his 'Révolutions de France et de Brabant,' No. 56, ' Paris ought to be looked upon less as an individual town than as the common country of all French people. Paris is to France what the Communal House is to a town?'

vocation of the deputies of the Convention. What soul, however cold, would not catch fire; however narrow, expand at the contemplation of so lofty a destiny?'

Who then prevented the attainment of this result? Why, in spite of its prodigies, did the Convention end in that military despotism, the Empire? And again, why, in spite of its tragic divisions, has it renovated the world, from end to end? Our age persists in propounding these formidable questions, which the future alone can solve. Fiévée, in a book in which many correct ideas are mixed up with a few errors, has tried to show that the Revolution ended fatally in the dictatorship because, in it, *opinions* clashed with *interests*.[1] The terrible dramas of which the Assembly was at once the theatre and the victim are more correctly explained by the ignorance of the members concerning their adversaries and their best friends. They did worse than forget themselves: they never knew themselves. Suspicious of each other, and even of themselves, they quarrelled in the dark. A scarecrow affrighted them: the scarecrow of fear and of ignorance— ignorance of everything, and fear of everything— and yet (explain the marvel who will) this fear urged a handful of men to acts of immortal courage, and cowardice became heroism as rapidly as rashness degenerated into vileness.

First came a terrible misfortune, an alarming and sinister event, which may be expressed in one word —September. The massacres of the Carmelites, of the Abbaye, and of La Force could not fail to divide for ever men who were made to be united: the Dantonists

---

[1] 'Des opinions et des intérêts pendant la Révolution,' by J. Fiévée. (Paris, 1809: in 8vo.)

and the Girondins.   The friends of Brissot and of Vergniaud never forgave Danton for that frightful day
on which workmen, armed with sabres, scythes, or
clubs, strangled or cut down prisoners, priests, women.
It has been affirmed that Danton *organised* the
massacres of September ; this however history denies.
Royalist writers have stated that Camille Desmoulins
was a party to the crime ; the assertion is false. 'But,'
it will be objected, 'he was the means of saving
the Abbé Bérardier, formerly his preceptor at the
college of Louis-le-Grand ; he sent him a safe-conduct
in his prison.'   The fact simply proves that he
wished to set his old professor at liberty ; but it does
not prove that he was even in the secret of the massacre.   Who is Camille's principal accuser in this
matter ?   Roch Marcandier—his countryman, formerly
his secretary ; one under obligations to him, and who,
after having worked with him in his most violent publications, turns against him, attacks and calumniates
him.   Another accuser is Peltier, formerly the editor of
the 'Actes des Apôtres,' who, in his 'Histoire de
la Révolution du 10 août,' openly accuses Danton and
his two secretaries, Camille Desmoulins and Fabre
d'Eglantine.   But the testimony of Peltier is more
than suspicious : he hates Camille, and even maligns
Lucile because she is his wife.   The opportunity
was too good to be allowed to escape.   When a
crime is anonymous, or multiple, like that of September, nothing is more easy than to inculpate the
innocent.

Fate willed that the man who could have saved
the Revolution, and made it fruitful and lasting,
should be regarded by the Girondins as 'the man of
September ;' that Danton should bear the burden of

the crime of the multitude. These two groups of devoted men, each equally ready to found the Republic (for, now-a-days, who would venture to accuse the Gironde of Royalism ?) contended with each other, instead of uniting their forces. The Dantonist party would have been the strength of the united body, if union had been possible. The Gironde was its tongue, as we know only too well ; the Dantonists would have been its muscle.

Let us pause for a moment before this group of men, in whose hands the fortune of the French Revolution once rested, who sacrificed their future reputation and their existence to their country, and whose death was a crime. Nearly all young—for the complete renovation of a community could only be effected by vigorous arms—their reward has been the heaping of boundless accusations upon their memory.

The foremost among them, he who gave his name to the party, was Danton. The *Dantonian* policy, to speak the language of positivists (*we* say, Dantonist) emanates from him alone. This man, *with the face of a bull-dog*, as Roederer said, whose aspect struck terror, and whom Claude Fauchet called 'the Pluto of eloquence,' had nevertheless an attractive expression of goodness and frankness. ' Do I look like a hypocrite ?' Danton cried, looking his judges straight in the eyes. His stately and massive form was that of a Hercules ; he had a powerful voice and bold gestures ; and was more careful in his dress than has been admitted. He was hot-tempered, easily moved to anger ; he needed a well-turned-down collar in which to move his bull-neck ; his hand was frankly held out to his friend, but terrible to his adversary. This man was in himself a power, a born Tribune. He was an educated man, whatever may be said (the composition of his library, which he daily consulted, proves this[1]); and he loved his home better than out-door life; but his eloquence electrified from the steps of the tribune and thundered from its height, he was the voice of the country in danger. His cry, 'Dare, and dare yet more!' accompanied the roar of the alarm-gun. None better than he was formed to sound 'the charge upon our enemies!'[2] Terrible as he was, Danton was still human. In this great revolutionist there was a large heart. He had the heat, the fire and the smoke of Diderot, and the mirth of Kleber. His logic was prompted by his passion, and his passion was that of the multitude. More than all beside, throughout that gigantic series of trials, and in the midst of that awful storm, he suffered from the insult offered by foreigners to France. His dream was—the freedom of his country by the agency of patriotic effort. He has been accused of loving pleasure: he loved, in truth, nothing but his fireside. 'Have I time for conspiracy?' he will hereafter ask those who accuse him. 'I love my wife too well to steal an hour from her.' Twice this man displayed for the woman of his choice a love passionate and well nigh fierce.[8] On

[1] For an account of Danton and his private life, see Dr. Robinet's book, which is full of facts, and also the remarkable work of M. Alfred Bougeart.

[2] 'The tocsin that is about to sound,' he exclaimed (September 1792), 'is not an alarm-signal; it is the charge upon the enemies of our country.'

[8] Danton was born at Arcis-sur-Aube, October 26, 1759. His father was Jacques Danton, *procureur* to the bailiwick of Arcis. Georges-Jacques Danton married, in June 1787, Antoinette-Gabrielle Charpentier, who died February 10, 1793. In the month of June Danton married Sophie Gély, who, on becoming a widow, married M. Dupin, a councillor of the Cour des Comptes.

his return from his mission to Belgium, the 'Journal
Français,' intent upon *administering a kick behind to
the Jacobins* (I am quoting the Royalist press) greeted
him with the cry : ' Here comes the butcher of September ! ' His first wife having died during his
absence, he had her body exhumed, that he might
gaze upon her once more. What a picture ! I know
not one more dramatic in this succession of striking
episodes.

The Girondins crushed Danton by the sinister date
—September, as the Jacobins afterwards immolated
him with the terrible word, *virtue* ; when he was
reproached for his heat, his impetuosity, the ebullitions
of his French blood, like the son of Rabelais. When
that time came, he shrugged his shoulders and said,
' I prefer being guillotined to guillotining.' How
could history forget this saying ? An irresistible
sympathy attracts even his enemies to Danton.
His large-hearted and manly pity draws all hearts.
This man had no power of hatred in him. Did
he not offer to make peace with the Girondins
and to withdraw to Bordeaux as a hostage ? Did
he not say of an adversary, ' I often meet X. . . .
who blackens my character ; but I remember having
seen him struggling with adverse fortune, and I pity
him ? ' [1]

Bold, strong in combat, Danton accepted beforehand the responsibilities and the vicissitudes of the
struggle. He wrote to Courtois (de l'Aube) on the
subject of the war in the north, which had not a

---

[1] Unpublished ' Notes ' of Courtois (de l'Aube). Courtois may be
blamed for his bitter animosity against Robespierre in his ' Rapport
sur les papiers saisis,' but no one can deny that his ' Notes ' are lifelike
and truthful.

fortunate beginning : 'Whatever misfortunes may be caused by the present war, they must always be less insupportable than slavery!' And yet he was not without his moments of discouragement in such a vortex, in the midst of divisions, condemnations, and oratorical duels, whose arena was the scaffold. How many times he thought of withdrawing to Arcis-sur-Aube, there to *plant cabbages !* 'I would indeed willingly retire from the thick of the fray,' he said; 'but how, after having played such a part ?' The time was not far off when he would cry out, 'I am sick of men ;' but when, notwithstanding, he was to show them how a man should die; how, at two paces from 'nothingness,' a man may lay claim to a place in the Pantheon.

'The arbitrary stamp of the opinion of the moment,' said Courtois (de l'Aube), in the unpublished 'Notes' which it has been our privilege to consult, 'may cling to his memory—dishonour it even, if possible; but when there are only republicans in France, this truly great man will enjoy the esteem of posterity.' The truth is, that Danton was a great Frenchman, who felt the heart of outraged France beat within him. He met menace with menace. Without personal ambition, he was largely ambitious for his country; he panted to behold her free. Unlike those common minds who sacrifice everything to popularity, he would willingly have sold his favour with the masses cheap, to lay the foundation of the liberty of his country. He did not think that France was necessarily incarnate in a few individuals ; and, like Luther, whom he resembled in the bent of his mind, and in the temper of his 'Table Talk,' he bowed down before the 'Herr Omnes,' 'Monsieur Tous.' 'Cannot we tear Robespierre's skin without making patriotism bleed?' he asked, with his scornful laugh.

At the opening of the Revolution, he who has been represented as 'a lawyer without a case,' was, if not rich, at least in easy circumstances. (Hentz, in his unpublished 'Memoirs,' relates that he was in tatters. The inventory of his wardrobe shows us, on the contrary, that it was well stocked and cared for.) He was a citizen of Paris, industrious, working hard in his study, performing, with profit to himself, the duties of solicitor to the King's Council.[1] The Revolution carried him away, tore him from

[1] M. Campardon found in the National Archives, among the papers of the Commissaries of the Châtelet, the following, which relates to a complaint of Danton's in 1787, that he could not work in consequence of the noise made by his neighbours :—

'This day, Thursday, May 17, 1787, at eight o'clock in the evening, at our house and before us, Jean Odent, etc., M. Georges-Jacques Danton, solicitor to His Majesty's Council, living in the Rue de la Tixeranderie, opposite the street of the Deux-Portes, in the parish of St. Jean, appeared ; the same said to us, and declared, that yesterday in the evening, towards a quarter-past or half-past eight, he engaged a lodging on the first floor, above the *entresol*, in a house in the Rue Guénégaud, and gave the earnest-money for it to the Sieur Paschal, proprietor or principal occupier of the said house ; but that, having become aware of the vicinity of a locksmith and a saddler, whose trades necessitated the use of a hammer, and were the cause of much noise, and very hurtful to persons studying, he wished to avail himself of the power granted to all occupiers in like circumstances—that is, to re-demand of the said Sieur Paschal the earnest-money he had deposited yesterday ; by this only making use of the same power as the said Paschal would have to return the said earnest-money to the applicant before the expiration of the twenty-four hours, during which he ought to have made enquiries concerning the said applicant ; but that, not having found the said Paschal at his house, whither the said applicant had gone, this day, at seven o'clock in the evening, he had betaken himself to five of our colleagues successively, without finding them, and at last came to us to make the present declaration and protestation, that his occupancy of the said lodging is null and void, reserving to himself, in case of difficulties on the part of the said Sieur Paschal, the right to sue if he thought fit.—Signed Odent ; Danton. National Archives. Commissaries to the Châtelet ; file 4075 ; Commissary Odent.' An unpublished fragment.

his study, and thrust him into the popular meetings. He arose in the district of the Cordeliers, like a Mirabeau formed for the clubs, the orator of the populace, and their mouth-piece. His impassioned and genial eloquence, teeming with good-humour and energy tempered by compassion, pleased the mob, and went straight to the hearts of the masses. At the time of the massacres of September—that crime, which once more we call anonymous, that frightful massacre to which fear prompted a handful of scoundrels, and which was allowed to take place—Danton laid claim, through Thuriot, to the Dictatorship for himself. The Girondins have accused him of taking refuge on the 2nd of September at the Champ de Mars. He was there, in fact; he was waiting. There were twelve thousand men there. With these, had he been master, he would have scoured the streets, and his powerful voice would have driven the maddened crowd to the frontier.[1]

The massacre of September was the mortal wound of the Revolution. Those hideous deeds, for which Marat and his friends were, after the crowd, solely responsible, separated the Gironde from the Dantonists,

---

[1] Another tradition tells us that Danton lived close to the scene of the massacre. Some years ago, in Paris, a *maison Dautruc*, Rue de Vaugirard, was pulled down at the time of the extension of the Rue de Rennes. Charles IX. had confiscated this house from the Huguenots, and given it to the Sieur Dautruc, one of his favourite huntsmen. Until late years the house remained in the family. The family of Dautruc had Danton for their lawyer at the Council; the tie was strengthened at the time of the events of 1792, and Danton was in this house on September 2, it seems, when the massacre at the prison of the Carmelites took place. From the cellars of this house wine was served out to the *Septembriseurs.* Finally, it is asserted that in this house the robbery of the *garde-meuble* was planned with Lebrun and Tondu. This is a tradition not to be passed over unnoticed, but I do not attach much importance to it. What is certain is, that the crime of September stains the memory of Danton, but that he was innocent of it.

and destroyed this league of men which would, I repeat, had it remained unbroken, have laid the foundation of liberty. In vain does Danton speak (March 10, 1793) of those ' days of blood which every good citizen has bewailed,' and try to demonstrate that 'no human power was in a position to check such an outbreak ; ' he will never be forgiven for it, although he deplored it deeply. The Gironde continued the war. Danton had, far more than any of the Girondins, practical eloquence, a clear insight into events and the popular sense ; he was also as strongly opposed as they to any negation of our national temperament, to that puritanical rigidity which is incompatible with the French mind. Doubtless he would have prevented the Girondins from rushing into the federalist movement in the face of the foreigner, into that idea which divided, weakened, and broke up France; an idea which, by a strange irony, the Hébertists of 1871 borrowed from the Girondins of 1793.

But the fatal error of these men was their mutual misunderstanding. They condemned each other too often on calumnious evidence. Danton helped on the downfall of the Girondins, whom he did not hate ; he only wished to weaken their power in the Assembly ; but he awoke, scared, to find that he had co-operated in their death. ' Do not make the first split in the Assembly,' Danton cried out to the Girondins, at the time when they demanded the prosecution of Marat. After May 31, the Assembly was more than split up ; it was decimated ; it was bleeding to death. Danton had not intended May 31 to be a day of slaughter ; but, in these critical times, the axe was not to be played with. The excited and irresponsible crowd, urge on the arm that would willingly hold back the knife.

To slaughter the Gironde was to promise Danton-ism to the executioner. Besides, Danton had not pre-served his dauntless daring, since the murders which had mowed down so many and such various talents, so many heads full of thought and charm. Thence-forth the excesses which he had hoped to govern and moderate revolted him. Those with whom he strove were the infuriate madmen of the time. This Titan wrestled with the men of the Commune. Hébert and his followers succumbed in the struggle; but if the Committee sacrificed Hébertism, they only did so with the intention of punishing Dantonism. As we shall see presently, it was a double blow; Robespierre and the members of the Committee struck both the *infuriates* and the *moderate party*, within a few days of each other. Then there remained only the '*purs.*' They did not perceive that the Revolution was dead, and that their turn was coming! The majority of the tremblers asked no better than to revolt against the Committee, and to avenge those whom they had just sacrificed.

O eternal cowardice of mankind !

'Some days after the fall of Danton, Camille Desmoulins was at the sitting of the —— *Thermidor*, in which Robespierre cruelly and ironically abused the unhappy victims of his barbarity. " I perceived beside me," says Courtois, " a citizen who, at those portions of the tyrant's discourse most loudly applauded by the majority of the Convention, clapped his hands also, with all his might, and looked laughingly at me. I thought I could discern that his applause was not sincere, and I answered him by a smile which let him understand that I was not duped by his acting. He came close to my ear, then, and said in a low voice : ' If it cost me the pair of gloves with which I am applauding (his hands were bare), I would willingly sacrifice them to be guaranteed, at that price, the

fall of the monster who occupies the tribune at this moment.'
I told him to restrain himself. He pressed my hand, his
eyes filled with tears, and he disappeared."' [1]

The revolutionists forgot that the trembling
majority, who had too long applauded all these proscriptions, was composed of courtiers and sycophants
as little convinced as this *admirer* of Robespierre. 'I
drag Robespierre with me!' said Danton in his
death hour. But Vergniaud had done the same, and
the sacrifice of so many men, devoted at least to the
public interests, could only end in France being flung
at the feet of a victorious soldier, worn out, with
her legislative power decimated, disheartened, and
discredited.

II.

Let us now pass in review the group who are
shortly to sit together upon the benches of the accused :
Hérault de Séchelles, Westermann, Philippeaux, Fabre
d'Eglantine, the *Dantonists*, the companions and friends
of Desmoulins.

Hérault de Séchelles, called *the handsome Séchelles*,
a man of sensitive mind, dashed with bitterness and
haughtiness, brought into the Dantonist party a lofty
and profound intelligence, eloquence remarkable for its
vigour, and unflinching courage. These qualities he
had placed at the service of the popular cause, since
the commencement of the Revolution. Born at Paris
in 1760, grandson of René Hérault, lieutenant-general
of police, and enemy of the Jansenists, who, from 1725
to 1739, had filled Paris with spies and policemen ; son

[1] Courtois (de l'Aube). Unpublished Notes.

of Hérault de Séchelles, colonel and commandant of the regiment de Rouergue, who was killed at the battle of Minden, in trying to break through the impenetrable English infantry with his squadrons—Marie-Jean Hérault de Séchelles belonged to the privileged caste. At twenty, he was an advocate at the Châtelet, and, hailed as a rising orator. He had also been particularly well received at Court.[1] The Duchess de Polignac, his cousin, was eager to present this Cicero in his twentieth year, this intelligent and charming young man, to the Queen. In spite of a certain rigidity of manner, and his evident distaste for royalty, the Court was pleased with him ; and pronounced this well-made

---

[1] With respect to Hérault, I find in the ' Journal de Paris ' of August 7, 1785, the account of an assize at the Châtelet, in which Hérault de Séchelles, the Crown lawyer, spoke for the last time prior to taking his place in Parliament as attorney-general. 'The speech of the young magistrate,' says the ' Journal de Paris,' ' did not aim at florid eloquence ; his style was calm and tranquil, like that of the law. It indicated that repose of the passions, which is so necessary for the mind in search of truth. Conviction and light came gently and by degrees from his words, without any parade of reasoning, without any of that sort of syllogism which is not reason, and offends against taste ; but by the connexion of facts, of documents, and of laws, and the concise development of one and the other, he arrived at his conclusions through the evidence. He might have almost dispensed with drawing his conclusions. They had been heard in the laws, whose intentions and wisdom he had so clearly shown. The tone of his eloquence was wisely fitted to the nature of his case, and the universal interest he inspired showed itself in the general applause, which he seemed to wish to make over to the orators who had spoken before him. The homage he paid them seemed merited, but especially that awarded to M. de Sèze, son of a celebrated lawyer in the Parliament of Bordeaux, and whose talents are of great promise.

' This speech of M. Hérault de Séchelles was the last he was to make at the Châtelet, and all dreaded to hear the end ; the young orator himself shared this feeling, and he gave expression to it with touching eloquence in his farewell to the president. All the magistrates and the court shared his emotion, and the audience accompanied M. Hérault de Séchelles to his carriage amid prolonged applause.'

Alcestis to be distinguished looking. Hérault was handsome. Virgil says :

> Gratior et pulchro veniens in corpore virtus.

The Queen herself deigned to embroider a scarf for him when he was made attorney-general at the Châtelet. 'The wife of the King,' says Camille, 'has sent the black girdle to the young and handsome Séchelles.' But an ardent love of liberty, a deeply-rooted conviction that the nation must perish if prompt recourse were not had to reforms, had already made Hérault de Séchelles an adversary, almost a rebel. In the Parliament he strove against Dambray on behalf of reforms in the government; on July 14 he did better than this : he enrolled himself among the stormers of the Bastille. Hérault was then nine-and-twenty. Two years later he was deputed to the Legislative Assembly by the Paris electors.[1] He was to be among those who cried out that France must answer foreign insolence by war (January 14, 1792). Hérault, too, demanded and obtained that the country should be *declared in danger.* Refusing the post of mayor of Paris after August 10, he entered the Convention as the representative of the department of Seine-et-Oise. On the 2nd of June, when Henriot came, at the head of his artillery, to threaten the Convention, and, with eighty thousand men and a hundred and sixty-three cannon at his back, to demand the arrest of the proscribed Girondins, in the name of the insurgents, Hérault, president of the Convention, went down into the court of the Tuileries, which was invested by the

---

[1] See the Complementary Documents for a speech by Hérault and a harangue by Danton.

insurrectionists, and endeavoured to calm the mob. To Henriot's words—' The people have not risen to listen to fine words; it is the traitors they want! Give up the traitors, or go back to your place '— Hérault de Séchelles replied, as coldly as the law: ' Seize the rebel!' But Henriot cried out, in a voice of thunder, ' *Men! to your guns!* ' Hérault was carried by the crowd into the Convention, and the Assembly had to deliberate under the menace of the bayonet, while Marat embraced Henriot, hailing him as ' the saviour of the country!'

Hérault, at least by his attitude, seems to have responded to Henriot's rude command by ' *Members! to your places!* ' The next day he, with Danton and Lacroix, demanded the arrest of the revolutionary general. Hérault, who afterwards elaborated the project of the Constitution presented by the Committee of Public Safety, was about to have the honour of presiding, on August 10, 1793, at the first national fête dedicated to the French Republic. He it was who, in the *Place de la Révolution*, standing at the foot of an enormous funeral pile on which were heaped the emblems of royalty, cried aloud to the crowd and waving a lighted torch: ' Perish the signs of slavery! Let nothing remain immortal but the love of virtue! Let the plough, the wheat-ear, the cap of Liberty, the wonders of art which adorn and enrich society, form for the future the Republic's sole decorations! Hallowed earth! be covered with these true riches, and refuse to bring forth aught which can only serve the purposes of empty pride!' Then, amid the acclamations of nearly a million of men at this popular auto-da-fé, Hérault applied his torch to the pile, which was speedily swallowed up by the devouring flames;

all that had been the admiration, the adoration of former days : the crown, the royal mantle, the *fleurs-de-lys*, the escutcheons, the fragments of the throne—that throne which the Emperor Napoleon afterwards defined as '*four boards covered with velvet.*' The proclamation of the new Constitution, that of '93, was about to follow this vain ceremony ; vain, for what avails it to pull down what the future rebuilds ? It is impotent folly to wreak our anger upon inanimate objects, when we ought only to contend with ideas ! We amuse ourselves childishly with signboard and symbol reforms and revolutions ; and punish *things* for the deceptions which *men* have practised upon us. There is, however, a wide interval between the ceremony which Hérault de Séchelles presided over, and the impious destruction of monuments and works of art, into which the mob has too often allowed itself to be led.

Hérault, rich, proud, and popular, made a great impression on that famous day upon the ' Republican multitude,' to use an expression of Louis XV. to the Duke de Choiseul some years before. His figure was tall and erect, he had a straight nose, a finely-cut mouth, a plump face, slightly tinged with red, a double chin, and powdered hair ; and he wore, according to the coloured portrait engraved by Quenedey, and bequeathed to us by the *Physionocrate*, a white waistcoat and an elegantly cut coat striped with blue. The gentleman always peeped through the democrat ; or, rather, Hérault was one of those who prove that democrats know how to retain good taste and elegance of manners. His caste could not forgive him for having enrolled himself on the side of the nation against the cause of the king. Their hatred was great towards one whom they called 'a renegade.' Lavater, who

P

had known Hérault, once wrote to him that 'such a man as he could no longer remain the accomplice of a few coarse, ignorant, and stupid scoundrels!' Hérault was at a sitting of the Committee of Public Safety when the letter reached him; he smiled and said, 'These people do not understand our situation!'

He received many similar letters, also threatening, insulting and anti-patriotic ones like the following anonymous letter, which is in a feigned writing, imitating the printed character of the documents in the Archives to be found on the files of papers relating to the Dantonists:

'M. HÉRAULT,—That factious wretches, infamous scoundrels, who have risen out of the mire, should conceive and execute every imaginable crime, to maintain the authority they have usurped, will not surprise persons who know the rabble and its ferocity; but that a French gentleman, promoted to the highest dignities, a magistrate entrusted with the maintenance of the laws, a Hérault de Séchelles in short, should consort with and preside over this unruly horde, should betray his class, and assassinate his king—*this* is the excess of rascality and abomination.

'But the time of vengeance approaches, and these corrupt rulers, who have ruined their country, already watch with terror the approach of the punishment due to their crimes. The people, deceived in every way, greet this coming justice with smiles; they have seen with indignation the impudent and lying announcement of the unanimous acceptation of the *brigandage* called the Constitution, while it is notorious that the tricks of a few members of the primary assemblies have supplanted the real vote of the people. Among a thousand examples it will suffice to cite this one:—The canton of Tirepied, in the district of Avranches, having unanimously (*sic*) rejected the Constitution, the deputy, chosen to attend the Bacchanalian orgies of August 10, refused to give in a negative vote; but all the voters having withdrawn, the superintendents of the proceedings took upon themselves to return an affirmative vote, and the deputy charged himself with its delivery.

'The same trick has been played throughout all France; but what will these impotent stratagems avail? Has crime blinded you so that you cannot see your approaching downfall? You are going to excite the people to rise in a body;— what folly! what monstrous iniquity! But will the people lend itself to this project, visibly impracticable as it is, and which, besides, can but hasten the success of the Powers whose advance can no longer be arrested? How can you doubt that, if the people rise, it will only be to turn against you? The people see clearly, now, that those scoundrels who, under the false appearance of their well-wishers, persuaded them to lend themselves to their manœuvres, will sacrifice them to prevent, or rather to stave off, the punishment that threatens them: the people are ashamed of their blind credulity, and will be the first to punish these scoundrels for their crimes.

'Farewell, Hérault! Before three months elapse I shall have the pleasure of seeing you expiate on the wheel the blood of your king and of all the brave Frenchmen who have been sacrificed to your criminal and ferocious madness: York, Ricardo, Cobourg, Nassau, Brunswick, and Condé are my securities for this, in spite of the great general Houchard.

'August 10, 1793, the Fifth Year of all the Crimes.

'P.S. I have just heard that the company of Shoeblacks in London have taken the decree issued against Pitt into careful consideration, and return thanks for it to their brothers of the Convention.'[1]

What could anyone expect that men, inflamed as Hérault was with the love of the nation, should feel on reading such threats as these? They burned with anger to know that Frenchmen loudly and shamelessly desired the success of Condé, allied with Cobourg, Brunswick, and Nassau. This proof of the Royalists' complicity with foreigners excited still further the fierce zeal of those legislators, whose passion was their country.

[1] National Archives; Committee of Public Safety, c. vii. 4608.

Hence their fury and their excesses. Moreover, Hérault de Séchelles was destined to die, not because he had been too cruel, but because he had tried to save a woman, an *émigrée*, from the grasp of the law. Already denounced on December 16, 1793, by Bourdon (de l'Oise) as an ex-aristocrat, and for receiving nobles at his house, and defended on that occasion by Couthon and Bentabole, he was again to be denounced in March 1794 for having been cognisant of the presence of a woman at the house of Simond, the deputy (du Mont-Blanc). In fact, a woman, an aristocrat, had taken refuge at Simond's, and the law of March 4, 1794, interdicted all communication with those accused of conspiracy under pain of being regarded as an accomplice. In December 1793 Hérault attempted to defend himself. 'If the accident of my birth is a crime that I have to expiate,' he said, 'be it so ; I tender my resignation as a member of the Committee of Public Safety.' But this resignation was rejected ; in March 1794 Hérault made no attempt to exculpate himself. He seemed tired of life ; he did not resist the order of arrest ; he did not retort upon his accusers. He entered the prison of the Luxembourg like a man who had expected worse than a prison.

Some time before he had been in the habit of going every day, as one might go to a theatre, to the corner of the Tuileries, to see the condemned pass by in the tumbrils ? One of his friends met him there, to his great surprise. 'What ! do I find you here, Hérault ?' said his friend ; 'you, who have judged those who are passing by ?' 'Yes ; it is I,' he replied. 'I have come to see the Republic in its death-throes, and to learn how to die !'

How far away were those days when Hérault, sent

to Savoy by the Convention, made a poetical pilgrimage
to Les Charmettes, and had a tablet of white marble
(now defaced) placed upon the house which had witnessed the loves of Jean-Jacques and Madame de
Warens. No doubt he then wrote the inscription and
the verses upon the tablet :—

> Réduit par Jean-Jacques habité,
> Tu me rappelles son génie,
> Sa solitude, sa fierté,
> Et ses misères et sa folie.
> A la gloire, à la vérité,
> Il osa consacrer sa vie,
> Et fut toujours persécuté
> Ou par lui-même ou par l'envie.

The admirer of Jean-Jacques was no longer the
lover of aught but rest—I would almost say, of the
grave. He too felt himself, like Danton, 'sick to death
of men.' And yet, only one year before, what a refined
and brave spirit had been that of Hérault de Séchelles !
An unpublished private letter, relating to his mission
in Savoy, paints him as he was in February 1793. It
shows us a brilliant imagination, a keen and rapid
intelligence, an acute understanding, abandoning itself
entirely to the delightful chit-chat of a letter to his
colleagues who had been sent to Nice, and is indited
with charming and sympathetic ease. It is eminently
characteristic, and deserves to be preserved :—

'Moutiers en Tarentaise, February 26, 1793 : Year II.

'My dear colleagues,—I have had news of you three
times : three letters from Grégoire ; three words from Jagot.
I have had a laugh over your freaks, I have made the gravest
beings in all Chambéri laugh at them : it seems to me that the
Provençal spirit has already taken possession of you. Your

sayings are all witty sayings. (Vous ne dites pas un mot qui ne soit un bon mot.)

'Die! you have not seen Saint-Pierre d'Albigny. Heavens! what an enchanting spot! And no one at Chambéri spoke of it to us. Nature in the Alps in her most whimsical mood, with all the coquetry, all the most refined arts of her wild toilet—waterfalls, *maisonnettes*, vistas, immense masses, fir-trees, flowery plains, limpid streams, poplars, in fact everything! In vain have you lived in eternal spring, and made love under the olive-trees ;—die, and die twice over, that you have not seen Elysium—Tempé—Armida—Eden—Albigny!

'Now I am going to speak of something very different. Cavelli is a deputy ; he passed at an evening sitting, like a bad decree. Gavard passed yesterday at a morning sitting.

'How plainly I recognise my friend Jagot in your new *Misanthrope* in three acts, killing all the men and kissing all the women!

'Reassure yourself, Grégoire! The two mistakes in your epistle to the *Valaisans* will be, or rather already are, corrected. A young French abbé, who was passing this way, spent a morning in doing you this service. Five people have already asked for your work. I have certain means of getting it to its destination. It goes the day after to-morrow.

'But, respecting your speech upon the oath, just listen to the abominable bad turn those beggarly rascals did us. Fancy, at the same time that they were trying to kill us with their filthy libels, they took it into their heads to deprive us of the means of defending ourselves, by shutting up the printing-presses in the Alps.[1] Consequently, Gowin corrupted our workmen. That fine fellow, Champ-d'Avoine, spent three days, and often far into the night, in chasing them from hiding-place to hiding-place, and from tavern to tavern. At last he caught them and put them in prison, with the alternative of remaining there or of working. However, they preferred the latter. Well, what do you say to that ? Is it not treacherous ?

'B which means, Grégoire, your speech, which is a sheet

---

[1] Alpes Maritimes.

and a half long, has been set up, and the proofs have been
corrected by me. Of the first sheet, there are still seven
pages of copy to set up. These fellows are doing this now
under compulsion, and with the cudgel of Liberty held over
them. You will make your appearance. And I? Shall
I not appear too, after you; I, a layman; I, unworthy; I,
profane? Just fancy! *M. Gobemouche* has set me going.
I have written a pamphlet, in a spirit of buffoonery. Irritated
by the visits of electors and priests on the subject of the
oath, I imagined a dialogue in which all these fellows should
take a part, which should contain all their propositions and
all their objections. See what man is! As I have already
told you, I formerly treated this subject and studied it
thoroughly in Alsace. All my ideas have come back to me. I
have written a work of fifty pages; I did it in a day and a half;
I did it without reading it over; I sent it sheet by sheet to
the press. Let Grégoire (whom I quote somewhere) tell me if
there are any heresies in it, and I will submit like a Fénelon.

'All this is great fun. I will send you my work by the
first post. It is being printed.

'My letter is dated from Moutiers, and it is time to tell
you that I am at Moutiers. What a country for a man who
has come from Saint-Pierre d'Albigny! O nature! Here
I have a brown wrap consisting of eight mountains. Day
hardly breaks here. The sun takes leave of the place for eight
months in the year. Moutiers is all but a sinecure to him.
You will confess this is very hard upon a town in which there
used to be an archbishop's palace, a parliament, an excise-
office, a mint, &c., for the good of twelve hundred inhabitants all told. I arrived at night. I have not seen anyone
yet. I shall see the municipality, the club, and the bishop,
and then be off.

'By the way, they say the bishop is a good fellow, and
has not forbidden anyone to take the oath. He is himself
halting between two opinions. I will give him a shove this
morning. Our friend Simon remains at Chambéri, detained
by the business of his diocese.

'And now I must tell you of a new plot of that execrable
municipality and town of Chambéri. Fancy, my dear fellows,

that insatiable Chambéri wanted to take away the bishop's house from Annécy and have it itself. They have made every effort to induce the old aristocrat bishop of Chambéri to take the oath. They destroyed a letter of his to the Pope, and he has cheated them by adding to it a private letter. This attempt will either place the bishopric at Chambéri (if the Pope will consent, which is not to be thought of), or paralyse the Electoral Assembly, and prevent it from nominating a bishop. At all events, it baulks Annécy. I possess this specimen of mean Italian trickery. I have not had time to copy it for you; you shall have it on my return. But be easy; we will out-general those rascals.

'Many clerics have fled from the mountains to Geneva, in Switzerland. However, they leave their friends their address, and I feel sure they will come back.

'Lyons is in a hateful state of ferment. I prophesy that the Assembly will be obliged to send down more commissaries.

'Eighteen ecclesiastics of the neighbouring departments, propagandists of the oath and of patriotism, have arrived here. They are first going to rig up their platform in Chambéri, to make themselves known, and from that to make themselves desired. This will puzzle the club a little.

'Farewell, my Nizards. With you at least stabbing is done gracefully. I leave you to go and preach to an old bishop. I embrace you both and Arnaud, like Saint-Pierre d'Albigny. Make a copy of my letter, so please you, that I may refer to it hereafter.'[1]

Under the elegant lucidity of the style of this letter the disappointed man can be detected; he who has made the sacrifice of his life, and, like a true son of the eighteenth century, is only seeking to make a good use of the remnant of existence. In truth, Hérault was essentially a son of the eighteenth century. He

[1] I have to return my best thanks to Madame Charras, who kindly allowed me to take a copy of this precious autograph letter from the important album she possesses, and which contains many fragments, doubly interesting from a literary and an historical point of view.

had, like Camille, its solid learning and its cultivation of mind. In 1788, Hérault de Séchelles had begun a collection of thoughts, which J. B. Salgues republished in the year X. (1802), under the title: 'The Theory of Ambition; first published under the mock title, Codicille politique et pratique d'un jeune habitant d'Epone.' The original work was revised by Hérault in the prison of the Luxembourg. He was putting it into a new form up to the moment when he was summoned to execution. A curious book is this half-posthumous work; a book of psychology, or rather of physiology, and quite modern in tone. Hérault's bitterness of spirit appears here undisguisedly; he was saddened, tired of mankind, disheartened, and almost sickened, but still and always faithful to the law of justice.

Hérault exacts from man that he shall demand his strength, his glory, and his happiness from himself:

'Believe thyself, know thyself, respect thyself. The practice of these three maxims will make man healthy, enlightened, good, and virtuous.

'Each individual (he says again) is the centre of the universe. An individual idea is but the representation, the copy, of an individual. Each individual idea may therefore be the centre of all others.'

I know what will be said to this, I foresee the objections. This theory of Hérault's is nothing but the code of selfishness. Not so! *Egotism*, Goethe would reply; that is to say, respect and culture of the *me*, absolute knowledge of this *me*, which ought to lead to the knowledge of others.

Many modern ideas, brought forth and grown up since Hérault's time, will be found in his pages, in which, strangely enough, we meet with evidences of

the handsome Séchelles' utter severity towards women ;
he was as implacable to them as are those disappointed
melancholy men who owe women a grudge :

'Take (he said) the idea of weakness from a woman.

'Women oftener rule vain men than proud men. These
latter only want a woman, and that from time to time. The
former always want to be preferred, and, *above all, to seem so.*

' *Venus sæpe excitata, raro peracta ingenium acuit.'*

Sometimes Hérault's precepts are weighty and
high-minded ; at others they affect a cutting and be-
wildering irony. Now he is a stoic, full of the
sternest principles; anon he is a cruel satirist, who
takes pleasure in throwing, as it were, a mourning veil
over life. Listen to him ! there is in him, by turns,
something of Marcus Aurelius and of Swift :—

' *Have a high idea of your powers, and then work ; you will
treble them.*

' *We make great progress only at the time when we turn
melancholy—at the time when, discontented with a real world,
we are forced to make for ourselves one more bearable.*

' *Fly from what is little, and seek what is great.*

' *Society is the cure for pride, and solitude for vanity.*

' *Man is only great in proportion to the continuous esteem
he has for himself. Therefore, avoid the meaner part and the
company of unworthy men ; the disdainful end by forcing
their fellows to believe in them.'*

This is the lofty thinker, the manly and daring
moralist. But, suddenly, the satirist lets his shrill note
be heard, and the author of the ' Théorie de l'ambition.'
displays a disdain of the human race which I am very
sure he did not feel. I can only see a vindictive
irony, after the pattern of Larochefoucauld, in the precepts which Hérault de Séchelles lays down for those
who are ambitious of literary glory :—

'*Praise those with whom you converse for the things upon which they pride themselves most, in order that you may get a chance of being praised yourself.*

'*Tell many people that your reputation is great; they will repeat it, and these repetitions will make your reputation.*

'*Slip in your praise of a man between two censures, so as to enhance the criticism by the contrast.*

'*Put problems into your books and your conversation without giving the solution; riddles, without giving the answers; so as to bring yourself into request, and to fix attention upon the author: people do not forget the names of places at which, in spite of themselves, they have had to stop.*[1]

'*Never stand on the defensive when attacked, but be always ready for the attack, either in word or in act.*'

The few pages of the 'Traité d'ambition,' in which Hérault, with rigid exactness, studies man and mankind from a purely physical point of view, are perhaps the most curious and the most significant in all this singular, startling, and little known book. Hérault had not been the friend of Lavater some years before for nothing. He skilfully applies the reflections and the researches of the master :—

'*The female brain* (he says) *must be carefully distinguished from the male brain. The first is a sort of matrix; it receives and it gives forth, but it does not produce.*'

A materialist idea if you like, but clear, absolute, and well stated. Hérault condenses his thought still more in the observations which follow :—

'Eye steady ; thoughts and will steady.

'Eye unsettled ; thoughts and will unsettled.

'Visual ray downcast; sign of a proud, disdainful, and passionate character.

[1] This was Honoré de Balzac's opinion : 'I let fall here and there, in my books, a few incomprehensible ideas, so that the public may think me, at least in these special points, superior to themselves, and in consequence respect me.'

'Visual ray upward ; sign of a timid, humble, and retiring character.

'Visual ray level ; sign of an equable, constant, sociable character.

'Double voice, double character.

'As the texture of the skin, so is the texture of the opinions and of the style.

'By comparing the form, the colour, the physiognomy, the tone of voice, the appearance, and, in one word, the external qualities and the movements of a man with the external qualities of animals, we can, by the known constitution of the latter, discover the hidden constitution of the former. Example : the cry of the peacock, and the noise that it makes with its feet to get itself looked at, greatly resemble the loud voice and the noise that those people make, in putting themselves forward, who like to parade themselves and to attract notice.'

Everyone may criticise or verify the observations Hérault de Séchelles has made. They are undoubtedly interesting, and this 'Théorie de l'ambition' shows us clearly that the author was a hard thinker, and a man of vast knowledge ; one of those *masculine brains* of which he speaks. Not in vain had he received the education of the eighteenth century ; sound, full of facts, rich in ideas, not in mere words. He had, at the same time, its gracefulness—as we have seen in his letter to his colleagues—and its feeling ; the lines written upon Les Charmettes, the remembrance of Rousseau evoked at Savoy, and afterwards in his prison, have shown us that ; above all, he had its vigorous science. At twenty-five, in 1785, did not Hérault de Séchelles publish a 'Visite à Buffon,' which even then disclosed a remarkable writer and, better still, a philosopher ?[1] It was a curious, a life-

[1] Reprinted by J. B. Noëllat in 1802, under the title of 'Voyage à Montbard,' and followed, in this new edition, by 'Réflexions sur la

like portrait of the author of the 'Histoire Naturelle.' Madame de Polignac's nephew was greeted by the aged Buffon as an acquaintance. 'We have been looking out for each other this long time,' said the great writer, on receiving his young admirer at Montbard.

Hérault describes the fine, noble, calm face of this old man of seventy-eight years, whose sole weakness was to rate his fame below his title—that of 'Count.' 'I stammered a few words, being careful to say *M. le Comte*, for in that none must fail. I had been warned that he had no dislike whatever to this way of addressing him.' Can we not see the scarcely hidden smile of Hérault, in these lines—do we not discern that in 1785 the young aristocrat is indifferent to his own nobility of birth? The revolutionist already whispers in this sceptic's words.

This picture of an *interior*, this portrait of Buffon, when all but an octogenarian, taken three years before his death, is a finished painting. It would be worth while to have it reprinted, and we should there see a Buffon who is little known, who treats religion as a purely human institution, 'which must be respected outwardly.' A calumny! cries Noëllat, who re-edited the work. It is the fact that in 1788 Buffon did ask for the Viaticum. It is certain that Hérault de Séchelles had no other intention in speaking thus than to praise Buffon's independence of mind.

In order to be thoroughly acquainted with this Hérault de Séchelles, who was so eloquent, so enchanting, so much petted and praised, we ought to read the fragment upon 'La Conversation,' in which he deli-

déclamation,' by a fragment upon 'La Conversation,' by an 'Eloge d'Athanase Auger,' and by 'Pensées et anecdotes,' which are also by J.-M. Hérault de Séchelles.

neates with a touch, a stroke of the pencil, or a turn of
the hand, the celebrated talkers who thronged the
saloons before '89, and each of whom made his personal
mark upon the French mind.   They all live once more
under his pen ; one line is enough to call them forth—
here is Delille, witty and elegant, a thorough Academician ; here Ducis, of the grand and polished manners ;
Garat's way of holding up his head and knitting his
brows ; Cérutti's precise speech ; the *nipping pincers* of
Chamfort's genius ; the verbose audacity of the Abbé
Fauchet ; the sudden harangues and the loud voice of
D'Eprémesnil ; Lavater's lively and expressive mien ;
Marmontel's continual and thoroughly French talk ; the
grave, large-minded, enlightened disposition of Condorcet, with a dash of malignity ; and reminiscences
of Rousseau, who *punctuated* his words so well, and
of Diderot, who brightened them up like a sunbeam.
There is nothing Hérault de Séchelles does not
remark and quote as an example, even to the 'silence
of the celebrated Franklin.'   With all these men did the
future member of the Convention mix, and closely did
he study them.   ' For a long time,' he said, ' I acted the
part of a listener.'   It is by knowing how to fill this
part that we learn to perform every other.   The best
method whereby youth may learn (a method forgotten
now-a-days) is to hearken to the aged.

The young magistrate, the future conqueror of
the Bastille, borrowed a new charm, fresh knowledge
and wit, from the company of these eminent men.   He
fought for the future with the elegant manners of a
man of the past ; the democrat set the high fashion
to the gentry.[1]

Such was Hérault de Séchelles—fascinating and

---

[1] The family of Hérault de Séchelles still exists.   According to
authentic information, the elder branch of the Héraults (which befor

sparkling, the true type of the *grand seigneur*, who was also a man of letters, devoting himself entirely to the popular cause, yet preserving the refined manners of a caste which he had not yet ceased, as he said, 'to combat and to despise.'

La Morency, whose autobiographical romance, ' Illyrine, ou l'Ecueil de l'inexpérience,' contains more than one valuable historical detail, has given us several life-like traits of the physiognomy of the man whom she calls ' *the delicious Séchelles.*' She describes the apartment on the second floor of No. 16, Rue Basse-du-Rempart, in which Hérault lived ; the *immense library* of the member of the Convention, and the private room in which he received his guest, ' hung with English paper, of a yellow colour, •with arabesque borders ; Cupids painted on the ceiling ; a couch, a mirror from the top to the bottom of the wall ; pots of flowers in the window, and blinds which only admitted a half-light.' There was something of the Epicurean, or at least of the Athenian, in this Montagnard. One morning Hérault said to Morency—to that woman whom for a fleeting moment he loved—' I want to live quickly ;—and when *they* take my life, *they* will think they are killing a man of thirty-two, and I shall be eighty ; for I shall have lived ten years in one day !' [1]

the abolition of the rights of primogeniture, bore the title of De Séchelles, has very rich descendants near Tours.

[1] ' Illyrine, ou l'Ecueil de l'inexpérience,' by G. de Morency (3 vols. in 8vo.), Paris, in the year VI., can be had of the author, Rue Neuve-saint-Roch, No. 111 ; at Rainville's, the publisher, Rue Féron, No. 991 ; at Mademoiselle Durand's library ; Favre's library at the Palais-Egalité, and from all the sellers of new publications, with this motto :—

' Ce monde est une comédie
Où chaque acteur vient à son tour,
Amuser les hommes du jour
Des aventures de sa vie.'

Epître à Sophie, par le citoyen Alibert.

III.

Pierre Philippeaux, born in 1759, at La Ferrière-aux-Etangs, in L'Orne, had been judge of the court of Mans, before the 'Revolution, and was returned by La Sarthe to the National Convention, in '92. There, he voted for the death of the king, and at the same time called for an appeal to the people; and he, who was accused of being the accomplice of Dumouriez, demanded that three hundred thousand *livres* should be promised to anyone who would deliver up the treacherous general to his country. It was a sinister proceeding, to set a price on such a deed. Honest and upright, of unequalled probity, but easily blinded concerning men, while faithful to principles, gentle and firm at the same time, Philippeaux had voted against the Girondins, and repented it afterwards. When sent into La Vendée to re-organize the administrations, which were tainted with federalism, he from the first opposed the plan proposed by the generals and deputies assembled at Saumur, '*the Court of Saumur*,' as he called it. Agreeing with the military staff of Nantes, Philippeaux wished to subdue La Vendée by sending into it flying columns, which should multiply, escape, appear, disappear, scatter and

This *collection of follies*, as the author says, possesses some interest. We see in it several illustrious members of the Convention in undress: Quinette, who writes to Illyrine : '*Adieu, Lili; I will go and federate with you in three or four days, July* 14;' Fabre d'Eglantine, 'a little man, whose eye expressed genius, and his voice feeling;' then Madame de Sainte-Amaranthe, who draws forth this cry from La Morency—'How beautiful she is ! how superbly handsome !' Illyrine relates that one day Hérault was supping at her house with a friend, who said to him, 'Hérault, do you stand well with Robespierre?' He reddened, and retired early, in tears, giving this excuse—'I have to make a report for to-morrow.'

form again, fighting after the fashion of the Vendéans, opposing a man-hunt to the war of ambuscades.

Rossignol and Ronsin, on the contrary, would not attempt to measure themselves against the Vendéans without a considerable force. But while they were concentrating this force, the civil war continued its ravages, and spread like a conflagration, or rather—for the word used at the time was correct—like a canker. The Committee of Public Safety approved of Philippeaux's measures; but the flying columns were beaten and dispersed. Philippeaux, who was recalled, defended himself as he best could. He defended himself indeed, after French fashion, by straightway attacking his enemy.

On the 18th *Nivôse* he made a deliberate attack upon those whom he called '*the executioners of La Vendée,*' and, like Camille, later on, he demanded clemency for the Vendéans. Useless cruelties and senseless tactics he denounced with terrible vehemence. 'What have you done, you unlucky fellow?' a friend said to him, when the sitting broke up; 'you have let loose the War Office, the Committees, the Cordeliers, and the Commune upon yourself!' In fact, the Convention had been unanimous in deciding against La Vendée.[1] Philippeaux persisted. This was the same man who afterwards wrote to his wife from his prison: 'It is glorious to suffer for the Republic and for the good of the people.' 'I have sacrificed personal interest to the higher interest of public affairs.' And, after his death, he left a fresh

---

[1] The Breton Lanjuinais, in his loyal indignation against the insurgents, not only wished (like the Gironde) the rebellious Bretons to be sent before the revolutionary tribunal, *but even the goods of those who had been killed to be confiscated.* Cambacérès suggested military justice. —Michelet, 'Histoire de la Révolution Française,' vol. v. pp. 431-432.

proof of his courage and boldness in speaking the truth. ('Réponse de Philippeaux à tous les défenseurs officieux des bourreaux de nos frères dans la Vendée,' at Paris, *de l'imprimerie des femmes,* in the year III.) His wife published this document, which is a kind of last will and testament.

Philippeaux—severe even to injustice upon Bouchotte (the records of the war give evidence of this)—had been the judge of the operations in La Vendée.

Westermann was the general of this war in La Vendée, which was made known in Paris by the member of the Convention. Westermann was forty-three in 1794, having been born on September 5, 1751, at Molsheim (Alsace). His father, a surgeon in that town, had given him so good an education, that, after having served at fifteen in Esterhazy's regiment, at eighteen in the *petite gendarmerie,* which he left in 1773 with the rank of a non-commissioned officer, we find Francis-Joseph Westermann, in 1775, at twenty-four, advocate to the Superior Council of Alsace (in proceedings instituted against him, and of which the papers still exist in the National Archives). Truth compels us to say that these proceedings (of which nothing has been said until now) do no honour to the morality of Westermann. Was he driven to theft by necessity? I do not know; but the fact is that F.-J. Westermann appeared before the commissioner, Joseph Chenon the younger, on Saturday, September 16, 1786, on the charge of having stolen a silver dish, with a crest engraved upon it, from the *sieur* Jean Creux, hotel-keeper in Paris, Rue des Poulies. Westermann, then lodging at the Hôtel de la Marine, was taken into custody. A month later, October 20, 1786, the plaintiffs withdrew their accusation by their notary; but the

' instruction ' remains, and can unfortunately be substan-
tiated. Before that, in March 1775, Westermann had
been accused by Dumouchet, a slop seller, of the theft
of two waistcoats. He was also compromised in I
know not what robbery of plate with a certain Roch
de la Verdure, whom Westermann accuses of being the
only one guilty. He was taken up a second time on
January 4, 1776, and set at liberty on the 10th of the
same month ; and then he at once entered the regiment
of Royal Dragoons, to be for the third time arrested
and accused, eleven years after, in 1786.

Strangely enough, Westermann was brought on
September 16 before Commissioner Chenon, to answer
to the charge made by the eating-house keeper Jean
Creux; and fourteen days after, before the commissioner,
Chenu, another personage, more famous than Westermann—Saint-Just, then aged nineteen—was brought up
to account for several articles—a silver basin, a goblet,
a flagon, some silver cups, some gold lace, a ring, a
pair of pistols mounted in gold—which he had taken
with him when running away from his mother's house.
Saint-Just, who had to expiate this freak by a year of
seclusion—demanded by his mother, not by the law, at
La Dame Marie de Sainte-Colombe at Picpus—ought
to have derived a little indulgence for human weakness
from his own experience. But Saint-Just, stubborn
before the commissioner who interrogated him in 1786,
and protesting that he had done no more than possess
himself of his own property, and had a right to do as
he chose—Saint-Just was afterwards implacable towards
those whom he accused—and accused, wretched man !
in the name of *virtue !*

Westermann, at least, tried to make up by a
daily sacrifice for the faults for which man had not

condemned him, but which his conscience did not pardon.

He is to be seen everywhere, risking his life like a man who is weary of living. Brave to rashness, daring to a fault, throwing himself in the way of sword and bullet, Westermann seemed really to have no relish for anything but death. Alsace made him sheriff of Strasburg, then member of the municipality of Haguenau; August 10 found him a soldier once more, commanding the sections, who were eager for the fray. On that stormy day Westermann multiplied himself, sword in hand, his coat off and his shirt sleeves tucked up to the elbow; that day Westermann was the right arm of the battle. We might have wished for a soldier freer from reproach, but not for a braver. Danton and his friends were then ignorant—and all the world, even history, was until now ignorant—of the antecedents of this intrepid soldier who had some heroic qualities, and who fought like a Trojan and died like a hero. Once more I discern a yearning for death in his frenzy for fighting.

The Executive Council had, on September 14, 1792, nominated Westermann to the post of adjutant-general. The warrior of August 10 set out for Dumouriez' army. Made colonel of the Legion of the North, September 27, 1792, he felt happy; he knew himself to be powerful. His artless pride betrays itself in a letter, dated October 3, in which, writing to a friend, Westermann is quite proud, poor man! of having dined at the Prussian camp, during a suspension of arms.

I admired this Westermann, and my imagination made a brother-in-arms to the great and valiant Republican Kléber of this Alsatian officer; but truth will out, and military courage, however magnificent, cannot condone everything.

LETTER OF OCTOBER 3, 1792.

' To Citizen Philibert, at Strasburg.'

'I am chief of the Legion of the North, staff-adjutant of the army, and commissary-general of the Executive Power. I have been to the Prussian camp to dine with the King of Prussia. For the time I am all-powerful. What can I do for you? Would you like the post of that imprudent Ehrmann (the son)? I will have him dismissed and the post given to you. I have had Thomassin dismissed.[1]

'WESTERMANN.'

The *all-powerful* Westermann had only to wait: less than two years later he might have bethought himself, in his turn, of claiming the favour which he now offers with such frank pride. Let us say briefly, that he asked for nothing, and suffered death with admirable composure. The rough soldier did not give the lie to his life in his last hour.

In January 1793 he was detached from the army in Belgium to join the army in Holland. There he fulfilled his functions as adjutant-general so well that Breda and Gertruydenberg were forced to surrender. But General d'Arçon received the keys. Westermann, in a fury, complained to Dumouriez, and talked of favouritism ; Dumouriez sent him to Turhout with the Legion of the North.

The check at Aix-la-Chapelle placed Westermann's troops in a perilous situation, but the intrepid commandant opened a passage for himself to Antwerp by keeping up a brisk fire, night and day ; and when he reached Antwerp, the fortress had just surrendered.

[1] See ' L'Amateur d'autographes' of July 16, 1863, No. 38.

Westermann and his soldiers were taken back to the French frontier by an Austrian escort. Once on French soil, he was arrested. Lecointre (of Versailles), deputed by the Convention to examine into the charges against Westermann in the name of the Committee of Public Safety, after having read all the documents in the suit—even those of the citizens of the section of the Lombards, which recapitulated the soldier's antecedents—proposed that it should be decreed that there was no reason to find Westermann guilty. This was on May 4. ' Had he saved liberty by his single arm,' Legendre had said some months before, ' and were he a rascal, he ought to be punished.'

May 10, 1793, Westermann set out for La Vendée as general of brigade. Impetuous, enthusiastic, kindling the zeal of the conscripts, rousing his soldiers to enthusiasm, he was the real chief of the advance guard ; and after having surprised Parthenay, he purposed to crush La Rochejaquelein and Lescure together, before Châtillon, besieged by *les blancs*. The Royalist chiefs gathered together a considerable force ; but this mattered little to Westermann. He broke through the hostile army, on July 3, entered the town, delivered the prisoners, and taking up his position on the heights which command the town, he sent for help to Biron. The victory was won ; he only required supports, but, in the night, one of those foolish panics, too common, alas ! among French troops, seized upon his soldiers. All fled. The torrent carried Westermann away with it. Guns and ammunition—all were abandoned ! The Convention called Westermann to strict account for that day, which Madame de la Rochejaquelein, an inimical witness, declares in her ' Memoirs ' to have

been one of glory for Westermann, whom she represents as irresistible at the head of his hundred
hussars. He appeared at the bar of the Convention on
July 17, and the military tribunal of Niort, before
which he was referred, acquitted him, 'with honour,'
on the 29th August.

It might be interesting to trace the charges to
which Westermann's too hasty conduct gave rise.
Here is the identical text of a letter (I shall cite
others) addressed by a soldier, named Baré, to his
father, who sent it, at the time of the trial of the
Dantonists, to Fouquier-Tinville, as an accusing
document :—[1]

'Saint-Maixent, July 24, 1793.
'The second year of the French Republic.

'My dear Father and Mother,—In answer to your letter
of the 18th instant, which I received on the 21st, I must tell
you I was bivouacking, so could not write sooner to enquire
after your health ; as for mine, it is very good. I can only
give you a few details of our situation, for I have not as yet
mastered them all, since we left Paris. On arriving at Niort,
we were put to sleep in the church of Notre Dame, with only
straw to lie upon, after having marched a hundred and ten
leagues ; while the others were quartered upon the citizens ;
for one prefers sleeping in one's trousers to lying on bare
boards. First, we remained eight days in the church at Niort,
after that we slept two days in a bed, after that we set out
on our way to Tours. When we arrived at Poitiers, we
received orders to return to Saint-Maixent, and from thence
to Parthenay, to rejoin Westermann's army, which had gone
to Châtillon. The day after we arrived at Parthenay we
received orders to set out for Bellessuire at four in the
afternoon. Three hours after we beat the retreat, for Westermann's army had been defeated ; nothing was left but the

---

[1] This letter, in the original, with its remarkable orthography, will be
found in the Appendix.

cavalry ; as for the infantry, there was none remaining. We returned to the heights at Parthenay, where our two battalions bivouacked. At three o'clock in the morning, General Westermann reviewed us, and we remained at the bivouac. The day after we were sent to take up another position. Here there was a misunderstanding ; for on being taken down a declivity there was a cry of " treason." The general was informed of this, and was told that it was our captain Rouy ; and all the while he was not there, having gone to the hospital with a man who had received a shot in the arm, during the afternoon. While I was looking about for a dinner in Parthenay, the commandant of our battalion—the same who had told the general it was our captain—said to me : " Here's a fine business ; your captain and the captain Baré will have their heads broken." I, who knew nothing about it, asked why? He told me we were betrayed, and left me in great agitation. This increased when I saw General Westermann at that moment pass with his cavalry, which was going to the bivouac ; and I said to one of my comrades, that if they were going to kill my captain I would desert, since one was no longer allowed to open one's mouth, for I saw the general behaving like the absolute master, without assembling a council of war, and not choosing to listen to Captain Rouy, who told him he did not know what was meant. General Westermann, like a despot, told him he would make an example of him, and said to him, " Kneel down." This the captain did at once ; whilst the grenadiers were ready to fire, and the light cavalry faced our battalion, the general having said that if they budged an inch he would cut them to pieces. The moment the captain was on his knees, his son threw himself into his father's arms, saying that he would die with his father. At the same time a commandant of a battalion d'Orléans said to the general that the troops begged for mercy for the captain. He did not want it, for he had done no harm. See the reign of Liberty ! I leave you to think how terrified we were at seeing justice administered on the spot. However, as if in mercy, the general said to the captain, " Get up." This man, who had not been guilty, had no need of a pardon ; for we can only forgive a criminal. Let us pass over this. From that moment the general could not endure us. We left Parthenay the same night to return to Saint-Maixent, where the general had the troop put into beds, and our Paris battalion was chosen out to be quartered at the bishop's house. Here we have been for three weeks, which shows that the Parisians are loved. I do not know why; there are townspeople who are quite astonished; for five thousand men have been lodged in this town, and there were not two thousand of us when we came here, and there are not five thousand of us yet. This is how we are placed. I think they are sorry to see us in these countries. We are nearly all married and fathers of families, and this is our recompense. Westermann has set out for Paris. Citizen Daillac has replaced him; it is not Daillac now—I think it is General Vajusquit—and this is why I beg you to let me know if Westermann is in Paris, and what news there is of him, for I am still at my post; but if Westermann comes back to this country, I shall be obliged to run away, for if he were to know what I have written, he would have me killed. Yet we sleep on the ground by choice, always. Another thing I will tell you, that I have received a letter from my wife which has given me great pleasure. As for the cabinet of which you speak, pray do with it as if it were your own. I hope, nevertheless, to return before long. I beg of you to be very careful to whom you show my letter. I end, my father and my mother, with hearty love,

'Your son,
' E. P. BARÉ.

'Let me know what the news is about Westermann and Paris.'[1]

This letter shows the necessity imposed upon Westermann for raising the tone of the troops, which were as yet undisciplined, and I know not a better eulogium upon a general than to say he contrived to conquer with such soldiers. Furious at

---

[1] ' National Archives.' Trial of the Dantonists.

the check he had received on the 3rd July, Westermann, with the vanguard, carried Châtillon, entered Beaupréau, pursued the Vendéans beyond the Loire, with his jaded troops ; harassed the Royalists in Poitou, and on the 13th December attacked them in the town of Mans.   This was a terrible battle.   Three times was Westermann repulsed by the Vendéans, who fought with intrepid courage.   Three times he fell upon them to dislodge them.   Marceau arrived during the action bearing a letter from the representative Bourbotte, sent by the Convention to the armies of the West.   'Cease firing,' was Bourbotte's order. Marceau spoke of choosing a better position before Mans.   'The best position,' Westermann replied, ' is in the town itself.   Forward !'   And, in spite of the darkness, the battle began afresh.

Westermann, who was wounded, bleeding, and black with powder, had two horses killed under him. He never relinquished his post or his sword.   He entered Mans sword in hand.   The Vendéans being driven back, he pursued them.   Twelve days after, with Kléber, he crushed them at Savenay.   La Vendée has had no more formidable adversary than this Alsatian, who marched, half-clothed, at the head of the battalions, and imparted to his soldiers the intoxicating foretaste of victory.

On January the 4th, 1794, Westermann returned to Paris.   The hero of La Vendée had no suspicion that death awaited him there.   He was about to be regarded as the prime mover of the Dantonist party.   The Committee of Public Safety heard with mistrust the clanking of the sword of the warrior of the 10th August in the lobbies of the Tuileries.   On the 6th January, the general was dismissed.   Westermann seeing the

danger, wished to forestall it by marching upon Paris, as
he had marched upon Châtillon and upon Mans. He
proposed to carry off the Committees. Danton refused.
Westermann disgraced was speedily to become Wes
termann accused. He must often have felt himself a
prey to melancholy and to disgust. He had had his
luggage and his weapons taken to the Rue Meslay, to
the house of Citizen Le Loir, who had let him a
lodging. At the bottom of a trunk Westermann carefully preserved the different epaulets which marked
the stages of his various ranks—the worsted epaulet,
the silver epaulet, and the golden epaulet. He contemplated them sorrowfully sometimes ; as a soldier
without arms, a warrior in repose, he waited. For
what ? An opportunity ;—the first shot fired. Here,
in the Rue Meslay, he was arrested by order of the
Committees.

Fabre d'Eglantine, born at Carcassonne, December
28, 1755, was, together with Desmoulins, secretary to
the group of which Westermann had been the arm.
Amiable and elegant, of less corrupt morals than has
been supposed, this writer of *chansons*, who wrote the
couplet for Simon, the musician, ' Il pleut, il pleut,
bergère,' and for Garat the romance, ' Je t'aime tant,
je t'aime tant ! '—this man of letters, whose principal
comedy, ' Le Philinte de Molière,' is much above the
rank of second-class works ; this worldling who united
idyll to tragedy, gracefully paraded his fancies amid
the tempests of the Revolution. ·His real name was
Philippe-François Fabre. While still a youth he was
the winner in the ' jeux floraux ' of Toulouse, and
added to his name that of the golden Eglantine
awarded as a prize to his verses. He was born a
dramatic poet. His genius was essentially comic.

He said one day to Arnault, his colleague, ' Between the moment in which I give you this snuff-box and the moment in which you give it back to me there is a comedy.' This saying is charming, most characteristic and personal. ' And while saying this,' adds Arnault, ' he improvised a plot üpon the event. He saw comedy everywhere.'

He even saw it, unfortunately for him, in the Convention and in public affairs. I am convinced that he was innocent of the falsifications of which he was accused (January 13, 1794), with respect to the decree relating to the liquidation of the *Compagnie des Indes*. But the man who dared accuse the Girondins, in his deposition against them, of complicity in the robbery of the *garde meuble*, deserved to be calumniated in his turn, that he might know how heavily the charge of infamy falls upon the accused. Fabre was, moreover, to have the honour of being accused by Hébert, and to be treated as one of the moderate party. At such a time this was at once a threat, a danger, and a distinction.

Such were the principal personages in the group of the Dantonists to which Camille Desmoulins belonged, at least in death. Bazire, the generous-hearted, was attached to it by pity and fate. But I pass over— for I am far from looking on them as combatants in the same cause—scheming financiers like D'Espagnac and foreigners like Gusman, the Spaniard, and the two Austrians, the elder and the younger Frey, with whom the revolutionary tribunal coupled Danton and Camille.[1] In the light of the future, we need only class with

---

[1] I find in a work published upon Danton—(see the newspaper ' La République Française ' of September 25 and November 3, 1873), respecting the articles there given by Dr. Robinet to the ' Revue Positive ' upon the *Procès des Dantonistes*, the following curious information :—

the vanquished, those men with whom they were proud to brave death for their political faith.

'There was much to say about the Austrians, Frey (or rather Frei), and the naturalised Spaniard, Gusman. Regarding the two Austrians, M. Robinet is astonished that the author of "Anacharsis Clootz" should hold them in high esteem, and he even points out that the Baron de Trenck denounced them as spies. Setting aside what the Baron de Trenck may have said, and without being explicit here as to what this Prussian was himself doing in France, we may tell M. Robinet that the elder of the two brothers, Junius, is the author of a " Philosophie sociale," dedicated to the French people, which appeared some days before he was arrested ; that in this book Junius makes all society rest upon the principle of individual preservation, and pronounced, "like a free man," against certain propositions of Jean-Jacques. We believe this publication contributed to the arrest of the two brothers, inasmuch as Robespierre, in drawing up his report against Chabot, seems to aim at the philosopher in Junius, whom he represents as "always dreaming, pen in hand, of the rights of man, and bent double over the works of Plutarch and Jean-Jacques." It *is* therefore possible to honour the two Austrians, although step-brothers to Chabot, as the author of "Anacharsis Clootz " has done.

' M. Robinet should at least have given these victims their right name, which we find in the gaolers' book. We read there—Eschine Portock. This name is assuredly inexact ; but, however it may be, it would none the less be a help in the researches which might be made, either in Vienna or in Moravia, into the origin of these two foreign patriots. And, at the same time, why not make enquiries about their sister Léopoldine, the natural daughter, it was said, of an eminent personage in Vienna. Who knows if, one day, it may not be discovered that the beautiful Léopoldine was one of the seventy-four natural children of the Emperor Leopold, and then, how strange it would be should the capuchin Chabot prove to be the nephew of Marie Antoinette.

' But since we are upon strange coincidences, let us point out one suggested by Gusman, the Spaniard. M. Robinet gives some valuable information concerning this grandee of Spain, who was a small, muscular man, of fiery temper, like Marat, whose friend he was. Who knows whether, in prosecuting his researches, M. Robinet might not have discovered in this friend of Marat's one of the ancestors of the ex-Empress of the French ?'

These exceedingly interesting details have probably been given to us (the article is anonymous) by M. George Avenel, one of the men most competent to treat of the history of the French people, and whose life-like studies of Pache and his friends deserve especial attention.

CHAPTER V.

I.

IT was Friday, the 21st September, 1792, little more than one month after the 10th of August. In the palace of the Tuileries, the Convention recently established by the popular vote awaited the members of the Legislative Assembly, who were about to place the fate of France in the hands of the new tribunes. At a quarter past noon the Legislative Assembly met. François de Neufchâteau was spokesman and made over the ' reins of government ' to the Convention.

' In nominating you,' he said, ' the primary Assemblies have sanctioned the extraordinary measures necessary for the welfare of twenty-four millions of men against the perfidy of one.'

This announcement was applauded. The National Convention quitted the hall of the palace of the Tuileries and repaired to the Riding-school, where the legislative body sat. The usual occupants of the galleries were in attendance. They saw their deputies passing, and greeted them with acclamations. Pétion took the President's chair. Condorcet, Brissot, Vergniaud, Camus, Lasource, Rabaut, Saint-Etienne, occupied the bureau.

Two hours after, a proposition made by the man, who years afterwards as a senator, first demanded, and then proclaimed, the downfall of Napoleon, was put to the vote.

There was a profound silence.

The motion of Grégoire, ex-curé of Embermesnil, was adopted amid frenzied shouts and clapping of hands, and, from the tribunal of the Convention, these words fell, like the death-knell of the monarchy :—

' *The National Convention decrees that royalty is abolished in France !* '

Shouts and acclamations were heard ; the enthusiasm spread, thundering from the galleries. 'Long live the nation!' the occupants cried, in their intoxication. The light cavalry, organised into free companies, swore to conquer or to die. To the Austrians who were bombarding Lille, to the foreigners who advanced upon Paris, to the kings who declared war, France replied : *Kings are no more !* Before setting out for the Pyrenees, the Alps, or the Rhine, the soldiers offered two days' pay. Drunk with love of their country, happy and proud, they paraded before the Convention, then in the first flush of victory, and of its conviction that the liberty of the country was for ever established. When the sitting broke up at four o'clock, the shout of the Assembly spread throughout Paris, and from Paris over the world, with its decree :—

'Royalty is no more! Royalty is abolished!'

Alas for those sublime defenders of a liberty which we have not yet been able to establish. for which we still grope in the dark; their bones lie in the catacombs, in dungeons, in the lime of the Madeleine or the mud of Clamart. But what of that? Sacrifice is never fruitless; self-devotion is never vain; and, despite every deception, every trial, ultimate success belongs only to the right,

On the eve of the same day on which Grégoire, the *schismatic priest*, as the Royalists called him ever after, carried the vote for the Republic, the cannonading of Valmy proved to foreign nations that France was still living. Chambéry was occupied by the French three days later, on September the 23rd; Nice on the 28th; Spires on the 30th; Worms on October the 4th; Lille, which had been besieged by the Austrians, beheld their departure on the 8th. On the 22nd there was no longer a Prussian in France; on November the 2nd there was not an Austrian in France, except the Queen. What intoxicating success! The Republic was synonymous with Victory.

But if the nation seemed to have only one mind against the enemy, she had millions of hands wherewith to rend and ruin herself. It is not our intention to follow the phases of those struggles, which made the 'first breach' in the National Convention, then decimated, and finally disgraced it. Once more, it must be borne in mind that this is a history of a man, or of some few men, not of an epoch.

The Convention had abolished royalty; now it struck at the king. Thirty years after the trial of Louis XVI., the aged and upright Lakanal wrote to David (d'Angers) with respect to his vote for the king's death :—

'As for me, I followed the line of my duty and my convictions, and twenty-two years of exile have but confirmed me in the belief that I thereby justified the confidence of my constituents. . . . 1st. We had the right of judgment. The decree of the Legislative Assembly, given in Vergniaud's report, said: The interest of the public demands that the French people should manifest its will by the vote of a National Convention formed of representatives invested with *unlimited* powers by the people. 2ndly. *Two millions of addresses* congratulated this courageous Assembly upon the judgment which it had passed upon the perjured king.' [1]

Camille Desmoulins, who voted for the king's death, mingled facetiousness with condemnation, and produced loud murmurs by wording his vote thus: 'Manuel, in his "opinion" of the month of November said : A king dead is not a man the less. I vote for death, perhaps too late for the honour of the National Convention.' [2]

[1] Unpublished letter. Madame de Charras' collection of autographs.

[2] Had he received the following letter from his father?

'My dear son,—You can immortalise yourself, but you have only a moment to do it in ; this is the warning of a father who loves you. This is pretty nearly what I should say in your place : " I am a Republican in feeling and in act, and have given proof of it. I was one of the first and most eager to denounce Louis XVI. ; and for these very reasons I decline to vote. I owe this to the strictness of my principles ; I owe it to the dignity of the Convention ; I owe it to my contemporaries and to posterity ; in a word, I owe it to the Republic, to Louis XVI., and to myself."

R

Under circumstances such as these, Camille ought to have learned from Lucile to restrain his natural tendency to extremes. What a pity that this beloved wife had not taught him to combine dignity with moderation and firmness. But Camille, who was an indifferent speaker, and who made no figure in the rostrum of the Convention (he was a member of the 'Comité de correspondance,' and was more in his place there), chafed at his second-rate position, and thought, no doubt, by displays of this kind to maintain his popularity and his reputation as a pitiless Frondeur. Even Lucile indulged at that time in flights of fancy and imagination, and we find evidence of the exaggeration of her ideas in some of her writings.

For instance, she writes concerning Marie-Antoinette, soon to be accused like Louis XVI.,[1] and sacrificed even more uselessly than he :—

'This is between ourselves, so that you may have the sole merit ; I only wish to be able soon to comment upon the affair to your advantage, and for your peace of mind and my own, for I am your best friend.

'January 10, 1793.'   'DESMOULINS.

[1] Two years before, Camille Desmoulins had ventured to write of her, whom he called 'the *Austrian*' (following in this the example of the Comte de Provence, afterwards Louis XVIII.) as the *wife of the great man-eater* :—

'Many patriots continue to regard Marie-Antoinette as irreconcilable with the Constitution. All the public papers announce that she found this note in her plate at dinner, on Sunday : *At the first cannon ball your brother orders to be fired against the French patriots, your head will be sent him.* Perhaps the anecdote is apocryphal, but so many journals published it, that the note might as well have been actually put under the Queen's plate ' (' Révolutions de France et de Brabant ').

A pamphlet of the day amuses itself over the anger the Queen would feel on reading Desmoulins' attacks upon her :

' Request of the Queen to the heads of the tribunal of police of the Hôtel de Ville at Paris.

' The humble petition of Marie-Antoinette of Austria, Queen of France, spouse—often separated in body, and always in interest,—of His Majesty Louis XVI., formerly King of France and Navarre, and as such authorised to sue for her rights by action-at-law.

' She complains of Desmoulins, who calls her the *king's wife*, and

'WHAT I WOULD DO IN HER PLACE.

'If Fate had placed me on the throne, if I were Queen, and if, having wrought the misery of my subjects, a certain death awaited me, as the just punishment of my crimes, I would not wait for the disorderly populace to tear me from my palace and drag me, with infamy, to the foot of the scaffold; I would forestall the attack, I say, and by my death overawe the whole world.

'I would have a large enclosure made ready in a public place; I would have a funeral pile erected and surrounded by barriers; and three days before my death I would have my intentions made known to the people. Within the enclosure and opposite the funeral pile I would have an altar erected.

'During those three days I would pray at the foot of the altar to the great Master of the universe; the third day, the day of my death, all my family should accompany me to the funeral pile, in mourning. The ceremony should take place at midnight and by torchlight.' [1]

It was, therefore, not Lucile who could have re-

demands that he shall be, not shut up in the Bastille—since, in consequence of the insurrection of the people of Paris, the prison of the Bastille is no more in existence—but confined as a madman in some prison.'

[1] On the other hand, Lucile wrote in her red copy-book the following verses, which she had either heard in the street, or which had been com-posed by some poet-friend :—

Complainte de Marie-Antoinette, Reine de France.

(Sur l'air de la Complainte de Marie Stuart, Reine d'Angleterre.)

De votre reine infortunée,
Français, écoutez le remords ;
A la coupable destinée
Demandez raison de mes torts.
Près de mon palais solitaire,
Autrefois plein de faux amis,
Du peuple j'entends la colère,
Il m'accuse, et moi je gémis.

A tous les coups mon âme est prête,
Mais où m'entraînent ces bourreaux ?
Où suis-je ? J'entends sur ma tête
Se croiser de fatals ciseaux.

R 2

called Camille into the path of moderation at this time, or kept him in it. This gay young girl, who died like a Roman, lived like an Athenian; loving— more than that, adoring her husband, but knowing neither how to counsel nor how to restrain him. In May 1793 Camille, urged on by Robespierre, published his 'Histoire des Brissotins' ('Fragment de l'Histoire secrète de la Révolution'). In the struggle between the Gironde and the Mountain, he took a decided part against the Gironde. His style had never before been so aggressive. He spoke of the rascality of Brissot, the hypocrisy of Roland, Gensonné's complicity with Dumouriez, Guadet's venality; and in order to secure ' a fowl in the pot for everybody ' (alluding to the historical saying of Henri Quatre) he proposed that the Brissotins should be ' vomited forth' by the Convention, and the Revolutionary Tribunal 'amputated.' An awful pamphlet! Desmoulins was to be tremendously punished for it, by finding the accusations he had made against the Girondins turned against himself. He accused them of an Orleanist and Anglo-Prussian conspiracy, and he was, together with Danton, sentenced to death for having been the Duke of Orleans' friend, and the contriver of an imaginary restoration of the Monarchy!

> On m'arrache le diadème,
> Un voile est posé sur mon front,
> Je vais donc survivre à moi-même ?
> Non, je mourrai de cet affront.

> ᐧO vous, pastourelles naïves,
> Qui portiez envie à mon sort,
> Dans quelques romances plaintives
> Placez mon nom après ma mort.
> Dites de Marie-Antoinette
> L'ambition et les malheurs ;
> J'expire un peu plus satisfaite
> Si votre reine obtient des pleurs.

Events followed in due political order. The Girondins, enamoured of liberty, had blundered by demanding the impeachment of Marat, without calculating that his popularity as a constant remembrancer of old popular grudges would ensure his acquittal, and that Marat would be returned upon their hands, in greater favour than ever, by the verdict of the revolutionary tribunal. Marat's triumph was the first severe shock to the Gironde. What man so powerful as the *people's friend*—its evil genius—after such an acquittal?

Bailly has painted this scene in a picture, which is placed in the Museum at Lille, and which gives an effective idea of the intoxication of the mob. It is lifelike and charming; the painter has made an idyll of one of the fatal storms of the Revolution. We expect to find something wild and savage like the *Marat* of David, but we behold a festive scene after the manner of Greuze. The *people's friend*, carried on the shoulders of stalwart fellows, is sweetly smiling upon the crowd with the air of a passionless sage, just rescued from the grasp of death, and who salutes the life for which he cares little. The market-porters, clean, spruce, and neat, like the bridegroom of a comic opera, wave their broad felt hats with enthusiasm. A comfortable, fatherly-looking citizen stands with folded arms, in the attitude of one of Jan Steen's or Adrian Brauwer's Flemings, contemplating this good M. Marat, just taken out of the hands of the judges. Women, dressed in pale grey silk, coquettish and charming, one of them holding by the hand a child in the costume of the National Guard (the fashionable attire), mix with the crowd, which seems not so much shouting for joy at seeing a tribune again, as deeply

moved at the sight of a father. The background of
the picture is, however, sombre, despite its silvery tone;
the long chill lobby of the tribunal, the two heavy
square columns plastered over with lime, the windows
with half-broken panes, the terrible little door with
its sculptures representing the law, the dismal gallery,
throw a solemn and lugubrious air over the picture,
otherwise as radiant and gay as a Kermesse by Teniers
or a *Cinquantaine* by Knauss.

This false move cost the Gironde dear. Instead
of going to the Abbaye, Marat, henceforth invincible,
re-entered the Convention, and again stood erect before
those whom the Vendéan journalist disdainfully calls
'statesmen.' Nevertheless, it was not Marat, but Robespierre, who dealt the Gironde the hardest blows, and
Camille, ruled just then by Maximilien rather than by
Danton, and more Jacobin than Cordelier, held the
pen while Robespierre,—I will not say dictated,—but
advised. Thence came the ' Histoire des Brissotins,'
a collection of calumnies, of petty gossip, and of murderous outbursts.

This cruel pamphlet had an enormous success.
More than four thousand copies were sold. It was—
and Camille boasts of it ! (see his letter to his father)—
' the *precursor* of the Revolution of May 31, the *manifesto.*' In fact, the ' Histoire des Brissotins ' served to
precipitate the fall of the Gironde ; and by inditing,
soon after, the ' Adresse des Jacobins aux départements
sur l'insurrection du 31 Mai,' Camille believed he had
done the Republic good service.

A thunderclap opened his eyes, or rather, he awoke,
as with a start, from his culpable error, at the sound
of Sanson's knife falling upon the necks of the Brissotins. What ! Boyer-Fonfrède, Ducos, Isnard, Girey-

Dupré, Carra, Valazé—are these the men whom he had wished the Convention to *vomit forth ?* Well! it was done now. But denunciation cannot be played at. The fatal heedlessness of Camille was to cause him bitter remorse. The Convention would not content itself with weeding out some; it would proceed to sacrifice. It condemned to death, as Royalists, Guadet and Lasource, who had divulged Lafayette's project of marching upon Paris—aye, as Royalists and accomplices of that Dumouriez whom Brissot and his friends (see Garat's ' Mémoires ' and the ' Considérations de Mallet du Pan ') suspected at the very time (March 10, 1793), when Robespierre still declared, ' *I have confidence in Dumouriez.*' The men whose federalism—dangerous no doubt in the face of the enemy, and at the time proposed,—was, nevertheless, an idea taken up later by the ' decentralizers ' of the Committee of Nancy in 1866, and, as I have already said, in 1870, by the most furious enemies of the Gironde, the very heirs of the Commune, were about to be accused of having sought to dismember France. These men were to be sacrificed because of the senseless, wicked saying of Isnard, which threatened Paris with being ' razed ' to the ground ; and yet Barère had said almost the same ! [1]

Camille, who would have wished to save the Girondins, helped on their condemnation. Danton, also, who offered them to go to Bordeaux as their hostage, would willingly have rescued them from death ;

[1] The saying of Isnard, in May 1793, a saying which hastened the climax, had been uttered by Barère at the sitting of March 10, 1793, without exciting a murmur ; on the contrary, *he* was applauded.

Barère (' Moniteur' of the 12th, p. 243) : ' The heads of the deputies are held in trust for every department of the Republic. (*Repeated applause.*) Who then would dare touch them ? The day of this impossible crime, the Republic would be dissolved and *Paris annihilated.*'

and Bazire, the upright Bazire, whom Chabot dragged down with him, hid his brief from the Committee of Public Safety, as if concealing the names of the accused would save their heads. When the sentence was pronounced (October 31), Camille, pale, in tears, cried out, striking his breast and his forehead :—' Ah! wretch that I am, it is I who am killing them, it is my " Histoire des Brissotins !" And they die Republicans !' On hearing the charge of Fouquier-Tinville, Camille would fain have blotted out his falsehood with his tears.   Vilate relates this moving scene :—

' I was,' he says, ' seated with Camille Desmoulins on the bench placed before the table of the jury. When they re-turned from their deliberation Camille advanced to speak to Antonelle, who came in one of the last. Surprised at the alteration in his face, Camille said to him, rather loud : "I pity you ; yours are terrible functions ; " then hearing the decla-ration of the jury, he threw himself into my arms, in distress and agony of mind : "O my God ! my God ! it is I who kill them ! my ' Brissot unveiled.' O my God ! this has destroyed them !" As the accused returned to hear their sentence, all eyes were turned on them ; the most profound silence reigned throughout the hall ; the public prosecutor con-cluded with the sentence of death. The unfortunate Camille, fainting, losing his consciousness, faltered out these words:—" I am going, I am going, I must go out." He could not.' [1]

Thus came swift remorse. But all the tears, all the sobs of Camille, could not efface from remembrance his attacks upon those of whom he said :

' Necker, Orléans, Lafayette, Chapelier, Mirabeau, Bailly, Desmeuniers, Duport, Lameth, Pastoret, Cerutti, Brissot, Ramond, Pétion, Guadet, Gensonné, were the impure vases

[1] ' Les Mystères de la Mère de Dieu dévoilés,' third volume of the ' Causes secrètes de la Révolution,' of the 9th to the 10th Thermidor ; by Vilate, ex-juror of the revolutionary tribunal of Paris, in detention, p. 51.

of Amasis, of which was formed, in the matrix of the Jacobins, the golden statue of the Republic. Until these our
days it was held to be impossible to found a Republic except
upon the virtues, like the ancient legislators ; but it has been
the immortal glory of this society to create the *Republic with
vices.*[1]

Now he wept over these pages, bitterly, but in vain.
He wept ; but, as Shakespeare says : '*All the perfumes
of Arabia will not sweeten this little hand.*'

I know, through information given me by M. Labat
the elder, that one evening in that mournful summer of
1793, Danton and Camille Desmoulins had walked to
the *Cour du Commerce*, along the Seine, by the quay
des Lunettes, and, thinking of that 31st of May, which
was to end in the events of the 31st of October, Danton
pointed out to Camille the great river in which the rays
of the sun, setting behind the hill of Passy, were reflected so vividly that the river looked like blood.   'Look,'
said Danton—and, like Garat, Camille saw the tribune's
eyes fill with tears—'see, how much blood !   The Seine
runs blood ! Ah ! too much blood has been spilt !
Come, take up your pen again; write and demand
clemency—I will support you !'

Before that, at Sèvres, Souberbielle had exclaimed :
'Ah! if I were Danton!' and Danton had replied :
'Danton sleeps ; he will awaken !'

Danton's awakening was to be a plea for clemency.

Danton wanted to go and rest at Arcis for a
while. Weariness had come upon him, bitter weariness. The back of the Colossus was breaking.

Camille Desmoulins, too, was tired out. Even
before the death of the Girondins, before the scene
related by Vilate, he had felt remorse and depres-

---

[1] '*Histoire secrète.*'

sion. After August 10, 1793, he seems, judging by his letter to his father, to envy his brother, who had fallen, fighting for his country. His life, so happy until now, so full of charm, with Fréron, Brune, Madame Duplessis, Lucile, was growing gloomy and filled with fatal presentiments. Too long had he been thoughtless, happy, bewilderingly happy. He had seen Fréron-*Lapin* (rabbit) playing with the rabbits in the garden, *Patagon* (Brune's surname among this young and playful group) wandering under the trees of Bourg-la-Reine with *Saturn* (Duplain, of the Commune). The young rabbit (little Horace), his mother-in-law Melpomene ; the pranks in the gardens, when Lucile, the *indefinable being*, threw *potfuls of water* at Fréron, who only laughed ! All this was far off. Happy laughter of bygone days ! Camille was to hear it no more ! He now dreaded the loss of his son—'this child, so loveable, and so much loved.' 'Life,' he says, 'is made up of evil and good in equal proportions, and for some years evil has floated around me without touching me, *so that it seems to me my turn to be engulphed must soon come.*' Where were his quips now ? Where was his bitter sarcasm ? Camille was a father, a husband, a friend. The spoilt child of fortune is punished by the course of events, and he who defended yesterday attacks to-day : he undertakes the defence of General Dillon, a prisoner in the Madelonettes.

'*Everyone has had a Dillon,*' he said afterwards, when before the tribunal, he was reproached for his connection with this open or covert Royalist, formerly an adherent of Marie-Antoinette, and who was accused of having acquainted the Prussians with the movements of the brave and unfortunate Custine, in '92.

A friend of M. de Pastoret related that he was Dillon's aide-de-camp, and saw the general go every night from the French to the Prussian camps. But Camille was volatile, and defended whom he pleased ; so that it gave rise to the remark that this fascinating Dillon, formerly noticed by the Queen, had made a still more profound impression upon Lucile Desmoulins. Who says so ? Desmoulins himself, in a tone of banter, astonishing enough :—

'But do you know Dillon well ?' he was asked in conversation. 'Of course I know him. Have I not got myself into a scrape for him, against his will ?' 'Your wife knows him better than you do.' 'What do you mean ?' 'I am afraid of annoying you.' 'Don't be frightened.' 'Does your wife often see Dillon ?' 'I don't think she has seen him four times in her life.' 'That a husband can never know ;' (and as I did not seem agitated) 'since you take it so philosophically, you must know that Dillon betrays you as well as the Republic. You are not a handsome fellow.' 'Far from it.' 'Your wife is charming, Dillon is still handsome ; the time you pass at the Convention is very favourable, and women are so fickle !' 'Some, at least.' 'I am sorry for you ; I liked you because of your "Révolutions," which delighted my wife in the country.' 'But, my dear fellow, how is it you are so well informed ?' 'It is the public talk, and five hundred persons have told me of it this morning.' 'Ah ! you reassure me ; already, like the daughters of Prœtus,

"In lævi quærebam cornua fronte."

I am believed to belong to the kingdom of Buzot, which is much worse than belonging to it in reality, according to La Fontaine's testimony. But let your friendship make its mind easy ; I see plainly that you do not know my wife, and if Dillon betrays the Republic as he betrays me, I will answer for his innocence.'

Camille was a spoilt child ; but whatever allowance one may make for his humour, here one must cry *hold !*

He goes too far. Certain things are not to be told to the outer world, and this lover of antiquity ought to have remembered that the gynæceum was sacred. Lucile's devoted love for him was a surer guarantee of her virtue than this almost sacrilegious pleasantry. Yet, under this raillery, pity was hidden; Camille was defending an accused man, and may therefore be forgiven.[1]

It appears that from this time forth Camille was actuated by only humane feelings. He desired to create a reaction against the Reign of Terror, against the fury of the people. But he was borne down by the popular feeling. The vulgar orators of the clubs, gifted with that 'aristocracy of the lungs' on which he rallied Legendre, either did not allow him to speak or shouted him down. 'It has been said that in every country under an absolute government, the grand way to succeed is to be commonplace. I see that this may be true of a Republic.' Success, even the success he loved so much, mattered little to him now. 'Of what importance is success to me ? But I cannot bear the sight of all this accumulated injustice, ingratitude, and wrong.' He was haunted by the thought that the men killed in war or otherwise— *have children, have*

---

[1] Dillon addressed the following letter to Camille :—

'Madelonettes, July 26, '93, 7 P.M.

'This tremendous business of mine, now become so simple—thanks to your kindness, to your courage, and above all to your fair-dealing, holds by only one thread, which is frightfully elongated by the laziness of your cousin, Fouquier de Tinville. Three days ago the president of the tribunal pressed him to make a report ; the period allowed him expires to-morrow, Saturday. See him, I beg of you ; induce him to finish, as he promised. He knows my innocence ; my request is worthy of you, my kind and upright defender ; only a word from your cousin is wanted. See him very early to-morrow morning ; let him say this word, and give back to the Republic a man who only aspires to save it from the tyrants who are advancing with rapid strides.'

fathers also. And after having cursed war, the fancy took him to go and be killed in La Vendée or on the frontiers, 'to free himself from the sight of so many ills.'

'Farewell,' he said to his father, 'I embrace you ; take care of your health, so that I may press you to my heart if I am to outlive this revolution.' [1]

If the liberty of the press had not been left him, Camille would have been completely beaten down and without hope. But, thank God, he says to himself, we can fight against ambition, cupidity, and cheating. 'The condition of things, such as it is, is incomparably better than four years ago, because there is a hope of "amendment."' And he was tempted then to repeat the cry, which served as a motto to his 'Lettre au général Dillon,' *Give me my inkstand !* '

II.

Camille was to seize his inkstand again soon, and to wield a pen as valiant in demanding clemency as it had been in the attack. The 'Vieux Cordelier' was about to appear—the 'Vieux Cordelier,' that indestructible monument of compassion, of generous ardour, of courage, and of humanity.

The death of the Girondins had left profound sorrow and overwhelming bitterness in the heart of Danton. 'I could not save them,' he said to Garat, speaking in distress and consternation that bowed his athletic form ; 'and great tears,' adds Garat, 'fell

---

[1] See ' Œuvres de Camille Desmoulins ' (Charpentier's edition, 2 vols. 1874, vol. ii. p. 373).

down the face whose lines would have served for that of a Tartar.' This man, who had tried to rally the Girondins, who cried out in speaking of them 'They refused to believe me!' who had offered them—I repeat it to his honour—to withdraw to Bordeaux as a hostage of the final peace he offered them; this all-powerful tribune had not been able to save even Ducos, not even Vergniaud; and Saint-Just soon after reproached him with having *held out his hand* to the latter. Weary of the conflict, cast down, broken-hearted, *sick of men* (these words of his have been already quoted), he had left Paris towards the middle of October 1793,[1] and he had gone, towards the end of November (about the 15th or the 20th) to Arcis-sur-Aube, where he wished to remain, and cultivate his garden, like Candide. There, at least, in his native home, under his mother's roof, he could breathe, he could forget. He wished to be far from Paris, during the slaughter of October 31, when the purest blood of the Gironde was to be spilt. He regained his old self by his mother's side, with old Marguerite Hariot, his nurse, and his rough shell fell off; he again found room for affectionate feelings, for tenderness, and forgotten aspirations. It seemed to — him, on arriving from Paris at this little town in Champagne, that he had passed from the atmosphere of a blacksmith's forge into the restful air of an oasis. It is told in the place that while he was chatting in the evening at the fireside, telling his mother that he should soon return to Arcis not to leave it again, the

---

[1] Sitting of October 12 :—'The president informs the National Convention that Citizen Danton, deputy, asks for leave of absence that he may go to Arcis to recruit his health. The Convention grants the leave.'

townsfolk came out of curiosity (and some in horror), and flattened their noses against the window-panes of Madame Danton's house, to get a look at the face of the Titan of the Revolution. And when they saw him, tranquil, dreamy, melancholy, or sometimes laughing, they withdrew astonished and subdued.

This rest of Danton's, this retreat, which may be compared with the short visit Robespierre made to Ermenonville on the eve of Thermidor, was a fleeting abdication which proved ruinous to him. When he returned, his powerlessness to check a fatal movement of the Revolution—(a powerlessness visible before his departure, since all his efforts to save the Gironde were vain, and his attack upon the Committee of Public Safety, on September 25, had ended in a victory for Billaud-Varennes and Robespierre)—was complete. During the weeks Danton had passed at Arcis, the government had been proclaimed *revolutionary* until the conclusion of peace. (Saint-Just's Report, October 10).[1] Amar had secured, almost by intimidation, the death of the Girondins, and the Committee was more formidable than ever. This Committee, formerly proposed by Isnard, who was to be its victim, might, perhaps, have been governed by Danton ; but he had—from weakness, or rather from a total want of ambition—refused to become a member of it. At the end of 1793 he only reckoned one friend in it (Thuriot

---

[1] Saint-Just said :—'The laws are revolutionary ; those who execute them are not. The Republic will only be established when the will of the sovereign (people) represses the monarchical minority and *rules it by the right of conquest.* Prosperity is not to be hoped for so long as one enemy of liberty draws breath. *You have to punish not only traitors but the indifferent ; you have to punish all who are passive in the Republic, and who do nothing for her.'*

having sent in his resignation) Hérault de Séchelles, of whom the Committee speedily rid itself.

In truth, Billaud-Varennes and Saint-Just reigned. Robespierre was popular and powerful with the Jacobins at the Convention, and in the Committee. The Reign of Terror was the order of the day, that terrorism of which a Revolutionary writer, M. Louis Blanc, has candidly admitted that it *wore out* the Revolution. In vain Saint-Just gave it the name of *Justice*; Billaud-Varennes, that outspoken patriot, as Camille called him, frankly called it Terrorism, and desired that name to be associated with it. 'How many traitors,' said Saint-Just, 'have escaped the Terror which talks, but who would not have escaped Justice, which weighs all crimes in her hand?' Billaud-Varennes, more intractable, did not understand any distinction; he only wished to terrorise. He it was who, vexed at the efforts of Robespierre, which were feeble enough, hastened, in concert with Saint-Just, the fall of Danton, Camille, and their friends.

Camille Desmoulins, besides, had been imprudent enough, at the time of the 'Lettre au général Dillon,' to make enemies of two all-powerful men, Saint-Just and Billaud-Varennes. He had at the same time, and in the same document, accused Billaud of cowardice and Saint-Just of conceit.

'Why,' he wrote to Dillon, 'why did you say in the presence of many deputies that, when Billaud was a Commissioner of the Executive Power in your army in the month of September, he was in such a fright one day that he begged you to turn tail, and that he has looked upon you askance ever since, and as a traitor for having made him face the enemy? Judge if the bilious patriot will forgive you for this jest, any more than he will forgive me for repeating it.'

And further on, in a note upon Saint-Just :—

'After Legendre, the member of the Convention who has the highest opinion of himself is Saint-Just. One can see by his gait and bearing that he looks upon his own head as the corner-stone of the Revolution, for he carries it upon his shoulders with as much respect as if it were the Sacred Host. But what makes his vanity killing is, that some years ago he published an epic poem in twenty-four cantos, entitled "Argant." ' (It is 'Organt.' Camille is quite capable of maliciously misprinting the name.) [1] 'Now Rivarol and Champcenetz, whose microscope, used in the interests of the "Almanach des grands hommes," not a single verse, not a single hemistich in France, has ever escaped, have in vain gone in search of this; they who have hunted up even the least little scrap of literature, have not seen Saint-Just's epic poem in twenty-four cantos. After such a misadventure, how can he show himself?' [2]

For these personalities Camille was to pay dearly. Neither Billaud nor Saint-Just was likely to forgive them. But all this makes it evident that Desmoulins, even before he wrote the 'Vieux Cordelier,' had

[1] Page 52.

[2] The following notice is to be found in the 'Révolutions de France et de Brabant' :—'"Organt," a poem in twenty cantos, with the following motto : "*Young man, have you said good-bye to good sense?*" And the following preface : "I am twenty ; I have done ill ; I can yet do better." ' (No. 6, p. 283.) 'In the Portefeuille de Camille,' published by M. Matton, in a letter from Saint-Just to Desmoulins, in which the future accuser of Camille writes to him, 'Your country is proud of you !' Saint-Just describes himself in this letter as amusing himself at the château of the Comte de Lauragnais with cutting off the heads of the ferns. With respect to 'Organt,' Grimm's 'Literary Correspondence' alludes to this poem, in the month of June, 1789 (vol. v. part 3, p. 178, edition of 1813) :—'"Organt" (first attributed to M. de la Dixmerie, the friend of the famous Chevalier d'Arc, the author of "Lutin," of the "Sibylle Gauloise," of "Toni et Clairette"), seems to be the work of a young man who has read "La Pucelle" too much, and not enough ; too much, for every moment we find reminiscences or awkward imitations of the French Ariosto ; not enough, because he rarely catches his wit, his elegance, or his genius.'

S

decided on risking a struggle with the Committee.
Once more it was Danton who gave the signal
for clemency. Robespierre had advised Camille to
demand that the Committee should arrest the
course of the Reign of Terror ; but he deserted his
friend midway. Danton, however, persevered to the
end—his own death. These two men had already
originated, as we have seen, the idea of the *Committee of
Clemency*; to Camille belongs the honour of giving it
form and substance.

The moment seemed well chosen; not doubtless
from the point of view of personal prudence, but from
that of public utility and the national welfare, from a
Republican point of view above all ; for it was important that the Republic should at last realise its theories ;
should be generous, liberal, and fraternal. The Convention, which had become, in the hands of the Committee,
and according to Isnard (confirmed by Sieyès at the sitting
of the 4th *Germinal*, year III.), a *machine for decrees*, regained a little heart and spirit when accents such as
Bazire's were heard. 'When,' exclaimed this man, he who
had tried to save the Girondists by hiding the '*dossier*'
under the papers of the Committee —'when will
this butchery of deputies cease ?' It was time that the
long-stifled cry of pity should find eloquent utterance.[1]

---

[1] It has been very justly remarked that the struggle between the
Committee of Public Safety and Danton had its counterpart in England.
The debates of the English Parliament at this epoch afford evidence of
this. The political destiny of Danton was intimately united with that of
Fox. Lord Wycombe and Sheridan had already spoken of peace. 'I have
always been,' said Fox, 'for treating with the French Jacobins.' Fox had
pressed for peace, Pitt continued the war with energy. The downfall of
Fox deprived Danton of a great deal of power. These are points of
view that can only be indicated in a note in such a work as this, but
which ought to be developed in a general history, or readers will fail to
understand the synoptical picture of French history at this epoch.

This cry was Camille's. The 'Vieux Cordelier' came out on the 15th Frimaire, year II. (December 5, 1793), two days after a sitting of the Jacobin club, at which Danton had demanded that they should set at defiance ' those who would carry the people beyond the limits of the Revolution, and who proposed *ultra-revolutionary* measures.' His speech had been received so ill that Robespierre had been obliged to defend him. Here was sufficient proof that Danton's popularity and influence 'in; the club were irrevocably lost. What matter! Fight they must. Besides Robespierre's, influence would suffice, at a pinch, to conduct the enterprise to a happy end. 'Victory is with us,' Camille wrote, after the first number of his 'Vieux Cordelier,' ' because, amid the ruins of so many colossal civic reputations, Robespierre's is unassailed ; because he lent a hand to his competitor in patriotism, our perpetual President of the "Anciens Cordeliers," our Horatius Cocles, who alone held the bridge against Lafayette and his four thousand Parisians.' Then, addressing Robespierre, he said : ' In all the other dangers from which you have delivered the Republic you have had companions in your glory ; but yesterday alone you saved it.'

It is therefore clear that these men were allies at the beginning of this movement ; that Robespierre, like Danton, wished to end the Reign of Terror. Camille wrote, and they dictated. But Maximilien regarded even the first number of the new publication as compromising ; Billaud-Varennes and Saint-Just frowned at it ; Robespierre required Camille to submit the proofs of the forthcoming numbers to him. In the second number of the 'Vieux Cordelier' Robespierre's influence is clearly perceptible; he was then preoccupied with ridding himself of Chaumette and Anacharsis Clootz, guilty, in his eyes, of having put into too life-like a form the philosophy of the eighteenth century. Alas! Camille again, and for the last time, handled the instrument of death. The former virus was still in his ink, and the pantheistic dreamer Clootz, he who formerly called Desmoulins *'illustrious patriot, intrepid Desmoulins'* (see Clootz' letter, August 28, 1790); he whom Camille in his turn called '*Our friend Clootz; Baron in Prussia, Citizen in Paris,*' and of whom he said, 'A *Prussian Anacharsis* is indeed a rare being!'—Anacharsis, the citizen of the world, and Anaxagoras, the humanitarian philosopher, felt its effects.

Chaumette, who had offended Camille by calling himself Anaxagoras, and who was one of those who obtained the abolition of the lash, and of corporal punishment in schools, the suppression of lotteries, the closing of gaming-houses, the daily opening to the public of those libraries which under the monarchy had only been opened two hours a week;—Chaumette, who wrote to his friend Thomas on his becoming a priest, 'As well that walk in life as another; the essential is, to be an upright man,' was far from being dangerous. Whilst many of his colleagues in the Commune gained an evil reputation, he was occupied in organising benevolent schemes. He obtained that the patients, hitherto crowded in the

---

[1] Here are a few autographic lines which depict this mystical personage :—' Strong in virtue, one hand resting upon the breasts of nature, with the other I shall repulse all the sophistries of knavery.—ANACHARSIS CLOOTZ.'

hospitals, sometimes five or six together, should each thenceforth have a separate bed ; that books should be sent to these hospitals ; that a separate building should be assigned to the use of lying-in women ; that the atrocious treatment of the insane should be amended ; that the blind, who were lodged in the Quinze-Vingts, should receive five sous daily ; that means should be taken to assure an asylum to the indigent and the aged. This victim of Camille's bitter pen helped to found the Conservatoire of Music, and procured the suspension of the Vandal restoration of pictures at the Louvre, which certain superintendents have since ventured to resume. He brought wooden shoes into fashion, that leather might be left to the soldiers, the defenders of the country, who were marching barefoot through snow and mud. Finally, he demanded equality of burial, and wished (a dream, but a beautiful one !) that the winding-sheet of every citizen in his coffin should be a tri-coloured flag. For all this, Camille rallied him none the less cruelly. He helped to doom him. Let us turn the page ; I am in haste to reach the sublime hour of Camille's life. At last he published his third number ; he called Tacitus to his aid : the hand so adroit in Picard and Parisian satire seized the red-hot iron of the Roman, and branded on the forehead those whose cry was for a perpetual Reign of Terror :—

'In ancient days in Rome (says Tacitus) there was a law which specified what were State crimes and crimes of lèse-majesty, and those were punished with death. Under the Republic crimes of lèse-majesty were reduced to four kinds : abandoning an army in a foreign country ; exciting seditions ; maladministration of the public affairs and money by the members of constituted bodies ; degrading the majesty of the Roman people. The Emperors needed only to add a few articles to this law in order to include whole cities in a proscription. Augustus was the first to extend the law of lèse-majesty, within which he comprised all writings called "anti-revolutionary." Under his successors the extensions ceased to have any limits so soon as words had become State crimes; thenceforth, one step changed simple looks, sorrow, compassion, sighs, and even silence, into crimes.

'It was a crime of lèse-majesty or "counter-revolution" that the town of Nursia raised a monument to its inhabitants who were killed at the siege of Modena, fighting under Augustus himself, it is true, but then Augustus was fighting against Brutus.

'It was a crime against the revolution that Dibonius Drusus asked the fortune-tellers if he should not one day be possessed of great riches. It was a crime against the revolution that the journalist, Cremutius Cordus, called Brutus and Cassius the last of the Romans. It was a crime against the revolution that one of Cassius' descendants had a portrait of his ancestor in his house. Mamercus Scaurus committed a crime against the revolution by writing a tragedy in which were certain verses capable of a double meaning. It was a crime against the revolution that Torquatus Silanus had spent money; that Petreius had had a dream about Claudius; and that the wife of Claudius had had a dream concerning Appius Silanus, was counted a crime on his part. It was a crime against the revolution that Pomponius, a friend of Sejanus, had taken refuge in one of his country-houses. It was a crime against the revolution to complain of the misfortunes of the times, for this was to sit in judgment on the government. Anti-revolutionary crime was implied in the non-invocation of the divine genius of Caligula. For having failed in this, numberless citizens were torn by scourges, condemned to work in the mines, or thrown to the wild beasts; some were even sawn in two. It was a crime against the revolution that the mother of the consul Furius Geminus, mourned for the death of her son.

'It was necessary to rejoice in the death of a friend or relative, if one wished to escape death oneself. Under Nero,

several whose relatives he was about to put to death went to return thanks to the gods ; and illuminated their houses. At least
it was necessary to wear a contented air, a frank and serene
countenance. There was fear lest even fear should be accounted guilt.

' Everything gave umbrage to the tyrant. Was a citizen
popular ? He was the prince's rival, who might excite a
civil war. *Studia civium in se verteret, et si multi idem
audeant, bellum esse.* Suspected.

' Did a man fly from popularity, and keep by his fireside ?
This retired life had made him noticed, and had gained him
consideration. *Quando metu, occultior, tanto famæ adeptus.*
Suspected.

' Were you rich ? There was imminent danger that the
people would be corrupted by your gifts. *Auri vim atque
opes Plauti principi infensas.* Suspected.

' Were you poor ? Then, O invincible Emperor, we
must watch this man closely ; there is no person so enter-
prising as he who has nothing. *Sylla inopem, inde præcipuam
audaciam.* Suspected.

' Were you of a grave, melancholy disposition, or carelessly
dressed ? You were in affliction because public affairs were
going on well. *Hominem bonis publicis mæstum.* Suspected.

' If, on the contrary, a citizen enjoyed life and had in-
digestion, he was amusing himself because the Emperor had
had that attack of gout (which, happily, would be nothing) ;
it was necessary to make him feel that his Majesty was still
in the prime of life. *Reddendam pro intempestivâ licentiâ
mæstam et funebrem noctem quâ sentiat vivere Vitellium et
imperare.* Suspected.

' Was he virtuous and strict in his morals ? Good ! A
new Brutus, who aspires, by his pallor and his Jacobin wig,
to censure an amiable and well-curled Court. *Gliscere æmulos
Brutorum vultûs rigidi et tristis quo tibi lasciviam exprobrent.*
Suspected.

' Was a man a philosopher, an orator, or a poet ? Becoming, indeed, that he should have more renown than the
rulers ! Was it bearable that more attention should be paid

to an author in the gallery or the pit than to the Emperor in his private box? *Virginium et Rufum claritudo nominis.* Suspected.

'Finally, had a man acquired a great reputation in war? He was all the more dangerous. With an incapable general there are some resources. If he be a traitor he cannot deliver up the army to the enemy so effectually as if he be clever. But if an officer of merit, like Agricola, turned traitor, not a man would resist him. It was best to get rid of such generals. At least the Emperor could not be dispensed from removing them from the army. *Multa militari famâ metum fecerat.* Suspected.

'It is easy to see that it was still worse to be the grandson or connection of Augustus; such a one might one day pretend to the throne. *Nobilem et quod tunc spectaretur e Cæsarem posteris!* Suspected.

'And suspected persons under the Emperors were not only sent, as with us, to the *Madelonettes*, to the *Irlandais*, or to *Sainte-Pélagie*. The sovereign sent them an order to summon their doctor or apothecary, and to choose, within twenty-four hours, the sort of death they liked best. *Missus centurio qui maturaret eum.*

'Thus, it was not possible to have any quality, unless it were one that might be used as an instrument of tyranny, without awakening the despot's jealousy and exposing oneself to certain death. It was a crime to hold a high post, or to tender one's resignation; but the greatest crime of all was to be incorruptible. Nero had so utterly destroyed honest people, that after he had rid himself of Thrasea and Soranus, he boasted of having banished even the name of virtue from the face of the earth. When the Senate condemned each of them, the Emperor wrote a letter of thanks to it for having caused *an enemy of the Republic* to perish; just as Clodius the tribune erected *an altar to Liberty* on the site of Cicero's dismantled house, whilst the people shouted, "*Long live Liberty!*"

'One was condemned because of his name and that of his ancestors; another, because he possessed a beautiful house at Alba; Valerius Asiaticus, because his gardens had taken the fancy of the Empress ; Statilius, because his face had displeased her ; and a multitude of others for no conceivable cause. Toranius, the tutor and old friend of Augustus, was proscribed by his pupil for no reason, except that he was an upright man and loved his country.   Neither the prætorship nor his innocence could save Quintus Gellius from the bloody hands of the executioner ; Augustus, whose clemency has been vaunted, tore out his eyes with his own hands.   Men were betrayed and stabbed by their slaves or their enemies ; and if they had no enemies, an assassin was found in a guest, a friend, or a son.   In one word, during these reigns, the natural death of a celebrated man, or of a man in a high place even, was so rare that it was gazetted as an event, and handed down by the historian to the memory of future ages.   Under this consulate, says our annalist, there was a pontiff, Pisonius, who died in his bed : this was looked upon as a marvel.'

Is this all ?   No.   A   blind and generous fury seemed to have taken possession of Camille.   He was fairly launched.   Sensitive and impressionable, he excited himself to that work of humane reaction which, whatever Tissot and Louis Blanc may say, did no harm to the Republic.   'The anti-revolutionists clapped their hands,' says M. Louis Blanc.   That may be, but, at that moment, the ultra-revolutionists were more dangerous to the Republic, perhaps, than its bitterest enemies.   They did more than fight against her : they compromised her.   They were, as has been well said, to the Revolution what the 'Jacques' were to Etienne Marcel, the Anabaptists to the Reformers, and the Iconoclasts to the proud Huguenots of Flanders.   These '*enragés*' pushed the 'purging out' and 'death' system to the point of madness.

The name of *enragés* was at first given to the members of the left of the Constituent Assembly, the adversaries of the *Noirs* ; it dated, in fact, from the

Manége.   The Royalists then applied it to the men of movement.   Later, this name indicated the *exaltés.* Marat applies it to Jacques Roux, Leclerc, and Varlet. Until the beginning of 1793 the *enragés* were confounded with those who were afterwards called Hébertists.   All were ultra-revolutionists ; but the shades of the *ultra* party, to which Desmoulins ingeniously opposed the *citra,* are not clearly defined.   On the 10th of March and the 31st of May, 1793, the *enragés,* acting in concert with others rather than on their own account, took the stage and played a part.   On the 31st of May they were in the vanguard.   Later, they aspired to be the bulk of the army—what am I saying ?—to be the grand Staff of the nation.   After the victory, they began to display themselves under their true aspect, to manifest their doctrines distinctly ; they appeared as socialists ; they were Cordeliers, not Jacobins.   They attacked the Constitution, and then all parties fell upon them, and pursued them with animosity until they were crushed. They held out a hand to the socialists at Lyons. Leclerc is the connecting link between Lyons and Paris, between Chalier and Jacques Roux.   Looking everywhere for help, they enlisted the ' women of the Revolution.'   The men of the party were Varlet, J. Roux, Leclerc, a certain Dubois, whom Robespierre (at the end of *Ventôse,* year III.) designates as a confederate of Jacques Roux ; among the women, the notorious Rose Lacombe had already appeared.   Probably they knew Babeuf.   Even in 1792 confused rumours of Communism had arisen.   Danton, a practical man, saw that Babeuf was a dangerous dreamer, a seductive and terrible sophist.

Camille was determined to harass them.   His third number had appeared on December 15 ; his

fourth number was for sale on December 20. It was
in everyone's hand. Camille complained that it was
sold at 'an exorbitant price.' France, which is gene
rous, humane, foolish, but not cruel, thoughtless but
not implacable, recognised itself, so to speak, body and
soul, in those eloquent and heart-inspired pages. Yes,
their source was the heart, whence come, not only great
thoughts, as Vauvenargues says, but great resolutions
and great deeds.

Like a man in love with pure liberty, Camille
uttered a great cry for clemency :—

'Liberty,' exclaims Camille, 'has neither old age nor
infancy; she has but one age, that of strength and vigour.
This liberty, which I worship, is not an unknown deity. We are
fighting in defence of the good things which she puts into
the possession of those who invoke her : these good things
are the Declaration of Rights, the sweetness of Republican
maxims, fraternity, holy equality, and the inviolability of
principles. These are the footprints of the goddess, these
are the signs by which I distinguish the nations among whom
she dwells.

'If by liberty,' he says again, 'you do not mean, as I do,
principles, but only a bit of stone, then never has there been
an idolatry more stupid and more costly than ours ! O my
dear fellow-citizens ! shall we so far debase ourselves as to
fall at the feet of such divinities? No ; liberty, the liberty
that comes down from heaven, is not a nymph of the opera ;
it is not a red cap, a dirty shirt, or tatters. Liberty is happiness, reason, equality, justice ! . . . .

'. . . . Would you have me acknowledge her, fall at her
feet, spill my blood for her ? Open the prisons of those two
hundred thousand citizens whom you call "suspects," for in
the Declaration of Rights there was no prison for suspected
persons, but only for felons. Suspicion has no prison, it has
the public prosecutor ; there are no suspected persons but
those who are accused of crime by the law. Do not believe that
this measure would be fatal to the Republic, it would be the

most revolutionary step you have ever taken. You wish to exterminate all your enemies by the guillotine ! But was there
ever greater folly ? Can you bring one to the scaffold without
making to yourselves ten more of his family or his friends ?
Do you think that these women, these old men, these egotists,
these laggards of the Revolution whom you shut up, are
dangerous ? Of your enemies, none remain to you but the
cowards and the sick ; the brave and the strong have emi-
grated ; they have perished at Lyons or in La Vendée ; the
rest do not deserve your anger.'

It was done : Camille had given vent, as Michelet
says, ' to that divine cry which will touch all hearts for
ever.' The nation thrilled at the sound like the
earth at the touch of spring. Only the blind, the
inflexible, the obstinate, and the men whom Desmoulins calls ' patriot adventurers, who profit by revolutions,'
were angered by these appeals for clemency. If this
ray of true liberty had but fallen upon France in those
first days of 1794 ; if the Reign of Terror had been
ended, if a reconciliation had been at this time effected,
while the heads of so many generous, intelligent, and
courageous men had not yet fallen, what evils would have
been avoided, what fresh trials, what reactions far
more dangerous than mercy to the Republic, would the
country have been spared !

The terrorists did not understand this. Robespierre,
scared by the protests which the ' Vieux Cordelier'
excited, broke with Camille. The anger of his allies,
the Jacobinical madness, as the English said, would soon
have reached him, for it was about to strike Camille.
Maximilien contented himself, soon after, with defending
his friend in such a fashion that Camille Desmoulins
took the defence for an attack, and was angry.

' *O my dear Robespierre*,' says Camille in his fourth

number — (thus avowing that Robespierre was, so to speak, standing behind Desmoulins whilst the latter wrote his articles)—'*you have already come closer to this idea*' (that love is stronger, more lasting than fear) '*in the measure which you have had decreed.*' Maximilien must have been in despair at seeing that 'his old friend' was revealing him so openly. From that time forth Robespierre allowed Camille to risk his life, and Desmoulins had no support but Danton, who, at least, did not dissuade him from pleading the cause of clemency.

Camille mentioned Philippeaux in terms of praise —Philippeaux the brave denouncer of Ronsin in La Vendée. Camille had attacked Hébert,[1] whose advice might still be followed by the Paris populace, and who had alarmed the Committee of Public Safety.[2] Camille was to be attacked for all these

---

[1] 'Let the people,' said Hébert, a little time before, 'gather in a body to-morrow at the Convention, surround it as they did on May 31, and not quit their post until the National representatives have adopted proper means for our safety. Let the revolutionist army set out the moment the decree shall have been issued ; *but, above all, let the guillotine follow every line, every column of the army.*'—Sitting of the Commune, September 3, 1793; 'Républicain Français,' No. ccxciv. ; 'Journal de la Montagne,' No. xcvi. ; Buchez et Roux, xxix. p. 23.

[2] It might be interesting to show what the official functions of this Committee were, according to the 'Almanach' of 1773 :—

'The Committee is established by the decree of October 2 last. It consists of thirty members ; a considerable number, but hardly sufficient for the many operations and the assiduous labour involved in their functions.

'These thirty members are nearly all chosen from the Legislative Assembly, re-elected for the National Convention.

'It may be said that this Committee has no other functions than to watch over the general safety of the State ; and with this object, it should have relations with every place and citizen in the Republic.

'In this supervision, which excepts nothing that relates to the general safety, four objects are especially notable.

writings in the Jacobin club. On the 1st Nivôse, Nicolas, the 'hard-hitter' juror and printer of the revolutionary tribunal, who escorted Robespierre with his flunkeys armed with sticks, declared from the rostrum of the club, that 'Camille Desmoulins had been within a close shave of the guillotine for a long time !' This was a terrible saying. Camille tried to turn it off with a jest; but it was a death-knell sounding its sinister warning in his ear. Let us do Desmoulins justice: it did not make him relax in the accomplishment of his task. Denounced, threatened by Hébert, treated as a 'political blackguard,' a 'scoundrel,' a 'renegade from Sansculottism,' a 'miserable intriguer;' accused by the 'Père Duchesne' of 'speaking the language of the fops whose company he frequented, and whose sentiments he shared as well as their language;' he persisted in his work. 'You, the friend of counts and marquises,' Hébert said to him; 'you, the guest of

'The Committee is charged :

' 1. To watch the enemies of public affairs in Paris, and to interrogate them when arrested, in order to discover plots, their authors, their chiefs, and their agents.

' 2. To find out and prosecute the fabricators of false *assignats*.

' 3. To have those who are denounced to it as agents of foreign Courts, and all those who trouble public order in any way whatsoever, arrested.

' 4. And, finally, to watch equally closely those whose names are in the *Liste civile*—that is, in the list of the men who were sold to the late king.

'By another decree of the same day, October 2 last, the National Convention bestowed another function upon this Committee ; authorising it to receive an account of all arrests relating to the Revolution which have taken place throughout the Republic since August 10 ; to take cognisance of their motives ; to inspect the correspondence of arrested persons, and, generally, all the documents tending either to their justification or giving proof of the matters of which they were accused, so as to make a report to the National Convention, upon which it shall come to such determination as it may think fit.

'The report of the Committee upon this last subject should be printed and sent to the eighty-four departments.'

that D'Orléans of whom you now speak no more, because you would rather not remember your days of distress, now that you live like a Sybarite (*sic*). You blush to recall the Hôtel de la Frugalité, where we used to meet, side by side with honest masons and poor workmen, worth more than you and I.' This was a strange reproach to come from the pen of Hébert, who wore gloves, and really lived, as he says, 'like a dandy,' all the time he was writing his infamous publications. Under these reproaches lay blood and death ; but Camille did not flinch. The man who has been accused of want of self-command when confronted with the guillotine, did not hesitate for a moment to continue the fatal work he had begun. Camille met these accusations by a series of personal denials which were rather successive attacks upon his enemies. And what attacks! those whom he strikes down rise no more. So long as the name of Hébert survives in history, he will carry Camille's marks :—

'Do you not know, Hébert, that when the tyrants of Europe wish to vilify the Republic, to make their slaves believe that France is covered with the darkness of barbarism, that Paris, the city of Attic glory and taste, is peopled with Vandals, they insert fragments of your writings in their newspapers ? As if the people were as ignorant and as stupid as you would have Mr. Pitt believe them to be ; as if no one could speak to him but in language like yours, as if such were the speech of the Convention and of the Committee of Public Safety ; as if your filthiness were the nation's ; as if a Paris sewer were the Seine !'[1]

---

[1] Hébert's answer has been little quoted. In it he rallies Camille, reminding him with irony, which unfortunately hit the right nail on the head, that he had not always been so tender and pitiful.

'Here, my brave *sansculottes*,' said Hébert, 'here is a great man whom you have forgotten ; it is truly ungrateful of you, for he declares

It is plain that Camille did not mend his ways. Hébert redoubles his fury; he speaks thus of Desmoulins: 'A little ass with long ears (the ânon des Moulins of the Apôtres), who never was mouthed or spurred, has been straining every nerve these last few days. After having pleaded the cause of dandy Dillon and maintained that, without the protection of the "red-heels" (a mark of nobility), the Republic could not be saved, nowadays he turns champion of all the — — who are in quod.' But Camille was afraid neither of Hébert's attacks nor of Robespierre's countenance. He cared not to follow the prudent counsel of Pollionus : ' *Never write against him who can proscribe thee.*' And as for his Committee of Clemency, in spite of the threats of Nicolas and the *enragés*, in spite of the censure of Barère, he maintained its principles and cried out, like Galileo, when condemned by the Sacred College, ' It moves for all that.'

III.

The fifth number of the 'Vieux Cordelier,' dated the 5th *Nivôse*, year II. (December 25, 1793) was, how-

that, without him, there would never have been a Revolution. Formerly he called himself " Procureur-Général de la Lanterne." You think I am speaking of that famous cutthroat whose celebrated beard made the aristocrats take flight ; no, he of whom we speak boasts that he is the most pacific of men. To believe him, he has no more gall than a pigeon ; he is so sensitive, that he never hears the word guillotine without shivering to his very bones ; he is a great teacher who, in his own person, has more wisdom than all the patriots put together, and more judgment than the entire Convention ; it is a great pity that he cannot speak ; or he would prove to the " Moniteur " and the Committee of Public Safety that they have no common sense. But if he cannot speak, master Camille can make up for it by writing, to the great satisfaction of the *modérés*, Royalists, and aristocrats.' (' J. R. Hébert, author of " Père Duchesne," to Camille Desmoulins and Company.')

ever, not for sale until the 16th *Nivôse* (January 5,
1794). The sixth, dated, by mistake, the 10th *Nivôse*
(December 30), did not come out until the 15th
Pluviôse (February 1794). This No. VI. was to
be the last which should appear in the lifetime of
Desmoulins. In it Camille had begun what he called
his *political credo*; but at the seventh number Desenne
his publisher took alarm, and refused to print it. Those
sheets, covered with Desmoulins' close handwriting,
frightened him. The seventh number did not appear
until *Prairial*, year III. (June 1795), on the day
after the outbreak whose history we have related.[1]
But Desenne only issued fragments of it in 1795, and
M. Matton, senior, the inheritor of Camille's manuscripts, and who published the ' Œuvres ' of his famous
relative, did not give No. VII. complete in 1834. In
an article in the ' Complément de l'Encyclopédie
moderne,' [2] the late Edouard Carteron, keeper of the
National Archives, who was well versed in the history
of the Revolution, has printed, under the heading
' Indulgent,' some pages from this No. VII. which
may still be regarded as unpublished or at least
unknown.

They are taken from the collection of Baron de
Girardot, of Bourges. M. Carteron copied them from
the manuscript itself, ' consisting of several loose
leaves, which were formerly a continuation of each
other.' Other fragments are copied from the original
by Panis, a Dantonist and Camille's friend. They
will be found interesting. There are, among them,
certain pages which do not figure in the ' Œuvres ' of
Camille. What an uproar they would have created

---

[1] See the ' Derniers Montagnards.'
[2] Firmin Didot.

T

at the Jacobins and the Cordeliers may be guessed on perusing them.

FRAGMENTS OF THE 'VIEUX CORDELIER.'

1. 'It is under the mask of patriotism, and contrary to that sensible maxim from which Machiavel so strongly recommends a sovereign never to swerve,—*Ministers and generals should have honours, high posts, and riches heaped upon them, so that they cannot hope to gain so much by treason as by fidelity*—that the Convention first decreed that the *maximum* of the retiring pension of a citizen who had been general-in-chief, and had exterminated the enemy, could only be three thousand *livres* ; and then the deputy Chabot, who had just acquired a hundred thousand crowns by his marriage, proposed, in order to make himself popular, that ministers, generals, and deputies should only have the same pay as the soldiers. When we remember that retrenching half-a-crown a month from his salary deprived Portugal of Magellan's services and discoveries, and when we see folly of this kind presiding at our deliberations, should we not be tempted to think that Pitt himself has a seat on the benches of *la Montagne ?*

'It was under this mask of patriotism that, in order to disgust with office any citizen of talent who might have been useful to the Republic, and by the removal or disgrace of all men of merit, so that the most important places were left to men whose ignorance was as useful to our enemies as if it had been treason—denunciation falling unceasingly upon all who had distinguished themselves—we had arrived at such a happy state that there did not remain at the head of our eleven armies a single man who, I do not say knew, but who had even learned the profession of war. By these perpetual denunciations, the only generals in those two campaigns in which a siege or a battle could be cited which did honour to the commandant and not to the valour of the soldiers or to French impetuosity—Dillon, Custine, Aubert-Dubayet, Harville, Lamarlière—and, indeed, all our generals in succession, have been thrown into prison or dragged to the scaffold. In one single campaign, all that history relates of the Carthaginians, who crucified their generals, we have surpassed by the guillotine ; and the French nation has not hesitated to pronounce against itself a judgment which will stain it for ever ; for, if all the generals whom it has condemned have in truth been traitors, it follows that our nation, with its boasted loyalty, has included, in two years, more traitors than all other nations together, since, throughout the entire history of the Roman Republic, only two generals were traitors.

'When will this denunciation tire itself out? It alone promoted the officer to the rank of general, the journalist to the Ministry, and the deputy to the Committee of Public Safety! It alone could, on the morrow, command the applause of the tribunes for the representative of the people who had been most decried the day before. Had Robert laid hands upon some rum? He denounced General Bouchet, a soldier without reproach, a venerable old man ; was applauded by the galleries, and believed himself once more popular. Had Duhem misconducted himself in his mission to the North? Had he levied, for his own table, two thousand bottles of excellent " emigrant wine," by an order to the representatives of the people addressed to the department of the Pas-de-Calais? To make himself popular again, he severely denounced Lamarlière, who was in prison, after having sung his praises as commissary to the army. In order to regain his popularity, he made a deposition against the " Twenty-One," which would have stifled the faction at its birth, and spared you much evil if it had been done in time. Thus he effaced the memory of his requisitions. Chabot made that famous deposition against his one-and-twenty colleagues in which the most shameless false witness comes to light in more than one place ; and believed he had effaced the memory of his marriage. Each thought his sins washed out by a little word, not of penitence, as formerly, but of denunciation, true or false. This man denounced some one to save his own fine house ; that man, that he might be forgiven for the mission from which he had returned ; the proconsul, in order to get back to his province ; this one, to get a seat at the Committee of Surveillance; that one, for a seat at the Committee of Public Safety; one, to be president; another, to be secretary; and Levasseur, to prove that he had (not) been the first to give the signal for flight in the fatal sortie from Cambray, positively said that, returning from the fight, where he had had his horse killed under him, he had met with General Houchard behind a hedge, covered with wounds from head to foot, and he accused him of cowardice! What must have been Hébert's feelings, after having denounced so many for six months, on seeing Paré, who had never denounced anyone, preferred to himself as Minister of the Interior. It was easy to see, in "La grande colère du Père Duchêne" of the day after, that he could not pardon Thuriot and Danton for this preference. What, then, is this unquenchable thirst of ambition? And ought not Hébert, whom all Paris has seen distributing theatre tickets under the vestibule *des Italiens*, to be contented with his scarf, with the forty thousand *livres* a year given him by Bouchotte, the Minister, as the subscription of the eleven armies to the inestimable "Père Duchêne;" with making France tremble at his denunciations and bringing her on her knees before his Jacqueline? With what rapidity a Republic rushes towards ruin, when denunciation has become the shortest road to success, as it was under Tiberius and the worst of the emperors; when, every day, the denouncer, sacred and inviolable, made his triumphal entry into the palace of the dead, and received some rich *inheritance*; when all these denouncers arrayed themselves in fine names, and were called [1] Cotta, Regulus, Cassius, Severus! But such is the danger of the best institutions; Marat's denouncers had contributed not a little to clear the soil of France, and prepare the way for the Republic. At his death, the altars raised everywhere to the deputy who, for four years, had exercised the functions of *denouncer in general*, the feasts, the solemn processions in his honour, his apotheosis in all the sections, procured him successors who surpass him in zeal. The honours of the Pantheon granted to Voltaire, to J.-J. Rousseau,

---

[1] Anaxagoras (Chaumette); Anacharsis (Clootz); Fabricius (Paris, recorder of the Revolutionary Tribunal).

and to Descartes, will not give them too many imitators. Let him refuse who will to arrive at glory by the road of genius; it is the *narrow way*. But so soon as public opinion makes the imitation of Jean-Paul Marat—the physician born at Neufchâtel whom Voltaire ridiculed so much—the acme of civic perfection, and the sure means of perching oneself, one day, upon the high altar of the Pantheon, the pride which moves the heart of man, and the desire to leave one's memory behind and to make a name, are sure guarantees that the mob will rush into so broad and easy a road to immortality. Thus, Quintus Cicero, not being able to attain to his brother's elevation by eloquence, endeavoured to make as great a name for himself by the severity of his judgments, and made his government of Asia nothing but a record of crucifixions and torture. Before long, Marat's successors had left him far behind, and the "Père Duchêne" could look upon the *Friend of the People*, who had acquitted Ducos and Fonfride with contempt, as a mere Brissotin.

'Thenceforth, there was emulation among the Commissioners of the Convention, who travelled through the departments, as to who should eclipse the glory of the great Marat and, in his turn, multiply statues of himself like the sand of the sea. "I have changed all the federal administrations, from the president of the department down to the mayor of the village; taxed the rich, like a true Revolutionist; pulled down the bells; shut up suspected persons; guillotined all the royalists: such is the summary of my journey," Laplanche said, on his return from Loiret-et-Cher;[1] when, that he might obtain the honours of triumph, he threw down before the Convention more chalices, ciboriums, and Sacred Hosts, than Hannibal's courier did rings of the Roman knights after the battle of Cannes.

'At this recital, inserted in the "Bulletin," Laplanche's trophies disturbed the repose of Fouché of Nantes at Nevers, and he at once made an anti-episcopal visit to his diocese, not leaving in the whole department of La Nièvre a single paten, altar-cruet, or thurible; and instead of the one waggon that Laplanche had sent to the Convention, he sent seventeen

---

[1] 'Moniteur' of the 30th of the first month, p. 122, 2.

cartloads of sacred things. It was laughable to see the representatives of the people laying their hands upon all these symbols of fanaticism, servitude, and ignorance.

'But the other deputies' mission in the departments was one of chains and tears. If certain commissioners had had secret instructions to fulfil their duties in such a manner as to make the Republic hated, they could not have acted otherwise than as they did. André Dumont[1] counted his prisoners only by the twenty or thirty tumbril loads. "In leaving Montreuil," he wrote to the Convention, "I bring with me forty-four carts[2] full of suspected persons ;" and he alone made more French people prisoners in one department in fourteen days, than the army of the North did Prussians, English, and Austrians in the whole campaign. In vain was liberty of worship guaranteed by the Constitution : "You shall confess that you are harbouring quacks (priests ?), or you shall go to prison."[3] In his letters to the Convention, he speaks of his prizes with as much emphasis as if he had gained them by boarding dismasted ships, covered with wounds, and after twelve hours' fighting. "Victory !" he exclaims ; "I send you an ex-count d'Hervily, who had buried his title-deeds and his plate sixty feet below ground ; and ten other rascals of his stamp." Now who is this d'Hervily? An hypochondriac ex-nobleman, an octogenarian at thirty-six, wasted by medicine rather than by illness, who had buried his title-deeds and his plate, when his estate, near Péronne, was surrounded by the Uhlans, who had just burned the villages within three-quarters of a league of his château. Who were *the ten rascals of his stamp ?*[4] I know one among them, a

---

[1] See André Dumont's letters : 1. 'Moniteur' of September 10, 1793, p. 1075, col. 1 ; 2. 'Moniteur' of September 16, p. 1098, col. 3 ; 3. 'Moniteur' of September 25, p. 1137, col. 3.

[2] 'Moniteur' of October 6, 1793, p. 1187, cols. 2 and 3 ; 'Moniteur' of 18th of the first month, p. 74, 1.

[3] 'Moniteur' of the 1st of the second month, p. 124, col. 2 ; *cf.* 'Moniteur' of the 5th of the second month (October 26, 1793), p. 143, cols. 2 and 3.

[4] See the 'Vieux Cordelier,' p. 81 and following ; Matton's edition, concerning Vaillant, Camille's cousin, who had been arrested for having given a bed to Citizen Nantouillet.

relative of mine, whose rascality consisted in having received a man at dinner, at his country house, who had lived at Péronne for five months, had mounted guard there, received his rents there, in a word, was a French citizen, but whom André Dumont accused of having made a journey to London ; as if, before receiving a citizen. into my house, I were obliged to enquire of him where he had been and what he had been doing since the Revolution ! This is one of André Dumont's ten rascals.[1]

'Even André Dumont has, however, been surpassed by his colleague Dubouchet, in the department of Seine-et-Marne. Commissioner Rousselin's letter would have already covered him with ridicule,[2] if one could laugh while a whole province weeps. The decree of the Convention,[3] which forbade the sending of commissioners into the departments in which they were born—a wise decree, in that it prevented the deputies from being influenced by their relatives and friends—had the defect of exposing the deputies, in a country they did not know, to the suggestions and deceits of false patriotism, on the 'alert to deceive them ; and the complaints which arose on all sides against Dubouchet, fall less upon him than those in whom he placed confidence. Dubouchet, on arriving at Melun, enquired for the most ardent patriot ; and a grocer was pointed out to him as the Marat of the place. This fellow took care of his own customers, and found suspected persons only among those who did not deal with him.'

(END OF THE FIRST FRAGMENT.)

---

[1] See the 'Moniteur ' (for the other Hébertist manifestations of André Dumont) of 15th *Brumaire*, year II. p. 184, 3 ; 17th *Frimaire*, year II. p. 309, 2 ; 23rd *Frimaire*, p. 334, 1 ; of the 3rd *Nivôse*, p. 375, 3 ; 14th *Nivôse*, p. 418-19.

[2] 'Moniteur,' 24th of first month, p. 96, 1 ; *cf.* 'Moniteur,' 29th of first month, p. 118, 1 ; where is a reply to Rousselin's denunciation of Dubouchet, deputy of Rhône-et-Loire ; 'Moniteur' of 3rd *Frimaire*, p. 255, 2 ; 'Moniteur,' 29th *Frimaire*, p. 358, 3.

[3] Decree of July 5, 1797.

N.B.—The original is identical with Panis' copy. The different sheets on which Desmoulins wrote this long fragment, are separated from each other in Baron de Girardot's portfolio. Panis copied the sheets before they were dispersed.

Second Fragment of the 'Vieux Cordelier.'

For the first fragment (as above) M. Carteron had had— 1st, Panis' copy; 2nd, some loose sheets in Baron de Girardot's portfolio; but, on these sheets, which are in Camille's handwriting, being put together, they are found to match perfectly; they have, without any doubt, served Panis for his copy.

The second fragment (the present one) has been restored from the same sources. Panis' copy was made from Camille's manuscript; but Panis, being an ignorant man, could not read some words, such as non causa pro causâ. *Camille's manuscript is composed of a single sheet, recto and verso; there was certainly a beginning and a continuation.*

For the first (above mentioned) the beginning is wanting; but the manuscript ending at the bottom of a page and the rest of the sheet being blank, this fragment may be held to end with these words: 'who did not deal with him.'

'. . . . While so far on my way, I did not fail to visit our wise men. What was my surprise to hear hardly any discussion! It seems that the rostrum of the Convention has become as dangerous as a campaign in La Vendée under certain generals of whom you know. If a deputy feel himself obliged to declare his sentiments, good or bad, nothing is more pleasant for the Republican who follows these sittings than to observe with what *ifs* and *buts*, *yeas* and *nays*, what concessions, circumlocutions, corrections, and oratorical precautions, he envelopes his meaning, for fear the guillotine should find a way to the neck of it; how he foresees future contingencies, and how he parries in tierce and in carte all M. Renaudin's interrogatories.

'Not one of you dares give utterance on the morrow to the opinion you have agreed upon the day before. Each of you waits for the others. It seems that the most incorrupt of

deputies is he who, never having opened his mouth throughout the session, will be able to say on coming away from
the Convention : " God be praised ! Let Fouquier-Tinville
come when he will ! I defy him to find a flaw in my
opinions ! " If this goes on, the nation, in order to have
faithful and irreproachable representatives, cannot do better
than elect Carthusian monks, who, without breaking their
vow of perpetual silence, will only have to stand up and sit
down, according to the applause of the galleries, and at the
back of Hébert (or [1] Vincent). I have often thought already
that you looked, in your gloomy silence, not like the conscript
Fathers, but the Fathers of La Trappe or of Sept-Fonds ; [2]
or rather, after hearing you a hundred times disapproving
of the measures proposed, but keeping your places, and not
daring to ask leave to address the Assembly, I protest whilst
you sat listening to stump-orators who put you far above
the Greeks or the Romans, I, on this celebrated Mountain,
have merely seen mice deliberating, while no one dared to
bell the cat.

'Whatever may have been the degradation of past generations, until now it has been held that a man may say everything if he do but know how to say it. We know how
Abraham, in his walk with God in person—having to treat of
a very difficult matter, nothing less than to ask the Immutable
God to revoke his sentence upon Sodom—skilfully extricated
himself from his difficulty by the help of a figure of rhetoric.
" Lord," he said, " if there had been only five hundred patriots
who were not accomplices in the crime, would you spare [3] the
houses ? " " I would spare them," said God. " But even if
I were to rub out a cipher, and there were fifty, would you
spare them ? " " I would." " But if I rubbed out the last
cipher—if there were only five just patriots ? " " Even then,"
replied the good God, " I would grant a reprieve."

'I allow that a Republican would have been more candid ;
he would have said to God : " There is a flaw in the reasoning

---

[1] These words ' or Vincent' are erased.
[2] An abbey of the Cistercian order, near Moulins.
[3] 'not' is wanting in the MS.

here that is called in logic *non causa pro causâ*,[1] and you lay the blame on the walls ; pardon me, but . . . ."

' " The walls also, great Lord, have they . . . . ? "[2] After all, from the creature to the Creator [from the clay[3] to the potter] there is so great a distance that Abraham is quite excusable ; and the watch should be allowed, in speaking to the watchmaker, to use these circumlocutions and periphrases. But I cannot forgive the revolutionary government of Billaud-Varennes and the *reign of terror* he has made *the order of the day*, in that, although it is constantly declared that *all men are equal* and *that the time has come for plain-speaking*, you, the representatives of the people and clothed with the dignity of the first magistrates, far from speaking as equals to equals, cannot even, by exerting all your rhetoric,[4] and resorting to every imaginable circumlocution, utter an opinion adverse to the one in favour ; that you dare not say that you differ from Ronsin with respect to Lyons ; and since, by his avowal, there are fifteen hundred patriots[5] in *Commune-affranchie*, you share the sentiments of God the Father at least with regard to the houses. I contend that such servility has never before been seen, not only from man to man, but from the servant to the master, and the clay to the potter : I contend that we have never been so enslaved as since we have called ourselves Republican, that we have never grovelled so abjectly before men in credit and in place as since we have spoken with them hat on head.'

These fragments clearly show the state of Camille's mind at the beginning of the year 1794, the spring of which was to witness his death. Miot de Mélito, in his ' Mémoires,' shows him to us saddened and beset by fatal presentiments. ' The few words he let fall,' says Mélito, ' were confined to enquiries into or observations

---

[1] Panis could not read this.
[2] Words wanting in the MS.
[3] Erased in the MS. The words occur again in the page following.
[4] In the MS. and Panis' copy ' réthorique.'
[5] See the ' Vieux Cordelier,' p. 69, Matton's edition.

upon the sentences of the revolutionary tribunal, the kind of punishment inflicted upon the condemned, and the most noble or most decent fashion in which to prepare for it, or to endure it.[1] He was weary; he felt that all was lost; and that he had brought about not his own destruction only, but that of his family. Already two commissioners of the section Mucius Scævola, the section of Vincent, Hébert's friend, had searched the house of M. Duplessis, Camille's father-in-law, following up the perquisition by a seizure which had called forth a protest at the Convention from Danton, supported by Romme, against the seizure of certain objects of art; nor was this all : although he had not married an Austrian, like Chabot, Camille had, like the ex-Capuchin, to defend himself for having *married a rich wife.*

'I will say but one word of my wife' (he answered Hébert on this subject in a touching tone, and with more emotion than was usual with him); 'I had always believed in the immortality of the soul. After sacrificing my personal interest so many times to the liberty and happiness of the people, I said to myself, in the heat of the persecution,—"There must be a reward for virtue elsewhere." But my marriage is so blissful, my domestic happiness so great, that I feared I was receiving my reward on earth, and I lost my faith in immortality. Now your persecutions, your invectives, and your cowardly calumnies, restore to me all my hope.'.[2]

Alas! at the moment when he spoke of his 'great domestic happiness' Camille felt it was already slipping from his hold, disappearing, passing away,

---

[1] 'Mémoires of Count Miot de Mélito,' second edition (1873), vol. i. p. 44.
[2] The 'Vieux Cordelier,' No. 5. See 'Œuvres de Camille Desmoulins,' vol. ii. p. 213. Charpentier's edition.

leaving to the unhappy man no more than a shadow! Despair, disquiet, fear, had entered into the house, which Sylvain Maréchal had called in days past—how long past!—the dwelling-place of innocence.   There is a letter of Lucile's, broken-hearted and despairing, which she wrote to Fréron, then at Toulon, and which gives the keynote of this tragic time; it has been already quoted, but only partially, in the ' Histoire des Tribunaux,' p. 283, and in E. Lairtullier's book, ' Les Femmes célèbres de 1789 à 1795.'   It follows here, in its entirety, just as I copied it from the original.[1]

Fréron was far away; he had been absent for eight months at the siege of Toulon; he writes to Camille, ' You know I love your wife to madness;' he wishes his two children to be called, one Camille and the other Lucile (these children of Fréron's both died in infancy, as their namesakes died in the flower of their age). He misses the *lapin*, the friend of Bouli-Boula— Desmoulins' nickname—and of *Rouleau*—Lucile's nickname; he regrets ' the thyme and wild herbs with which Madame Desmoulins' pretty, dimpled hands had fed him;' he recalls the past; the idylls, the willows, the graves, and the bursts of laughter of that Lucile who read Young and Grécourt at the same time; he sees her ' trotting about in her room, gliding over the polished floor, sitting for a moment at her piano, and whole hours in an easy-chair, dreaming, giving the reins to her imagination, then making the coffee with a filtering-bag, behaving like a sprite and showing her teeth like a cat.'   What a sweet portrait of Lucile, and how one feels Fréron was right, more right than he thought perhaps, in saying he loved her, and that her

---

[1] This letter, with its strange orthography, will be found in the original in the Appendix.

melancholy, mingled with her sweet laughter, had charmed him. 'Farewell! madly, a hundred-fold madly loved *Rouleau,*' he said to her. And he mimicked her language after having described her attitudes. 'What is that to me? It is as clear as the day.' The 'rabbit embraces the whole warren, until he can return to frisk upon the grass of the Bourg-Égalité!' Then, thinking of Camille, of the 'Vieux Cordelier,' of the denunciations to which he was exposed, the future reactionist of the days following Thermidor advises—a thing to be noted!—that the *loup-loup* (Camille) should bridle his imagination with regard to his Committee of Clemency. 'It would be,' said Fréron, 'a triumph for the counter-revolutionists. Do not let his philanthropy blind him; but let him wage war to the knife with all these patriot-adventurers.' Now, it is this letter which Lucile answers, trying to make the friend at a distance understand the terrible and pressing danger of a situation of which he is ignorant.

'24th Nivôse, the second year of the Republic one and indivisible.

'Come back, Fréron, come back quickly. You have no time to lose; bring with you all the *Vieux Cordeliers* you can meet with; we have the greatest need of them. If it had pleased Heaven not to have ever dispersed them! You cannot have an idea of what is doing here! You are ignorant of everything, you only see a feeble glimmering in the distance, which can give you but a faint idea of our situation. Indeed, I am not surprised that you reproach Camille for his Committee of Clemency. He cannot be judged from Toulon. You are happy where you are; all has gone according to the wish of your heart; but we, calumniated, persecuted by the ignorant, the intriguing, and even by patriots; Robespière (*sic*) your *headpiece*, has denounced Camille to the Jacobins; he has had Nos. 3 and 4 read, and has demanded that they should be burnt; *he who had read them in manuscript. Can*

you conceive such a thing?[1]   For two consecutive sittings
he has thundered, *or rather shrieked,*[1] against Camille. At
the third sitting Camille's name was cancelled. Oddly
enough, he made inconceivable efforts to have the cancelling
reported ; it was reported ; but he saw that when he did
not think or act according to [*their*[1]] the will of a certain
number of individuals, he was not all powerful. Marius[2]
is not listened to any more, he is losing courage and vigour.
D'Eglantine is arrested, and in the Luxembourg, under
very grave charges. So he was not a patriot! he who had
been one until now! A patriot the less is a misfortune the
more.

'The monsters have dared to reproach Camille with having
married a rich woman. Ah! let them never speak of me ; let
them ignore my existence, let me live in the midst of a desert.
I ask nothing from them, I will give up to them all I possess,
provided I do not breathe the same air as they !' (Here let
me note a detail which gives a sinister air to this document,
about which hangs the savour of death. Lucile let fall a blot
of ink, and, her pen marking badly, she tried to make it better
by drawing lines and zigzags on the margin, which render
this letter still more curious and precious.) 'Could I but
forget them, and all the evils they cause us! I see nothing
but misfortune around me. I confess, I am too weak to bear
so sad a sight. Life has become a heavy burden. I cannot
even think—thinking, once such a pure and sweet pleasure—
alas! I am deprived of it. . . . My eyes fill with tears. . . .
I shut up this terrible sorrow in my heart ; I meet Camille
with a serene look, I affect courage that he may (*not lose his* ;[3])
keep up his.

'You do not seem to me to have read his five numbers.
Yet you are a subscriber. Yes, the wild thyme is *gathered,*
quite ready. I plucked it amid many cares. I laugh no
more ; I never act the cat ; I never touch my piano ; I dream
no more, I am nothing but a machine now. I see no one, I
never go out. It is a long time since I have seen the Roberts.

[1] Struck out by Lucile.   [2] Danton.
[3] Struck out.

They have got into difficulties through their own fault. They are trying to be forgotten.

'Farewell, lapin, (*thou*[1]) you will call me mad again. I am not, however, quite yet; I have still enough reason left to suffer.

'I cannot express to you my joy on learning that your dear sister had met with no accident [and in Paris]; I have been quite uneasy since I heard Toulon was taken. I wondered incessantly what would be their fate. Speak to them sometimes of me. Embrace them both for me. I beg them to do the same to you, for me.

'Do you hear! my *loup* cries out: Martin, my dear Martin, *here, thou art come that I may embrace thee*;[1] come back very soon.

'Come back; come back very soon; we are awaiting you impatiently.'[2]

Marius not listened to! We are calumniated, persecuted! D'Eglantine is arrested! 'I cannot even think.' What a picture! Cannot we imagine the forced smiles, the heavy hearts, and the pale faces? Nevertheless, Camille persisted in his enterprise, in spite of the advice given him.[3] Letters like the

---

[1] Struck out.

[2] Copied from the original.

[3] Dialogue between Camille Desmoulins and myself when his fifth number was about to come out:—

'Mon cher Camille, il faut de la prudence,
En toute chose. Eh ! m'en suis-je écarté?
Qu'ai-je donc fait ? J'ai dit la vérité ;
En homme libre, avec toute assurance,
Je veux la dire. Ah ! garder le silence
Serait trahir mon auguste devoir.—
Mais Robespierre est forcé de se voir
Dans vos portraits. C'est l'unique remède,
Pour le guérir. A femme ou fille laide
Il ne faut pas présenter un miroir.'—

'Le Chiffonier,' by P. Villet, author of the 'Rhapsodies.' Paris, at all rag-merchants, year VIII.

following, which reached him from the prisons, spurred him on, strung up his courage by echoing his cry for mercy.

' Quintidi, Nivôse.

'Eternal thanks for your noble and touching idea of a Committee of Clemency. But alas! they will cut down too many. At the moment when your fourth number was brought me yesterday, I was reading the eighteenth chapter of the philosopher Seneca's treaty on Clemency, and I had paused at those memorable words of Augustus : *Vitam tibi, Cinna, iterum do, prius hosti, nunc insidiatori ac parricidæ.* Citizen, as virtuous as you are enlightened, when you say that this Committee of Clemency would put an end to the Revolution, the proof of your words is in this same chapter of Seneca's : *Post hæc nullis amplius insidiis ab ullo petitus est.* May the genius of humanity, which has inspired you with so beautiful a commentary on the "*Let us be friends, Cinna,*" convince our rulers that there can be no Constitution without morals, and that justice is the best and only policy. Ah ! if they had the noble courage to say to the two thousand citizens whom they call *suspect,* "Let us be friends," with those two words they would save the Republic far more surely than with the million men armed for its defence.

'If I recover my liberty, the first use I will make of it shall be to converse with the friend whom misfortune has given me ; but I despair of it if we are to be dragged from Committee to Committee, and if the Convention, in its justice and its wisdom, does not abridge the length of this labyrinth.

'Must it then be, under the rule of liberty as under the iron hand of despotism, *that evil is poured out all at once, but good drop by drop !* Do not fear to compromise yourself by whatever your noble heart may inspire you with in my favour, and rest assured, man after my own heart and mind, that the strictest examination into my conduct and principles can never be too severe for my wishes.

' AMABLE LATRAMBLAYE.' [1]

[1] Unpublished letter.

On the other hand, Camille received letters demanding from him

And at the same time another faithful friend wrote encouragingly to Camille :—

' 11th Nivôse, year II.

' How I thank you, my dear Camille, for your precious gift! In truth, since the Revolution, I have not read anything which has afforded me so much pleasure! What a delightful night you have given me while on guard! Thanks to you, I found Cicero and Voltaire awaiting me there. My friend, I am not a fanatic, nor an enthusiast, nor a man to pay compliments ; but if I should happen to survive you, I mean to have your bust and to carve on it :—" Wicked men would have had us accept liberty kneaded together of mud and blood ; Camille made us love it, carved in marble and covered with flowers."

' Let Robespierre stick to the Committee of Public Safety,

accusations and proscriptions of the persons denounced in them. I will only quote one, taken from his unpublished papers :—

' 20th Nivôse, year II. of the French Republic, one, indivisible, and imperishable.

' LIBERTY, EQUALITY, OR DEATH.

' *Denunciation to the Committee of Public Safety.*

' *Pitt and Cobourg* have, perhaps, never to their knowledge had a more useful colleague than the puppet *Bouchotte.* His stupidities, his incapacity, and his negligence are equivalent to the greatest treachery.

' Rivalling his idiotic predecessor, whom I have followed closely for a twelvemonth, he has, contrary to the text of the decrees, withdrawn from the military levy a battalion of young men whom I offer to the Republic ; far from *sansculottising* the generals, he has manned the staff with fops and Royalists like himself, and, if possible, of even less value.

' He makes the Republic pay for seven hundred thousand able men, and a large number are incapable of service. He has supplied the armies with generals who are fools as well as rascals ; and retained thieves, brigands, and even nobles everywhere, even in the commissariat. Finally, I offer any information and disclosure the Committee may require concerning this petty captain of Esterhazy's.

' Health and fraternity.

' HÉDOIN, Republican.

' Born 1739; forty years in the army ; first Vice-President of the section Lepelletier, at Rheims.'

Danton to the rostrum, and you to your pen, and soon the
French will find they owe to you three an ever-increasing
happiness. But, the more I reflect the less I comprehend
your incomprehensible Lucile. What have I done to give
her so mean an idea of poor Polichinelle? Only yesterday
she would not lend me your paper for fear it should not be
to my taste.

'What! If I have loved liberty, even as it is roughly
sketched by artists often unskilful and unfaithful, was I not
sure to adore it when traced, after nature, by the painter who
has inherited the brushes and colours of Cicero, Lucian, Voltaire, and that child of Nature, Lafontaine!

'As a punishment, this Lucile, as ugly in mind as in body,
must send to her dear Polichinelle the MS. in which is "La
fleur que j'aime," your "Révolutions," all your works, and the
numbers present and to come of your "Vieux Cordelier."

'You may easily believe I should have much more pleasure
in fetching them myself; but, for fear of disturbing you, I
prefer giving you my address; thus you can let me know,
if, by any chance, you have a few minutes to give me at your
fire-side. You might as well come to see me one of these
mornings while I am getting up, and share the breakfast of

'POLICHINELLE.

'P.S. Although rather rare, I look upon the books I present
you with as more useful than valuable. They are the most
suitable for you which my little library affords, but the whole
is entirely at your service.

'Good-bye; I am chattering to you and forgetting that I
have stolen away from the guard-room for my dinner. I must
run back, and beg you will not spare the citizens *Rouleau,
Roulette,* and *Daronne,* for I have a little spite against them.'

Some days later Brune breakfasted with Camille,
but he was depressed, uneasy, full of mournful presentiments. Desmoulins, on the contrary, by a reaction
not uncommon to such excitable natures, had regained
confidence, and on Lucile saying to Brune, as she poured
out his chocolate, 'You see he must perform his mis-

sion,' 'Pooh!' Camille said, quoting Latin to please the lover of Horace, 'let us eat and drink, for to-morrow we die.' This was a frequent saying at this critical time.

M. D——, formerly a lecturer at the College which Camille had attended, met him in the Rue Saint-Honoré, a few days before his arrest. 'What are you carrying there, Camille?' he asked, pointing to a packet of newspapers under Desmoulins' arm. 'Some numbers of my "Vieux Cordelier;" will you have some?' 'No, no; they burn.' 'Coward!' returned Desmoulins. 'Have you forgotten that passage of Scripture, "*Edamus et bibamus, cras enim moriemur*"?'

'We die!' Poor Desmoulins little thought how truly he spoke. The rupture between Robespierre and himself was complete, as we have seen by Lucile's letter to Fréron. It is said that the rupture had its rise in Camille's having imprudently lent ' L'Arétin,' illustrated with obscene pictures, to Elisabeth Duplay, the youngest daughter of Robespierre's landlord. Maximilien's anger was great against Camille, 'this corrupter of youth.' This anecdote is, however, impossible to verify. Perhaps Robespierre was secretly vexed with Camille, because when he asked for the hand of Mademoiselle Adèle Duplessis, Lucile's sister, he had been very gently refused. I imagine the father, M. Duplessis, did not wish to give his second daughter to a political man. Hence his refusal, no doubt. It is probable that Camille pleaded his friend's cause. However that may be, Robespierre's heart reverted to the daughter of the joiner Duplay, whom indeed it is known he loved with a profound, austere affection.

The time was at hand when the rupture between

Camille and Maximilien was to be made public. On the 7th of January, at the Jacobins Club, two days after the appearance of the fifth number of the ʻVieux Cordelier,ʼ the question was under discussion as to whether Fabre d'Eglantine, Bourdon (de l'Oise), and Camille Desmoulins should be expelled from the society. Three times their names were called, and no one replied. ʻVery well,ʼ said Robespierre, ʻcite them before the tribunal of public opinion; let it judge.ʼ At that moment Camille presented himself. He was required to render an account of his connection with Philippeaux. Camille replied that the Club was deceived, and that the accusations brought against him were false. But this was not the real gist of the debate. The Jacobins wanted to blast the ʻVieux Cordelier.ʼ If Camille had come out vanquished, if *ʻpurifyingʼ* had been decreed, all would be over; the guillotine would be near at hand. At that time the way to the scaffold was made up of several stations; *ʻpurificationʼ* was the first. Camille had not spoken upon the chief accusation ere Robespierre demanded leave to speak.

ʻWhile energetically blaming the "Vieux Cordelier,"ʼ says Charlotte Robespierre, in her ʻMémoires,ʼ ʻMaximilien tried to justify their author. In spite of his immense popularity and his extraordinary influence, his words were received with murmurs. Then he saw that, in endeavouring to save Camille, he would destroy himself. Camille did not give him credit for the efforts he made.ʼ

The truth is that Robespierre, wishing to turn aside the wrath of the Jacobins, thought it necessary to sacrifice the work in order to save the author. ʻCamille,ʼ he said, with a certain irony, and in a dry tone which must have deeply irritated the impressionable Desmoulins, 'Camille is a spoilt child ; he had a good disposition ; bad company has led him astray. Saint-Just afterwards made use of these words in his murderous report, for which Robespierre furnished him with materials.

'Finally,' said Robespierre, in conclusion, 'we must deal rigorously with these numbers, which even Brissot would not have dared to acknowledge, but we must keep Desmoulins among us. I demand, for example's sake, that these numbers be burnt before this society.'

Burnt! burnt by the Jacobins, as the 'France libre' had been by order of the Toulouse Parliament! Truly, it was too much for Camille, who did not in the least understand Robespierre's aim. He drew himself up, looked Maximilien in his face, and said, in a clear voice, which contrasted with his usual stammering, 'Well said, Robespierre ; but I will answer with Rousseau : *Burning is not answering !*'

Robespierre was surprised at so sudden a retort. He did not expect it. He thought Desmoulins would understand the meaning of his tactics. 'His friend's' exclamation irritated him in his turn, and he changed his tone. 'Learn, Camille,' he said, 'that if you were not Camille, you would not be treated with so much indulgence! The way in which you attempt to justify yourself proves to me that your intentions were bad.' 'My intentions!' replied Camille; 'but you knew my intentions! Was I not at your house? Did I not read you my numbers ?' 'I only read one or two ; I refused to hear the others !'

In this way the duel of words went on, impetuous, hasty, retort succeeding retort, like rapid passes between fencers with uncapped foils; whilst the public, the witnesses, the excited crowd of the Cordeliers, eagerly watched both, with evident partiality for *Robespierre the incorruptible*, who had been Camille's defender a moment before, but was now his accuser. In vain did Danton intervene, trying to persuade Camille that 'he should not take fright at the rather severe lesson Robespierre in his friendship had just given him.' To appease him was impossible. The strife continued. 'Well then,' exclaimed Robespierre, 'let them not be burnt; let them be answered for.' And, amid the murmurs of the audience, a secretary read aloud the fourth number of the 'Vieux Cordelier.' Camille and Danton must even then have felt they were lost. On January 8 (19th Nivôse) the Jacobins again returned to the 'Vieux Cordelier.' The third number, that terrible document in which the word *suspect* resounds like the mournful refrain of a song, was read by Momoro, who, in June 1789, had been afraid to print 'La France libre,' and who now accused Desmoulins of moderantism. The reading was received with gloomy silence. Then Robespierre again spoke; to his mind Desmoulins was 'a whimsical mixture of truth and falsehood, of political talent and chimeræ.' Besides this, 'whether the Jacobins expelled or detained Desmoulins mattered little; *he was but an individual.*' The affairs of the public only had real importance. Its interests were just then menaced by two classes, the *citra*-revolutionists and the *ultra*-revolutionists; and these two factions 'understand each other like brigands in a wood.' 'And,' added Robespierre, 'Camille and Hébert are equally wrong in my eyes.'[1]

[1] See in Courtois' book the sketch of a speech in which Robespierre attacks both *factions* at once:—'One preaches severity and the other

Thus, after the month of January, Maximilien's project is quite plain; it was necessary for him to rid himself both of *modérés* and *exagérés*, of *indulgents* and *enragés*. The see-saw condition of his mind had come to an end. It only remained for him to strike.

Somehow this long discussion seemed to have turned to Desmoulins' advantage. He was not expelled from the club of the Jacobins, and the title of Cordelier was restored to him. He might think himself safe— *he was lost!*

At the end of this volume will be found the testimony of Robespierre's sister, in which she tries to make out that Maximilien really wished to save Camille. Authentic evidence proves that Robespierre drew up, for Saint-Just, an accusation of Desmoulins. The rough draft of a report, which was published by M. France in 1841 from the autographs, does not admit of a doubt that Robespierre inspired the *Chevalier porte-glaive.* What a strange destiny was Camille's, to be treated as vain, foolish, and versatile by him whom he had called in days gone by his dear Robespierre![1] Camille, as we have seen, was variable in his opinions about men. He had, for the most

---

clemency; one counsels weakness and the other folly. . . . The two factions *meet and blend with each other.'* Robespierre in this document calls Desmoulins' *libels* the *gospel* of the aristocrats, and treats Westermann as a *ridiculous braggart.*

[1] Robespierre's relations with his former fellow-scholar at Louis-le-Grand were odd enough. The two college friends lost sight of each other for a short time. Robespierre wrote to Desmoulins on June 7, 1790, to protest against an anecdote related by Camille. Robespierre did not say, on the little Dauphin applauding the Mirabeau decree on May 22, 'Oh! let the brat clap his hands!' In this letter Robespierre, stiffly enough, calls Camille *Sir* :—

'Sir,—I have read in your last article,' &c.

'You are quite in the right,' replied Camille, 'but you might at least salute an old comrade with a nod. I do not love you the less for

part, two judgments touching the same personage. One man alone had fascinated and conquered him, once and for ever; he whom he called, after 1791, *the stoutest athlete among patriots, the sole tribune of the people who could have obtained a hearing in the Champ de. Mars*—Danton; and Danton's influence urged him on to pity and to pardon. Therefore Camille broke finally with Maximilien.

The seventh number, which was destined to be a posthumous one, is full of direct, fiery, daring, and desperate attacks upon Robespierre; upon Vadier, who, on the 16th of July, 1791, said, in the tribune

being faithful to your principles, even though you are not faithful to friendship.'

Later, Camille said concerning Maximilien:

'One cannot speak of Robespierre without thinking of Pétion.'

' Deux gens de bien à Versailles vivoient ; '

as was said in the time of Turgot and Malesherbes.

In this same year (1790), in reference to Robespierre's speech in reply to Cazalès against military chiefs, martial law, &c.; and after having repeated these words of Robespierre's, that *orator of the people*, ' Do not let us place the fate of the Republic in the hands of military chiefs ; do not let us give way to the murmurs of those who prefer a peaceful slavery to a liberty bought by sacrifice, and who show us incessantly the flames of a few burning castles,' Camille expresses himself thus : ' Oh, my dear Robespierre ! it is not long since we were sighing together over our country's servitude, since, drawing from the same sources the sacred love of liberty and equality, amid so many professors whose lessons only taught us to detest our land, we were complaining there was no professor of cabals who would teach us to free it ; while we were regretting the rostrum of Rome and Athens, how far was I from thinking that the day of a constitution a thousand-fold more noble was so soon to dawn upon us, and that you, in the rostrum of the French people, would be one of the firmest ramparts of this budding liberty !' Finally, in his sixty-fifth number of the ' Révolutions de France et de Brabant,' Camille says again: ' Robespierre, not Robertspierre, as some journalists affect to call him, apparently thinking this name more noble and softer, and who are igno-rant that this deputy, no matter how he called himself, would always bear the most glorious name in France.'

of the NationalAssembly : ' I adore the monarchy and abhor the republican government !' upon David, ' who has dishonoured his art by forgetting that, in painting as in eloquence, the fount of genius is the heart;' upon Héron, La Vicomterie, &c. It is the song of the swan; a song of glowing indignation and of generous hate. But this song was not to reach the world until after the death of the singer.

IV.

The Dantonists and Hébertists were irrevocably condemned.

Hébert's friends tried to excite the Parisians to revolt in the spring of '94, but unsuccessfully. Carrier, who had returned from Nantes, spoke in the rostrum of the Cordeliers of 'a *holy insurrection.*' They made the attempt. Vincent carried a resolution that the picture of the ' Rights of Man ' should be veiled with black crape until the *moderates* were annihilated. Hébert threatened, stormed, and the *grande colère du Père Duchesne* waxed terrible. Vain threats. Saint-Just ascended the rostrum of the Convention, and denounced the Hébertists, whom he accused of being partisans of the enemy; and on the 24th of March Hébert, Momoro, Clootz, and Chaumette were executed.

The *Ultras* were no longer to be feared, it was the turn of the *Citras* to tremble. The Committees had broken up the revolutionary army; renovated and disciplined the Commune; regenerated—that is to say, weeded out, the Cordeliers. They now turned their whole strength against the Dantonists. To strike down Danton, to seize upon Camille, unpopular though they were in the eyes of the Club, would be no easy task.   How many members might not still start up to defend them !   And what audacity would it not require to accuse Desmoulins of *royalism* and Danton of treason !

The Committees manœuvred skilfully.   First they put aside Hérault de Séchelles, the only friend of Danton who sat on the Committee of Public Safety. Hérault, tired out and disheartened, allowed this to be done.   He was charged with having taken home with him the papers of the Diplomatic Committee; of having carried on a correspondence with Proly, Pereyra and Dubuisson, which was false ; and of having given shelter to an *émigrée,* which was true.   On the 26th *Ventôse* he was arrested, and the Convention confirmed the arrest, the next day, on the report of Saint-Just.   This Saint-Just, *the exterminating angel,* the *knight sword-bearer,* had returned from the army. of the North, to perform the office of accuser with unrelenting severity.   He spoke in his weak but resolute voice, with a sinister conciseness.   Of Hérault, and later on of the other Dantonists, he seemed, according to the report of an eye-witness, to say, by voice and gesture, ' You are only asked for a little impure blood.'

Hérault's arrest was a direct threat to Danton. His friends warned him.   They knew that Billaud-Varennes and Saint-Just were ready to ask for the heads of all the *moderate party.*   Danton shrugged his shoulders.   ' Nothing can be done,' he said.   ' Resist ? shed blood ? Enough blood has been shed ; I would rather shed my own.   *I prefer being guillotined to guillotining.'*   And when they spoke to him of flight, the grand soul of the patriot breathed forth his ardent love for France in words which will echo through the ages : ' We cannot carry our country on the soles of our shoes ? ' He repeated too, as did Camille, the dignified saying of the Duke of Guise : ' They would not dare ! ' (His answer was more coarsely worded.)

They did dare, however. A month previously Billaud-Varennes had denounced Danton to the Committee of Public Safety,[1] but Robespierre had risen in a fury, saying, ' You want to destroy the greatest of the patriots.' At the close of the night-sitting, which decided the arrest of Danton and his friends, Robert Lindet and the aged Rühl—who moreover had not signed the decree for the arrest—warned him, through Panis. ' Danton,' said Doctor Robinet (' Comment se tuent les Républiques,' articles on ' La Politique positive '), ' Danton had not gone out of his house. Sitting at the fireside in his study, leaning over the hearth lost in thought, from time to time he roused himself from his immobility to poke the fire violently ; then he would heave deep sighs and utter broken sentences. At other times he rose abruptly, and walked with long strides through the room ; then throwing his arms round his nephew, from whom we have this account, he embraced him with emotion.' Panis' visit, although he was agitated and troubled, and besought Danton to fly, did not move Danton. Yet the danger was urgent. Billaud-Varennes, who, according to Tissot, afterwards repented of having said it, had already coolly declared, with bitter resolution, ' Danton has conspired ; he must die ! ' Robespierre and Saint-Just agreed with him. Maximilien made the

---

[1] See the speech of Billaud, of the 9th *Thermidor*.

rough draft of the act of accusation, and gave it to Saint-Just, who put it into shape with the dexerity of hate, and the terrible implacability of conviction. Then, pale, overwhelmed, and careworn, Robespierre with-drew, in the March morning, to his little room in Duplay's house, where he remained shut up while Danton, Camille Desmoulins, Lacroix, and Philip-peaux were arrested.[1]

There are dark hours in a lifetime when mis-fortunes come all at once. While Camille's arrest was being deliberated upon at the Tuileries, the unhappy man received the following letter from his father—poor Madame Desmoulins was no more !—

'My dear Son,—I have lost the half of myself. Your mother is no more. I have always hoped for her recovery, which has prevented me from telling you of her illness. She died to-day, at noon. She is worthy of all our regrets ; she loved you tenderly. I embrace your wife, my dear daughter-in-law, very affectionately and sorrowfully, and little Horace. I will write more to-morrow. I am always your best friend,

'DESMOULINS.'

Camille's grief was profound ; his eyes were still red with tears when the patrol, charged with the duty of arresting him and Danton, took possession of the approaches to the *Cour du Commerce.* The first words that Camille uttered when he heard the dull sound of the butt-ends of the muskets on the pavement were : ' They have come to arrest me.' Lucile listened to him, and looked at him bewildered. She felt as if she

---

[1] The official Report of the arrests is signed by Billaud de Varennes, Lebas, Barère, Carnot, Prieur, Louis (du Bas-Rhin), Vadier, Collot d'Herbois, Vouland, Jagot, Dubarru, Saint-Just, Amar, La Vicomterie, M. Bayle, Élie Lacoste, Robespierre, and Couthon.

should go mad. Camille was calmer than might have been expected. He dressed himself, embraced his child, took from his library Young's ' Night Thoughts ' and Hervey's ' Meditations among the Tombs,' and then pressing to his heart his weeping wife, whom he adored, their lips met for the last time in an agonising kiss made bitter by burning tears.

Lucile, maddened, distracted, clung to him ; nothing but a swoon could have separated her from her Camille. Desmoulins and his friends were carried off to the prison of the Luxembourg.

Camille Desmoulins seemed to have lost all hope when he entered the Luxembourg. It has been said that he felt himself condemned beforehand. His letters, his admirable letters, the most touching and sorrowful that love could dictate to a human hand, are full of dreadful presentiments and sad reminis- cences. He sees from his prison window the garden of the Luxembourg, where he had passed ' eight years with Lucile.' 'A glimpse of the Luxembourg brings back to me a crowd of remembrances of our love.' How long ago that seems ! And he dreams of his wife, of his child, of Madame Duplessis. He is near them ' in thought, in imagination, almost by touch.' ' Alas ! no, Lucile is far away, little Horace has been torn away from him.' ' I throw myself on my knees, I stretch out my arms to embrace thee ; I shall never find my poor Loulou again. . . .' and a tear, dropped on the paper, cuts short this mournful sentence.

He tried, however, to encourage his friends. Why need he fear ? 'My eight republican books will prove my justification. They are a pillow upon which my conscience can rest while awaiting the sentence of the tribunal and of posterity.' Posterity ! Camille was right; posterity has not failed to absolve him, forgetting his sarcasms, remembering only his tears.

Camille was soon attacked by fever. He wrote to Robespierre. He could neither sleep nor eat. He had appetite for nothing except the soup that Lucile sent to him. 'Send me,' said he, 'a lock of your hair and your portrait.' When he slept for an instant, how rejoiced he was, for he dreamed of her! 'One is free in sleep. Heaven has had pity on me. For a moment I saw you in my dream; I embraced alternately you, Horace, and Daronne' (his mother-in-law) 'who was with you; but our little one had lost an eye by a disease which had attacked it, and the sorrow of this accident awoke me. I found myself in my prison. Day was breaking. . . . I burst into tears, or rather I sobbed, crying out in my tomb: "Lucile! Lucile!" Oh, my dear Lucile, where are you?'

This was the incessant cry of the unhappy man, to whom love and sorrow dictated these heart-rending words, which thrill one like a Shakespearian drama.

'Yesterday,' writes Camille, 'when the citizen who brought you my letter came back, "Well, you have seen her?" I said to him, as I used to say to the Abbé Landreville' (the confidant in Lucile's and Camille's love affairs), 'and I caught myself looking at him as if something of you lingered about him or his clothes.'

'I have discovered a chink in the wall of my room,' he continues, 'to which I put my ear, and I heard the voice of one who was ill and suffering. He asked me my name, and I told him. "My God!" he cried on hearing this name, falling back upon his bed from which he had risen, and I heard distinctly Fabre d'Eglantine's voice. "Yes, I am Fabre," he answered me; "but you here! has the counter-revolution come then ? " We dared not speak to each other, however, lest hatred should envy us this poor consolation, and if it became known, we should be separated and more closely imprisoned, for he has a fireplace in his room, and mine would be a handsome room if a dungeon could be so.

' I see the fate that awaits me,' writes Camille, after the first examination. 'Good-bye, my Lolotte, my dear Loup ; say farewell to my father. You see in my fate an example of the barbarity and ingratitude of men. My last moments will not dishonour you. You see my fears were well founded, and my presentiments true. I married a wife heavenly in her virtues ; I have been a good husband, a good son, I should have been a good father. I carry with me the esteem and regrets of all true Republicans, of all men of virtue and who love liberty. I die at the age of thirty-four years, but it is marvellous that I have walked for five years along the precipices of the Revolution without falling over them, and that I am still living ; and I rest my head calmly upon the pillow of my writings, which, too numerous as they may be, all breathe the same philanthropy, the same desire to make my fellow-citizens happy and free. The axe cannot touch *them.*

' I see that power intoxicates the greater part of mankind, and all say, like Dionysius of Syracuse, " Tyranny is a fine epitaph." But be comforted, disconsolate widow ! the epitaph of your poor Camille is still more glorious ; it is that of Brutus and Cato, the tyrannicides. Oh, my dear Lucile ! I was born to write poetry, to defend the unfortunate, to make you happy; to form a little Otaheite of our own, with you and your mother, my father, and some of our friends, who are after our own hearts. I have dreamed of a Republic such as all the world would have adored. I could never have believed that men could be so ferocious and so unjust. How could anyone think that a few jests in my writings against the colleagues who provoked me would have effaced the memories of my services ! I do not deceive myself in believing that I die a victim to these jests and to my friendship for Danton. I thank my assassins that they kill me with him and Philipp-eaux ; and since my colleagues have been cowardly enough to abandon us, and have lent an ear to calumnies that I do not know, but I dare affirm are of the grossest nature, I say that we die victims to our courage in denouncing traitors, and to our love of truth.

'We carry with us this knowledge, that in us die the last of the Republicans. Pardon me, my dear one, my true life, that I lost when we were separated, for occupying myself with memory. I had far better busy myself in making thee forget. My Lucile, my dear Louploup, my darling, I conjure you, do not call upon me ; your cries will rend my heart even at the bottom of my grave. Care for your little one ; live for my Horace ; speak to him of me. Tell him, hereafter, what he cannot as yet understand, that I should have loved him well. Notwithstanding my punishment, I believe that there is a God. My blood will wash out my faults, my human weaknesses ; and for the good I have done, for my virtues, my love of liberty, God will reward me. I shall see you again one day. O Lucile ! Annette ! Feeling as I do, is death so great a misfortune, since it delivers me from the sight of so many crimes ? Good-bye, Loulou, my life, my soul, my divinity on earth ! I leave thee to good friends—all the sensible and virtuous men who remain. Good-bye, Lucile ! my Lucile ! my dear Lucile ! Good-bye, Horace, Annette, Adèle ! Adieu, my father ! The shores of life recede from me ! I see you still, my Lucile, my beloved ! I see her, my Lucile ! my bound hands embrace you, and my head as it falls rests its dying eyes upon you !'

Was no voice raised in favour of Camille ? Did no help come ? Were his old friends dumb, his relatives inactive ? No. Legendre raised his voice in the Convention in favour of Danton and his friends. He demanded that the arrested deputies should be brought to the bar of the Convention. 'They ought to be accused or acquitted by you,' he said. But it was not to the bar of the Convention, but to the benches of the Revolutionary Tribunal, that Robespierre, Saint-Just, Billaud and Couthon resolved to drag the '*indulgents*'. Legendre's speech was drowned by murmurs.

Legendre had had the courage to say, ' I believe Danton to be as innocent as I am.' He was obliged to retract these words, and to make an apology during the same sitting. Legendre's courage did not last long.. 'Legendre,' said Robespierre, 'has spoken of Danton because 'he thinks a privilege attaches to this name. No ; we will have no more privileges ; and no more idols !' *No more idols !* The words were noisily applauded. Legendre trembled when he heard Robespierre add, ' I say that he who trembles at this moment is guilty.' He turned pale and stammered ; a little later, and he will call his friends 'the guilty ones.'

And then Saint-Just rose to speak : it seemed as if an angel of death had appeared upon the rostrum and was uttering words of doom. His first words were terrible, and he went straight to the point : ' The Republic is the people and not the renown of a few men !' He spoke with fierce pride of the sacred love of country which sacrifices everything, hurls down Manlius, drags Regulus to Carthage, sees Curtius precipitate himself into the gulf, unmoved, and of that doctrine which subjugates morality and right to a sinister theory. He denounced, in succession, Hérault, whom he called a conspirator ; Danton, whom he charged with cowardice ; Camille, whom he accused of shameful vices ; and Fabre d'Eglantine, whom he skilfully represented as the head of the faction. Why ? Because Fabre had been accused of forgery ; and it was necessary to stigmatise these men, whom they were not contented with putting to death, but must also dishonour. Saint-Just addressed his arrested colleagues, as if they had been present. ' False friend,' he said of Danton, ' only two days ago you spoke against Desmoulins, your tool, whom you had ruined !'

x

He said of Camille that he was first 'a dupe and afterwards an accomplice.' Then that he 'passed Camille by with contempt,' he was 'wanting in character.' He knew quite well that he was not striking at Camille, but at Danton. 'Poor Camille!' says Michelet with deep emotion, 'what was he? A charming flower which grew upon Danton; one could not be touched without the others being uprooted.'

I know nothing to compare with this speech of Saint-Just. It is like a murderous weapon of finely tempered steel. All of which he accused the Dantonists, of conspiring with Dumouriez, of complicity with Orleans, of royalism and corruption, was false, but it was put forward with such cleverness and such unmoved conviction! This man believed he was doing a duty. 'Fatal blindness!' cries M. Ernest Hamel, an historian who is friendly to Robespierre and Saint-Just. 'The error of a generous and stoical mind, which saw crimes where there was doubtless much frivolity and perhaps a little corruption.'[1] With all due respect for M. Hamel, can we accept this peculiar *stoicism* which immolates men because, looking at it from Saint-Just's point of view, we consider them frivolous, and 'perhaps' a little corrupt?

It was in the name of I do not know what super-human virtue, unattained by mortals who possess that weakness—a heart, that Saint-Just demanded the death of the Dantonists at the hands of the Convention. The Convention received Saint-Just's speech with unanimous and repeated applause. The members trembled before him, and Couthon, praising their docility, cried, 'The Convention moves, like armies, at quick march.'

[1] E. Hamel, 'Histoire de Saint-Just,' vol. ii. p. 164.

Less than four months afterwards it was against Couthon and his friends that the word 'quick march' was given. Lucile traversed Paris, trying to reach Robespierre's ear, that she might move him to pity. She tried to induce Madame Danton to go with her to Duplay's house. Robespierre was invisible. She then wrote. Her letter is that of a madwoman, but it is touching. M. Ed. Fleury has given it in full :—'Camille saw the growth of your pride. . . . But he recoiled from the idea of accusing his college friend, the companion of his labours. That hand which has often pressed yours, forsook the pen before its time, because it could no longer hold it to trace your praises. And you have sent him to death ! You have then understood his silence !' She wandered round the Luxembourg trying to see Camille, and to speak with him from afar by signs. She endeavoured to save him, and by the attempt lost her own life—a touching image of womanhood is this heroine of conjugal love, who determined to follow her husband even to death !

The charges, or rather the pretended charges, against the accused, were ready. 'We must divide the work between us,' Herman wrote to Fouquier ; 'it belongs of right to the public prosecutor.' The most petty informations, the most unworthy reports, the meanest accusations, were heaped together with perfidious skill. They took into account against General Westermann the letter of a Parisian soldier fighting in La Vendée, the son of Paton the tailor, who accused his chief of having led the soldiers badly. This letter, dated from Sables, August 27, 1793, with its astonishing orthography, witnesses against Westermann, accusing him of being a Royalist. 'If General Westermann had been a brave man, we should not have lost so many citizens at Châtillon.' And it was actually at the battle of Châtillon that Westermann, in order to encourage his soldiers, cried out to them, pointing to his breast, 'Comrades, kill me, or follow me to battle!' This Paton forgot. He hated his commander. And, further on, Paton says: 'I am very tired of fighting in La Vendée. The generals would like the war to last for ever.' What was Westermann's crime? He had repressed the excesses with which his troops revenged those of the Vendéans with inflexible severity. He declared that those who pillaged were savages. 'We burned everything as we passed,' says the letter before quoted, 'and we took the cattle and the corn, because the law ordered us; and then we were told that we were brigands, pillagers, and incendiaries.' And such a deposition as this, the ridiculous complaint of a cowardly discontented soldier, tired of fighting, is affixed to the charges against the General of La Vendée, accepted and signed by the public prosecutor!

Anonymous reports arose against the brothers Frey, 'who were born Jews under the name of Tropuscka; they are Moravians, and ennobled under the name of Schönfeld.'

'There are two brothers here, and eight in the service of Austria. The citizen, their sister, was baptised three years ago. There are also two sisters in Vienna, of whom one only has been baptised, and is kept by a German baron. The eldest Frey, who is in Paris, is married; his wife is in Vienna with her two daughters and a son of sixteen, who has been placed in the revolutionary army, where he passed for Frey's nephew. They are not known to have any money, but are in debt in Germany, &c.' These facts are certified to by Frederich Dietrichsten, a prisoner in La Force, before G.

Haussman, who signs the paper, and by C. Wartz, a physician living in the Rue Saint-André-des-Arts, at Mail's house, a vinegar-maker.[1]

In another report about the Freys, it was pretended that they had been sent as spies to France by Joseph II., the emperor 'being aware that the children of Israel surpass all other nations at this kind of work.' 'They are called the "gentlemen." They made their appearance, it is said, at Strasbourg. They kept open house and crept into the popular societies. The elder Frey insinuated himself into the Orleans Club of the Palais Royal. In one word, these so-called Freys are egotists, immoral persons, full of tricks and intrigues, who, under the mask of patriotism, gratify their passions by serving the enemies of the Republic who pay them.'

The ex-capuchin Chabot had married a sister of these Freys, and this was an unpardonable crime in the eyes of certain suspicious patriots.

The following documents received by Fouquier-Tinville reveal an odious and deplorable inquisitorial system :—

'Citizen Public Prosecutor,

'In compliance with the decision of the National Society of the Electoral Club, I send you in its name the enclosed papers, and beg you to send back the rough draft of the petition when you have made use of it, if you should think fit to do so.

'Health and fraternity,

'HUET, *Secretary.*

'Paris : this octidi Germinal : second year of the
French Republic, one and indivisible.'

And the resolution is added to this letter of Secretary Huet :—

[1] National Archives, C. W., 342. No. 648.

'On the twenty-fourth day of the second month of the second year of the Republic, the Electoral Club, seeing :—

' 1st. That no compact can ever be made between the good and the bad, between free men and slaves, between the defenders of tyranny and the conquerors of liberty, between the regenerators of France and savages :—

' 2nd. That the tyrants themselves, under whom the nation has grovelled during so many centuries, only reached the height of their crimes and the maximum of the execration of the people when they married foreign wives :—

' 3rd. That among all the women who shared their crimes, the Austrian women carried off the palm of evil, even from the Medicis :—

' 4th. That every man who wears foreign stuffs is a counter-revolutionist ; who, despising public opinion, dares to appear in the livery of our enemies, reducing our beloved artisans to poverty :—

' 5th. That at a time when the regeneration of morals has stigmatised celibacy among men, at a time when the immolation of so many patriots has left to the care of their brethren, for whose liberty they died, so many virtuous wives and daughters ; it is an immoral act, it is wasting the most precious treasures, to despise the virtues, the tenderness, and above all the misfortunes, of these Frenchwomen, whom the interests of the public reduce to celibacy ; and that he who seeks a foreigner, and above all an Austrian, is the enemy of these Frenchwomen, an *émigré* in heart, and one who deserves to be struck out of the list of Frenchmen, and off the roll of free men:—

' 6th. That he who thus despises public opinion, and takes to himself a foreign wife, subjects beforehand his patriotism to her charms, and cannot hope from such an impure stock for any but a mongrel breed, unworthy to be enrolled among the children of the country ; and, finally, that he degrades himself by thus adopting the manners of savages :—

' 7th. That as public opinion has pronounced that every man charged with high functions and missions who takes a rich wife is—1st, an avaricious man who aspires to riches and is unworthy to defend the cause of the unfortunate ; 2nd, a man suspected of venality, and who marries that he may hide under the pretence of a dowry the fruits of his treason ; it is, therefore, a crime to play with the decrees of public opinion, and to brave the execution of them.

' 8th. That the crime is greater in those whose functions are more eminent ; that venality destroys a great number of indigent people ; and is also worse when the culprit is a representative. . . .

' Compelled to make known to all true representatives the voice of public opinion resounding (constantly [1]) from the celebrated *Montagne*, compelled to honour morality in the face of the universe and to honour virtue (only [2]), the society declares that, in virtue of the eternal laws of reason which precede and dictate their decrees, the deputy Chabot (having allied himself with savages, and being united to the blood of our enemies [2]) has lost the esteem and confidence of patriots, by having married a foreign woman who is rich and an Austrian.

' The present resolution shall be carried by two commissaries to the Convention, to the Jacobins, and also sent to the sections, to the departments, to the commune, and to all patriotic societies, and shall be posted up.

Then, under the presidency of Grandvallet, the society ordered these minutes to be sent to the public prosecutor, in the name of the Electoral Club.

It was not altogether unreasonable that a man who ' united himself with a slave,' an Austrian, at the moment when France was invaded, should inspire horror. Public feeling, which acts by instinct, cannot comprehend certain alliances at certain times.

There are terrible epochs when the blood of different races cannot mix except on the battle-field. But, because a man is guilty of a weakness, is that a reason for accusing him of infamy, as the National Society

---

[1] Added.   [2] Scratched out.

of the Electoral Club accused Chabot, on septidi of
the third decade of Brumaire, in the second year,
under the presidency of citizen Rose?[1]   Let us also
remark, in passing, the strange difference that existed
between the extreme opinions of 1794 and those of
1871.   In 1794 a horror of foreigners was prevalent.
Patriotism is firm, resolute, deeply rooted, invincible

---

[1] Extract from the deliberations of the National Society of the Electoral Club, at a sitting in the ex-bishopric :—

Presidency of Citizen Rose.

From the minutes of the sitting of septidi of the third decade of
Brumaire.   What follows has been literally extracted :—

' A member denounced the great immorality of Chabot, deputy to the
Convention, and the way in which he had profaned his character as a
deputy by giving bail, with Bazire and Thuriot, for a great criminal, and
in giving his vote for establishing in the Convention a "right side," which
was always opposed to the Montagne.

' A report of what had passed on this subject was made to the Convention and to the Society of the Jacobins, from both of which societies these
three deputies have been expelled.

' The society decides to present a petition to the Convention to pray
that it may be declared infamous for a free man, after the epoch of 1789,
to be married to, or marry, a foreigner, until other nations shall have
become as free as the French nation.

' And that every deputy who shall prefer his own interests to the
public good shall be declared unworthy to represent the nation.

'(Signed)   EYNAUD, *Acting Secretary.*
' A true copy :
' HUET, *Secretary.*'

This Chabot, though little deserving of sympathy on the whole, took a
personal share in the acts of June 19, 1792 ; but he did more on the 9th
and 10th of August following.   After having traversed the Faubourgs, he
appeared, accompanied by a sapper of the Marseillais, before the Committee, and said with deep agitation, ' The people do not appear to be
greatly excited ; if at nine o'clock the sections have not risen, this brave
man you see here' (pointing to the sapper) 'shall cut off my head, my
bleeding body shall be dragged through the streets of Paris, and all the
friends of liberty will cry out, "Behold the work of the tyrant."'—' Memorial
or Historical Journal, Impartial and Anecdotical, of the French Revolution,' by P. C. Lecomte, 3 vols. year IX. (1801).

and profound in proportion as it is narrow. In 1871 cosmopolitanism, the idea of an international question, invaded and enfeebled men's hearts.

An anonymous denouncer asserted 'that Lacroix and Danton, while in Brussels, sent a carriage into France packed with table linen, belonging to the Governess of the Low Countries, and which was worth a considerable sum, about two or three hundred thousand livres. This linen'—so said this unsigned note—'was registered at the commune of Bethune, and hence it was discovered that the two deputies had appropriated the linen. This fact is well known to two representatives of the people, the citizens Le Bas and Duquesnoy.' So be it ; but was enquiry made of Le Bas and Duquesnoy into the truth of this denunciation ? No, certainly not ; neither Le Bas nor Duquesnoy, the future victim of Prairial, in the third year, can be cited as witnesses. Lacroix demanded that Pache, mayor of Paris, Legendre, Callou, Jagot, Robert Lindet, Gossuin, Merlin (of Douai), Guitton-Morvaux, Rose, 'who kept the tavern of la Grange-Batelière,' should be heard in his favour. This just request was not granted. Never was a trial more infamously conducted.

Among the papers more particularly relating to Camille Desmoulins is the following list of witnesses to be subpœnaed, in the handwriting of Fouquier-Tinville :

PANIS,
BOUCHIER SAINT-SAUVEUR,
ROBESPIERRE (scratched out).
ROBESPIERRE (scratched out again).

None of these witnesses were subpœnaed. As to the accusation, brought against Danton and Lacroix, of having stolen a carriage full of table linen ; they were obliged to defend themselves before the tribunal, without being allowed to bring forward witnesses in their favour.   'I bought six hundred livres' worth of table linen in Belgium ; it was a good bargain,' said Lacroix.   And said Danton :   'It will be seen from the minutes that there was nothing of mine in this carriage, which it is pretended was full of plate, except my clothes.'[1]

Fouquier and Herman endeavoured to collect crushing testimony against the accused.   There are manifest proofs in documents, which may be called bloodthirsty, of the animosity which they displayed against Danton and his friends.   Fouquier made a long list of criminating documents which were to be arranged and grouped in such a manner as to form, as it were, a fasces of instruments of death.   They gathered together all that Danton had said, that Desmoulins had written, that Hérault had thought, in the past.   The list is long ; the public prosecutor demands :—

'The extract from the deliberations of the Electoral Assembly of the department of Paris, in which Danton was named administrator of the department.

'What was said in the journals of the same date.

'The letter of Laz-Cazas (*sic*) which reports in detail a sitting of the Committee ; such details could not have been given by anyone but Hérault.

'*Documents to be sought for.*

'The journals of October and November 1792, in which Danton's opinions may be found relative to—

'Marat,

'Roland,

---

[1] Notes (destroyed) of Topino-Lebrun, Archives of the Prefecture of Police.

' The war with England.

' (In the margin, *Les Révolutions de Paris.*)

' Those journals in which are given the details of the sitting of the Committee of General Defence at which Danton was present with Pétion, Brissot, &c.

' The journals which announce the retirement of Danton to Arcis-sur-Aube at different times, and particularly after the affair of the Champ de Mars.

' The journals which mention the supper which took place at Talma's house, when Dumouriez went to Paris in the January of 1793, and the appearance of Dumouriez at the different theatres with Danton.

' Look for (under the seals at Debenne's)

' Details of May 31 and June 2, as to what Hérault, Lacroix, and Danton said relative to Henriot.

' The numbers of the "Vieux Cordelier."

' Philippeaux's letter to the Committee of Public Safety, and his other pamphlets.

' The portrait of Marat, by Fabre.

' Camille Desmoulins' speech as counsel for Dillon.

' Levasseur's pamphlet entitled " Philippeaux painted by himself."

' Philippeaux's catechism.'

It will be seen by this document how clever Fouquier was in grouping together the most dissimilar counts in an indictment, and in giving a culpable air to actions and words in which the accused had taken no part. To give but one instance—Hérault de Séchelles is made responsible for this letter of Las-Casas ;—he was unquestionably ignorant of its existence. It is interesting, as illustrative of the state of thought at this time, and it will be found at the end of the volume, among the supplementary documents. The thorough bad faith of the judges, who regarded these men brought before them for judgment as guilty in advance, comes out, plainly, from a study of this trial.

It would have been useless to appeal to their conscience, to sentiments of honour and justice, of which they were ignorant. Deaf to the voice of justice, Fouquier, Herman, and their followers aimed at nothing but the conviction of those whom the Committees looked upon as enemies. A voice of authority and integrity was, however, to make itself audible to Fouquier-Tinville. Camille Desmoulins' father, that respected servant of the law—whom we have seen, in his love of justice and meekness, conjuring his son to moderate his revolutionary ardour—came forth from his silence and retirement to petition those who were seeking the life of his son. In his touching and noble letter he does not demean himself to supplicate or to flatter, but, on the contrary, he preserves the calm and dignified attitude of a man who asks for justice, not favour. Having to beseech Fouquier, he does not call him 'his dear relation,' as Fouquier had called Camille. A magistrate, he speaks to a magistrate, gravely, but with a broken heart. This noble document has been hidden until now among the papers of the tribunal, but it will serve henceforth to complete the austere and venerable picture of the father of Camille Desmoulins :

'*To Citizen Fouquier de Thinville, Public Prosecutor*.

'Réunion-sur-Oise, formerly Guise,
15th Germinal, 2nd year of the Republic.

'Citizen and fellow-countryman,—Camille Desmoulins (my son), I speak from sincere conviction, is a true Republican, a Republican in feeling, in principles, and, so to speak, by instinct. He was Republican in heart and in choice before July 14, 1789, and he has been so in reality and deed ever since. His perfect disinterestedness and love of truth, two distinguishing virtues of his, which I have instilled into him from his cradle, and which he has invariably put in practice, have kept him on a level with the loftiest aspirations of the Revolution.

'Is it likely, is it not even absurd to suppose that he has changed his opinion, that he has renounced his character, his love for liberty, for the sovereignty of the people, his favourite and beloved design, at the moment when it has succeeded so brilliantly, at the moment when he had opposed and defeated the cabal of the Brissots ; at the moment when he had unmasked Hébert and his adherents, the authors of a deep conspiracy; at the moment when he believed the Revolution accomplished, or about to be so, and his Republic established by our victories and triumphs over our enemies without and within ?

'Are not these improbabilities sufficient to remove from my son even the shadow of suspicion? And yet he lies under the weight of an accusation as grave as I believe it to be calumnious.

'Confined to my study by my infirmities, I was the last, owing to the care that was taken to hide it from me, to hear of this event, which is calculated to alarm every true Republican.

'Citizen, I ask of you but one thing, in the name of justice and of our country—for the true Republican thinks of nought besides—to investigate and to cause the examining jury to investigate the conduct of my son, and that of his denouncer, whomsoever he may be ; it will be soon known which is the true Republican. The confidence I have in my son's innocence makes me believe that this accusation will prove a fresh triumph, as well for the Republic as for him.

' 'Health and fraternity from your compatriot and fellow-citizen Desmoulins, who until now has held himself honoured in being the father of the foremost and most unflinching of Republicans.[1]

'DESMOULINS.'

[1] Unpublished letter.
I quote as a cruel antithesis to this letter one addressed two years before to Camille by the public prosecutor Fouquier, who, less dignified than M. Desmoulins the father, lays a stress upon these words, ' My dear relation.' Camille was, in fact, his distant cousin :—

Fouquier did not receive this letter, doubtless, until it was too late, but it certainly did not disturb the serenity of the purveyor of the iniquitous severities of the law. Camille Desmoulins was already dead when the letter of the father, asking for the life of his son, arrived. Camille, who was imprisoned in the Luxembourg, underwent his first examination on the 12th Germinal ; we give it here in its entirety :—

'To-day, being the 12th day of Germinal, the 2nd year of the French Republic, one and indivisible, at 11 o'clock in the morning, We, François-Joseph Denizot, one of the judges of the revolutionary tribunal established in Paris by the law of March 10, 1793, without recourse to the Court of Appeal, and in virtue of the powers granted to the tribunal by the law of April 5 of the same year, assisted by F. Girard, to whom we have administered the oath as deputy-registrar of the tribunal in one of the halls of the auditory of the palace [erased in the printing] in the presence of Gilbert Lieudon, deputy public prosecutor ; have transferred [have had

'August 20, 1792.

'Until the ever-memorable day of the tenth of this month, my dear cousin, the title of patriot was not only a reason for exclusion from every office, but even furnished a motive for persecution; you are an example in your own person. The time has at length arrived, it is to be hoped, when true patriotism will triumph over and conquer the aristocracy ; it would be indeed wrong to doubt this, after the election of the patriotic Ministers just given to us by the National Assembly. I know them all by reputation, but I am not so happy as to be known to them. You alone can be useful to me through your acquaintance and connection with them. My patriotism is known to you, as well as my capacity in legal business. I flatter myself that you will make interest for me with the Minister of Justice to procure me a situation in his office or elsewhere. You know I am the father of a large family, and not well off. My eldest son, who has fled to the frontiers, has been a great expense to me, and is so still. I count upon your old friendship and your willingness to oblige. I recall to your remembrance Deviefville, our common relation, whose position is more distressing than I can describe to you.

'I remain, my dear cousin,

'Your most humble and obedient servant,

'FOUQUIER, lawyer.'

brought from prison scratched out] *to the prison* formerly called the Luxembourg, and caused the prisoners to be brought into a private room, where we have asked them their names, ages, professions, country, and place of residence.

'The undermentioned replied :

'*Q.* What was his name ?

'*A.* Benoît-Camille Desmoulins, aged thirty-four years, born at Guise, department of Aine, lawyer and a deputy to the National Convention, living in Paris, Rue du Théâtre Français.

'*Q.* Had he conspired against the French nation by wishing to restore the monarchy, by destroying national representation and the Republican government ?

'*A.* No.

'*Q.* Had he counsel ?

'*A.* No.

'We nominate, therefore, Chauveau de Lagarde.

'Examination read to accused, who affirmed it and signed with us.

'CAMILLE DESMOULINS.
'F. GIRARD.
'LIEUDON.
'DENIZOT.
'A. G. FOUQUIER.'[1]

Camille had been interrogated first. After him Danton, Lacroix, and Hérault underwent the same process. To the question, 'Have you conspired against the Republic?' Hérault replied that 'such horrible thoughts' had never entered his 'mind or his heart.' The attitude of the Dantonists was admirable. From the moment of their entrance into the Luxembourg until the hour they left the Conciergerie they were firm and dignified. Above all, Danton. 'I have in my character a good deal of the gaiety of a Frenchman,' he had said, on March 16, at

---

[1] Trial of the Dantonists. National Archives.

the Convention in his last speech but one.[1] This
gaiety did not forsake him on entering the court of
the prison, where he found Hérault de Séchelles
playing at nine-pins.

Danton said to the prisoners: 'When men do
stupid things, we must know how to laugh at them.
But if reason does not come back to this nether earth,
what we have seen is as nothing to what we shall see.'
He perceived Thomas Paine, the defender of the
Revolution against Burke, whom the votes of the
electors of the Pas-de-Calais had made a deputy to
the Convention, and the political tempest had made a
prisoner.

'What you have done for the happiness and the
liberty of your country,' said Danton to him, 'I have
vainly tried to do for mine! I have been less fortunate!' What a contrast between these two men, thus
meeting in the court of a prison—Thomas Paine, as
we see him in Arano's beautiful engraving, cunning
and supercilious, at once a cynic and an enthusiast,

---

[1] This is, in my opinion, the most characteristic of Danton's speeches.
It is, however, not one of his most important harangues.   After the
reading of a petition from an orator of one of the sections, praying to be
allowed to sing the praises of the Convention to the accompaniment of an
organ at the bar of the Assembly, Danton recalled the Convention not to
decency, as Marat had once done, but to good sense :—' The hall and the
bar of the Convention,' said he, ' are intended for the solemn and serious
utterance of the will of the citizens ; no one can be allowed to change
them into a mountebank's platform.   I have in my character a good deal
of the gaiety of a Frenchman, and I hope to preserve it.   I think, for
instance, we ought to give our enemies a ball ; but here we should rigidly,
and with dignity and composure, occupy ourselves with the greater interests of the country, discuss them, sound the " charge " upon all tyrants,
point out and strike down all traitors, and beat to arms against all im-
postors.   I do full justice to the civic loyalty of the petitioners, but *I
demand that henceforth nothing shall be heard at the bar of the Assembly
but reason in prose.*'   This was like a smile under the axe.   Three days
after, March 19, Danton delivered his last speech, which referred to the
accusation against Bouchotte. ·

with a long thick nose, slightly inclining towards a mouth of remarkable thinness, a pointed and grace-fully modelled chin, and a countenance indicative of both feeling and intellect. His costume is an elegant imitation of Franklin's, and his hair is powdered. He is a vigorous man somewhat past fifty. At his side stands Danton, upright, bold, almost defiant, and replying to this formalist like a true son of Rabelais, ' I am to be sent to the scaffold. Well, I shall go merrily ! '

The prisoners were at first confined *au secret*, but when the indictment had been made known to them, they were conducted to the Conciergerie. Lacroix and Danton went smiling, Philippeaux looked proud and unmoved, but Camille was sorrowful. ' On just such a day as this,' said Danton, on arriving at the Concier-gerie, ' I got the Revolutionary Tribunal established ; I beg pardon for it from God and from men ! But then, it was not out of inhumanity ! I meant to pre-vent fresh massacres like those of September ! ' He spoke aloud in his prison, so that the others might hear. ' I leave everything in a muddle,' he repeated ; and he added : ' It is better to be a poor fisherman than to govern men ! '

On the 13th *Germinal*, the accused—condemned beforehand—appeared at the tribunal. In order to degrade Danton, he was coupled with a robber, d'Espagnac. The ' *fauteuil* ' was given to Fabre d'Eglantine. The jury had been taken from among the *solides* : they were Renaudin, the musical-instru-ment-maker, whom Camille in vain challenged ; Trinchard ; Leroy, nicknamed *Dix-Août*, Desbois-seaux, Lumière, Souberbielle ; Topino Lebrun, who afterwards testified, in history, against the infamy of such a trial. Whatever M. Ernest Hamel may say in his conscientious ' Histoire de Robespierre,' it is perfectly true that Souberbielle said to one of the jury whom he saw weeping at the idea of condemning Danton, 'Which is more useful to the Republic, Danton or Robespierre ? ' ' Robespierre.' ' Very well ; then Danton must be guillotined.' M. Moreau-Chaslon has related the anecdote on the authority of Dr. Dubois (of Amiens), who had it from Souberbielle himself.

The judges were Herman, president, with Masson-Denizot, Foucault and Bravet as assessors. Fouquier-Tinville and Fleuriot-Lescot, his deputy, were also present.

' I am thirty-three, the age of the *sans-culotte* Jesus ; a critical age for every patriot,' replied Camille, on being interrogated.

' My name is Georges-Jacques Danton, law-adviser to the former Council, and afterwards a revolutionist and representative of the people,' replied Danton. ' My dwelling ? Soon to be nowhere ; after that, in the Pantheon of history. Formerly street and section Marat.'

Hérault de Séchelles, Chabot, Bazire, Delaunay (d'Angers), Lacroix, Fabre, Philippeaux—all of them de-puties—Westermann,[1] the Abbé Sahuguet d'Espagnac, Junius Frey and Emmanuel Frey—Chabot's brothers-in-law—Jacques Luillier, attorney-general of the depart-ment of Paris (the only one who was acquitted), Deiderichen, solicitor to the court of the king of Denmark, and André Guzman, a Spaniard ; all an-

---

[1] Westermann's answer was sublime : ' I demand to be presented naked to the people,' he said. ' I have received seven wounds, all in the front ; I have received but one in the back—it is this indictment !

swered in their turn. The oldest of these men was forty-one; the youngest, Claude Bazire, who died because he would not desert Chabot, was twenty-nine. By coupling the Austrians, the Spaniard, and the Dane with the Dantonists, and mixing up the matter of the suppression or falsification of the decree of the 17th *Vendémiaire* concerning the *Compagnie des Indes*, which referred to Fabre, with the accusation touching Danton, it was intended, I repeat, to discredit the whole '*batch*' in public opinion. Danton was quick to feel this, and protested against being confounded with scoundrels. Moreover, he boldly confronted the Public Accuser, and his powerful voice drowned the tinkling of the president's bell. 'Do you not hear my bell?' cried Herman. 'A man defending his life despises a bell and cries aloud,' replied Danton. This famous trial lives and breathes in the notes of Topino-Lebrun, which will be found at the end of this volume, and which utterly discredit Coffinal's version of it.

While they were judging, or rather sacrificing, the Dantonists, the mob, anxious, uneasy, yelling, *making a tail*, as we call it, from the door of the old Court of Appeal (it was the hall in which the Revolutionary Tribunal held its sittings, and it was burned in May 1871), filled the whole of the hall now-a-days called the *Pas-Perdus*, and the Cour du Harlay, skirted the walls of the Palais de Justice, stretched as far as the quay, thronged the Place Dauphine, made a bend at the Pont-Neuf, and reached to the Mint. This surging sea of human beings literally throbbed at every incident of which the hall of the formidable tribunal was the scene. Danton's every word was repeated as if by electricity, passed on from mouth to mouth, and instantaneously reached the Mint, thanks to this human telegraph. The thunder of Danton's voice was like the match to a train of gunpowder.[1] Michelet has related, and attested by witnesses, that the windows of the revolutionary tribunal being open, the sound of Danton's voice could be heard on the other side of the Seine.

And what said Danton? Never did man defend a menaced life with so much courage and yet so much disdain. Confronted with the guillotine, the tribune, for a moment jaded and downcast, once more became a Titan. David's pupil, the painter and juryman, Topino-Lebrun, who was afterwards executed, has transmitted to us, in his notes, the correct version of Danton's last speech.[2] While Danton spoke, Topino-Lebrun wrote. The juror's notes, unique in history, were burnt in the month of May 1871,

---

[1] These authentic and accurate details were given to the late M. Labat, senior, the director of the archives of the Prefecture of Police, who transmitted them to us through one Collet, employed, in 1793, at the Hôtel de Ville (stores office). The same man, on going to the town hall to his usual post on the 10th Thermidor, perceived a large crowd in front of the Hôtel de Ville. A sentinel asked him, 'Where are you going?' 'To my office,' replied the official. 'But do you not see what is passing?' some one said to him. 'What?' '*What* is passing or *who* is passing, which ever you like.' Collet looked; between two ranks of soldiers were marching the officials at the Hôtel de Ville. The scaffold was then not far off for them.

[2] François-Jean-Baptiste Topino-Lebrun, born at Marseilles in 1769, was sent to Rome to study painting Here he met with David, who took him back to France as his pupil. More than once in his functions as a juror, instead of *daubing with the red*, according to his master's saying, he was merciful and acquitted; his Republican convictions were profound. He was implicated in Babeuf's affair, but acknowledged to be innocent; later, however, in 1800, he was arrested as an accomplice of Arena, in that affair in which the police of Fouché played a prominent part, and was condemned and executed with J. Arena, Cerucchi, and Demerville. He asked to die with his face unveiled. It may be safely stated that Topino-Lebrun was innocent. Of his pictures there are very few. At the exhibition of 1797 he exhibited a Death of Caïus Gracchus, which the *Directoire* gave to the town of Marseilles.

in the Palais de Justice, with many other valuable documents of a similar kind. Fortunately, owing to the kindness of the late M. Labat, I had already taken a copy of these notes. I had then no notion that they would be destroyed and that I should have preserved them to history.

Nothing can exceed the sublimity of Danton's defence. The notes of Topino-Lebrun faithfully give us its incoherence, its singularity, its surprising mingling of heroism and magnificent buffoonery. Fancy one of Shakespeare's characters blending tragedy with comedy, and casting his sarcasms in the teeth of his accusers, and you have Danton. He jested, he brought forward proofs of his innocence, he thundered, he sneered; he was crushing; he was superhuman in his audacity and profoundly human in the words, all on fire with pity and gentle hardihood, that found their source in his inmost feelings, in his breast, in his heart. With what dignity did he spurn the shameful accusations heaped upon him! How high he held his head before insult! How he seemed to dilate and grow before his abashed enemies, who indeed were able to kill his body, but could not tarnish his fame!

' I sold to the enemy!' he cried. 'A man of my stamp is priceless. Where is the proof? .... Let him who accuses me, according to the Convention, give the proof, *the semi-proofs*, the signs of my venality!'

And when he was opposed by the pretended testimony of an anonymous *patriot.* 'Where is this patriot? Let him come hither! I challenge contradiction! Let him come forward!'

Then, turning round, like a wounded lion, he faced those of his opponents whom he knew and whose hatred had betrayed itself. 'Billaud-Varennes,' he said, 'cannot forgive me because he was once my secretary!' He dwelt, with the pride of a soldier after the fight, on the active part he had taken in the deeds of August 10; he showed in figures the sums entrusted to him for his mission to Belgium, and fully accounted for the expenditure. His hands were clean.

> 'I had 400,000 *livres*; 200,000 *livres* for secret service; I spent them in the presence of Marat and Robespierre. I gave 6,000 *livres* to Billaud for the army. I have accounted for 130,000 out of the other 200,000; and as for the rest, I handed it to Fabre, empowering him to pay the commissioners sent to the departments. He was cashier, and I only employed him because Billaud-Varennes had refused. I still believe Fabre to be a trustworthy citizen.'

Certainly Danton defended himself there in a manly and convincing manner; but his heart prompted the truest and most mighty eloquence, when, overflowing with the love of his country and the Republic, he besought his enemies to forget their resentment, as he forgot his anger, to think of nothing but France and the dangers still threatening her. 'Let patriots rally round each other, and then, if we can subjugate ourselves, we shall triumph over Europe.' 'I would embrace my enemy,' he added, with that Shakespearian vehemence of his; 'I would embrace him for the sake of the country, for which I would willingly give my body to be devoured!'

In the presence of death there came to him a clear perception of the morality even of that sanguinary Revolution in which 'brethren turned enemies' would destroy each other. Each he held to be useful in his turn, even the fiercest. 'Marat, with his volcanic temperament; Robespierre, tenacious and firm.' 'And I,' he added, '*I was useful in my way!*'

Then, at last, disgusted and disheartened by the attitude of the tribunal; 'I am refused any witnesses,' he said, shrugging his shoulders, 'so I will defend myself no longer!' 'I beg to apologize,' he added, as he sat down again, 'if I have spoken with too much warmth. It is my nature.'

And with one last cry of haughty prophecy: 'Before three months are past,' he said, 'the people will tear my enemies to pieces.'[1]

It is easy to conceive that sayings such as these, repeated, as we have seen, by the anxious crowd, who began to manifest its sympathy with the accused (nothing works up the masses so much as physical courage, and a lofty attitude in the presence of death); it is easy to conceive that such a defence seemed dangerous to the judges of the Revolutionary Tribunal. They turned pale as they sat.

In the papers relating to this trial (c. iv. 342), in the National Archives, are to be found proofs of the confusion into which both Herman, the president, and Fouquier-Tinville, the prosecutor, were thrown. They passed slips of paper to each other, covered with hasty writing, and which, having remained among the documents, testify to their uneasiness at Danton's attitude, when, with head erect and mighty voice, the accused became the accuser.

'*To Fouquier,*' wrote Herman. '*In half an hour I shall suspend Danton's defence; we must enter into greater detail.*'

Fouquier to Herman: '*I have a question to put*

---

[1] We give in the 'Pièces Justificatives' all we have been able to preserve of Topino-Lebrun's valuable notes.

to Danton with respect to Belgium, when you have finished yours.' 'We must,' says another note, 'only broach the question of the business in Belgium with Lacroix and Danton, and when we have gone so far (*a dash*) *we must get on.*'

We must get on ! By this one saying the true aspect of the trial is placed before us. In fact, it did *not get on.* On the 13th *Germinal* (3rd April) Herman, taking fright at the vigour of the accused, had abruptly. adjourned the court, and Fouquier went to enquire of the Committee if it were necessary to hear the witnesses whom the accused demanded should be subpœnaed. The answer was in the negative. On the 14th *Germinal*, Danton electrified his judges, and Desmoulins moved the bystanders to pity. On the 15th, the accused, being denied their witnesses, energetically protested against this violation of right, and Fouquier addressed himself to the Convention to obtain its help against their '*indecorum*.' On the 16th, the Dantonists, already destined to the scaffold, were refused permission to speak. It was necessary to impose silence upon those formidable lips, before they could be sealed by death.

'Provided they let us speak *freely*,' Danton had said, 'I am sure of confounding my accusers ; and if the French nation is what it ought to be, I shall be obliged to ask mercy for them !'

Who knows if this magnanimous dream of Danton's (the saying, it is well known, is Royer-Collard's) would not have been realised, if Fouquier and Herman had not suddenly called to their aid the most iniquitous of decrees ?

When, later, Fouquier-Tinville had himself to appear before his judges, the evidence of Nicolas-

Joseph Pâris, called Fabricius, registrar to the Revolutionary Tribunal, revealed the odious machinations of this trial of the Dantonists :

'It was in this affair that the deponent (N.-J. Pâris) saw the Committee of Public Welfare and General Safety employing the most refined Machiavelism, and Fouquier as well as Dumas lent themselves basely and willingly to the perfidious projects of these two Committees, who wanted to sacrifice the most enlightened citizens and the stoutest defenders of our liberty, that they might more surely establish their own tyranny and the barbarous system they have carried on since. This is what the deponent saw and heard in the course of that affair, for ever memorable by the crimes then committed, and a lasting misfortune for the country. At eleven o'clock the accused were brought into court. After the reading of the indictment, Westermann and Sulier were sent for, and tacked on to Danton, Camille and Philippeaux, as the latter had been to d'Eglantine, Chabot and Despagnac, in such a way that, in this matter, three groups of persons were included who had never seen or known each other ; a refinement of perfidy often made use of by the Committees and still oftener by Fouquier, confounding men of the highest probity, the most intrepid defenders of our liberty, with mean scoundrels and declared enemies of the Revolution. At this sitting Camille Desmoulins challenged the juror Renaudin, giving his reasons for the challenge, which seemed to be well founded. Fouquier ought to have prayed the tribunal to decree according to the challenge, but they wanted a juror like Renaudin too much, and they took good care not to accede to the challenge ; they did not even take it into consideration. The accused seeing a marked partiality on the part of the tribunal, which was surrounded by members of the Committee of General Safety, who were behind the judges and the jury, demanded that several deputies, to the number of sixteen, should be heard as witnesses. Danton also prayed that the tribunal should write to the Convention, to demand that a committee, composed of its members, should be nominated to receive the protest that he, Camille, and Philippeaux wished to make against the system of dictation exercised by the Committee of Public Welfare.   These demands were not acceded to ; they were rejected by the president and by Fouquier and his worthy friend Fleuriot, who filled, conjointly with Fouquier, the post of public prosecutor ; and as the tribunal had no valid reason for opposing a demand that could not be refused without injustice, the president broke up the sitting.

' The next day the hearing began very late ; some questions were put to one of the accused. Danton asked leave to speak that he might reply to the accusations brought against him ; it was refused at first, under pretext that he should speak in his turn ; he insisted ; at length leave could not be denied him any longer ; he took the indictment, and as every count was unsupported either by proof or by documents, and even devoid of any probability, it was not difficult for him to justify himself. A great part of the audience applauded his justification ; this was not what the tribunal wished. The president withdrew his permission under the pretext that he was tired and that each prisoner must be heard in his turn. Danton would not be silent until the president had promised that he should be permitted to speak the next day in refutation of the other counts of the indictment which he had not been allowed time to touch upon ; and then the sitting was brought to a close.

' The next day the hearing again began very late, so that the time might be taken up and none left for the dreaded truth to come to light. Before the end of the three days, after which it was proposed to tell the jury that they were sufficiently informed as to what had happened, the accused having entered, Danton demanded leave to continue his justification ; this was refused him on the pretext that the other accused must be interrogated concerning the acts imputed to them. Danton, Camille, Philippeaux and others again demanded the presence of some deputies who were their colleagues, and that the tribunal should write to the Convention in order that a commission might be nominated to receive their protest, and appeal to the people against the refusal to hear those witnesses. It was at this juncture that Fouquier, instead of acceding to the just and well-founded claims of the accused, wrote a letter to the Committee of Public Welfare, in which he described the accused as in a state of revolt and demanded a decree. It was a decree of outlawry that Fouquier demanded, as will be seen by the sequel ; he wanted it badly, as for an instant virtue and innocence had made crime turn pale. Even Fouquier and his worthy associate Fleuriot, atrocious as they were, the judges and the jury, were thunderstruck before such men, and for one moment deponent thought they would not have the daring to sacrifice them.' He did not then know the odious means employed to this end, and that a conspiracy was being fabricated at the Luxembourg, by the aid of which, and Fouquier-Tinville's letter, the scruples of the National Convention were overcome and a decree of outlawry was obtained. This fatal decree arrived, it was brought by Amar and Vouland. Deponent was in the Hall of Witnesses when they arrived ; they were pale ; anger and terror were painted on their countenances, so much did they seem to fear their victims would escape death ; they greeted deponent, who, wishing to know what there was fresh, accosted them. Vouland said to him : " *We have them, the scoundrels ; they were conspiring at the Luxembourg.*" They sent for Fouquier, who was in the court. He appeared at once. On seeing him, Amar said to him : *"Here is what you want."* It was the decree of outlawry. Vouland said : " *Here is something to put you at ease.*" Fouquier replied with a smile : "*We wanted it badly enough.*" He re-entered the court with an air of satisfaction, and read aloud the decree and the declaration of the iniquitous Laflotte, which everyone knows ; the accused recoiled with horror at the recital of such a falsehood. The unhappy Camille, hearing his wife's name, gave vent to cries of distress, and said : " The wretches, not satisfied with assassinating me, they will kill my wife too ! " During this scene, distressing to honest and feeling hearts, the members of the Committee of General Safety, placed below the benches and behind Fouquier and the judges, were rejoicing with barbarous glee at the despair of the unfortunate men whose death they were compassing. Danton saw them and pointing them out to his companions in misfortune, said: "*Look at those base assassins, they will hunt us to death.*" The accused demanded leave to show the absurdity and improbability of this conspiracy ; they were answered by the breaking up of the sitting. During the three days which had elapsed since the commencement of this affair, the members of the Committee of General Safety, and particularly Amar, Vouland, Vadier, and David, had not left the court. They came and went, fidgetted about, spoke to the judges, the jury and the witnesses, told all comers that the accused, Danton particularly, were wicked men, conspirators. Dumas, Artur and Nicolas did the same. The members of the Committee of General Safety corresponded from thence with the Committee of Public Welfare. The next day was the fourth day ; the members of the Committee of General Safety were at the tribunal before nine o'clock. They went to Fouquier's private room, and when the jurors were assembled, deponent saw Herman, the president, with Fouquier, come out of the jury room. At this time Amar, Vouland, Vadier, David, and other deputies known to deponent as members of the Committee of General Safety, were in the refreshment room (*remained* [1]) next to the jurors' room, from which what took place in the latter was audible. Deponent is ignorant of what passed between Herman, Fouquier and the jury ; but Topino-Lebrun, one of them, told him that Herman and Fouquier had persuaded them to declare that they were satisfied with the evidence, and that, in order to bring them to that determination, they had painted the accused in villanous colours, as conspirators, and had displayed a letter which they said came from abroad and which was addressed to Danton. The court opened, and the jury declared themselves satisfied with the evidence.

'From that moment the accused appeared no more in the court. They were shut up separately in the prison and sent to the scaffold on the same day by Fouquier.[2] While the jury

---

[1] Erased in the minutes.

[2] Written in the margin. Nevertheless several witnesses were summoned at Fouquier's request; only one was heard on the first day, and he spoke in exculpation of the accused.

was deliberating, the deponent was in the registrar's office below. He heard a noise in the direction of the staircase which led to the jury-room ; on going to the entrance of the office, he saw the jurymen coming out, with Trinchard at their head. With the exception of a few, they looked like madmen ; rage and anger were pictured in their countenances. As Trinchard approached with a furious air, and using the most violent gestures, he said : " *The rascals shall perish.*" Not wishing to witness such horrors any longer, deponent withdrew, groaning over the misfortunes which were overwhelming the Republic and those still greater which such tyranny presaged. The next day he went to the tribunal with the firm resolution that it should be for the last time, being determined to give in his resignation. Fouquier having asked at the registrar's office for a copy of the list of the jury, deponent took it to him, wishing to know what use he was going to make of it. He was in the refreshment room ; he took his pencil and by the side of several names he made a + on the margin. Deponent perceived that he marked with an *f* one who had been concerned in the business of the day before. He made a remark to that effect. Fouquier replied : "*He is fond of reasoning, and we don't want people who reason; we want this business done with.*" Deponent could not restrain a movement which showed he did not approve ; he observed it, and looking fixedly at deponent, he said : " Moreover, it is what the Committee of Public Safety wills." [1]

What more dramatic than such a recital as this, so terrible in its candour ? Fabricius relates this tragic episode as no other could. In the autograph MS. of this deposition, it is easy to read the word *weak* ('foible') effaced, which explains the letter *f* that Fouquier-Tinville used. The public prosecutor was,

[1] National Archives (Fouquier-Tinville's trial, deposition of Pâris, *alias Fabricius, Ventôse,* year III. portfolio W, 501). Fabricius was arrested the day after that on which Fouquier looked at him so fixedly. The decree of the 22nd Thermidor gave him his liberty and his post at the tribunal.

otherwise, as has been seen, fully satisfied, and he had not been kept waiting for the demand he addressed to the Convention.

'We foresee that the only way to make them keep silence,' he had written, ' would be by a decree.'

The decree was made on the 15th Germinal after a report of Saint-Just, to which was added the reading, demanded by Billaud-Varennes, of the denunciation of the spy, Alexandre Laflotte, who accused Arthur Dillon of having joined with Lucile Desmoulins to effect the escape of the accused.

Saint-Just found sophisms with which to crush his enemies, condemned from the first. He turned even their indignation into a crime. ' *What innocent man,*' he said, ' *has ever rebelled against the law? We want no other proofs* of their criminal attempts than this audacity.' We must quote, besides, the most striking passages of this report which Vouland and Amar brought in with such good will. The fragments of phrases that are printed in italics are underlined in red pencil (by Fouquier, no doubt) in the original :

Extract from the minutes of the National Convention, the fifteenth day of Germinal, the year II. of the French Republic, one and indivisible.

REPORT MADE IN THE NAME OF THE COMMITTEES OF PUBLIC WELFARE AND GENERAL SAFETY.

' The public prosecutor at the Revolutionary Tribunal *has informed us* that the revolt of the culprits has caused the deliberations of justice to be suspended, until the National Convention shall have deliberated.

'You have escaped dangers, the greatest that have ever threatened liberty ; now all the accomplices are discovered, *and these criminals at the very feet of justice,* intimidated by the law, divulge their secrets. Their despair, their fury, all announce that their apparent good faith was the most hypocritical snare ever laid for the Revolution. What innocent man ever rebelled against the laws ? *We want no other proofs of their criminal attempts than this audacity.* What ! the men whom we have accused of having been the accomplices of Dumouriez and d'Orléans, the men who have but made a revolution in favour of a new dynasty, the men who have conspired for the misfortune and the slavery of the people, *put the finishing touch to their infamy.*'

'If there are men who are true friends of liberty, if the energy which belongs to those who have undertaken to deliver their country is in their hearts, they will see that there are no more hidden conspirators in Paris, but that these are *barefaced* conspirators, who, counting upon the aristocracy with which they have been acting for several years, call down the vengeance of crime upon the people. No ! liberty will not recoil before her enemies, and the coalition is discovered. *Dillon,* who ordered his army to march upon Paris, has declared that the wife of Desmoulins had received money in order to promote a rising for the assassination of patriots and of the Revolutionary Tribunal.

'We thank you for having put us in the place of honour. Like you, we will shield our country with our bodies. Death is nothing provided the Revolution triumphs ; the day of glory was that on which the Roman Senate fought against Catiline. Such a day would consolidate the public liberty for ever.

'Your Committees answer to you for heroic watchfulness. Who can refuse you his veneration in this terrible moment when you are combating for the last time the faction which was indulgent to your enemies, and which now regains all its fury to fight against liberty ?

'Your Committees hold life cheap ; they set a high price on honour. People ! You shall triumph. But may this experience make you love the Revolution for the perils to which she exposes your friends ! *It was unexampled that your justice should be insulted,* and if it has ever been so, it was only by insensate *émigrés* in prophesying tyranny. These new conspirators have offended the public conscience. What more do we want to complete our conviction of their crimes? Unhappy men! They confess their crimes *by resisting the laws.* It is only criminals whom stern equity terrifies. How dangerous were all those who hid their plots and their audacity under the mask of simplicity. At this moment there is *a conspiracy in the prisons in their favour.* At this moment the aristocrats are bestirring themselves; the letters that are about to be read to you will show you your danger.

'Is it by a privilege that the accused are insolent? Let us then recall the tyrants Custine and Brissot from the grave; *for they had not, at least, the terrible privilege of insulting their judges.*

'In the country's peril, in the post of majesty in which the people has placed you, mark the distance which separates you from the culprits. It is with these views that your Committees propose to you the subjoined decree (side A).

'And upon the motion of a member, the National Convention decrees that the report of the Committee of Public Welfare, the official report of the administrators of the department of police of the township of Paris, shall be sent to the Revolutionary Tribunal with an injunction to the president to read them aloud during the sitting.

'Decrees further that the report and the papers be printed and inserted in the records.

'*Signed by the inspector,* AUGER.

'Compared with the original by us, Secretaries to the Convention, at Paris, the 15th *Germinal,* year II. of the French Republic.

'PEYSSARD, LEGRIS, BÉRARD, M.-A. BAUDOT.

'Initialled by the members of the Commission with

'A.-Q. FOUQUIER, LECOINTRE, BEAUPREY, GUFFROY.'[1]

---

[1] National Archives, C. W. 500. The decree A was to the following effect :—

It is worthy of remark, although a painful fact, that this decree of outlawry, presented by Saint-Just, was adopted by the Convention *unanimously* ! Unanimously these men, of opposite temperament and different opinions, declared that all the desired means were to be used in order to prevent the ' thwarting of the course of justice.' Not one voice was raised in protest against this outlawry ; not even that of the Dantonist Legendre, who might this time have placed his powerful lungs at the service of his friends. What ! among the *modérés* who, later, were to overturn Maximilien Robespierre—among those who would one day rise up against these *bloodthirsty* men, was there not one to protest in favour of Camille, guilty of compassion and condemned for his clemency ? Among those who knew well that Danton would have saved the Republic, and made it take root in the country, was not one to be met who would repel the stupid

Extract from the minutes of the National Convention, the fifteenth day of Germinal ; in the second year of the French Republic, One and Indivisible.

The National Convention decrees that the Revolutionary Tribunal shall proceed with the instruction relating to the conspiracy of Lacroix, Danton, Chabot, and others.

The President shall make use of every means which the law permits to make his authority and that of the Revolutionary Tribunal respected, and to repress any attempt on the part of the accused to trouble public tranquillity and to hinder the course of justice.

It is decreed that all persons accused of conspiracy who shall resist or insult the national justice shall be outlawed and receive judgment on the spot.

(Signed by the Inspector) AUGER.

Compared with the original by us, Secretaries to the National Convention, Paris, the fifteenth Germinal, the second year of the French Republic, One and Indivisible.

BERARD, M. A. BAUDOT, LEGRIS, *Secretaries.*

Initialled by the members of the Commission,

A.-Q. FOUQUIER, L. LE COINTRE, BEAUPREY.

Z

accusation of *royalism* launched at the man of the 10th August? What a miserable spectacle! And how sights such as these make us despise the baseness of these cowardly and trembling assemblies, always ready to attack, to banish, to sacrifice others, in order to escape the danger which they thought was hanging over themselves! There are unfathomable vilenesses in human nature; and those, indeed, are unhealthy times in which fear—hideous fear—reduces culprits and cowards to the same level. We shall return presently to the denunciation of La Flotte which was to bring the unfortunate Lucile to the scaffold. La Flotte accused Arthur Dillon of having planned with the Conventionalist Simon to excite a rising in the faubourgs, whilst Lucile Desmoulins was to endeavour to move the people to pity. The unhappy Camille had learned, at the moment when his own life was threatened, that he was to be doubly stricken through this beloved being, whose only guilt was the bearing of his name. Lucile arrested! Lucile too in danger! What poignant grief must have wrung the husband's heart! It was, in truth, the last drop in the cup. Camille's fury and that of the other prisoners thenceforth knew no bounds. Herman, the president, fortified by the decree of the Convention, did not care much, as we have seen by the deposition of the registrar Fabricius, about their redoubled rage and despair.

He proceeded to order the prisoners to be removed from the court. This was equivalent to outlawry.

'But,' exclaimed Danton, at this virtual condemnation, 'no documents have been produced against us. No witnesses have yet been heard.'

'It is infamous!' said Lacroix. 'We are judged without being heard,' said another. 'The brigands!

the assassins!' 'All deliberation is useless!' 'This is not judging; it is killing!' 'Let us be led at once to the scaffold!'

Thus did the cries of these unhappy men mingle in a confused sound of complaint and insult; but the judges remained impassible. The President ordered the *gendarmes* to remove the prisoners. Then ensued a terrible scene. Danton cast a contemptuous look at his judges, as a last defiance, but Camille clung to his seat, and refused to walk out. Three men laid hold of him, tore him from his place, and literally carried him out. Desmoulins' last cry was an invective.

These terrible scenes had not failed to make an impression as profound as it was strong upon the minds of the jury. Whilst they were deliberating, there was a momentary rumour in the tribunal that 'the majority would vote for the innocence of the accused.' Afterwards Lecointre declared that at that very moment, Amar, Voulland and Vadier passed through the refreshment-room, going in company with Fouquier, in search of Herman, the president, to persuade him to 'use all possible means to obtain sentence of death.' Fouquier replied, in his examination,[1] that he had 'not even any remembrance that citizens Amar and Voulland had transmitted him the decree of the 15th *Germinal*, and, as for the citizen Vadier, he had not known until long after that he had been in the tribunal.' 'He did not come,' added Fouquier, 'to my private room, nor did I see him in the court.' Vadier was there, however.

In short, the terrible questions were to be submitted to the jury; and Trinchard, who was their chief, and who

---

[1] See the papers in his trial at the National Archives.

bestirred himself so zealousy to obtain a condemnation, had not long to wait.

The following are, word for word, the questions submitted to the jury :

Questions.

'CITIZEN JURORS,—

'There has existed a conspiracy tending (*sic*) to restore the monarchy, to destroy the national representation and the Republican government.

'1st. Is Jean-François Lacroix, lawyer, deputy of the National Convention, convicted of having taken part in this conspiracy ?

'2nd. Georges-Jacques Danton, lawyer and deputy.

'3rd. Benoît-Camille Desmoulins, lawyer and deputy.

'4th. Pierre Philippeaux, lawyer and deputy.

'5th. Marie-Joseph Hérault de Séchelles, deputy.

'6th. François-Joseph Westermann, deputy.

'Are these convicted of having taken part in this conspiracy ?

'There has existed a conspiracy tending to defame and vilify the national representation and to destroy the Republican government by bribery.

'7th. Philippe-François-Nezaire-Fabre d'Eglantine, author, deputy to the National Convention ; is he convicted of having sold his vote as a representative of the people ?

'8th. Joseph Delaunai, lawyer, deputy to the National Convention ; is he convicted, &c. ?

'9th. François Chabot, ex-Capuchin, deputy to the National Convention ; is he convicted, &c. ?

'10th. Claude Bazire, archivist of the former "States of Burgundy" ; is he convicted of complicity with Chabot and Delaunai, for having concealed the revelations of their criminal manœuvres which they made to him, or having concealed the proposals made to him ?

'11th. Marie-Réné Sahugnet Despagnac, ex-abbé, purveyor to the armies of the Republic ; is he convicted of having taken part in the conspiracy ?

' (We pass over the names of the other prisoners.)

' The declaration of the jurors (*or jury*) is in the affirmative to all these questions ; negative only with regard to Lullier.

' HERMAN, *President.*

·' DUCRAY, *Recorder's clerk.*'

At the demand of Fouquier, public prosecutor, the tribunal ordered at once that, in consequence of ' *the indecorum, the sneers, and the blasphemies of the accused* in the presence of the tribunal, the questions be submitted to the jury and the intervening judgment pronounced in the absence of the accused.'

Herman and Fouquier had indeed deserved well of the Committee of Public Welfare.

CHAPTER VI.

I.

IT was done! The Dantonists were to die! While the jury still deliberated, hesitating, in spite of Fouquier, Herman, and Trinchard, to commit this judicial murder, the printers were setting up the types for the text of the death sentence, so that the public criers might announce it at once to the crowd. The accused, who had been reconducted to the Conciergerie, after being dragged from their benches, awaited there the sentence which they now knew to be inevitable. Danton spoke calmly and proudly to the clerk, Ducray, who soon came to read them the sentence of death. (They were taken one by one to the waiting-room to hear this read.) ' It is useless ; you may take us at once to the guillotine. To your judgment I will not listen.' Not one of the others would listen to the reading of their sentence. What use was it ? ' We are assassinated,' said they all ; ' that is enough.'

Camille Desmoulins crouched in a corner of the

prison and wept. He thought of his young wife, whom he must leave in the power of his executioners. He repeated with sobs the sad farewell he had written to his Lucile, on the eve of the trial. 'Horace! Lucile! My Horace! My beloved! What will become of them?' This was weak, perhaps, but Camille had not shown himself weak during the Reign of Terror, when he demanded clemency for all its victims. Let another reproach him with these tears shed for himself, for his vanished happiness, for his home into which dark death had entered, striking down with one blow both husband and wife, and leaving an infant, orphaned even in its cradle. I can only remember, for my part, the cause of his death. When he wrote the 'Vieux Cordelier,' Camille knew well that he ran the risk of dying on the scaffold erected for waverers. But he knew too that a word of pity would help to overturn the devouring guillotine. This word of pity he had repeatedly uttered. He whom Lamartine has called 'a sniffer of the wind,' had at any rate scented the storm, and gone to meet the breath of the tempest half way, tired of being blown about like a wisp of straw. His self-sacrifice will be eternally reckoned to Camille. As for his tears, has not posterity wept with him? Be that as it may, Camille Desmoulins will always live in the imagination of the people, standing on the table of the Palais Royal, or, heart-broken, calling upon his Lucile at the foot of the scaffold.

Danton, too, had to leave a young wife whom he adored; but he was of a manlier nature, and, besides, he had learnt to despise the joys of life, having already drained the cup even to its bitter dregs. He stood firm at the approach of death, which could neither disturb his peace nor blanch his cheek. He who said in his prison, as Riouffe tells us, that Robespierre, Billaut, Collot d'Herbois, and others were all 'Cain's brethren,' was determined to show his destroyers that a Danton dies as he has lived. His last words and thoughts, during the hours of his life now fleeting so rapidly away, were all tinged with the manly energy and cutting sarcasm which formed a fundamental part of his nature. Sometimes he would reason quite calmly about the judgment that would be passed upon him by future ages. 'I have the consolation of knowing,' said he, 'that the man who goes to his death as the leader of the *faction of indulgence*, will find favour in the eyes of posterity. Besides,' he added, 'suppose they persevere in these severities. When the condemned march to the scaffold laughing, it is time to break the scythe of death.'[1] As if to prove that laughter, contempt of the scaffold, insolent bravado in the very face of death, might be heard even in the executioner's cart, he turned to Desmoulins, and, half sneering at his tears, said : (this saying has been attributed to Lacroix) 'What will you say when Sanson cuts your spinal cord in two ?' A terrible jest! It is the jocoseness of a Titan who braves not only death, but suffering! What insolent defiance of the deadly knife about to fall on him! What supreme scorn of the sudden death awaiting that body now so full of life and strength! It was Danton, too, who, even on the way to the scaffold, said to Fabre d'Eglantine, who was lamenting over the unfinished comedy in verse, 'L'Orange de Malte,'[2] that he, the dramatist, would never be able to complete : 'Vos vers! Bah! dans une semaine

---

[1] 'Notes de Courtois' (de l'Aube).
[2] It has been lost.

vous ferez assez de vers.'[1] Danton's wit is akin to some
of Shakspeare's jests.

Then Danton, resuming his gravity, nobly added :
' We have finished our task ; let us take our rest.'

The hour was approaching. The executioner
arrived with his assistants to perform the toilet of the
condemned. Camille still struggled. He resisted to
the utmost, and just as it had been necessary to carry
him to the dock, so they had to tie him to his seat while
the collar of his shirt was cut. We are informed that he
asked Danton to place between his bound hands a locket
containing Lucile's hair, which he had hitherto worn
next his heart. Danton complied ; then gave himself up
in his turn to the scissors and cords of the executioner.
There was upon his terrible face a smile of contempt.

Chabot embraced Bazire, and said to him : ' It is for
me that you are to die ! Poor Bazire, what have you
done ? '

There were, in all, fifteen condemned, who were to
die together. They filled two tumbrils, which were
waiting for them, surrounded by *gendarmes*, in the
court of the Palais de Justice, before that terrible gate
which may be seen to this day. The crowd, pressing
against the railings, waited, impatient to see Danton
again. Camille Desmoulins stepped into the tumbril
the last but one. Danton followed him. He placed
himself between Camille and Fabre d'Eglantine.
Their elbows touched, and Danton's chest served as a
support to Camille's shoulder. ' The —— fools ! ' Danton said, as he looked at the crowd. ' They are waiting to cry *Long live the Republic !* as we pass. In an
hour's time the Republic will no longer have a head ! '

---

[1] This horrible calembour, which turns on the identity of the words
vers (verses) and *vers* (worms), is untranslatable.

The tumbril moved on, and the gendarmes sword in hand spurred their horses. There was a terrible surging in the immense crowd which filled the approaches of the Palais de Justice, lined the quays, and formed a howling and yelling escort for the awful cartload up to the *Place de la Révolution.* Danton looked at this crowd, this nameless monster, ready for every excess, for any reaction—ready to elevate tyrants to apotheosis, or to drag the just to the shambles. He looked at the masses, the true criminals of the terrible 2nd of September, so fresh in his own memory. Among this moving heap of sightseers were some infatuated beings who merrily sang the Marseillaise; but there were others, fewer and more intelligent, who, as they saw Danton, Camille, Hérault, and Philippeaux pass to the scaffold, asked themselves had the counter-revolution begun? What thoughts must have crowded upon these men, who, as they passed out, pinioned, to die for the people, were insulted by them? The laughter of the crowd at the ex-Capuchin Chabot may be excused; but at Danton, who would have led the people to the frontier and have made heroism spring out of rags! at Desmoulins, who, at the dawn of the revolution, had shown the crowd the way to the Bastille! What bitter reminiscences passed through the minds of those so soon to be cold in death! As a drowning man sees, like a lightning flash, at one glance, his earliest memories, his first joys, his old loves, thus Camille lived his past life over again—his walks in the Luxembourg, his dreams of liberty, the scene of his first meeting with Lucile, the feverish happiness of his married life, his domestic joys, his chats at the fireside with Brune or Fréron, his long watchings by the cradle where the little

Horace slept! What! had all vanished? Was all annihilated? Every turn of the wheel of the death-cart brought him nearer to the inevitable end. And, waiting on these fair dreams, was Sanson, below.

Then, wild with rage and despair, Camille tried to break his bonds, and, tearing his shirt to rags, so that his lean shoulder, neck and chest showed through the tatters, he made a last appeal to the crowd—an appeal more utterly thrown away on that heaving sea than if it had been shouted in the desert, where at least the echoes would not have answered by insults. 'You are deceived, citizens,' he cried, in hoarse tones. 'Citizens, your preservers are being sacrificed! It was I, who, in '89, called you to arms. I raised the first cry of liberty! My crime, my only crime has been pity!' Vain words! The condemned, like the conquered everywhere, met with nothing but abuse. 'Be quiet,' said Danton to him, 'and let the rabble be!' [1]

Evening was at hand. The weather was superb, as it was indeed during the whole of that terrible spring of 1794, so beautiful, so brilliant, so lovely, that old men

---

[1] See the account of the death of Camille by Beffroy de Rigny (le cousin Jacques). The author begins by stating his surprise that Camille, who had pistols and daggers to excite the people to revolt, did not find any to defend himself with at the moment of his arrest, or to shoot his judges through the brain when brought before the Revolutionary Tribunal. But he adds : ' Camille made incredible efforts to escape from the hands of these wretches, who were the lowest of the hangers-on of the tyrants, so that he went to the scaffold absolutely naked down to the waist, his shirt being torn in rags.

' *I saw him* passing along the space before the Palais to the *place of blood*, speaking to those near him with a scared look and in wild agitation ; his face distorted with the convulsive laughter of a man out of his senses.

' Thus perished, at the age of thirty-four, Benoît-Camille Desmoulins, the dupe and the victim of the madness of the eighteenth century,' &c.— *Dictionnaire-Néologique des hommes et de choses*, par le cousin Jacques. Paris, an VIII. t. ii. p. 480.

said 'such weather had not been seen within the memory of man.'

The tumbril advanced slowly, pressing back the crowd. The academician Arnault, who saw it pass, has drawn, in his 'Souvenirs d'un Sexagénaire,' an indelible picture of this group of young and courageous men, dragged to the scaffold: Danton's unblanched face wore an expression of contempt and disdain. Hérault de Séchelles, whose face also wore its natural hue, appeared more like a spectator than an actor in the drama that was being played. He looked at the surging sea of faces, ferocious, indifferent, or compassionate, with the phlegm of a painter who studies the ocean during a tempest. Fabre appeared to be overwhelmed; Camille Desmoulins spoke, called out, and appealed continually to the crowd. As they passed a café, Danton perceived that David was making a sketch of the martyrs. 'Knave!' he called out to him. They passed before Robespierre's house; the windows were closed as if for a funeral, those windows which four short months afterwards were smeared with blood by the crowd in its delirium. Camille Desmoulins tried to make his terrible curses reach the ears of Maximilien. 'My assassins,' he cried, 'will not long survive me.' Thus was Danton's ejaculation at the trial repeated before the house of their enemy.

A few more turns of the wheels, and then, beyond the immense crowd that filled the *Place de la Révolution*, the condemned could perceive the hideous machine, which, notwithstanding its rust, glowed in the setting sun. There were gathered together multitudes of human beings, eager to see how the *Indulgents* would die. In the streets off the Place the taverns were full of men drinking, who sang and chinked their glasses.

A ray of the sun reddened the great plaster statue of Liberty, which Madame Roland had saluted in dying, on which pigeons, indifferent to scenes which inflame the passions of men, had peaceably made their nests. The lilac trees were in full bloom on the terraces of the Tuileries. All this beauty of the opening year marked out the tragic scene with greater distinctness. The glory of the April evening made this frightful deed all the blacker.

The tumbril drew up at the foot of the scaffold. The executioner began his work. Hérault de Séchelles, still calm and resolute, was the first to descend from the cart. He looked in the direction of the *Garde-Meuble*, and saw a woman's hand, which from between the half-opened blinds waved a last farewell to the dying man, as if to say : ' Thou wert loved ! ' It is known that he tried to embrace Danton, to press his cheek to the cheek of his friend. Sanson's assistants prevented this. Danton shrugged his shoulders. ' Fools,' he said, ' you will not be able to hinder our heads from meeting presently in the basket ! ' He continued to scoff at death. Hérault mounted the guillotine, appeared standing on the platform, and while the crowd repeated his name, he was bound to the plank, his head severed from the trunk, and he was no more.

Lacroix was the next executed.[1]

---

[1] Arnault, in his ' Souvenirs,' is severe upon Hérault. In some fragments of the writings of André Chénier are some cutting lines which, we are told by the relative and editor of André, M. Gabriel de Chénier, portray Hérault de Séchelles. In the third volume of the edition of the ' Œuvres poétiques ' of André de Chénier (Iambes, xi. p. 291, edit. A. Lemerre, 1874) I find the following : ' Who is the big brown fellow

Then came Camille's turn. He recovered under the knife the calmness he had lost on the way thither.

'Thus, then,' he said bitterly, as he looked at the clotted and gory arms of the guillotine, 'the first apostle of Liberty ends!' and then drawing attention to the lock of Lucile's fair hair, which he had held clasped tight within his fingers the whole way from the Conciergerie, he said, 'Have this sent to my mother-in-law! . . . . O my poor wife!' They pushed him under the knife, and his head fell.

Danton was the last to die. Arnault, who saw him standing erect upon the dreadful platform, his feet in the blood of his friends, compared his firm and athletic figure, thrown out against the horizon, to one of Dante's conceptions. The setting sun shone upon his majestic countenance like the reflection from a forge. His head, which had been held up before the tribunal

(described in four, six, or at the most eight verses)? Have I not known him well in former days, with his long hair down his back, soiling the damask-covered chairs, sneering and saying nothing, yet aspiring to be called a wit, &c.? This certainly is H——. He is called Cicero among the lawyers, "et bel esprit chez les catins!"'

André avenges the wrongs of the Swiss and Collot d'Herbois in his iambics, but becomes defamatory in his verses when he attacks Hérault de Séchelles. He is no longer Archilochus, he is Zoïlus. All that can be said is that André did not understand Hérault ; in point of fact, he misunderstood him. The handsome Séchelles might have said, when he was dying, as the unfortunate Chenier said some months afterwards :

'*J'avais pourtant quelque chose là !*'

We must add a strange and dramatic incident. On the very day of Hérault's execution the theatre of the National Opera had a representation of a *sans-culottide* in five acts : 'The *Reunion* of the Tenth of August, or the Inauguration of the French Republic,' in which Hérault is seen in the act of burning the emblems of royalty. Thus, some hours after the execution of the veritable Hérault, a comedian makes his appearance on the stage, 'got up' perhaps after the portrait of Hérault de Séchelles by Laneuville.

haughtily, like that of one inspired, retained even on the scaffold its expression of power and command. He, too, was thinking of his wife. His courageous lips allowed these words to escape them : ' My beloved, I shall never see thee again ! ' Then, drawing himself up, and recovering his composure at once, he said aloud : ' Come, come, Danton, no weakness ! ' He looked the executioner in the face, and said in his sonorous voice :—' Show my head to the people ; it is worth while ; they do not see the like every day ! '

The last words of Danton were equivalent to a command, and the frightened crowd repeated the bold words, which he had uttered so loud that every one heard them. The bloody knife fell for the last time. Danton was no more. ' Kings are struck only on the head,' he had once said. It was on ' the head,' also, that they struck his eloquence, his courage, his boldness, his high spirit, which form the only royalty worth admiring.

And as with the Girondists, a few instants sufficed —one half-hour ; perhaps, alas ! less than that—for the sacrifice of the Dantonists.

The frightful promiscuousness of the punishment flung together trunkless heads and headless trunks in one hideous medley ; also many virtues and many vices ; the eloquence and patriotism of Danton, the wit and irony of Desmoulins, the military bravery of Westermann, the probity of Philippeaux, the elegance and profound faith of Hérault, and the skill and talent of Eglantine. A clerk registered, two days later, at the tribunal, a bloody heap of incongruous articles brought in by an assistant of the executioner—medallions, shoe-buckles, greatcoats, inkstands, pasteboard snuffboxes, cravats or neckties, ruffled shirts ;—

all that was left of the young men whose hearts had throbbed so warmly at the great names of Liberty, Fatherland, Freedom, and the Republic! Of all they had possessed, high spirit, courage, hope, error perhaps, but still generous error—of all that had throbbed, struggled, loved, suffered, what remained?

Corpses huddled into a trench in the cemetery of the Madeleine, the clothes at the registry office; as for their memories, they were already given over to the calumny of their triumphant enemies, and the ingratitude of those for whom they had died.

For, it was for us they fell. Labourers sacrificed in the early days, the days of darkness and bloodshed, they gave their existence for us without reckoning the cost, that they might assure to us a freedom yet to come. Eager to renovate the world, from a political, moral, judicial, legislative point of view—in a word, to found a new society, they banded themselves together against the past, and in the face of a furious opposition they organised a formidable struggle. Their life was a combat, and if—as we all hope—we succeed in establishing social peace, after so much sorrow, and so many crises, in this cruelly tormented country, to them our gratitude will be due. They have broken open the door that future generations may enter.

Undoubtedly their stern work has records which we would fain efface. In those troubled times while they were struggling, they held individuals too cheaply, forgetting the sacredness of human life, and that ideas are not destroyed when the body is slain. They were more revolutionary than republican, and it was time that the Republic should become a government and cease to be a revolution. But of what irresistible currents were they not the prey? Danton knew this well, he felt it fully, and he perished for having tried to establish liberty, in opposition to a superhuman and inhuman ideal, of which those whom he called 'the Jansenists of the Republic' would have made supreme law. He foresaw that such a method of government, antipathetic to the temperament of the French (these are his own words) would infallibly lead to a revolt; that is to say, to anarchy or reaction, and afterwards to a dictatorship. Behind Robespierre he descried Cæsar. 'The revolution,' he said, 'cannot be held to be really made while the people do not know how to profit by it.'[1] Therefore he tried to make the torrent return to the bed whence it had overflowed. Let those only count this a crime in him who do not regard pity, liberty, and justice as virtues.

'Danton killed by Robespierre,' writes Courtois, in his 'Notes,' 'is Pyrrhus killed by a woman.' The truth is that Danton killed by Robespierre, is Robespierre giving himself up to the scaffold, and that speedily. Robespierre had good reason to shut himself up in Duplay's house, while the tumbril in which Camille was seated was passing before the door. Only four months later, when he was seeking to save his own life, a voice called out to him, 'The blood of Danton chokes you!' Yet, not he more than others, had shed Danton's blood, and he certainly had hesitated to sign the order for the execution of Camille with Danton; but merciless consequences dragged the accusers in the train of the accused; and as Desmoulins had perished after the Girondists, so Robespierre and his friends were to perish after Danton and his friends.[2]

---

[1] See in the Appendix, Notes of Courtois (de l'Aube).

[2] The following epigram went the round of Paris after the execution

A A

Why did they not unite their efforts to found the
Republic? Why did they not abjure their resentments
and their prejudices, and so end the reign of hatred?

Danton, at least, knew not how to hate. He had a
large heart, in that athlete's breast of his. Although
he did not weep like Desmoulins, he was quite as
tender-hearted. Like Desmoulins, he was loved during
his life and after his death. Danton's father and
mother-in-law, M. and Madame Gély, who inhabited
for some time afterwards the house in which Danton
lived, in the Passage du Commerce, told M. Eugène
Despois, a young relation of theirs, from whom I have
the account, about Danton's domestic life, and how
loveable a man he was. This exact information, given
by the survivors, is very different from the pretended
traditions which make Danton out to be a man of
pleasure. The daily life of the tribune was that of
an honest citizen, loving his wife, his fireside, and his
books, preferring domestic joys to public greatness; at
once compassionate and terrible; one of those men who
may be compared to rivers whose overflowing fertilises,
and whose mighty waves carry men onwards to the
open sea.

In speaking of Danton, the venerable Madame
Gély, who had always been very pious, never failed to
say to the maternal grandfather of M. Despois: 'Ah!

of the Dantonists (see 'Memorial of the French Revolution,' by P. C.
Lecomte) :—

> ' Lorsqu'arrivés au bord du Phlégéton,
> Camille Desmoulins, d'Eglantine et Danton
> Payèrent pour passer ce fleuve redoutable.
> Le nautonier Caron, citoyen équitable,
> A nos trois passagers voulut remettre en mains
> L'excédant de la taxe imposée aux humains ;
> Garde, lui dit Danton, la somme toute entière
> Je paye pour Couthon, Saint-Just et Robespierre.'

my cousin, I am happy about our poor Danton's fate. M. l'Abbé de Kéravenant (the nonjuring priest who married Danton) followed him when he was led to death, and he took advantage of an instant when Danton looked at him, and made a sign of intelligence, to give him *mentally* holy absolution.' Danton could hardly, in the eyes of an orthodox person, be said to be fortified with the rites of the Church ; but the remembrance of the priest whom Danton saluted, and the conviction of the aged Madame Gély, prove two things—the calmness of the dying Danton saluting a friendly face in the crowd, and the manly goodness of the man who inspired such sympathies. Happy are those who die beloved! Their memory sooner or later will be avenged; their death will be regarded by some as a martyrdom, by others as an expiation, by all with regret.

To be loved! It is the ideal of happiness, and often it is salvation. To be loved! Camille Desmoulins was loved, and therefore is his memory living still ; therefore, notwithstanding the unpardonable excesses of his pamphlets, he is absolved, nay, more, he is held in honour, by those who admire his talents and compassionate his fate. The love of his wife, the romance of his life, have caused the reality of his history to be forgotten. At the sight of this pair who loved each other so much, and who were struck by the same knife within two days of each other, one is moved to sorrow. We no longer hear the sarcastic laugh of Desmoulins driving Brissot or Chaumette to the scaffold ; we no longer hear the grating of the rope slipping down the 'fatal lamp-post.' We only see this young man of thirty, dragged from the embraces of his wife, the prattle of his child, and flung into the bloody grasp of the guillotine. We hear only the immortal words he committed to paper, the letters over which he wept, scarce knowing what he wrote. Camille, ' the *gamin* of genius,' is transfigured by misfortune. It was the pen of a youth intoxicated with liberty which traced the 'France libre;' the stylus of a spoiled child wrote the 'Discours de la Lanterne,' certain pages of the 'Révolutions de France et de Brabant,' and 'Brissot démasqué;' but the hand of a man held the fiery steel of the 'Vieux Cordelier,' and the head of a man fell on the 16th Germinal, under the axe of Sanson.

II.

'THE wretches! not satisfied with assassinating me, they are going to kill my wife too!' Camille had said. At the same hour Madame Duplessis, in her terror, was writing a letter to Robespierre which remained un-finished and which never reached Maximilien, a letter in which the cry of Camille was repeated—'Robespierre, was it not enough to kill your best friend; will you also shed the blood of his wife?' Lucile had been de-nounced by a certain Amans, imprisoned in the Luxem-bourg—a miserable spy, a decoy of his fellow-prisoners; a *mouton*, who, in a letter to Robespierre, accused the ex-General Dillon of conspiring in favour of Danton, Camille, and Philippeaux. 'Dillon,' this Amans wrote, 'works in his office every night until five or six o'clock in the morning; he has a trustworthy messenger, who comes and goes with packets; suspicious-looking people come to see him, and speak with him privately. . . .'

It is not the first time, in fact, that we have had to notice the comparative liberty allowed to prisoners under the Reign of Terror.'[1]

Amans accuses Dillon of having money, and of fomenting a conspiracy. The agent, Alexandre La Flotte, soon gave a name to this imaginary plot. Fouquier complained that they meant to assassinate him, and the *conspiracy of the prisons* was created. Dillon, according to La Flotte, had concerted a project with Simond, the deputy (a friend of Hérault). They distributed money among the people. They sent 'persons' among the Revolutionary Tribunal. Desmoulins' wife, added La Flotte, is in the plot.[2]

---

[1] See the 'Memoirs' of Madame Roland in the prison of St. Pélagie. The 'Essais' of Beaulieu also show how the prisoners were allowed to go to the café of the Conciergerie, where (wonderful to relate !) 'there was,' he says, ' a good deal of gaiety.'

[2] There is a record respecting the Dantonists and the day after their death which will be read with interest, called the 'Rapport fait à la Société des Amis de la Liberté et de l'Egalité, séante aux Jacobins,' Rue Honoré, Paris, upon the conspiracies of Hébert, Ronsin, Vincent, and their accomplices ; of Fabre d'Eglantines (*sic*) ; Chabot, Delaunay d'Angers, Bazire, Danton, Lacroix, Hérault, Camille Desmoulins, Philippeaux, Westermann, and their accomplices, by Dumas, president of the Revolutionary Tribunal, one of the members of the society. Sitting of the 23rd Germinal (the eve of the execution of Lucile). The report speaks in the same breath of the ' enraged' and the ' indulgents.'

'The brigands,' says Dumas, 'who were bold usurpers, betrayed the cause of the people. A watchful government has followed them to the foot of the grave they dug for liberty, and the national justice has precipitated them into " nothingness." They are no more, and soon we shall say of their accomplices also, They have lived ! '

He calls the Dantonists, 'creatures and rivals of the immoral Mirabeau, the poor slaves of d'Orléans, who only attacked the king, never royalty.' He represents them 'as loaded with the spoils of Belgium and dreaming of themselves as new Cromwells.' What rhetoric ! ' You sold the welfare of the public,' he says to them, ' to the enemy very cheap.' Still the same system, which consists of confounding the friends of clemency with the forgers of the decrees of the Convention. .

[The society has stopped the printing of the present discours, and its distribution to the members, the people in the galleries, and the affiliated

The destruction of Lucile—a woman!—was decided upon. The Committee, not satisfied with having
silenced for ever the pen of the pamphleteer, determined to strike the author of the 'Vieux Cordelier'
another blow, through her who bore his name.

At the hour when the heads of Danton and Camille
fell, Vadier mounted the rostrum of the Convention,
and declaring that he had been present 'without
being seen, at the scandalous debates of the Revolutionary Tribunal,' asserted that Dillon and Simond
were conspiring now in their prison. 'They have,'
he said, 'organised a cohort of scoundrels, who are to
issue forth from the Luxembourg, with a password, to
occupy the avenues to the Committees of Public Welfare and General Safety, fall upon the members composing these Committees, and immolate them to their
fury.' 'And these men,' added Vadier, 'still breathe.'
Couthon succeeded him on the rostrum, and asked for
a fresh sentence of death. The following night, the
prisoners accused of having taken part in the 'conspiracy
of the prisons' were taken to the Conciergerie. Among
them were Arthur Dillon, the deputy Simond, the ex-
bishop Gobel ; Anaxagoras Chaumette, one of Camille's
victims; Grammont-Roselly, the actor, adjutant-general
of the revolutionary army, who had insulted Marie-
Antoinette as she went to the scaffold; Grammont-
Nourry, his son; Lambert, the turnkey; Beyssier, the
surgeon ; and the widows of Hébert and Camille.

What strange irony in the promiscuous joining together in condemnation and death of the *Jacqueline*
of Père Duchesne and the Rouleau, the *bon loup* of
Camille ! Thrown side by side, accused together,

societies. Signed, Veau, deputy-president ; Maillard, vice-president ;
Lequinio, deputy ; Voiron, Lassis, Leclerc, and Poidévin, secretaries.]

threatened with the same danger! 'They often sat on the same stone in the court of the Conciergerie,' says Riouffe,[1] 'and wept together.'

Certain gaolers of the Luxembourg, some old soldiers, of the army of Ph. Ronsin, a man-at-arms belonging to the household of the Count of Artois, Commissary Lapalue, Captain Lassalle of the merchant marine, Adjutant Denet, Lebrasse, a lieutenant of the *gendarmerie*, were imprisoned with the wretched women.

All these unhappy beings, threatened with a common accusation, were brought before the Revolutionary Tribunal as guilty of having conspired against the safety of the people, and of having wished to destroy the National Convention. To destroy the Convention! Lucile wish to do that! Fouquier-Tinville went still further in odious absurdity: he accused Dillon, Lambert, Simond, and Desmoulins' widow of having 'aimed at replacing on the throne of France the son of Louis XVI.'

'They were in the pay of the foreigner,' said the public prosecutor. Lucile exert herself to destroy the Convention, and place the Dauphin on the throne! All that she wished was to see Camille again, to save him if she could, or to find him again in death, if her efforts should prove vain. The unhappy wife never received those eloquent, sublime, and touching letters of farewell which Camille had addressed to her from his prison.[2] She had not been able to press

---

[1] 'Memoirs of a Prisoner,' p. 66.

[2] 'Before quitting the Luxembourg,' said M. Emile Campardon, 'Camille wrote his wife a touching letter. . . . When he arrived at the Conciergerie he gave it to Citizen Grossé-Beaurepaire, whom he found detained there, charging him to have it delivered to his wife. But Madame Desmoulins soon followed her husband to the scaffold, and this letter never reached her. Grossé-Beaurepaire gave it to Jules Paré, formerly Minister of the Interior, and a friend of Danton and Camille, in

a last kiss upon the paper blotted with Camille's tears.
She longed then, with feverish ardour—like that of
the martyrs eager to be delivered to the torturers—
for death which should reunite her with him whom
she had lost.

Before her judges she was calm and intrepid, but
withal womanly. She denied that General Dillon had
written to her, and sent her three thousand livres to
cover the expenses of an outbreak against the Convention. 'At least,' the president, Dumas, said to Dillon,
'you cannot deny having lighted the flame of revolt in
the prisons?' 'I said,' replied the ex-general, 'that if
the terrors of the days of September were to be re-
enacted in the prisons (as was reasonably supposed at
one time), it would be the duty of every brave man
to defend his life, to demand to be heard and judged
before he allowed himself to be sacrificed.' This was,
in fact, the only crime of the accused; they struggled
with the executioner for their own existence, or that of
those dear to them.

Lucile was guilty only of despair and love; she
had never conspired, she had but hovered around the
prison like a bird over its nest. She had called on
Camille's name, she had made mournful signs which
were intended to convey all her feelings, in one look,
one gesture. That was enough for her destruction.
She was condemned to death, after three days' deliberation, with eighteen others (all under twenty-six years
of age), on the 24th Germinal. Nearly all the condemned might say, with Chaumette, at the tribunal:
'You have decided upon my fate. I await my destiny
with calmness!'

whose possession it remained.'—*Le Tribunal Révolutionnaire*, vol. ii.
p. 254.

The astonishing serenity which Lucile had preserved during the trial, when there was a look in
her eyes as if she saw far beyond the judgment hall,
had given place to exultation ; and, on hearing the
sentence that condemned her to death, she raised her
head, and with eyes that glistened with the brilliancy
of fever, she cried, ' What happiness ! in a few hours
I shall see my Camille again.' And then her loyal
glance fell upon her judges. ' In quitting this earth,
to which love no longer binds me,' she said, ' I am
less to be pitied than you ; for at your death, which
will be infamous, you will be haunted by remorse for
what you have done.'

The tribunal condemned Hébert's widow with
Camille's widow. The ex-nun of the Convent of the
Conception, in the Rue St. Honoré, the woman whom
Fouquier accused of having employed ' her wit and
her charms to decoy men to conspire against her
country,' was to die with Camille's widow. In vain
did she declare she was pregnant. Théry and Naury,
the health officers, were of opinion that there were
no grounds for a reprieve. The wife of the inheritor
of Marat's tragic fame, and the wife of the promoter of
the Committee of Clemency, were to die on the same
day. But what a difference between these two women !
Hébert's widow felt it herself. One of the witnesses
on the trial of Fouquier-Tinville, Grandpré, deposed
that on the day the sentence was pronounced, Hébert's
widow said to Lucile : ' You are very fortunate ; nobody speaks ill of you ; there is no shadow upon your
character ; you will go out of life by the grand staircase.' Thus before their death these two beings, who
bore the names of men constantly hostile to each other,
became friends. The husbands had killed each other ;

their widows renounced their traditional enmity upon the steps of the scaffold.

What did it matter to Lucile whether she was accused or defended? She had no longer any pretext for living in this world. She was one of those heroines of conjugal love who are more wife than mother. Besides, Horace lived, and Camille was dead. It was of the absent only that she thought. As for the child, would not Madame Duplessis act a mother's part to him? The grandmother would watch over the orphan. If Lucile had lived, she could have done nothing but weep over the cradle, thinking of Camille.

Lucile dressed herself for death as if for a bridal. She displayed, I repeat, the holy exultation of a martyr. 'The blood of a woman drove the Tarquins out of Rome; so may mine drive away tyranny'[1] —are words imputed to her.

While Hébert's widow wept, Lucile smiled. She had cut her hair 'close to her head,' we are told by the executioner,[2] and she sent it to her mother, perhaps with a letter which she wrote in her prison—a short

---

[1] M. Ed. Fleury considers these words apocryphal, because they are not in accordance with the character of Lucile, which was simple, dignified, touching, and modest. Enthusiasm, however, does not exclude dignity, and we have seen from the memoranda of the young girl that Lucile was both enthusiastic and charming.

[2] 'The 24th saw many persons perish, among them Camille Desmoulins' wife and Hébert's wife. The first made much impression upon the public by her beauty and her demeanour. One man only dared to insult Lucile. This was that wretched Geoffrey, the author of the "Rougyff ou le Frankenvedette," a journal of blood and mud, whom Camille was weak enough to call "our dear Rougyff," and who wrote (No. 107): "The widows of Hébert and Desmoulins chatted with apparent calmness; but an observant eye could see that it was more the effect of a foolish pride in having played a part in the revolution!" And this man speaks of the *conceit* of the women in the face of the scaffold!'
—*Memorial of P. C. Lecomte*, vol. i. p. 276.

letter, but irresistibly touching in its devotedness, its resignation, its fervour :

'Good-night, my dear Mama. A tear drops from my eyes; it is for you. I shall fall asleep in the calmness of innocence.
'LUCILE.'

When the tumbril—the same perhaps which Camille had ascended a week before—arrived to carry away the condemned, the ex-General Arthur Dillon came towards poor Lucile bowing his head. 'I am sorry,' she said, 'to have caused your death.' Dillon smiled, and replied that the accusation against him was only a pretext, and was beginning to compassionate her in his turn, when Lucile interrupted him. 'Look,' she said, 'at my face ; is it that of a woman who needs consolation ?' In truth, she looked radiant. She had tied a white neckerchief under her chin. It covered her hair. She looked a little pale, but charming. 'I saw this young creature,' says Tissot, in his 'Histoire de la Révolution;' 'and she made an indelible impression on me, in which the memory of her beauty, the virginal graces of her person, the melody of her heart-stirring voice, were mingled with admiration of her courage, and regret for the cruel fate which threw her into the jaws of death a few days after her husband, and which denied her even the consolation of being united to him in the same grave.' Camille, 'that good fellow,' could have said nothing in his own defence but 'I am a child.' Lucile preferred to hold up her head and ask for death. 'They have assassinated the best of men,' she again said; 'if I did not hate them for that, I should bless them for the service they have done me this day.' Among all the heroic women who have died upon the scaffold, the youthful smiling face of Lucile stands out prominently, illuminated with a joyous light. It is the wife dying for the husband, a victim of passionate love of the noblest, holiest kind.

She bowed to Dillon, 'with playfulness,' as if she were taking leave of him in a drawing-room, and should soon see him again; then she took her place in the second tumbril with Grammont-Roselly and his son, who reproached each other with their respective deaths during the transit; Brumeau-Lacroix, Lapalue, Lassalle, and Hébert's widow. Lapalue was twenty-six years old, Lassalle was twenty-four. Lucile chatted with them pleasantly and smilingly. Grammont-Nourry having called his father a scoundrel, it is recorded that Lucile Desmoulins said to him, 'You insulted Antoinette when she was in the tumbril; that does not surprise me. Had you not better keep a little of your courage to brave another queen, Death, to whom we are hastening?' 'Grammont,' says an eye-witness, 'answered her with insults, but she turned from him with contempt.' Grammont-Roselly desired to embrace his son before he died, but his son refused that last embrace with the utmost brutality.

'Long live the king!' cried Dillon, returning on the scaffold to what he had been at Versailles.

Lucile said nothing; she mounted the steps of the scaffold with a sort of happy pride. They were for her the steps of an altar. She was going to Camille! This thought made her smile. The executioner looked at her, moved in spite of himself. She was, he has told us, scarcely pale. This young woman, who looked like a picture by Greuze, died like a Roman matron. The fair childlike head retained its expression of profound joy and passionate ecstasy, even when flung bleeding, into the blood-stained sawdust of the dreadful basket, by the brutal hands of Sanson's assistant.

III.

Thus, of those who, in the December of 1790, had been present at the marriage of Camille and Lucile, at St. Sulpice, three were dead : Brissot, Pétion, Lucile and Camille had disappeared. And in four months' time Robespierre was to die !

At Guise was an old man, overwhelmed with grief, whom sorrow was bringing down to the grave. In Paris was a broken-down man nearly dead with grief like M. Desmoulins, and an old woman mourning beside an orphan child. A few months later M. Desmoulins and M. Duplessis had both passed away. Political strife has always these dreadful after-consequences, and grief kills slowly those whom the steel has spared.

Madame Duplessis devoted herself entirely to the education of little Horace Desmoulins. She lived with her daughter Adèle, the betrothed of Robespierre, who survived until a few years ago, at Vervins, in M. Matton's neighbourhood. Philippeaux's widow, ever faithful to his memory, also devoted herself to his son.

These unhappy women lived for their respective charges, and nothing can be more touching than the correspondence between the survivors of such cruel trials. The letters, now published for the first time, will be found at the end of this volume.

Camille's faithful friend also watched over the little Horace. Brune wrote to Madame Duplessis as follows :

'I have just written to Fréron, as we agreed.

'This is what I think you ought to ask of him.

'1st. Being your children's friend, that he should take all necessary steps in Horace's favour with the Committees.

'2nd. That he should claim for him the family papers, and his father's manuscripts. The Committee of General Safety has the right to retain *temporarily* such as relate immediately to the welfare of the State. The others ought to be given back to the young orphan at once; they will serve for his instruction, they will teach him to know the authors of his being.

'3rd. That he should claim for Horace the family books; they also will be useful for his instruction; they are indispensable for the supply of his wants; besides, this justice has been already done to Citizen Boucher's widow, therefore there is a precedent for it.

'Committees composed of the friends of justice ought to be proud of being useful to the orphans of patriots.

'Fréron and his friends cannot refuse to act in concert with you. Greeting and friendship.

'(Signed)　　　BRUNE.'[1]

Oh! morrow of revolutions and of useless slaughter!

The time was not far distant when the Convention itself—that Convention which unanimously voted the arrest of Danton, Camille, and their friends—proclaimed that Desmoulins and Philippeaux had deserved well of humanity. On the 10th Thermidor, two months after the publication by Desenne of the seventh number of the 'Vieux Cordelier' (1795), Merlin de Thionville, Camille's friend and fellow-

---

[1] Unpublished.

worker, mounted the rostrum, and declared, amid unanimous applause, that 'flowers ought to be laid upon the tomb of the unfortunate Philippeaux, and upon that of Camille Desmoulins, who was the first to assume the tricolored cockade, at the Palais Egalité.' It was the green cockade, but Merlin de Thionville's idea, which was so much applauded, was a fitting tribute to him who had proudly called himself 'the first apostle of liberty.'

A year later, deputy Bailleul presented to the Council of the Five Hundred the report of a petition from the widows of Carra, Gorsas, Pétion, Valazé, Brissot, and Philippeaux, asking the nation's aid for themselves and their children. At the request of Goupillau, the name of Camille Desmoulins' son, 'who is in poverty,' was added to the draft of the decree voted April 28, 1796—

'In consideration of Camille Desmoulins, a representative of the people and a member of the National Convention, having been put to death for rising against proscriptions, and recalling principles of humanity, too long forgotten.' At the end of this sentence is recorded an annual grant of two thousand francs to Camille Desmoulins' son, to be paid him until he should have reached his eighteenth year.

The young orphan's life was short and sad.

In the year IX., he was placed at the Prytanée, in Paris (the same college of Louis-le-Grand where his father had dreamed), where he remained until schools were formed in the departments, of the *boursiers* from the Prytanée. Horace was to be sent, we learn from M. J. Quicherat, to the college of Bordeaux. 'It was a death-blow to Madame Duplessis. She laid her petition and her distress before the minister, Fourcroy, who was then director of public education; he imagined that it would be easy to erase the child's name from the list, but found himself powerless to do so. To save the poor woman from the alternative of being separated from her grandchild or of refusing the education that was to be given him, there was no other resource than to appeal to the kindness of the director of St. Barbe, M. de Lanneau. Although Desmoulins' name was in such bad odour, and Fourcroy's favour was so uncertain, M. Lanneau hastened to enrol the orphan among the number of his free pupils.[1]

Madame Duplessis did her best to protect her grandson's interests, like a brave woman who had been

---

[1] Jules Quicherat, 'History of St. Barbe,' vol. iii. p. 32, passage quoted by M. E. Campardon. We possess among our autographs the following letter from Madame Duplessis to M. de Lanneau:—

Sir,—Until now an illness, from which I hoped every day to recover, but from which I am still suffering, has prevented me from coming to pay you the tribute of gratitude I owe you. Believe, monsieur, I beg, that I look upon this hindrance as a new misfortune added to my sorrows. I am anxious to express to you the impatience and trouble it has caused me. I will devote the first strength of my convalescence to this duty. Until I can acquit myself of it, accept the assurance of my profoundest respect. I shall be able, I hope, soon to express this in person, accompanied by Camille's son.

Continue, monsieur, to watch over young Horace with the goodness of a true Mæcenas, such as you have shown yourself to be; and accept on this occasion with indulgence the assurance of grateful wishes and deepest respect.

Widow DUPLESSIS.

Bourg. Egalité : 4th Nivôse, year XII.

An anonymous note, appended to this autograph, contains these remarks by one of little Horace's masters :—

'I knew this child, a young pupil of the institution of St. Barbe, directed by M. Lanneau, and I was his master. He was a very amiable and interesting child. I have never heard him spoken of since, and if he be still alive, it is evident that he has not made so much noise in the world as his father.'

made martlike by trial. (See a letter of hers relating to her house of Bourg-la-Reine, in the Appendix.)

Horace died at Jacmel, in Hayti, where he perhaps met Virginie, the old negress, who is living to this day, and whose name must have reminded him of the proscriber of his father. She was Billaud-Varenne's widow. Virginie, now old and decrepid, still preserves the portrait of him whom Desmoulins ironically called ' *Le rectiligne.*'

Horace Desmoulins left a daughter, now Madame Broom, in Hayti, who inherited Horace's property, and had among other relics some spoons marked C. D., and Camille's drinking-cup. Also the following :—

1st. A diploma dated 16th (or 10th) November, 1816, given and signed by Charles-Philippe of France, Monsieur, Count of Artois, Lieutenant-General of the National Guards, authorising Horace-Camille Desmoulins, a lawyer, corporal of grenadiers of the National Guard, to wear the *médaille du Lys !*

The médaille du Lys ! What wonderful changes in this world of ours ! What would Camille have said could he have seen such a decoration on the breast of his son ?

2nd. A bachelor-at-law's diploma in favour of the same Horace-Camille Desmoulins, in the name of Napoléon, Emperor of the French, King of Italy and Protector of the Confederation of the Rhine—Paris, August 24, 1813 ; signed, Louis de Fontanes, grandmaster of the University.

3rd. A diploma of the Royal Arch. Mason Eagle Chapter, No. 54, at New York (April 5, 1824).

4th. A Certificate of the death of Horace-Camille Desmoulins.

Horace arrived at Hayti in 1817, and diĕd, like his father, at the age of *the sans-culotte Jesus* ; he was thirty-three years old, and the certificate gives us the date of his death, June 29, 1851.[1]

It was Madame Duplessis' fate to survive this child also. She lived, a relic of óther times, speaking eloquently of the tumultuous and eventful past. In her modest apartment in the Rue de la Sorbonne, forgotten, seeking retirement, and only opening her door to a few friends, she spoke softly of times gone by, and of great names departed. She recalled the romantic reminiscences, sorrowful at once and glorious, of the 14th of July, the 20th of June ; the dark tragedies of the 16th and 24th Germinal, the deaths of Camille and Lucile. Living thus, among the relics of her former life, Madame Duplessis and her daughter Adèle sometimes turned over the manuscripts of unpublished numbers of the 'Vieux Cordelier,' or the note-book of the poor young Lucile. She was like Rachel of old, less loud in her grief, but struck down as deeply, and like her refusing to be comforted.

To Madame Duplessis, history owes the restoration, in all its truth, of the vacillating but pleasing character of Camille Desmoulins. She has preserved and handed down to us the tradition of his troubled and tragic existence. She has pleaded, if I may say so, the cause of her children with posterity. And side by side with the young and smiling faces of Camille and Lucile, history has kept a place for the sorrow-stricken, serious, grave countenance of the aged white-haired woman, who survived all she loved

---

[1] We are indebted to the kindness of the distinguished doctor, M. Betonces of Hayti, for this information.

—a place which lasts longer than the glamour of popularity—longer than the clamour of hatred, which remains, when the Reign of Terror has long been over, like pardon, forgetfulness, consolation, reconciliation, and truth.

CONCLUSION.

IT is not without a certain melancholy that we re-open the annals of the past. History bears in its train, with its instructive lessons, its own especial sadness. What evils! What struggles! What destruction! What failures! What triumph of injustice! What terrible eclipse of right! What rude assertion of might! And, to recall only the period of those episodes which we have related, what hopes, brilliant at the beginning, and shattered at the end! If we were left with only the heart-breaking impression which every man with a heart must feel at the recital of such wholesale slaughter, we should shut up our book in despair, and ask ourselves whether the liberty the men of the eighteenth century desired so ardently to secure exacted so many sacrifices and so much blood? But it is from afar, from a distance, away from our own fireside, and as it were away from the centre of our present condition, now based upon equality, that the work of the French Revolution must be considered. Liberty it gave us only in part; but equality — which our national temperament, unfortunately, prefers to liberty—it established in reality and for ever. This is the great feat, the absolute result, which should console us for so many sorrows and make us forget them. This is what binds us, sons of the Revolution, to our tragic and magnificent past, to the bubbling crucible in which was elaborated modern society.

The Revolution will be to France what the Reformation has been to Germany—an era of remodelling, of fresh youth, and of new life. Each time we have frankly adopted its principles, we have felt stronger and more sure of ourselves. Each time we have denied them, we have become like a man who loses both his conscience and his confidence in himself. Come what may, the Revolution is to-day our great national tradition ; so true is this, that modern times admit of no form of government which does not proceed directly from the Revolution ; the Empire, which is a deviation from it ; or the Republic, which is its law.

But we must agree upon what is called the Revolution, and the time has arrived when we should accept nothing that is not fruitful and solid in it—political and social reform, generous ideas—when we should repudiate all that is theatrical and hurtful. Healthy ideas are to be found, codified, so to speak, in the ' Déclaration des Droits '; liberty is secured ; property is inviolable ; natural resistance to oppression is permitted ; in a word, the law has become the expression of the general will, and has a right to forbid only those actions which are hurtful to society ; public authority, the guarantee of the rights of each, is exercised for the advantage of all, and not for the private benefit of those in whom it is vested ; society having the right to call every public official to account for his administration. These are the true ideas of the Revolution ; its testament, I would say, if the Revolution were not still living, and if the benefits it desired to secure to future generations had not been taken from us only too often, and if we had not still to labour legally, without disorder or violence, for their security.

Our 'breakers ahead' are affectation, tragic grandeur, the love of fine words, of speech-making, of dramatic effect, which turned the Revolution into a tumultuous drama, at once terrifying and attractive —attractive in that it still further developed in the French that especial taste for outward demonstrations, for costumes, for shows, which lies at the foundation of the character of our race. The Revolution must not be confounded with revolutions. The Revolution is the complete reform of the ancient order of things ; revolutions are a series of shocks and of sudden ' *Coups d'état* ' which have more that once imperilled the very spirit of the Revolution.

It was to make an end of revolutions, tumults, and the *dog-days*,— as Camille Desmoulins said, in speaking of the outbreaks of the ' glorious faubourg ; '—it was to found liberty, to establish the Republic upon a solid basis, that the men whose history we have related risked and gave their lives. They were weary of magnificent but sterile demonstrations. The long lines of honest people offering the best of their goods to the country (a poor woman brought—do not let us laugh—*four eggs*, all she had to offer, to the country),[1] those manifestations of generous sentiments which spoke so loudly to the hearts of the masses had·

---

[1] ' Moniteur' of March 17, 1793, p. 346, 1 :
' I observe that a poor widow without any resources came to lay upon the altar of the country FOUR EGGS ; *it was all she had.* I regret not to be able to tell you her name.' (This widow was from Tarbes.) Féraud, deputy of the Hautes-Pyrénées, remarks this fact, and adds : 'A civic auction was at once opened, and the four eggs produced an offering of fifty *livres* for the war expenses.'—*Ibid.* (Sitting of Thursday, March 14, 1793.)

another side to them, when cunning men or madmen stirred up the mud in those grand and majestic currents. Danton was weary of these perpetual eddies. He knew that after the 10th of August came the dreaded 2nd of September. He wished to make the Nile return to its bed. Was this, as his mortal enemies called it, was this to be a counter-revolutionist? Yes, if by revolution we understand the perpetual abandonment to mere instincts. No, if we admit that the aim of the Revolution was the constitution of the Republic and the establishment of the laws. Like Mirabeau, Danton wished for *order* without the *ancient order*. He was right.

Doubtless the Reign of Terror, dear to Saint-Just under the name of 'justice,' and to Billaud-Varennes under the name of 'fear,' gave a sinister grandeur to the days gone by. Men's minds were invigorated by awe. See what dignity or poetry characterised their last hours. It was delirium, fever. They died like heroes, like Jean Petit, a volunteer in the first battalion of the Lombards, who said to the surgeon extracting the lead, 'Give me the bullet; I will send it back to the Austrians;' like the gunner who exclaimed, 'Pitt! your guineas would not have bought a drop of my blood, and I shed it all to-day for liberty;' like the man whom the Vendéans tortured because he had killed his king, and who cried out, with his feet upon the burning brands, 'Call him back to life, and I will do it again!'

All this is replete with tragic grandeur, sublime and wild. But did this national fever constitute, after all, a government able to secure what France had vainly demanded for nearly a century—a *morrow*? What had we come to, in 1793, and still more, in 1794, when Danton desired to ensure peace and liberty to France?

Camille Desmoulins propounded the question sorrowfully, with a sort of terrible presentiment :—

'Shall France,' he said, 'be a Republic, or will she seek in the Monarchy repose from her weariness of the continual treason of her representatives? Shall we form part of the Prussian or Austrian monarchies, or will France be dismembered into a federal Republic? Shall Paris, as the price of her civism and her sacrifices, be drowned in blood? Will you decree her entire destruction, the depopulation of the eighty-four departments, and perhaps fifty years of civil war? Shall it be a question whether the founders of the Republic are not worthy of death?'[1]

These were the thoughts and doubts which filled the hearts of some men then, and which, minus the threats of death, assail and profoundly disquiet the hearts of patriots now. 'What will France be? Whither is she tending? Will she be a Republic or a Monarchy? And—still more formidable question—will she be France?'

Alas! after having seen her fall so many times from liberty into despotism, free herself to-day to hold out her arms to the lictor's cords to-morrow—after having seen her hesitate, stagger, then rush blindly into the gulf, we ask ourselves, the terrible question which Desmoulins and Danton asked.

It is because they replied to this question that it was time to devote their lives to the *organisation* of the Republic—that is, to the welfare of the country; it is because they represented good sense, a clear view of the future, law and justice based upon pity and generosity, that I felt myself drawn towards them, and wished to add a page to their history.

They did not establish anything definitively because

[1] Speech on the trial of Louis XVI.

they died, because Robespierre himself fell in trying to take up, in another form, the task for which he assailed them so pitilessly ; they did not establish any-thing, and yet, on the day when the French nation enjoys peace and stability, it will be to them she will owe (and she will remember it) her emancipation and her new organization.

This day is perhaps far distant. The liberty of which Camille dreamed, that liberty which was the daughter of Athens reared under the sky of Gaul, liberty alike elegant and affable, is still far off. Until now we have preferred equality to liberty. We have let fall the substance for the shadow. What matters it to me that I am the equal of him who is not free ? What matters it to me that I share the rights of one whose right it is to grovel ? But equality fascinates, like a chimera, while liberty re-quires a loftier worship. This is the easy seduction of the one and the eternal charm of the other.

Let us then love and prefer, above all, the liberty which makes men honest and nations great. Let us love her, despite her excesses, and in order to hinder her excesses. A free people knows not the fury of nations that break their fetters and are but un-chained from time to time. Slaves only flock to the Saturnalia.

Let us not imitate these ancestors of the Revolution except in their probity and their uprightness, in those qualities which would easily make, despite its perils and trials, the epoch in which they lived more enviable than the degenerate times through which we drag our steps. Do not let our enthusiasm consist in a retro-spective passion for scarfs, plumes, or costumes. The Commune of 1871 has shown us what those traditions of

revolution, all display and sham, cost. Let us be of
our time, honouring the past for what was great in it,
but not seeking to begin it over again. The future
is made from to-day, not from yesterday. Let us try to
construct, not a revolutionary State always in effervescence, but a republican State, both solid and peaceable.

Let us cultivate our vines and our crops upon the
extinct volcano that none should rekindle; and while
the grumbling, the sullen roaring of the lava of hatred
shall pass away more and more with fresh generations,
let us think only of our mother, our country, whose
wounds are bleeding still, and of our betrothed—
Liberty, whom perhaps fate still reserves for our love!

It is with this prayer, this dream, that I wish to
conclude a book in which will be found, I think, hatred
of oppression, whatever it may be, and respect for
human life and liberty. But let us not forget the
Dantonists' death, that frightful sacrifice of devoted
citizens, while we say to ourselves that at least their
death was of some use. None of them in dying gave
the lie to their lives. As they lived, so they died. The
things of this world disenchant us often, but it would
be too bitter a thought that such sacrifices are useless,
and that the people for whom men such as these died
are incapable of being free, and will, as Tacitus says,
hurl themselves upon slavery. So many violent *Coups
d'état* of all sorts, so many successive deceptions, so
much ignorant despair, have perhaps at last accustomed
the nation to serve. Perhaps she feels lost without a
master. The restive horse wants the bit tightened, and
the manger full.

I will not believe this, and I will still hope.

'There shall be no *Brumaire* to obscure again the
great sun that only the blind do not see,' said

Bonaparte.   Peaceably, step by step, our France will make her way to a state of calmness and reparation where she will find once more her greatness and her *rôle.   The first of the everlasting flowers*, as a thinker who was also a poet called it, *the flower of humanity*, will once more shed its perfume.   And what joy would remain henceforth to the world if we should only prove to it that Cæsarism, open or disguised—that Cæsarism in which ended the Republic, the dream of Danton and Camille—is also the end of all human effort, of sacrifice, and of martyrdom ?

APPENDIX.

No. 1.

UNPUBLISHED FRAGMENTS OF CAMILLE DESMOULINS' WRITINGS.

All that comes from the pen of a great writer has a real importance, and especially whatever is left unfinished and can give, not a more perfect, but a more lifelike, idea of him. In certain fragments by political writers, as in a painter's sketches, though barely outlined, we discover the personality, the manner, and, as it were, the peculiar bent of the author's talent. The unpublished fragments which follow are therefore given as sketches. It will be seen in them how Desmoulins worked, making orderly notes tabulated as subjects and words, so that the journalist had at his disposal an alphabetical repertory, a portable arsenal of quotations. More than one article merely begun will also be found in these Notes. I have had to select from among them so as not to make my volume too large.

The authenticity of these Fragments is indisputable; M. Carteron copied them from Camille's manuscripts, in the possession of Baron Girardot; a piece of good luck by which we have profited, thanks to the politeness of M. F. Lock, who had these documents from M. Edouard Carteron.

Manners of the Romans.

Romulus divides the soil of the country into three parts: one for religion; another for the support of the government;

he distributes the third portion among the citizens. Hence, no taxes.

In the beginning there were patricians and plebeians in Rome ; but this distinction of the patricians in the beginning, the word *patrici*, meant only, some authors say, those who could give the name of their fathers. How many bastards there must have been in the thirty-five tribes !

The dignity of a prince of the Senate conferred only rank, without power. This post was, however, most honourable, because none but those who had led an irreproachable life could aspire to it.

When the Republic had become a flourishing state, each senator was obliged to prove possession of an annual income of forty thousand *livres*, and Augustus received a revenue of no less than sixty thousand *livres*.

The tribunes of the people convoked the Senate, and if any senators were absent they lost a certain fee. At Rome permission to speak was not asked ; the senators spoke in their turn.

If anyone opposed a decree, it was no longer a *senatus-consultum*, but was called the opinion of the Senate, *senatus auctoritas*.

At Rome the Senate was, properly speaking, only the ministry, the Council of State, the administrative body. The matters reported to the Senate, authors say, were all those which concerned the Republic ; but, 1st, the creation of magistrates ; 2nd, the legislation ; 3rd, deliberations concerning war and peace, were absolutely referred to the people. The Senate was so entirely subordinate to the Assembly of the people, that the people withdrew or restored its prerogatives at will. In the year 631 the tribune Sempronius Gracchus publishes a law which takes the judicial power from the senators and transfers it to the knights. What did the Emperors do in order to establish a despotism ? They began by transferring the *comitia* to the Senate ; they made over to them all the rights of the people, whom they thus despoiled of the legislative power and of their sovereignty. The *fasces* were lowered before the people in assembly, as were the colours before the king. The people were divided into thirty curiæ ; so soon as sixteen of these had given their opinion, the Assembly rose and the *plebiscite* was formed.

Varieties.

Two officers of the colonial regiment of Port-au-Prince narrate a touching anecdote ; an example of attachment and domestic virtue which only Eros, Antony's slave, has-hitherto offered, and which seems above human nature, and to belong only to dogs—animals, however, inferior to men in friendship. M. Monduit du Plessis, colonel of the regiment of Port-au-Prince, had a mulatto who was much attached to him. After the colonel had been hacked to pieces, the mulatto spent several days in gathering together his master's scattered limbs, and when he had done this, he dug a grave and buried them. For several days he was seen to shed tears over the grave, and he ended by shooting himself upon it with a pistol. He was found dead on his master's grave. When the first emotions of admiration aroused by this act were succeeded by reflection, an observer said, ' There are, then, men born to be slaves.' When death, which, in the old as in the new order, makes all ranks equal, had levelled every distinction between the colonel and the mulatto, might we not say that the latter, distracted by grief, still recognised a distinction between his master and himself—a distinction so deeply rooted that he would not even kill himself upon his master's body, lest their dust should mingle ; he only killed himself upon the grave ?

Mably.

' Money is the motive power of war,' said Aristias ; ' do you not see that our poverty does not permit us to have a fleet and to keep up an army?' 'These fine maxims,' says Phocion, ' would not have been heard when our fathers vanquished the Persians at Marathon and Salamis. They regarded temperance, the love of glory, courage and discipline as the sinews of war ; they despised money, which was useless to them ; they were poor, yet they built a numerous fleet to fight Xerxes : they constructed it out of the wood-work of their houses ; they did not pay their citizen soldiers, who had never commanded, and they vanquished the ten thousand immortals whose splendid achievements were the admiration of all Asia. If money be as powerful as Pericles called it, why do we not buy a Miltiades, an Aristides, a Themistocles, magistrates, citizens and heroes.

It is blasphemous to think that the gods make human reason contradict itself, by advising in the name of policy what it forbids in the name of morality. As for me, I make policy the servant of reason, and from that I see the happiness of communities arise.

Cyrus, wearied by the frequent revolts of the Lydians, ordered them to wear mantles and buskins ; he gave them entertainments, an opera-house, public walks, and enervated them by means of a circus and a pantheon.

Voltaire

calls the Witch of Endor, Mademoiselle d'Endor. He sings the praises of the journalist and his functions somewhere ; but after all we must say, as the magician Mambrès, in the 'Taureau Blanc,' says to the witch, Mademoiselle d'Endor : ' Comrade, your trade is a fine one, but dangerous ; and you run a risk of being hanged.'

It is not without reason that the ancients made young girls weep for their virginity before they were sacrificed ; meaning that there was nothing to regret in dying, when that was lost.

Mercury, the god of lawyers, thieves, and orators.

The minister who does not send in his accounts is like a man who, after having dined well, puts the forks and spoons in his pocket, and decamps without paying.

J.-J. Rousseau.

We are surrounded by people who complain of their lives. I ask if it has ever been heard that a free savage thought of complaining of his life or of depriving himself of it.

The conveniences of life soon lose their charm by use ; they degenerate into actual necessities, the loss of which is far more painful than their possession was pleasant.

When the ancients, says Gratianus, gave the ear of corn to Ceres as a legislatrix, and the name of Thesmophoria to a feast celebrated in her honour, they intended to signify that division of land had produced laws.

It is pleasant to hear Jean-Jacques exclaim at the simplicity of the manners of such great people as M. and Madame de Luxembourg. He weeps for joy, he wants to kiss the footprints of that good Marshal de Luxembourg who went out walking with one of his friends, a clerk of Britton's.

'Having finished reading " Julie," I at once began to read " Emile," that I might keep myself up in the presence of Madame la Maréchale.' What a mean creature !

' I received,' he says elsewhere, ' the greatest honour a man can receive : a visit from the Prince de Conti.' An honour which he shared with numerous prostitutes.

On reading his ' Confessions,' we say to him what he wrote to Voltaire : ' I do not like you.'

A Philosopher's Holidays (Materials).

We are doubly bound to pray for the emperors and the whole empire, because we know the end of the world and the miseries with which it threatens us are retarded by the Roman Empire.

In the public rejoicings, fires were made and tables were laid, people ate in the streets, they [1] . . . . in open day. The Christians took no part in all that . . . . [1] which drew down persecution. ' We are only of yesterday,' says Tertullian, in speaking of the Christians, ' and we are everywhere ; in your towns, your islands, your castles, your villages, your camps,. your tribes, in the palace, the Senate, in the public squares ; we leave you only your temples.'

The plays in Rome are excused on the ground, that men in masks took the women's parts ; but it is precisely men in women's clothes who are cursed by God in Deuteronomy.

[1] Erased in the MS.

C C

Tertullian compares with the feasts and pleasures of the heathen the pleasures of the Christians, and here they are, according to him: 'You trample the gods of the Gentiles under feet; you drive out devils, you heal the sick, you demand consolations. . . . These are the pleasures, these the plays of Christians.'

The envy of the clergy of the Roman Church of Tertullian, and the affronts they put upon him, drove him into the heresy of the Inontonists. Tertullian, in his treatise on the soul, believes that all souls remain in hell—that is, in the middle of the earth,—until the day of judgment, and that the (*blank*) of the saints were there relieved; he places the martyrs only in heaven.

Four Christian soldiers saw a young man being tortured, who, yielding to the pain, seemed about to renounce his faith; they began to grind their teeth with anger, to spread out their hands, and to make signs to him with their faces and their entire bodies. They were consequently led to the torture themselves.

And Satan entered. The sacrificing priest, surprised, hastened to Gregory, asking to be instructed, but the instruction displeased him. 'Never mind,' said B——, 'I will pass over my doubts, if you will command this stone to change its place and go to another,' which he indicated. Gregory having uttered the command, the stone, which was enormous, *limes agro positus*, set off at once and did not stop until it reached the place indicated by the heathen priest; who thereupon confessed Christianity.

In Origen we trace the pride and insolence of the bishops; we repulse the poor, we want to have body guards such as belong to kings.

Origen thought it necessary to observe to the letter the law concerning the first-fruits, also several others which had not been abolished by the Gospel; what he says of first-fruits, he says also of tithes, and what he says of fruit he also says of herds.[1] St. Cyprian attributes persecution to the relaxation of morals: women paint; men dye their beards, eyebrows

---

[1] Erased in the MS.

and hair ; many bishops quit their sees, abandon their flocks, go into the provinces, to frequent fairs and enrich themselves by traffic (*blank*). We are full of pride, jealousy, and division ; we neglect simplicity and faith, we have renounced the world in word but not in deed ; we please ourselves, and we are displeasing to everyone else. When the persecution of Decius was proclaimed at Carthage, the magistrates' tribunals were besieged by an immense crowd of Christians hastening to offer sacrifice to the gods. A cord was put round the neck of the priest Pionius to drag him to the temple in order to kill him ; six soldiers pulled at it with all their might, but he resisted so hard that they were obliged to force him into the temple with kicks. This Pionius was one of those most renowned among the Christians for science and philosophy.

Let those who have denied their faith, if at the point of death and no priest can be found, confess to a deacon, and having received the imposition of hands, let them go to the Lord in peace.—*St. Cyprian.*

Pertinent Allusions.

To people who come to hear sermons for the sake of the preacher's eloquence may be applied what Joseph said to his brethren who had come to Egypt in search of corn: *Non frumenti quæsitores, sed exploratores estis.—Massillon.*

M. le Brun carried off at twenty years of age the *accessit* of the Academy. In a notice of the young author's paper, Fréron ends with these words : ' Monsieur, France has already given birth to a great painter of the same name as yours ; there is room to hope that in our days *ut pictura poesis erit.*' —*Fréron.*

Erasmus loved to live at Basle ; he left the place sometimes, but always returned thither : *hic illius arma, hic currus fuit.* —*Bayle.*

The hypocrite covers his snares with the externals of religion. He displays a superficial piety so as to give freer course to his passions, and like the priests of the temple of Babylon, he offers all to the divinity in public ; in secret, and

by subterranean passages, he takes it all back for himself.—
Massillon.

At the Council of Trent, a French bishop complained of
the abuses committed in the disposal of benefices ; an Italian
prelate having said with a sarcastic smile, ' *Gallus cantat,*'
' *Utinam,*' replied the Bishop of Lavour, Pierre Danet, who
was French ambassador, ' *utinam ad hunc Galli cantum
excitaretur petrus, et fleret amare.*

Appropriate Applications.

The Cabal having suppressed the names of Pascal[1] and
Arnauld in the Lives of Illustrious Men, the public remembered what Tacitus says : *Præfulgebant Cassius et Brutus eo
ipso quod illorum effigies non viseretur.*

Some one said, pointing to Father Bauny, an extremely
lax casuist, *Ecce qui tollit peccata mundi.*

How many afflictions there are of which the consolation
is more difficult to bear than the affliction itself ! Joseph's
brethren hastened to wipe away Jacob's tears ; it was they
who had made them flow.—*F. de Neuville.*

The Duke of Burgundy showed the most vicious incli-
nations, but what plant could have remained diseased under
Fénelon's hands ? He smothered the germs of every vice in
his pupil, and made of him the amiable prince so much regretted
by our fathers. M. de la Harpe, in his eulogium upon Fénelon, supposes that when the education of this young prince,
already depraved, was committed to him, the good prelate
said in his heart what God said of man at the Creation :
' Let us make him in our image.' A sublime thought, and to
which it is impossible to add anything without weakening its
effect.

Polybius begged Cato to obtain from the Senate that the
exiles of Achaia, whom he had already sent back to their own
country, should be reinstated in all their posts and dignities.
Cato said to him : ' Polybius, you do not imitate the wisdom
of Ulysses ; you want to go back into the Cyclop's cavern for
a forgotten hat or girdle.'

---

[1] Desmoulins wrote *Paschal.*

Charles I. invented the word Demagogue.

The English people dragged the Protestant bishops out of the Upper House by their rochets, but they well deserved to be dragged out of it in another manner.

According to ancient law, Parliaments ought to have been held in London twice a year (?) The people wished the sittings to be triennial under Charles I. and the ministers ; afterwards they found it to their advantage to make them septennial.

This is what that animal, a king, is ! Charles I. in his book, written in prison, says : ' Good subjects do not consider it just that the condition of kings should be made worse by the amelioration of their own lot.'

Charles I. said to his Parliament, before accepting the new Constitution (*the nineteen propositions*), he must chew morsels of that kind before swallowing them : he must deliberate. 'But,' Milton said in answer, 'if the nation tastes nothing that he has not chewed, he must take the nation for a big baby in long clothes.'

Varia.

A young lady, before whom Voltaire was standing, having begged him to sit down, he said to her : ' No, mademoiselle, I am the audience, and I am looking at a pretty piece.' He said to Father Adam, a Jesuit who had criticised him : ' It is well known that Father Adam is not the first man in the world.'

We all like to see people whom we have obliged ; in consequence, kindnesses secure favour, and favour new kindnesses ; this is why the celebrated Comte de Grammont asked Louis XIV. one day for a crown, adding, that it was ' only the first kindness which cost.'

The Emperor of China never signs a death-warrant without preparing himself for it by fasting, and no one can sign a death-warrant but himself. In China, the sagacity which has discovered a culprit in spite of the shifts he used to escape, is less praised than the penetration of the judge who discerns innocence under the appearance of guilt.

In 1774 M. de Solar, a young officer of the Swiss Guards, gave a rare example of conjugal love. He put an end to his life by strangling himself with his hair, which was very handsome, and of which his mouth and throat were full.[1]

Cicero tells us that his friends left him legacies which increased his fortune by two millions (francs).

Who would venture to boast of his plate after what Pliny tells of a slave of Claudius, who had nine silver dishes, one of which weighed five hundred pounds; and that the granddaughter of Zollius, at an ordinary wedding-supper, displayed ornaments worth seven millions, 782,010 *livres*? Sixty years before, Æsop the actor had had at his table a dish of birds costing 19,453 *livres*.

Froissart remarks that Charles V. ennobled the profession of lawyers : *equites creati sunt.* In Savoy, in Italy, in Venice and in Spain, lawyers are noble by a real and transmissible nobility. It was the custom for Parliaments under Louis XII. to present three candidates for a vacant place, and the king then nominated one chosen from amongst the leading lawyers.

It was represented to Mazarin that the people were complaining of the taxes. 'Let them cackle,' he said, 'while we eat their eggs.'

In the times of Justinian, forty thousand bushels of corn were daily distributed to the people of Constantinople; that is, enough to feed two hundred and forty thousand men.

Pliny speaks of a sort of ballet executed by elephants; besides which, according to him, they walked upon the tight rope, and four of them carried a litter in which was another elephant. He also relates that one of these animals wrote on the pedestal of a trophy in Greek letters, 'I myself have traced these letters and dedicated the spoils of the Celts.'

The same author says that Strabo of Sicily was so sharp-sighted that from the promontory of Lilybæum he counted the vessels entering the port of Carthage, which is physically impossible, as the furthest distance the eye can reach is thirty leagues. Valerius Maximus, Cicero, Elienus, Varro, and Solinus, relate the same fact.

---

[1] Scratched out in the MS.

Barthol says that a man who had taught civil law for ten years was a knight, *ipso facto.*

During the proscriptions, Attilius the younger was invested with the toga of manhood before his majority, in order that he might be proscribed. A head was brought to Antony, who said, 'I do not know that man ; this is no doubt an affair of my wife's,' and he spoke the truth.

The emperor Otho III. had married a princess of Arragon, named Maria. While they were passing through Modena, the empress fell violently in love with a young Italian count ; he, just married and idolising his wife, met the empress's advances by excuses, and Maria, imitating Phædra and Potiphar's wife, accused him of having tried to seduce her. The credulous emperor had the young man's head cut off on the spot, but the young countess threw herself at the feet of the monarch, revealed the queen's crime, and demanded the ordeal by fire in proof of her words. She held the red-hot iron for a long time without being burnt, and Otho caused the empress to be burnt alive in the great square at Modena, and himself paid a heavy fine to the countess.

Formerly, the inhabitants of certain districts had the right to avoid imprisonment if they could find bail ; among these were Nevers, Saint-Geniés in Languedoc, and Villefranche in Périgord.—*Encyclopédie*, word *prison.*

According to the ancient laws of the kingdom, no one could be arrested or made a prisoner for any other cause than a capital and notorious crime.—*Ord. des rois de France,* vol. i. p. 12. If a citizen was arrested for any reason, unless indeed he was notoriously guilty, it was allowable to rescue him from his captors.—*Ibid.* vol. iii. p. 17.

A little bird, pursued by a sparrow-hawk, took refuge under the robe of Xenocrates ; he saved its life and gave it back its liberty, saying, 'Let us never deceive the hopes of those who have recourse to us.'

The laws of Draco punished idleness with death. A law of Solon decreed the same penalty against a magistrate who should be found drunk.

A royal edict in 1757 decrees that all authors, printers, or distributors of books tending to attack religion, to excite the public mind, and to impair the king's authority, be condemned to death; and the detestable Mugart de Vouglans inserted this edict in his compilation.

We may judge of the rank and preeminence of ecclesiastical dignities by one of the canons of the third Lateran Council, held in 1779. It is ordered that archbishops attending the council shall have only forty horses, bishops twenty, cardinals twenty-five, archdeacons seven, and deans two.[1]

Pliny says that Anaxagoras predicted the fall of a stone, which, at the time indicated, did fall into the Ægos Potamos. The astronomers of antiquity were more skilful than those of our day. We may judge of the knowledge of the ancients by this fact: Pytheus said that in the island of Thule, called by Virgil *Ultima Thule*, six days' journey from Great Britain, there was neither earth, nor sea, nor air, but a mixture of the three elements, in which it was not possible to walk on foot nor go in a vessel; he spoke of it as of a thing which he had seen.

Hippocrates begins his aphorisms with these grand words: 'Life is short, art is long, opportunity fleeting, experience dangerous, judgment difficult.'

Louis, King of Navarre, and Charles, Count de la Marche, both sons of Philippe le Bel, and who reigned after him, had married respectively—Louis, Margaret of Burgundy, and Charles, Blanche de la Marche, princesses endowed with many personal and mental charms. They passed the spring at the abbey of Montbrisson, where they gave themselves up to the pleasure of loving and being loved. The princesses had for lovers two brothers, Philippe and Gauthier de Launay. The two brothers having been found in the beds of the two princesses, were arrested and sentenced by the Parliament to be flayed alive and dragged by horses over a newly-ploughed field. In 1313 the Queen of Navarre was strangled with a winding-sheet at Château Gaillard.

According to Herodotus, Aristotle describes Babylon as so large a city, that the enemy having entered it at one end, the news of their arrival was not known at the opposite end

---

[1] Among the Jews, the law forbade a husband to leave his wife during the first year of marriage.

until three days after, in consequence of the distance of the two quarters from each other. There are few falsehoods of such magnitude, and Herodotus has here surpassed the passage in the Scriptures in which it is said that Jonah occupied three days in traversing Nineveh. Would it be believed that modern writers have exaggerated still more ; if we are to credit Marco Polo, Quincoy, a town in China, had seventy-two thousand stone bridges. Mendez-Pinto, Herrera, Mal-sonati, and Trigant have said of this town that a man on horseback can hardly traverse it in one day ; that it is thirty leagues in circumference, ten long, and fifteen wide ; that it has four hundred and eighty gates, and walls upon which twelve horses could go abreast.

We read in Josephus that it is established by the testimony of Hesiod, Argesilaus, Hellenicus, Nicholas of Damascus, Manetho, Berosus, Moschus, Estiæus, and Jerome of Egypt, that the ancients frequently lived a thousand years. It is related in the Life of Tamerlane that a man of Sogdiana lived three hundred and fifty years. Gassendi makes mention of a Persian who, in his time, was about four hundred years of age. Xenophon allots eight hundred to the king of I know not what island ; but all this is little in comparison with the life of Macrosiris, which avers that he had lived five thousand years.—*Huet.*

Among the Gauls, the fine for touching a woman's hand was fifteen *sols* ; for touching her arm, thirty *sols* ; for the elbow, thirty-five *sols* ; for the breast, forty-five *sols.*—*Lex salica*, title 25. The fine for rape was the same as for murder, two hundred pounds.[1]

Such is the inviolable respect due to forms that Scipio Africanus, being censor, did not dare to strike off the list of knights a certain Licinius, although he declared himself certain of his guilt, because no one presented himself to offer proofs.

The favourites of Richard II. caused a notice to be published in London that no one was to prefer any charge, no matter what, against them, under pain of confiscation.

---

[1] Erased in the MS.

At Rome, when a young man was called to the bar, it was a day of triumph in the family. Augustus, wishing his two sons to matriculate, at the same time demanded the consular dignity for them. Tiberius honoured with his presence the first appearance at the bar of his son Drusus, and of Nero and Drusus, his grandsons.

In 1763 Lord Ferrers, a blood relation of the Royal family of England, was hanged publicly in London for having killed his servant; this did not prevent his brother from taking his seat on the following day in the House of Lords.[1]

The Arcadians, after having put to death their king Aristocrates, a traitor to his country, caused these words to be engraved upon the column which they erected in the temple of Jupiter: 'Perjured kings are punished sooner or later by the aid of Jupiter. We have at last discovered the perfidy of him who betrayed Messenium. Great Jupiter be praised!'

Xenophon said, more than twenty centuries ago: 'The great difference Lycurgus has brought about between Lacedæmon and other cities consists in this, that there every citizen obeys the laws; he comes when the magistrate calls: but at Athens, a rich man would be in despair if he were thought to depend upon the magistrate.' This is precisely our case: the people is under the yoke of a law which is only an additional bondage, since it is not the safeguard of liberty, and all men of position consider it beneath them to demand redress of injuries from ordinary justice.

Mézerai wrote on the margin of his copy of Daubigné's 'Universal History': *Duo tantum hæc opto: unum ut moriens populum francorum liberum relinquam, alterum ut ita cuiquam veniat, sicut de republica merebitur.*

A charming religion is that of the Basilists and Carpocratians; they set forth that we were born in a state of nature, innocent, like Adam, at the moment of creation, and therefore ought to imitate his nudity; they detested marriage, maintaining that but for sin it would never have existed. In order to restore the innocent life of the earthly paradise and the pleasures of the Golden Age, they practised their rites in a

---

[1] It is hardly necessary to observe that Camille Desmoulins is mistaken in attributing this relationship to Earl Ferrers.

superb subterranean temple, heated by stoves, which temple they entered naked, both men and women. There, everything was permitted them, even unions which we call adulterous and incestuous, so soon as the chief of the assembly had pronounced these words from Genesis : ' Increase and multiply.'

Near Lake Morat, in Switzerland, over a heap of bones, there is still to be found the following sublime inscription : ' The Burgundians thought to conquer a free people : behold what is left of them ! '

The Christians.

The following fragments seem to belong to a work upon Christ. It is impossible to quote more than these samples. In what we suppress Camille makes no exegesis ; he jests and scoffs in the tone habitual to the eighteenth century, after the fashion of Voltaire, or rather of Parny.

.... Astonishing that anyone should ever have existed who dared to proclaim that he would disperse the darkness which has covered the universe since its birth, that he was the bearer of truth to men ; this truth, according to his account, he had brought from heaven. At least, it was not at the feet of sages and doctors that he had learned it ; he had not come out of their schools, but from the workshop of a poor artisan, to men who for thirty years had witnessed his obscure life amongst them. From handling the axe and the saw, from making ploughs and yokes, he came to people who had the soundest ideas of divinity, who had never erected altars to any man, and who were proud of their Law, the tables of which they believed to be written by the hand of God himself. To this people he announced himself as a legislator, and as a God, venturing to retouch the work of the Deity, and to teach a new doctrine. He did not attempt to establish it by disputation as do the philosophers ; he propounded it with simplicity and without argument. He chose his disciples from the lowest class of the people ; sent these men, who could not read, to instruct sages and nations ; predicted to them the success of their mission, the duration of his reign, even until the end of time ; and, to effect this great revolution, to per-

suade all nations, supplied them with only the simple formula :
'Jesus has said it.' That is to say : 'Greeks, Romans, nations
who look upon yourselves as the most enlightened of the universe, truth has issued from that corner of the world whose
people seem to you most stupid and despicable of all ; submit
your reason to the authority of a carpenter of this base nation,
overturn your altars that you may raise one to a Jew, who
died upon a gibbet, amid the insults and yells of his own
people, scoffing at his divinity. These dogmas which revolt
you and seem to you utter folly, you are to believe blindly;
walk no more in the steps of your fathers, who expiate in
another life by eternal torments the misfortune of not having
been able to hear us, and the error of their age. Instead of
a joyous religion, which teaches pleasure, and is suited to
every taste, a religion in which dancing, plays, feasts, and
pleasures are worship, and which had everything in its favour
except reason, embrace a religion which is not that of your
fathers, a religion which is sorrowful, austere, the enemy of
the gentlest desires of nature, which restrains joy, which only
promises reward to tears, to suffering, and to poverty, which
is only good for hospitals, a religion in which riches and
honours are of no value, grace and beauty of no use, in
which the wise and the gifted are to envy the poor in spirit,
which offers to its votaries a cross and a crown of thorns ; and
all this in order that they may enjoy in some third heaven,
a kind of felicity that the eye has never seen, and of which
no idea can be formed.'

Nevertheless the ancient cultus was abjured ; crowds threw
themselves into the bosom of that religion which has everything against it, and especially reason. If Jesus worked the
miracles which are related, I am not astonished; the resur-
rection of a dead man silences all objections and removes all
difficulties ; but you, who do not accept miracles, can you
explain the progress of a religion which is so irksome and so
oppressive . . . . which, in spite of hatred and . . . . through
opprobrium, the stake, the scaffold, and persecutions of all
sorts, advances so rapidly towards the conquest of the
universe ?

The Martyrs.[1]

. . . . How does the author of all evil profit by this ?

SOSTHENES.—I could wish God had only granted the gift of miracles to those who had received a mission from him. But, at least, there will always be this difference between the miracles transmitted to posterity by the annals of paganism, and those which Jesus worked, that the witnesses of the latter died to attest what they had seen. I say, with Pascal, ' I will believe witnesses who die for the truth they assert.'

NEARCHUS.—So you are persuaded to believe because of the crowd of martyrs who have shed their blood for their religion. If the priests of Esculapius had given their lives in testimony of the truth of the miracles they relate, you would then believe them also.

We do not see that the priests of any religion have died to attest the truth of the miracles which have been the foundation of that religion. But were they reduced to the necessity of dying, or of denying that they had seen these miracles? No Pagan government ever put those who maintained the truth of religion to this test ; if they had been reduced to such an alternative, how do I know what they would have done? I incline to think there were devotees among the priests who would have let their throats be cut to attest these miracles.

Obstinacy will undoubtedly make a man face death. Pellegrinus even ascended a funeral pile out of vanity, wholly and solely to make a show. Empedocles burnt himself for the same foolish reason. A coward will brave death and a forlorn hope to escape the charge of cowardice ; a poltroon will fight a duel in deference to public opinion. Did not the early Christians mount the scaffold rather than be accounted cowards and apostates? Those who denied their faith during the persecutions were held in horror by the faithful, who fled from them as the Jews fled from lepers. Ecclesiastical history tells us that the very peasants reproached them with their

[1] A passage also belonging to the work upon Christ.

meanness. What strength to resist torments must the thought have given them that they were going to be canonised and honoured, that they would be regarded as saints, as demigods! What pride for an artisan, for a man of the lower classes! 'My bones will be enclosed in a reliquary and kissed; I shall give my name to a day of the year; it will also be said that I have worked miracles, I, a poor mean slave! I shall have a tomb which will be venerated by posterity, where a temple will be built in which I shall be invoked!' They were so full of the thought of their apotheosis and of the name they would leave behind them, that a great number had the account of their martyrdom and of their visions in prison written. Their judges knew how much this prospect would support them in their torments, and therefore, to deprive them of such a stay, they were told before sentence was pronounced: 'Doubtless you imagine that women will come to collect your ashes, that they will wrap your remains in silk, and embalm them with perfumes? But do not flatter yourself, it shall not be permitted.' And let it not be said that it is only in later times these great honours were rendered to the martyrs, since we see that the faithful religiously kept the stones with which St. Stephen, the first martyr, had been put to death. And we are surprised that, full of these hopes and already surrounded by the aureole, the martyrs should have braved death—we who see thousands of soldiers face it daily in battle for five *sols*, without even the poor consolation of embellishing the gazette with a name to be forgotten on the morrow! In India, how many women have been burnt on the funeral pile of husbands whom they did not love, that they might be accounted faithful, and because it was the custom! Do we not daily see suicides descend tranquilly into the grave without any reason so far as we know? Let us confess it; a very little thing will sometimes determine a man to suffer death.

A citizen of Sybaris said that it was no wonder the Spartans sought to die in battle that they might rest themselves from so much toil and from their austere and rigorous discipline. Can we read what the fathers of the first centuries tell us of the lives of the early Christians, and not say the same of them ; and with much more reason, because beyond the tomb the Christians saw the heavens open, and an immortal crown as the reward of their sacrifice ?

Tragical death of my cousin Philippe.—His character.— Preface to his works.

. . . . Unfortunately he had taken the pistol which was loaded with bullets and cousin Philippe fell. I ran up in despair ; he was naturally melancholy, but had he been as great a jester as his brother Jacques, his gaiety might have deserted him. What was my astonishment when, pressing my hand, he said, ' At last I have some weight(lead) in my brain, late enough. How I regret not having foreseen that I should be killed ! I should have died speaking like Socrates and Seneca. What beautiful things I would have said ! My last conversation should have been the preface to my works, instead of leaving it to my editor to pass a preliminary eulogium upon them. I should have praised myself much better.' ' O my poor cousin !' I replied, ' most unfortunate of poets and of lawyers ! why should it happen that the first time you walked with a respectable woman at the Luxembourg, a bearded gallant should have taken advantage of your growing whiskers and thought he could insult her with impunity ? This is what one gets by walking with respectable women ! How much better if you had continued to follow the instructions of wise Cato, if you had only gone amongst prostitutes ; and how right is Horace, that eminently sensible man, when he says old Cato's apothegm is divine : *Inquit sententia dia Catonis.*' ' What memories you have just recalled !' replied Philippe. ' Why carry me back to that happy time when, as the day declined, cheating the vigilance of the porter, we escaped together from college to fly to the Palais-Royal, to that garden preferable to the garden of Eden, and by lamplight passed in review a much finer army than that of Xerxes. O charming and tender Rose ! Let us put these ideas away. Would you have me regret life ? This premature death is not a great misfortune for me. What should I have done in the world, a poet without patronage, and a lawyer without a case ? My imagination was failing. Women, pretty women I mean, of whom I have always been so fervent an adorer, the only beings whose divinity I never dared to call in question, no longer inspired me with religious sentiments, and I was becoming a complete atheist. I said of them still, like Jean the rake : " Under heaven is there a finer animal ? " but I no longer placed them upon an altar, and I happened sometimes to read Cicero or Desmoulins without my reading being interrupted by what devotees call ejaculatory prayers. What have I then to regret in life ? I should not have succeeded at the bar ; I cannot speak for a quarter of an hour without being hoarse. I had nothing in common with those who make large fortunes. Look at that man who can hardly carry his big brief bag. What advantage has he over others ? That of a watermill over a windmill. Just as the latter can only turn when the wind blows, so other lawyers can only speak when they have something to speak about, whereas he is always turning, like the mill on the river.[1] Nature having refused me this great talent, the resource of writing was left me ; but, I know not by what fatality, I could not exercise my faculties upon praiseworthy subjects ; nothing has ever struck me so much in my life.'

I.

There is this difference between the Monarchy and the Republic : that the reigns of the most wicked emperors, Nero, Tiberius, Claudius, Caligula, and Domitian, had a happy beginning ; the advantage of Republics is that they improve.

We have seen that Trajan said of his sword, *Pro me, si mereor, in me.*[2] Saying is not doing ; it belongs only to a senate to deal rigorously with the sovereign, and to send a hundred of its members to the Revolutionary Tribunal.

To be able to do everything, and to denounce, to be vanquished by ignorance (blank) with impunity, by calling oneself

---

[1] It is amusing enough to meet with this satire upon the legal profession from the pen of a lawyer turned pamphleteer. (J. C.)

[2] Aur. Vict. De Cæs. 13.—Dion, lviii. 16.—Cf. Pliny, *Pan.* 67.

a Jacobin or a Cordelier, is not this returning to the time when the slave might insult his master, the criminal might escape justice, the most infamous scoundrel [1] or most vicious woman might do every imaginable injury to a good man, and a senator, by wearing the image of Tiberius or Augustus?

Aquilius Regulus, the denouncer, was twice honoured with the consulate as a reward for his denunciations,[2]

· Usurping power by denunciation and means so base that they dishonoured power itself, denouncers were not more detested for their crimes than for the salary they derived from them.

The Convention would have done better to grant full liberty of speech, than to have missed so much important information. The sovereign whose ears are over-sensitive sees himself dethroned before he suspects that he is hated, and hardly knows an interval between the praise of flatterers and the guillotine.

The Romans allowed Sylla to live, the Syracusans Dionysius, the Athenians Pisistratus—despicable nations [3] who suffered little from the evils of tyranny, since they pardoned the tyrant.

Will not the world be reformed rather by patriotism than by Christianity? And is it not only one hypocrisy and one monkery [4] succeeded by another? Thus we have seen Fénelon and the solitaries of Port-Royal hated and persecuted as bad Christians, while others, contemptible and debauched, received applause and incense ; [5] the most stupidly ignorant, the most infamously voluptuous, the most violent bigots were regarded as the ornaments,[6] the fathers of the Gallican Church.

Doubtless Solon will succeed to Draco.

And yet, never were so many great men seen : Brutus,

---

[1] Doubtful—*blackened with vices* can be read distinctly.

[2] The two fragments are perhaps only one ; nevertheless, they are separate in the MS.

[3] Doubtful—the word *nations* only.

[4] There is *monkery* ; I was long inclined to read *mummery*.

[5] The word is very difficult to read, but I believe this reading is correct.

[6] *Sic* in the MS.

Scipio, Anacharsis, Anaxagoras, Gracchus, and my valet de chambre is Epaminondas.[1]

II. *My Tablets.*

Neque enim quum lectulus aut me
Porticus excepit, desum mihi : ' Rectius hoc est,
Hoc faciens vivam melius [sic dulcis amicis
Occurram; hoc quidam non belle ; numquid ego illi
Imprudens olim faciam simile ? ' Hæc ego mecum
Compressis agito labris] ; ubi quid datur otî,
Illudo chartis.—HORACE, *Sat.* I. iv. 133-139.

Claude de l'Étoile, one of the first Academicians who had the reputation of a *connoisseur* in his time, caused a young man, who had come from Languedoc with a comedy which he thought a masterpiece, and in which the academician pointed out a thousand defects, to die of grief. This great *connoisseur* said seriously that he would rather have written the last scene of the 'Danaïdes,' by Gombaut, than the best plays that had appeared in the last twenty years. And observe that Corneille's masterpieces had just then come out! In the same way Passerat declared that he would rather have written Ronsard's ode to the Chancellor de l'Hôpital than be Duke of Milan.

Under Tiberius, all people condemned to death who waited for execution, lost their property, and were deprived of burial. Those who had the courage to kill themselves were buried, and could make a will. It is astonishing that duelling was unknown to a nation by whom suicide was held in such honour. We need seek no other motive for this premium given to suicide than in the policy of the tyrant, who was pleased that those he had proscribed and condemned should appear to have condemned themselves.

[1] *Note* :—These two fragments (X. and XI.) are very difficult to read ; nevertheless, by means of a magnifying glass, I succeeded in restoring them accurately. At least, I think so. (J. C.)

These curious and important little notes, copied from the original belonging to Baron de Girardot, occupy the right-hand side of a page ; the last two begin the left-hand side of the sheet, which is unfinished ; the rest is blank.

The following passage in a letter from Cicero to Atticus is remarkable: 'If you would know why Clodius was pardoned, seek no further than the indigence and turpitude of his judges. . . .'[1] Not even in a gaming-house was so infamous an assemblage seen.[2] Crassus conducted the whole affair: he sent for the judges, made promises to them, offered them bail, and made them presents. Into the bargain, certain judges were to have the favours of several ladies of quality.'[3]

Harmodius and Aristogeiton, who had conspired against Hipparchus and Hippias, the two tyrants of Athens, were to stab them during a procession; as the procession was leaving the Bull's Eye, they saw one of the conspirators speaking familiarly to Hippias. Believing themselves betrayed, they determined to sell their lives dearly, and stabbed Hipparchus; Harmodius fell at the same moment covered with wounds. Aristogeiton, being arrested and put to the torture, accused the most faithful friends of Hippias, who ordered them to be executed on the spot. 'Hast thou more villains to denounce?' cried the tyrant in a fury. 'Only thyself,' replied the Athenian; 'I die, and in dying I carry with me the satisfaction·of having deprived thee of thy best friends.'[4]

Pisistratus, being accused of a murder, appeared before the Areopagus to justify himself, as though he had been the meanest citizen.

Otanes, after the death of Cambyses, proposed to establish a democracy; few in high places would do likewise.

What reflections are called forth by the conduct of Zopyrus, who, in order to deceive the enemy and open the gates of Babylon to the king his master, cut off his nose and his ears, and mutilated himself from head to foot—if the incident be true! Must we admire him as we admire ·Eros the

---

[1] Ab Attic. I. 16, vol. xxi. p. 86. Leclerc: 'Si causam quæris absolutionis, egestas judicium fuit et turpitudo. . . .'

[2] Page 88 : 'Non enim unquam turpior in ludo talario confessus fuit.'

[3] Page 90 : 'Biduo per unum servum, et eum ex gladiatorio ludo, confecit totum negotium: arcessivit ad se, promisit, intercessit, dedit. Jam vero (o dii boni !) rem perditam ! etiam noctes certarum mulierum atque adolescentulorum nobilium introductiones nonnullis judicibus pro mercedis cumulo fuerunt.'

[4] Thucyd.

slave, who set the example of death to Antony ? Or shall we call him a madman ? Racine, and our old Trivulcius, dying of grief at not having been saluted by the king, were sick of this same servile fever.

Histiæus of Miletus had raised all the Greeks of Ionia against Darius, but he had also prevented the destruction of the bridge of the Ister, against the advice of Miltiades, and had formerly saved the army of Darius from utter ruin in the expedition to Scythia. Darius would have forgiven him in memory of this service if his generals had not hastened to put him to death. The Persians rewarded crimes and benefits alike.

Darius, on learning the burning of Sardis, was so furious that he charged one of his officers to remind him daily to take vengeance for it. He must have been strangely absent-minded if it was necessary to remind him of the burning of this capital ! What an idea does this give us of kings ?

Aristides, when exiled, left Athens, praying for his country.

A violent storm having destroyed the bridge Xerxes had made, he ordered the workmen to be beheaded, and the sea to be whipped and branded with a red-hot iron.

The companions of Leonidas honoured by anticipation his death and their own by a funeral combat at which their fathers and mothers were present. They then conducted their relatives to a distance from the city, where they bade them an eternal farewell. Then it was that Leonidas said to his wife, who asked what were his last wishes : ' I wish you a husband worthy of you, and children who shall resemble him.'

Xerxes wrote to him : 'If thou wilt submit, I will give thee the empire of Greece.' Leonidas replied, ' I would rather die for my country than enslave her.'

The Duke de Richelieu, when shut up in the Bastile, was visited by two princesses of the blood royal, rivals, and both in love with him, who, disguised as servants, spent a hundred thousand crowns in bribing the jailors.

The day after the death of Louis XIV., the Parliament assembled, and received a lettre de cachet from Louis XV., aged five years. A lettre de cachet at five years old !

The peers would not uncover to the first President, while speaking. This affair made a great noise. The peers, said the Parliament in its memorial, venture apparently to include this assembly, the most august in the kingdom, in the tiers état.

A medal was decreed to the Duke of Bedford with this inscription : *For having planted an acorn.*

Henry IV. called himself *a bourgeois of Paris.*

A law of Athens forbade anyone under fifty years of age to speak in public.

Critias, one of the thirty tyrants, carried that ridiculous law by which it was forbidden to teach the art of reasoning.

In general, those who mix themselves up in public affairs are not disinterested, and the reflection of Demadus the orator, who found Phocion at table and was surprised at his extreme frugality, was a very just one: ' I am astonished,' said he, ' that, being content with so humble a repast, you take the trouble to mix yourself up in the affairs of the Republic.'

Aristides abolished that law of Solon, which only allowed such citizens to be raised to the magistracy as received from their land at least two hundred measures of wheat, oil, and wine, which was the ruin of the aristocracy of Athens. Mably says this was a great mistake.

No. 2.

Verses by Camille Desmoulins.

I. *To Miss L——, a young English lady.*

To the air *O ma tendre musette,* or to the air of the ballet of '*Armide.*' [1]

> Pardon, si, sur ses traces,
> On me voit chaque soir ;
> Mais pour suivre les grâces
> Est-il besoin d'espoir ?

[1] These verses are *unpublished.* They were communicated to us by M. C. Charavay. We give them merely as a curiosity.

Sans pouvoir m'en défendre
Mes jours vont s'écouler,
Le matin à l'attendre,
Le soir à l'admirer.

Cherchais-tu la plus belle
Qu'on trouve sous les cieux ?
Regardez : c'est bien elle
Que demandaient tes yeux.
Ne cherchais-tu que celle
Qui promit le bonheur ?
Eh bien ! c'est encore elle
Que demandait ton cœur.

Ta cousine est jolie ;
Mais seulement tu veux
Disputer à Fannie
A qui courra le mieux.
Oh ! prolonge l'enfance
Par ces jeux, mais pourquoi ?
Clarisse, l'innocence
N'a point d'âge pour toi.[1]

II. *To the King.*[2]

Qu'aujourd'hui mes vers, les muses une fois,
Au lieu de les flatter, épouvantent les rois !
Stupides citoyens, ô lâches que nous sommes !
Un homme ose braver tant de millions d'hommes :
Du front de l'artisan, du front du laboureur,
Il croit que pour lui seul doit couler la sueur,
Que les peuples sont faits dans nos tristes contrées
Pour payer les hochets à d'augustes poupées ;

[1] *Var.*—On dit qu'elle est jolie ;
　　　　Mais, détournant les yeux,
　　　　Tu provoques Fannie
　　　　A qui courra le mieux.

[2] This is one of the pieces that Camille found published in the 'Choix de Poésies révolutionnaires,' against which he protested, and of which only the first part had appeared in 1789.

Et que tout doit souffrir, afin qu'à Trianon
Nos maux fassent danser l'Autrichienne Toinon.
Claude sur les Français règne, et de Messaline
L'âge accroît tous les jours la fureur utérine :
Et quoiqu'un milliard coule dans le trésor,
Claude pour ses amants demande un fleuve d'or :
Car tel est mon plaisir, dit-il.   Dieux, quel langage !
Sommes-nous de vils serfs échus par héritage ?
Ah ! mon sang qui bouillonne à ces mots insolents,
M'avertit que je sors de ces antiques Francs
Qui, pour mettre leur *septre* (*sic*) en des mains plus habiles,
L'ôtoient aux fainéants, l'ôtoient aux imbéciles,
Et, maîtres d'obéir, ont du trône deux fois,
Car tel fut leur plaisir, fait descendre leurs rois.
Héritier d'Henri quatre et de Charles septième,
Est-ce donc à son fer qu'il doit le diadème ?
Croit-il parler en maître à des peuples conquis ?
Tout conquérant qu'il fut, même à ses Francs, Clovis,
S'il eût dicté pour loi sa volonté suprême,
La massue à leurs pieds l'eût étendu lui-même !
Apprends, mon cher Louis, mon gros benêt de roi,
Que tel est ton plaisir n'est pas telle est la loi ;
Rends compte, et l'on veut bien encor payer ta dette ;
Mais sois poli du moins quand tu fais une quête.
D'un gueux, dit Salomon, l'insolence déplaît,
Et c'est au mendiant à m'ôter son bonnet !

No. 3.

COMPLAINT AGAINST CAMILLE DESMOULINS AND GORSAS.

(*Unpublished document*).

In the year 1790, Thursday, September 23, at ten o'clock in the morning, before us, Marie-Joseph Chénon the younger, &c., appeared Charles-Francois-Marie-Joseph de Dortan, deputy from the bailiwicks of Dôle, Ornans and Quingey to the

National Assembly, living usually at Dôle in Franche-Comté, at present lodging in Paris, Rue des Orties, Butte St.-Roche, hôtel de Picardie ; who told us that Charles-Marie-Joseph de Dortan, his brother, knight of the royal and military order of St.-Louis, lieutenant-colonel of the Queen's regiment of cavalry, has addressed to him a certificated power of attorney procured from Thiébault and Bourgeois, notaries at Stenay, directing us to complain in his name, and to proceed against the authors, printers, and vendors of a certain periodical in which he was libelled, notably in a paper called : 'Courrier de Paris dans les quatre-vingt-trois départe- ments,' No. 21 ;[1] but as the author of this paper, in his third number of September 4, present month,. has made a sort of retractation, applicant could only complain in the name of his said brother of the authors of another paper called 'Révolutions de France et de Brabant, par Camille Desmoulins, de la Société des Amis de la Constitution,' with the motto *Quid Novi?* dated August 23, 1790, No. 39, in which it is said (p. 734) : 'The lieutenant-colonel of the Queen's regiment (cavalry), while manœuvring his regi- ment at Stenay, proposed that it should go over in a body to the Austrian service. It is true that the majority of the men refused, and that the left side gained the victory over the right ; but the commandant was not strung up to the lamp-post for a crime of high treason to the nation, which proves how much ground we have gained.' The applicant showed us No. 21 of the 'Révolutions de Paris,' as above dated and mentioned ; (we) have initialled it with him at the page 734, at the passage which concerns the brother of the applicant, and have annexed it to these presents.

The applicant, similarly, showed us the power of attorney of his said brother, procured as above mentioned, &c.

The applicant, in the name of his brother, makes the present complaint against the authors, printers, vendors and distributors of the paper, the 'Révolutions de France et de Brabant,' reserving the power to add to his complaint ; requiring in the terms of the said proxy, the assistance of the

---

[1] 'Le Courrier de Paris' is Gorsas' journal in its third form. See 'Deschiens,' 123.

minister of public prosecution, that he may obtain from justice all legal reparation due to his said brother, both damages and interest, &c., praying us to make record of his complaint.

(Signed) CHARLES DE DORTAN; CHÉNON the younger.
    (file 801). Commissioner CHÉNON the younger.

No. 4.

OBSERVATIONS UPON THE EXCHANGE OF SANCERRE, BY CAMILLE DESMOULINS.

(A pamphlet in 8vo. of eight pages—Analysis of the pamphlet.)[1]

The prayer of all French people is that the National Assembly should finish as soon as possible the great work of the Constitution, says Desmoulins at the opening of the pamphlet.

'This Constitution forbids the legislators of the country to be, in any case, the judges of their fellow-citizens, for then they would confound the legislative and judicial powers, and the liberty of the public would be in danger.

'The National Assembly would therefore, on one hand, violate the Constitution if it abandoned its labours to make itself the sovereign judge in private matters.

'On the other hand, it would be losing precious time at a critical moment for the empire; for we must not deceive ourselves, we are surrounded by powerful enemies, who threaten us from outside; hidden enemies, traitors, unnatural children within our walls burn with the criminal desire to overturn everything, to summon anarchy into the bosom of the country; to give back to the clergy their opulence and their egotism, to the nobility their oppressive prerogatives,

---

[1] This very rare pamphlet of Camille's has been too often spoken of for us to omit its analysis here; the more so as it contains some curious details about d'Espagnac, whom Hérault de Séchelles called 'that Spanish cheat.'

and to the former magistrature its old domination over the people.

'How then can a patriot have brought forward the affair of the exchange of Sancerre, on Thursday evening in the National Assembly, with which he well knows the Committee of Domains is occupied, but which it will not submit to the National Assembly until after it shall have received the most careful examination?'

(*Camille then attacks Calonne 'the depredator,' the ex-minister archbishop of Rheims, bankrupt, &c.*)

'In 1784 M. d'Espagnac owed the government a sum of five hundred thousand livres, which had been lent him for the aid of his brother-in-law, who had fallen into misfortunes and had rendered services to the State.[1]

'Not being able to put this sum back into the treasury, he offered the king the comté of Sancerre in payment; the king accepted the arrangement, and a quittance for five hundred thousand livres was given to M. d'Espagnac as an instalment on the value of his land.

'Some months passed; the ex-minister Calonne endeavoured to make the king give him the marquisate of Hatton-Châtel in Lorraine, near his property of Hannonville. In order to hold possession of it in a patrimonial manner, he contrived the plan of a contract, half rent, half exchange; he offered to M. d'Espagnac, in the name of the king, over and above his quittance of five hundred thousand livres, a further sum of five hundred thousand livres in assignats, payable in three years; and for the surplus, he presented him with domains, with power to sell them to the amount of the value of his land. M. d'Espagnac, in his penury, was obliged to accept whatever the government chose to offer; he would have preferred money; but, in fact, the sale of the domains which were to be handed over to him gave him the means to pay off his burthensome debts. . . .

'In fact, he consented that the price of the lands should be paid to him, as follows:

'A million in money or receipts, and the surplus in domains.

---

[1] In 1757, the army being in want of money, M. de Montmartel had provided the government with his paper.

'What was then called a domain of the Crown was in-alienable ; it could only be alienated by way of exchange.

'It was quite necessary to have recourse to this means, the only one which could then legalise the cession of Crown lands, the only one which could guarantee the domain from all damage. . . . The domains which the government in-tended to give him as the equivalent of the value of his land, were, in fact, ceded to him.

'M. d'Espagnac could have made a lucrative affair of the sale of these domains, but he did not ; he sold at the valua-tion price ratified by the upper courts and the council ; it was stipulated in the private contracts that the produce of the sale should be placed in the hands of M. Trutat, notary, to liquidate the fortune of M. d'Espagnac. The valuation began after the execution of the contract of exchange, and it would have been completely ratified if the Archbishop of Sens had not violated all constitutional law in order to annul the ex-change. He put a stop to the valuations in the king's name, and took M. d'Espagnac from his natural judges, handing him over to an illegal commission. The public only saw in this act of authority the punishment of the ex-minister Calonne, and did not perceive that their approbation of this violation of the rights of a citizen rivetted more and more firmly the chains of despotism, for law is one and indivisible for every citizen of the empire. To violate it, even in the case of a suspected parricide, is a social crime.'

(Desmoulins defends the exchange, or, if he finds a fault in it, he attributes it to Calonne ; he pleads for M. d'Espagnac, who—

in 1776, caused the revocation of the Edict of Nantes to be annulled ;

in 1781, was the first to propose the suppression of forced labour (*la corvée*) in the provincial Assembly of Berry:

in 1788, lost his military post for having dared to publish constitutional truth in his requests to the king ;

in 1789, at the time of the primary Assembly of the baili-wick of Blois, demanded that the people should have their representatives equally with the clergy and no-bility.

In fact, d'Espagnac always defended the rights of the people.

Moreover, in this affair he submits himself to the will of the Assembly.

Desmoulins finally demands that from three to four thousand acres of wood be taken from Calonne, who had caused them to be given to himself after the contract of exchange, and that an estimable citizen should be regarded apart from the operations of a minister so generally censured.

The tone of this pamphlet is far removed from the praises formerly bestowed by Camille upon *his dear Calonne.*)

No. 5.

AN ADDRESS BY CAMILLE DESMOULINS.

(*Unpublished document.*)

The 10th September, 1791.

Report made to the Procureur of the Commune upon an incendiary document signed Camille Desmoulins.

Commissary Gueulette thinks that M. le Procureur should prevent the consequences of the excitement which such a document may produce in the public mind.

The address is distributed throughout the entire section and other quarters. It is printed on red [1] paper, and, its heading, the expressions it contains, its insulting, indecent, and disgusting sallies .... bear all the characteristics of an inflammatory production, with the designation of the word *Passan* printed in large type and in a line by itself.

Having been composed, printed, and posted with the design of exciting all citizens to share with its author those sentiments of contempt which he impudently professes to entertain towards the members of the tribunal.

The said writing being seditious, inflammatory, and likely to disturb the public tranquillity, the commissary, having

---

[1] In reality the placard is rose-colour. This document was preserved in the Archives of the Prefecture of Police at Paris, now burnt down.

walked through the streets, found it posted up in the Rue du Monceau, St.-Gervaise, near the turnstile St.-Jean, and the stable-door of a house in which lives M. Mouricault, a judge of one of the district tribunals in the department of Paris. Upon the church-wall of the former parish of St.-Jean-en-Grève, the commissary saw the address, and a dozen people stopping to read it. We thought it the duty of our office to take down two of these papers, one from the wall of the said church, the other from the house of M. Mouricault, and, in consequence, we pulled them down in presence of the public, and, being in possession of these two papers, it seemed to us essential to give notice of them.

GUEULETTE, *Commissary* ; JOLLY, *Registrar.*

PLACARD.

ONLY UNSKILFUL DESPOTS USE THE BAYONET.

THE ART OF TYRANNY
IS TO USE JUDGES FOR SIMILAR PURPOSES.

TACITUS, a *factious* and *incendiary* historian.

PASSERS-BY,

I beg you to stop a moment and say to whom you would give the prize of virtue, if you had to choose between the benches of the convicts and the seats of the tribunal of the sixth arrondissement.

You have learned from the placard of *Santerre* that, false witnesses having failed, Bernard, the public prosecutor, supplied the false evidence by sending to the *Friend of the Citizens*, and signing with his own hand, a false *extract* from *depositions* which did not exist.

According to the same extract, sent to the journals by the sycophant Bernard, I understood they had made the lucky discovery of a false witness against me, and that the sixth witness had deposed, as the *Gazette des Tribunaux* asserted, 'that Camille Desmoulins had said at the Café Procope, *that the National Guard ought to be fired upon, and M. de*

Lafayette killed, and had also read aloud a petition in which he maintained that the *assignats* were the patrimony of poor. people.'

Instead of this deposition, what was my astonishment at the examination to find only the following :

'The sixth witness, Pierre l'Allemand, deposes that, *fif-teen days before the affair of the Champ de Mars,* he heard Camille Desmoulins reading aloud, at the Café Procope, a petition in which he maintained that *assignats* were the patrimony of the poor, *which is all he said he knew.*'

Citizens, you perceive that I never said the National Guard must be fired upon and M. de Lafayette killed. All this is an embellishment of the public prosecutor's.

There only remained the capital accusation of having read the petition.

But, 1st. How could the enunciation of an opinion upon the assignats, on the 3rd of July, be an event of the day on the 17th ?

2ndly. If it was a great crime to have read the petition in the afternoon, at the Café Procope, why did not the National Assembly denounce me for having presented it solemnly in the morning ?

3rdly. I have added the petition to the papers in the case. I defy the judges to find in it what the witness pretended I had read ; and if they find the proposition that *assignats are the patrimony of the poor,* I will consent to recognise MM. Clément de Blavet, Isnard, Lacaze, Robin, and this same Bernard,[1] as honest men who have never been set up to drive away too patriotic electors by decrees of adjournment.

What says this petition ? ' *That as a part of the assignats* (AND NOT ALL) represents Church property, of which one fourth was appropriated to the relief of the indigent, this *part* would not be diverted from its object if it were employed in procuring work for men who are in want of it.'

[1] I should myself be a calumniator as despicable as these judges if I did not except from this denunciation M. Mutel, whom I cannot praise too highly, and M. Recolene. Nevertheless, has a judge done enough for the oppressed by coldly washing his hands of the matter, like Pilate ? Is it not his duty to arise with the indignation of virtue and say, like Cato, to the judges, in the presence of the people : 'Scoundrels, I stand in the midst of you as in a gang of cut-throats'?

This, then, is my crime, that I enunciated in a café, a fortnight before the affair of the 17th, an opinion which I share with Fleury, D'Héricourt, all jurists, and all laws.

No, my crime is that I am incorruptible, that I have not chosen to make my pen the slave of any of the parties who have courted it and bargained for it; my crime is that I am the irreconcilable enemy of all enemies of the public welfare. This is the crime for which tyrants and slaves, the civil list and traitors, those who have sold themselves and those who would willingly sell themselves, cannot forgive me.

You see, citizens, that I only needed the petition to convict this witness of falsehood; and one of the judges has said publicly that there were no more charges, no more depositions, no more accusations, and yet the tribunal, sitting with closed doors, dismissed my demand to be remanded, at least, *for a further hearing.*

Thus I remain under an accusation, without any accusation!

I should have a fine pretext for crying out in the *lettre de cachet*, signed Bernard and Co.; but, once more, a patriot is now-a-days only too happy if he be not shot or imprisoned, and if he get off with not being sent to the Electoral Assembly. One only thing astonishes me, *i.e.* how it is that people are stupid enough to repeat daily, by calumnies, the royal prohibition of the *Chant du coq*, whilst one witness, or even none, was sufficient to let loose at the heels of Brissot, as at those of Danton, Legendre, Camille Desmoulins, &c., Bernard, the public prosecutor, who with one stamped page will do a hundred times more than Morande, the undertaker of defamation, with his long experience and all his reams of libels without a stamp.

CAMILLE DESMOULINS.

Elector of the section of the Théâtre Français.[1]

---

[1] In another placard Camille thus defended his title of Elector :—

Address of Camille Desmoulins, elector of the section of the Théâtre Français, to the Electoral Body.

Gentlemen,—Although an elector of the section of the Théâtre Français, have not received a letter of convocation.

No. 6.

CAMILLE DESMOULINS JUDGED BY HIS ENEMIES.

Camille Desmoulins, the beloved writer of the Parisian nation. Every orator has his arena and his audience; some take the rostrum, others the pulpit, others, again, the academical chair. M. Desmoulins sets up with his eloquence in the streets, and he has all who pass by for admirers. With three learned words, nation, lamp-post, and aristocrat, he knew how to bring himself down to the level of the honest butcher-boy and the modest fish-fag, and of all those new readers brought forth by the Revolution. Pens such as his are needed to lead the people, and to accustom them to having ideas. Voltaire and Rousseau, with their sublime writings, have done no more than enlighten and soften men. They have never disgusted them with the mônarchical yoke. Never would they, in order to civilise the people, have taught them their strength, and their highly lauded style would never have steeped France in blood. This is precisely what our public writers have contrived to do. Without their periodical harangues the French would still be contented slaves. Even now they would calm down and be weary of living only upon victims. But, happily, M. Desmoulins sustains their energy by his publications; he keeps, so to speak, their vengeance on the alert, and not one of his Nos. appears but blood is shed somewhere.[1]

In truth I am a journalist, and I am not ignorant that at the sitting of the 11th instant M. Barnave declared it to be the abomination of desolation that journalists should be nominated electors. But evidently M. Barnave could not have had my journal in view in this proscription, to which he and his friends did not disdain to put their hands, and of which they were the first lessors; besides the National Assembly contented itself with highly applauding this speech without branding as infamous a profession followed by a tenth of the numbers, to one of which it has given a place in the Pantheon.

My section has twenty-six representatives : to take away one would be to impugn the sovereignty of the people.

In a representative government, as the National Assembly has repeatedly said, the sovereignty of the people consists of the sole right to elect.

What remains to them of this paltry sovereignty is impugned, if their representatives are taken from them.

[1] 'Petit Dictionnaire des Grands Hommes de la Révolution,' by an Active Citizen, formerly *a Nobody*. At the Palais Royal, from the National Printing-press, 1790.)

No. 7.

HÉRAULT AND DANTON IN 1790.

A speech delivered by M. Hérault, elected judge of the tribunals of the six districts of the departments of Paris.

Gentlemen,—

I am not going to thank you, because you have forbidden expressions of gratitude ; but I may at least offer you the only homage worthy of you, an ardent and lasting zeal in the cause of liberty.

The choice of my fellow-citizens has surpassed my fondest hopes ; but at the moment when your votes have raised me to the rank of judge I ought not to listen to anything but the voice of my country. Thus, in the midst of a revolution which has changed everything, I owe it to you, gentlemen, to remain unchanged and still ready to consecrate my life to the maintenance of justice and to the interests of humanity.

Reply of the President.

Sir,—

The memory of those tribunals which you were defending by your eloquence, when public opinion had already pronounced against them, will soon exist only in history.

Such is the fate of things human. You have seen vast bodies fall which believed themselves immortal, but in the midst of ruin, merit and virtue still stand erect. They are the materials of the edifice which our freed hands are building up day by day. You ought to make a part of it. Justice, accustomed to your name, calls you into her new sanctuary. Famous in the rostrum when the voice of liberty dared not ask a hearing, you defended innocence and the laws with all your talents, with all your courage. But the people complained of your silence ; they called for you ; you have reappeared, you have listened to the voice of your country. She reigns over great minds ; in the midst of her children you have just solemnly undertaken to consecrate your life to her; she accepts your promise, and the Electoral Assembly in giving you its votes witnesses it.

Extract from the register of the Electoral Assembly of the department of Paris, sitting in the metropolitan bishop's house.

A speech made on September 17, 1790, by M. Hérault de Séchelles, nominated deputy of the department of Paris, to the Legislative Body in the winter sitting :—

Gentlemen,—

The first time I had the honour of serving the revolution in a public capacity was when it reached the judicial order. By their votes my fellow-citizens deigned to raise me to the honourable function of a judge, and this mark of their confidence renews in my heart the vow that I have taken, never to defend aught but the cause of right and humanity. It is very pleasant to me to be chosen a second time by the people, no longer to urge their interests in rights already established, but to find, if possible, new ones, and to represent them in all the majesty of their power. Until now I have only fulfilled among you the quiet duties of citizenship. As for the proofs of my patriotism, it was not under your eyes, but far from you, that I gave them; and however formidable the persecutions and the perils may have been to which the senseless rage of our enemies nearly made me a victim, you were not bound to know of them, nor to take them into account. But now, gentlemen, that through your goodness I have been invested with these high functions, where wisdom herself will be nothing without firmness, I promise you that the great cause of liberty, the sovereignty of the nation, the sacredness of the constitution, shall never have a more ardent defender. A great work has just been accomplished; the bark of France is at last constructed in the midst of ruin and clamour; and if, indeed, the storms growling in the distance ever become a reality, and if it be possible to believe that which it is not allowable to fear, she is about to be launched upon a tempestuous sea. Under such important circumstances, though I cannot hope to equal the brilliant intellects and talents of our colleagues, I can at least rival them in civic virtues. I will call to mind that I have lived all my life for justice, and this feeling is perhaps the one of all others that gives to man the truest courage and the most enduring energy. Without this, the revolution will not be made; this sustains it; and is a guarantee of its continuance for us, and its necessity for all peoples.

M. Pastoret, the president, replied to him :—

Sir,—

In those unhappy times, when, to use the expression of a great man, the law weighed us down like crime, you sought to alleviate its yoke, and your talents, adorned by tender sensibility, won for us the means of reconciling legislation with humanity. Then, eloquence was almost always condemned to take refuge in deserted temples, or to be lost among private interests in the sanctuary of the law. To-day she is more worthy of you and of herself. The orator exercises over us the most powerful of all magistracies, that of genius; and now, when the nation, once dethroned by kings, has reconquered its sovereignty, you ought to be proud of becoming the organ of its inalienable rights, and the firm support of its liberties.

Correct copy. GOUNION, *Secretary.*

Extract from the registry of the Electoral Assembly of the department of Paris.

Letter of M. Danton, elected administrator of the department :—

Monsieur le Président,—

I beg of you to announce to the Electoral Assembly that I accept the duties to which they have seen fit to call me. The suffrages with which the true friends of liberty have honoured me can add nothing to my feelings of duty towards my country; to serve her is a debt which is renewed each day, and which augments with each occasion for its acquittal. I do not know whether I deceive myself, but I feel beforehand that I shall not disappoint the expectations of those who have looked upon me as capable of uniting with the impulses of an ardent patriotism, without which we cannot contribute either to the conquest or the consolidation of liberty, that spirit of moderation which is necessary for enjoying the fruits of our happy revolution.

Eager to hail the last partisans of a broken-down despotism as my enemies, I cannot hope to silence calumny. I have on other ambition than to add to the esteem of the citizens who have done me justice, that of the well-intentioned men whom prejudice cannot long continue to lead into error.

Whatever may be the fluctuation of opinion concerning my public life, as I am convinced that it is important for the general interest that the supervision of public functionaries should be unlimited, and its exercise without danger, even for those who bring accusations as false as they are grave ; firm in my principles and my conduct, I engage to oppose to my detractors nothing but my actions themselves, and to avenge myself solely by showing more and more openly my love for the nation, for the laws, and for the king, and my eternal devotion to the maintenance of the constitution.

I have the honour to be, with respect, M. le Président,

Your very humble, very obedient servant,

(Signed)   DANTON.

Correct copy.   LACÈPÈDE, *Secretary.*

No. 8.

CAMILLE DESMOULINS AND DANTON JUDGED BY A CONTEMPORARY.[1]

I.

The section Lepelletier, regenerated after Thermidor, was very formidable in '93 for its terrorist inquisition. The Sainte-Amaranthe family having lived a long time in the Rue

[1] Extract from a very rare pamphlet, 'La Famille Sainte-Amaranthe,' by Madame A. R. (Paris, printed by V. Goupil and Co., Rue Garancière 5, 1864, in 8°.) The authoress is Madame A. R., whose works, published at the beginning of the century, had a well-deserved success. She died in 1852.

Vivienne, found themselves under the jurisdiction of its committee. The members who composed it were objects of horror to the family, and not one of them was ever admitted to the house.[1]

Among the most dangerous was Trial, who played buffoons' parts so cleverly at the Opéra Comique! What a perverse nature!

According to some of his friends, it appears that the rebuff Trial experienced from Madame de Sainte-Amaranthe, when he wished to be received at her house, was one of the principal causes of the fatal catastrophe. Amélie's mother could not bring herself to adopt the strange policy practised at a great number of fashionable salons, where extreme demagogues were admitted rather than moderate patriots. Alas! that policy did not save the unfortunate slaves of fear, who, however, regained their courage when they needed it to mount the scaffold. Madame de Sainte-Amaranthe consented nevertheless to receive Camille Desmoulins, whose talent, and heart perhaps, ought to have saved him from the excesses of the revolutionary fever. He was presented by M. de Laplatière, the editor of a journal of some influence, and whose moderate views proved that he did not share Camille's opinions. Anti-Dantonist as I am, I am forced to confess that he made himself very pleasant and was very good company on the only two occasions when he visited at Madame de Sainte-Amaranthe's. He was ugly, but it was a humorous

---

[1] The editor of the pamphlet 'La Famille de Sainte-Amaranthe' tells us that the author of these pages, the daughter of a financial administrator under Louis XVI., published some successful works in the beginning of the present century. None are more interesting than the present pamphlet. In it the folding-doors of the drawing-room of the ladies of Sainte-Amaranthe are thrown wide open. But the friendly hand has neglected to initiate us into the secrets of the boudoir. There is no mention of Hérault de Séchelles in the enumeration of the guests of Madame de Sainte-Amaranthe. MM. Auccanes, the Creole, de Fagan, de Miromesnil, Félix de Saint-Fargeau, the Parisian Alcibiades, figure in this gaming-house (the apartment in the Rue Vivienne); Dazincourt too, Fleury, Prince de Ligne, M. de Monville, who gave fêtes in the deserted house in the Forest of Marly; a flute-player whom Frederick II. called Apollyon, the Abbé Lajard de Cherval, brother to the minister of Louis XVI., Vicomte de Pons, a former suitor of Madame de Sainte-Amaranthe, M. de Morainville, M. de Langlade.

and pleasing ugliness. He replied with gracious gallantry to Amélie, who paid him a compliment upon the beauty of his wife.

'Yes,' said he, with that conjugal enthusiasm of which he has given so many touching proofs, 'yes, citizeness Lucile is very beautiful ; for she would be thought so even beside you.' He charmed M. de Sartines particularly by speaking with delight of the opera, the only thing in the world which was capable of rousing Amélie's husband to enthusism.

'The opera,' cried Camille, 'is the head-quarters of civilisation ; if that were shut up, we should fall back into barbarism.'

He has expressed nearly the same thought in an article of his 'Vieux Cordelier.' Would to heaven that his writings, his discourses, had been always so inoffensive ! He came a second time, but perceiving, I fancy, that Madame de Sainte-Amaranthe might have been more amiable than she was to him, he discontinued his visits. Far from complaining, she congratulated herself in speaking of it to me and to our good Colin, who said to her :

'You might have worse people at your house than Camille Desmoulins.'

'He is quite bad enough,' she replied, laughing.

Another Fragment.

Saint-Just, in his report of the 12th Germinal, 1794, speaks of Danton's presence at a conspirators' supper at the Sainte-Amaranthe's. Madame A. R. tells us about this supper, and the relations of Madame de Sainte-Amaranthe with Danton. The Sainte-Amaranthe family then lived at Sucy. The direction of the famous Number 50 had been given to M. de Mounier, who took it in the family's name. The village balls at Sucy threw Vauxhall and Ranelagh into the shade. She received besides. Félix de Saint-Fargeau, formerly a frequent visitor, rarely appeared. 'Since his brother's death, who was assassinated as a regicide, by the Paris *garde de corps*, this man, formerly so brilliant and frivolous, has become a scarecrow in appearance, and a demagogue in language.' One day a carriage arrived, in which were the Comte de Morand, 'little M. Poirson, French consul at Stockholm,' M. de Pressac, a witty talker, aide-de-camp to the Duc de Lauzun, and the Marquis de Fenouil, an ex-officer of the guards and brother-in-law to M. de Marbeuf. They had dinner. M. de Fenouil proposed to escort the ladies to Paris. The gentlemen were each, in his turn, to regale the ladies at a fashionable restaurant. M. de Fenouil himself, 'a handsome man,' chose Méot, MM. de Pressac and Poirson voted for Beauvilliers, and M. de Morand for the famous Rose, the keeper of the hotel Grange-Batelière. They went to a restaurant; then, after a long sitting at her dressmaker's, Madame Valandin, Amélie de Sartines appeared at the Opéra Comique, where the handsome Elleviou acted in 'Philippe and Georgette,' and cast many glances towards the box, while he sang expressively: '*Oh ! ma Georgette, toi seule embellis ce séjour.*'

The third day the dinner was at Rose's restaurant. M. de Morand wanted us to say 'The last is the best !' Alas ! we all repeated it ! We arrived there in high spirits, when Rose appeared with a concerned expression of face, and addressing himself to Madame de Sainte-Amaranthe, said :

'How very unfortunate I am, madame ! Preparations had been made to receive you in one of my finest rooms, when the citizen Danton ordered a dinner, and named the room he wished to have.' Poor Rose announced his discomfiture in despairing accents. M. de Morand was annoyed ; as for Madame de Sainte-Amaranthe, she began to laugh, and said : 'Honour to whom honour is due ; give citizen Danton our room, and do not put yourself out too much about it ; you can accommodate us in some other room—can you not?'

'Oh ! yes, madame, on the same floor, in a very nice room ; but not such as I wished to offer to madame.'

We went there. The dinner was splendid. Rose was determined to eclipse his rivals. We were almost gay, a little frivolous as heretofore. Fleury, who was one of us, had never been so amusing. We guessed when Danton and his guests entered from the sound of their voices ; but notwithstanding that they were so near, we could not distinguish what they said, although it did not the less interrupt our conversation. However, we soon resumed it. We were so glad in those days to forget ourselves sometimes!

'They are graver in there than we are,' observed M. de Morand, pointing to the room where the Dantonist party was. We left our room to go to the *Français.* 'Pamela' was acted. Some moments after our entrance a box opposite to us was opened.

'There is Danton,' cried M. de Pressac.

'He pursues us,' added Madame de Sainte-Amaranthe. Between the acts the fancy took her to look at him closer.

'Will you come with me, dear?' she said to me. 'The box next to his is vacant. Let us go there. Will you come, Amélie?'

'Oh! I shall remain here,' replied M. de Sartines; 'when I want to see wild beasts, I can go to the *Jardin du Roi.*'

M. de Pressac came with us; he assured us, laughing, that Danton would be flattered if he knew the reason of our moving.

'Yes,' replied my companion, 'he will think he has rallied all parties round him when he sees a royalist and a Girondin hovering about him.'

Having stayed half through an act in Danton's neighbourhood, she said to me : 'I have had enough; have you?' 'I have had too much,' I answered. Turning to our companion, she said aloud : 'Our first box was decidedly better; let us go back to it.' These words were intended to remove any idea of our appearance near Danton being intentional, for he and his friends had naturally looked at two well-dressed women. This, I swear, is the only connexion which ever existed between the family of Sainte-Amaranthe and Danton; they dined on the same day at Rose's restaurant, in totally separate rooms. I allow that there may have been a conspiracy in the room where the famous party leader was, but certainly in ours we were peaceable, almost gay.[1]

Madame A. R. relates, further on, the night journeys of Elleviou to Sucy; the alleys and paths of the garden had been pointed out to him. The arrangement of the lights was the signal agreed upon for his entry into the apartment by

[1] See the pamphlet, p. 112 and following.

the servants' staircase. History should not despise this information, which has its value. One day the democrat Chenard
learned from his friend Elleviou that it was said among them
that the nocturnal visitor was no other than Danton. It was
suspected that the fall of Robespierre was set on foot among
'these fair ladies.' All these made-up stories may have had
their effect. Chenard even asked Elleviou to appear before the
Committee of Public Welfare and declare that it was not Danton
who in disguise scaled the walls of the garden. Elleviou
would not do this. He ought to have repented of his refusal, if
the anecdote told by the author of this pamphlet is authentic.

No. 9.

DECREE OF ACCUSATION AGAINST THE DANTONISTS.

Decree of the National Convention on the eleventh day of
Germinal, second year of the French Republic, one and indi-
visible, accusing Camille Desmoulins, Hérault, Danton,
Philippeaux and Lacroix.

The National Convention, after having heard the report of
the Committees of General Safety and Public Welfare, decrees
accusation against Camille Desmoulins, Hérault, Danton,
Philippeaux, Lacroix, charged with complicity with Orléans
and Dumouriez, with Fabre d'Eglantine and the enemies of
the Republic, for having taken part in the conspiracy tending
to restablish the monarchy, and to destroy national representation and republican government ; consequently it orders
that they stand their trial with Fabre d'Eglantine.

Examined by the inspector.

(Signed)   AUGER.

Compared with the original by us the President and
Secretary of the National Convention, in Paris, eleventh
Germinal, second year of the Republic, one and indivisible.

(Signed)   TALLIEN, *President ;*

PEYSSARD and BEZARD, *Secretaries.*

In the name of the Republic, the Executive Provisional Council summons and orders all the administrative bodies and tribunals to enter the present law in their registers, to read, publish, post up, and execute it, in their departments and respective resorts. In virtue of which we have affixed our signature and the seal of the Republic. Given at Paris eleventh day of Germinal, second of the French Republic, one and indivisible.

(Signed) DESTOURNELLES ; (Countersigned) GOHIER.

Sealed with the seal of the Republic.

Certified copy.

(Signed) GOHIER.

A correct copy, collated by me, Registrar-in-chief of the Revolutionary Tribunal undersigned

N.-J. FABRICIUS.[1]

No. 10.

IMPOSITION OF SEALS AT WESTERMANN'S HOUSE.[2]

Section of Gravilliers—Committee of Supervision.

The thirteenth day of Germinal, second year of the French Republic, one and indivisible.

We, the undersigned, Commissioners of the Revolutionary Committee of the Section of Gravilliers, nominated to place

---

[1] National Archives, legislative and judicial section. (C. W. 342, No. 648 and following.)

[2] Westermann wrote to the Convention as follows :

'Saint-Maixent, 1st November, 1793, II. year of the Republic, one and indivisible.

'Citizen President,—I send the Convention the State seals and stamps of the pretended country conquered by the so-called Louis XVII., taken by me on my entry into Beaupréau.

'General of Brigade, WESTERMANN.'*

---

* Unpublished autograph, to be seen at the Museum of the National Archives. (See the important publication of M. Plon, *Muséum des Archives*).

the seals on the effects of the citizen Westermann, general of brigade, living in the Rue Mesllée, No. 63, arrested this day, by order of citizen Fouquier, public prosecutor to the Revolutionary Tribunal of Paris.

Being arrived, we found citizeness Anne-Louise-Joséphine Leloir, whom we had ordered to show us the effects belonging to citizen Westermann, which she did not refuse to do, declaring that all moveables belonged to him. So we carried away many trunks, as well as boxes, portmanteaus, arms, guns, hats, and other effects belonging to him ; also papers, from a room situated between the sleeping-room and drawing-room, having a window looking on the Rue Mesllée, and in the said room is a little alcove, where we shut everything up, and put seals on the door opening into the sleeping-room, and in the same room we have also put the watch that the citizen Westermann gave us at the Committee, in a small box, where he keeps his gold and silver epaulettes.

After having required the citizeness Leloir to give us proofs that the dwelling was hired in her name and to show us the receipts, she obeyed, and showed us the receipt for the last term, which proved that the dwelling was taken in her name.

And, finally, we have placed as guardian of the aforesaid seals, after having showed him and made him take notice that they were whole and entire, citizen Claude-Francis Menayant, who is engaged to represent us in this way every time that he shall be legally required. We have brought to our Committee a bunch of nine keys, which belong to the trunks and the articles under seal, and have drawn up this statement, and, after having had it read, have said it was declared, and with us has signed it.

Correct copy. HOUDEMARD, *Secretary.*

Citizen Varineau Antoine, aged 28 years, native of Daguenau, aide-de-camp to General Westermann, living in Rue Notre Dame de Lazareth, No. 130, showed us his passport from the minister, dated 12th Germinal, and good for six days, to be given up at his post, that he may rejoin his corps, which is at Poitié, making part of the army of the West; captain of the legion of the North, of the third company, 2nd battalion, and aide-de-camp since August 1793 (old style).

Correct copy. HOUDEMARD, *Secretary.*[1]

No. 11.

CHABOT—HIS WILL AND HIS ATTEMPT AT SUICIDE.

Chabot's will contains two full pages of close writing. I quote some lines of it :—

'I hope that the agents of England will not be much longer successful in misleading the French Government by a sect of so-called Catonists or Spartans, who neither know nor admire those who are courageous, and who live like Sybarites, while they recommend black broth to the favoured friends of the nation. The system preached by Saint-Just in particular will lead us to slavery, by a shorter road than the luxury which he declaims against. Men ought to be led to equality through the happiness of the greater number of those who work, and who add to the enjoyments of society by the development of their talents and their industry, and not through the privations of every individual.

'. . . . Chabot disowns the son of Julie Berger, but directs that he shall be maintained until his fourteenth year, recommending his parents to take care of his " very virtuous wife, and to console her."

' The two national domains of eleven thousand eight hundred livres were purchased with the money of my sister and mother, who for sixty-four years have practised economy, and gone through unheard-of toil to leave a competency to their children. My family has always lived by labour.

' I pardon,' he adds, ' my enemies from the bottom of my

---

[1] From the same file as the preceding document. Documents 9 and 10 are ill-spelt throughout in the original.

heart; if I have censured them a little too much in my memoir, I declare that the love of my country has been my ruling passion.

'The writings which I leave after me may do something towards the establishment of that happiness which, as I wrote long before Saint-Just did so, should be the aim of all societies. I have been guilty of weaknesses in my life. But the most disinterested philanthropy and respect for the laws of nature will secure for me pardon for some of the wanderings of my headstrong passions. I hope the Divinity, whom I adore, in spite of all the modern fanatics of atheism, will forget these, and will receive me into his bosom.

'I die exclaiming: Long live the Republic, one and indivisible! Long live her founders, her defenders, and her friends! War to the bloodthirsty, for they resemble despots of all sorts! Peace to all true friends of humanity! Down with the power of men! Long live that of virtue!

'FRANÇOIS CHABOT.'

The postscripts are in defence of Fabre and Bazire.

Bulletin of Chabot's health.

30 Ventôse.

We have found him easier; stomach still swollen, but rather less so; the urine difficult and painful to pass, also the motions; the head still affected, with mind wandering; vomiting from time to time.

The health officers of the police administration administered a purge to-day. Of this we do not approve; the treatment was premature, and calculated to augment the irritation and pain. Chabot is in a condition to be taken to-day to the hospital.

BAYARD, MAURY.

Guillaume Besse, turnkey (prison of the Luxembourg, section of Mucius Scévola), deposes:

About two o'clock he heard some one call out, 'Tell citizen Benoît to come up.'

Chabot had rung.   Besse went up.   He saw citizen Felette and Benoît, who were taking care of Chabot. He, being interrogated, replied :

'I shall not explain except to the Committee of Public Welfare or of General Safety.'

Besse did not know what poison the prisoner had taken. There was the word *topique* on the bottle.   Chabot, hearing the amendment of Billaud-de-Varennes to the act of accusations cried in the street, had drunk, calling out, 'Long live the Republic!'

About three o'clock, or a little past—for his watch did not go well—being in agony, he called the boy. Benoît came. 'Take my will, which is lying on the table,' Chabot said to him, 'and carry it to the Committee of General Safety, and say to my oppressors that I pardon them, because I believe that they have only pronounced sentence of death upon me to save the country.'

The administrators of police, Dangé and Cailleux, were summoned, then the physicians Markoski and Soupé. They administered an anodyne, such as laudanum, and ordered 'that every care should be taken of him that humanity and the nature of their functions demanded.'

(Signed)   FRANÇOIS CHABOT (upon the seal).[1]

No. 12.

TRANSLATION OF A LETTER WRITTEN BY THE SPANISH AMBASSADOR AT VENICE TO THE DUKE DE LA MENDIA.

July 31st, 1793.

My Lord,—Your Excellency doubtless already knows that on the 3rd of this month the Queen of France was separated from the Dauphin, which was done by the heads of Marat's party in the name of the Committee of Public Safety, who had no knowledge of it until it was over, and then did

---

[1] In the original, this and the preceding document are ill-spelt throughout.

not dare to offer any opposition. The Royalists think that they wish by this means to render the intrigues of that princess more credible. She persists in exposing herself to danger, notwithstanding the advice which it is more and more difficult to give her, owing to the severity with which she is treated and the constraint she is under, as you will see. The Commune of Paris pretend that an agent of the Prince of Coburg is in correspondence with the Queen; that Danton and Lacroix, who were of the *Montagne*, have become Girondins, and have had interviews with her Majesty; that the said agent is nephew to General Ferraris; that he comes to Paris, and returns on foot for fear of being known; that he set out at night on the 7th, carrying letters to the Queen; before she received them they had to pass through the hands of the Commissary of the Temple, in whom they thought they could confide, but the rascal carried them to his Commune, who had them copied. Upon this information the Commune turned accuser, and drew up a charge composed of seventeen articles. This critical situation is not less alarming than the suppression of the Committee of Public Safety and its re-formation. Nine of the principal Maratist leaders are members, Marat himself is president, Robespierre is secretary. They hope, however, to find a Royalist spy, disguised under a Maratist mask, amongst them. These scoundrels are known; we may expect anything from them. This idea alone makes one tremble.

I have already informed your Excellency, on the 17th of the current month, that a courier had arrived at Paris to announce the taking of Nantes by the army of Gaston. This news has been contradicted by letters written to Paris on the 13th, and it is feared that the Royalists, finding themselves masters of the suburbs, and that the skirmishes which have taken place in the streets of the town were to their advantage, congratulated themselves prematurely on having gained a complete victory.

Custine was defeated on the 3rd. On the 8th the details were not yet known in Paris, for the Commune, which seems to be much dispirited by them, kept them back. It was the same with the news of Wimpfen (Wimphen). He had brought his advance-posts up to the town of Caen, and taken several spare horses which were destined for the patriot hussars.

The Committee assembled at Bagatelle resolved that all possible measures should be taken to make the people consent to the Convention having a recess, at the same time remaining in Paris to receive what the Committee of Public Safety, the executive power, the department, and the Commune should send them.

The Commune is so strongly opposed to this project that it has not been carried out.

I do not know how they are to find generals. If the troops meet with any check, the generals are at once summoned before the bar of the Convention, and called to account by a decree of accusation. This is the case with Custine, Biron, Westermann, and Sandos, but most probably they will not obey the summons to the bar.

The reunion of the Marseillais and Lyonnais is still uncertain. In general the armies are for the Republic, but as the greater part of their leaders are Royalists, there is nothing to fear but from the soldiers, who will be easily persuaded to do all that the generals wish.

I have already told your Excellency that I had taken the liberty of giving notice to all the State inquisitors of the approaching arrival of Semonville. Neither he nor his companions have been seen. After the rigorous orders that have been issued, they could not pass through any town in this State. I have just heard that he had about two millions worth of diamonds belonging to the Crown. General Salis, who knows this, and who has much influence, has told his most devoted servants of it, pointing out to them the return routes by which he might pass. He has given orders that the diamonds and his papers should be taken from him. The Archduke of Milan will agree on his side as to the necessity for this proceeding.

Sainte-Croix has written to the Convention from Constantinople. I have already made you acquainted with his situation in that capital, and that the Austrian and Russian ministers carry on a brisk war with him, but that the English minister protects him and helps him to remain there. He is his intimate friend, a Jacobin by inclination, and does all he can to embroil the Porte with the Courts of Vienna and St. Petersburg..

(Signed)   CLEMENTE DE CAMPOS.

I have just heard that Marat has been killed by a woman twenty-two years old.

No. 13.

Copy of a note found among the papers of Baron Trenck, entitled *Note upon the cause of my arrest* :—

I know a Jew named Dobruska (or Doboufka), born at Nikelsburg in Moravia. He came to Vienna on account of his two very pretty sisters, who had ruined several young men of rank, and for that reason were publicly expelled from the city and the Austrian dominions. The Emperor Joseph made use of this Jew (who bought the title of Schönfeld at Vienna) as a spy during the sittings of the Hungarian Diet, where everybody knew him by this respectable title. I have seen him acting as such; I know him well; and I know that it was thus he gained free access to the Emperor Leopold.

Four months ago my wife wrote to me to be on my guard in Paris, because the cunning Jew Schönfeld was there, and that no doubt he would have instructions from the Emperor to do me harm. A favourite of the sovereign even gave me the same advice, out of friendship. I sought Schönfeld here, but did not find him. At length a Viennese came to tell me that he lived in the *Rue d'Anjou*, at a Royalist hotel, where he spent a great deal of money, kept open house for the Jacobins, among whom he played a great part; that he went by the name of Frey, and that he had given his sister, the celebrated virgin of Vienna, in marriage to the deputy Chabot, an ex-Capuchin.

I went immediately to him to make sure of my facts. I

F F

found the same Jew Dobruska, the Emperor's spy; he confessed, too, that it was he who, by means of one of his friends, had hindered my reception among the Jacobins, when I presented myself at their tribune, &c.

I have just heard that the wife and children of the Jew are at Vienna.

Paris, November 28, 1793.

(Signed) TRENCK.

Correct copy.

GUFFROY.[1]

No. 14.

THE ORDER FOR THE ARREST OF THE DANTONISTS (NOTIFIED 12TH GERMINAL).

To the citizens president, and judge of the Revolutionary Tribunal.

The public prosecutor, in consequence of the accusation by the National Convention, in its decree of 11th Germinal present month, against the above-named Camille Desmoulins, Hérault, Danton, Philippeaux and Lacroix, deputies; the said decree accusing them of complicity with d'Orléans and Dumouriez, with Fabre d'Eglantine and the enemies of the Republic, of having taken part in the conspiracies.

The said decree consequently ordering them to be tried with Fabre d'Eglantine.

Requires that, pending the decree of accusation under-dated, and to be put into execution as aforesaid, it be ordered by the assembled tribunal that, as quickly as possible, and by an usher of the tribunal, bearer of the undersigned order, Camille Desmoulins, Hérault, Danton, Philippeaux and Lacroix, deputies of the National Convention, and arraigned by the decree of accusation, be apprehended, taken up and arrested wherever they may be found, and their names

---

[1] All these papers are taken from the same file.

entered in the jail-book of the register of the Luxembourg house of detention, where they shall remain in prison. And also that the said forthcoming ordinance shall be notified to the municipality of Paris as well as to the accused.

Given at the office of the public prosecutor, 12th Germinal of the second year of the French Republic, one and indivisible.

Q. FOUQUIER.

The tribunal, acting upon the requisition of the public prosecutor, orders in consequence, that, with all promptitude in execution of the decree of the National Convention of the 11th Germinal, present month, and by an usher, bearer of the present order, Camille Desmoulins, Hérault, Danton, Philippeaux, and Lacroix, deputies of the National Convention, arraigned by the undersigned decree of accusation, shall be arrested wherever they may be found.

Given and decreed by the tribunal, 12th Germinal of the second year of the French Republic, one and indivisible, by citizens Martial Herman, president; Antoine-Marie Maire, Etienne Foucault, Gabriel Deliége, and Claude-Emmanuel Dobsent, judges; who have signed.

HERMAN, President.
DELIÉGE, DOBSENT, A.-M. MAIRE, FOUCAULT.

No. 15.

DANTON'S DEATH (RELATED BY AN EYE-WITNESS).

I was on my way to Méhul's house, which was in the Rue de la Monnaie, when I met in the Rue St.-Honoré the tumbril in which this revolutionary hero was presiding for the last time over his party, since shorn of its heads. He sat calmly between Camille Desmoulins, to whom he listened, and Fabre d'Eglantine, who listened to nobody. Camille was speaking with much vehemence, and throwing himself about, so that his torn clothes exposed his bare neck and shoulders, which were soon to be separated by the axe. Never had the life in him been more active. As to Fabre, motionless in his misery, weighed down by the suffering of the moment, and perhaps also by the remembrance of the past, he seemed hardly alive. Camille, who, in co-operating in the revolution had believed himself to be helping on a great work, still rejoiced in his delusion; he imagined himself on the way to martyrdom. Alluding to his last writings, he cried to the crowd, 'My crime has been to shed tears.' He was proud of his condemnation. Fabre, who had been led into revolutionary excesses by less generous feelings, was struck dumb by the voice of truth; he only saw the punishment at the end of the short way he had still to traverse.

Another face also attracted my attention to this tumbril of the condemned; it was that of Hérault de Séchelles. The peace which shone in the handsome face of the late Advocate-General was of a different sort from the calm of Danton, whose face was a caricature of Socrates. Hérault de Séchelles' calmness sprang from indifference, Danton's from contempt. Danton was not pale, but Hérault's face was tinged with so high a colour, that he looked more like a man returning from a banquet than one going to a scaffold. Hérault de Séchelles appeared to be detached from life, to which he had clung at the price of so much cowardice and so many atrocities. The aspect of this egotist astonished everybody; everyone asked his name, but as soon as they had heard it, they ceased to be interested in him.

An anecdote. Some weeks previous to this terrible day, Hérault had seen Hébert, Clootz, and Ronsin driven along the road which he was so soon to travel in the very same tumbril. 'I found myself on their road accidentally,' he said to the person from whom I learned the fact. 'I should not have run after the sight, but I am not sorry it came in my way; *such things are refreshing.*'

I entered Méhul's house, and my mind was full of what I had just seen. 'I should like to see the end of this tragedy,' I said to him, after I had finished in three words the business that brought me there. 'This Danton plays his part very well. We are all on the eve of such a day as is just ending for him ; I should like to learn how to go through it well also.' ' A study,' answered Méhul, who looked at things as I did, and who would have come with me if he had not been in his dressing-gown and slippers.

Meanwhile the fatal cart had continued its progress ; the execution had begun, when, having crossed the Tuileries, I arrived at the railing of the Place Louis XV. From thence I saw the condemned, not ascending, but appearing in turn upon the fatal platform, to disappear immediately by the movement of the plank on which they stepped—the bed on which their eternal repose began. The rest of the operation was hidden from me by the assistants. The accelerated fall of the steel alone showed me what was doing, what was done.

Danton was the last to appear upon the platform, red with the blood of his friends. At the foot of the horrible statue, whose enormous mass was outlined against the sky, I saw the tribune stand like one of Dante's shadows, and half illumined by the dying sun, looking rather as if new risen from the tomb than ready to go into it. Nothing was ever seen more brave than the demeanour of this athlete of the Revolution, more formidable than the expression of the face which defied the axe, than the bearing of the head which, though about to fall, seemed still to dictate laws! Terrible picture! Time will never erase it from my memory. I perfectly comprehend the feeling which inspired Danton to utter his last words, those terrible words, that I could not hear, but which were repeated to me in trembling horror and admiration. ' Do not forget, above all,' he said to the executioner, in the tone of one of the Gracchi, ' do not forget to show my. head to the people ; it is good to look at.'— *Souvenirs d'un Sexagénaire,* by A.-V. Arnault. Paris, Dafey, 4 vols. 8vo. 1833, vol. ii. p. 96 and following.

No. 16.

RECORD OF THE ENTRY IN THE JAIL-BOOK OF THE DANTONISTS' NAMES AND THEIR DELIVERY TO THE EXECUTIONER.

The 9 Germinal, 2nd year of the French Republic, one and indivisible, We, in virtue of a judgment made by the Revolutionary Tribunal and duly signed, and on the requisition of the public prosecutor, at the said tribunal, domiciled at his office near that of *Jah* (illegible) to the undersigned tribunal, caused to be taken from the house of detention the under-named, Fabre d'Eglantine, Delaunay Dangers, Chabot, Camille des Moulins, Lacroix, Philippeaux, Bazire, Hérault de Séchelles, Danton, and have confined and delivered them into the hands of the executor of criminal judgments, to be taken hence to the Place de la Révolution, there to suffer the penalty of death, which was done the same day of the discharge.

1. Fabre d'Eglantine.
2. Delaunay Dangers.
3. Chabot.
4. Camille des Moulins.
5. Lacroix.
6. Philippeaux.
7. Bazire.
8. Hérault.
9. Danton.

On the said day, 13th Germinal, the under-named, Fabre d'Eglantine, Delaunay Dangers, Chabot, Camille des Moulins, Lacroix, Philippeaux, Bazire, Hérault, Danton, all the nine, ex-deputies to the National Convention, were transferred from the prison where they were detained to this house, and inscribed in the jail-book of this register by me, undersigned, usher to the Revolutionary Tribunal, in virtue of the order of the said tribunal of to-day's date, made according to the decree of the National Convention of the same day for them to remain in this house, or in the prison of the tribunal, by reason of which citizen Richard, turnkey of the said house, remained in charge for the term fixed by the law, of which I have made them acquainted, speaking to them personally at the wicket as a free place; of all which, as aforesaid, I have at the present date made an act to one separately.

MONET.[1]

---

[1] Copied from the jail-book of the Prison of the Conciergerie, communicated by M. Labat senior. This book, which formed part of the Archives of the Prefecture of Police, is now destroyed.

No. 17.

CERTIFICATE OF THE DEATH OF CAMILLE DESMOULINS.

This certifies the death of Lucile-Simplice-Camille-Benoist Desmoulins, 16th Germinal (April 5, 1794), literary man, aged 33 years, native of Guise, district of Vervins, residing in Paris, Place du Théâtre Français.[1]

7th Floréal, 2nd year of the Republic.

No. 18.

THE CLOTHES AND OTHER EFFECTS OF THE CONDEMNED.

I.

18th Germinal.

Citizen Richard appeared ; and deposited :

747 livres 5 sols assignats.

An old gold watch, maker's name Romilly, Paris, with a copper key; another watch of gilded copper, without number or name, and on the dial-plate the name of Leblond; two pairs of silver garter-buckles, two steel ditto; one silver hat-buckle, one steel ditto; one pair of copper shoe-buckles; a locket set in copper; a large cardboard snuff-box, with a portrait; two other snuff-boxes, also of cardboard; a copper pocket inkstand; a pair of old silver buttons; ivory spectacles and other spectacles of silvered or plated copper; an overcoat of blue cloth; a thick iron-grey baize coat; a brown blouse; twelve pocket handkerchiefs of different colours; nine white handkerchiefs; five silk neckerchiefs; nine cravats or neckties; one cotton cap; three muslin collars; one frilled shirt. Richard declared that these articles belonged to the fifteen men condemned to death by the sentence of 12th Germinal, current month, of whom Lacroix

[1] Register of the Municipality.—*Dictionnaire de A. Jal.*

and Danton were two, but was not able to point out to whom the said effects respectively belonged, and signed, with me, the undersigned,

WOLFF. RICHARD.[1]

II.

7th Floréal.

Citizen Deguaigné, usher to the Revolutionary Tribunal, appeared; the same deposited at the registry the following objects :

A bolster ; a pair of sheets ; a pillow and its case ; two cotton counterpanes and one woollen ; a flannel waistcoat ; trousers and overcoat of white cloth ; a striped cloth waist-coat ; yellow cashmere breeches ; and one cotton waistcoat ; another of white flannel ; a woollen cap ; a cotton cap ; eight pairs of shoes ; six white handkerchiefs ; thirteen dinner napkins of linen or huckaback ; two stomach bands; two shirts ; a white double-breasted waistcoat ; a pair of shoes down at heel ; and a table-cloth, which he declared belonged to Danton, who had been condemned to death.

Also, the said Deguaigné deposited the following effects : a pair of sheets ; a ruffled shirt ; an overcoat and trousers of cloth ; four linen towels ; a cotton cap ; a handkerchief ; four bound volumes, which he declared belonged to Camille Desmoulins, who was condemned to death. Signed with me, undersigned registrar,

DEGUAIGNÉ. WOLFF.[2]

Prison of the Luxembourg.

Report of the administrators of the police department : Inventory—accompanied by the citizen Vignieul, member of the revolutionary committee ; citizens Guyard, ex-turnkey, and Mousset, guardian of the said seals, and citizen Bertrand, turnkey.

Having ascended to the apartments on the second floor, we verified the seals affixed to the door of the second room

---

[1] National Archives, W. 354, 2.   [2] Same file.

to the left, and on the three windows looking into the stable yard, which we found whole and entire, in the presence of the above named, in the order which follows :—

1. Musse.
2. Helle.
3. Citizeness Dapremont.
4. Lacroix (belonging to), who have fallen by the sword of the law :

> A small bedstead with sacking bottom.
> A mattress covered with checked tick.
> A horsehair under-mattress.
> An earthenware shaving-dish.
> An arm-chair covered with red and white striped Utrecht velvet.
> A night-stool, with two chamber utensils.
> A water-jug ; an earthenware inkstand.
> An iron spoon and fork.
> A steel garter buckle.
> A small table, with fire-screen.
> A straw-bottom chair, harp-shaped back.
> A toilet glass ; effects sent to agency of the National Domains.

5. Belonging to Danton :

> A sacking bed.
> A horsehair under-mattress.
> Two mattresses.
> A water-jug, with an earthenware lid.
> Three empty bottles.
> A tin coffee-pot.
> A hand-glass.
> A shaving-dish.
> A mother-of-pearl knife worked in silver.
> An easy-chair covered with flowered damask.
> A night-stool and two chamber utensils.
> A common straw chair.
> A small writing-table.
> A shovel and tongs.
> Two small candlesticks of copper gilt ; effects sent to the agency of the National Domains.

6. Belonging to Poire, upon whom the law has done justice.
7. Belonging to Simon, condemned to death.
8. Belonging to Fabre d'Eglantine, condemned to death:
   Two silver dishes.
   A pair of sheets.
   A large muff.
   An ivory telescope.
   Fifty bound volumes, thirty-nine 'Encyclopædia,' and
      six volumes, works of Molière.
   Two manuscript histories of the Revolution.
   An oil lamp.
   Three mattresses.
   A straw-bottom arm-chair with a harp-shaped back.
   A water-jug.
   A small bottle containing several prunes.
   A half bottle of brandy.
   An office seal.
   A pair of garter buckles.
   Seventeen sols in cash.
   A small organ.
   Ten large bottles.
   Have found more than a hundred and fifteen sols in
      paper money.
   More than thirty empty bottles.
   Three wax candles.
   A jar of gherkins.
   A tobacco jar.
   Two small ones for cream.
   A glass saltcellar.
   An oil cruet, and one broken.
   An earthenware chamber utensil.
   A lid.
   A small brown earthenware saucepan.
   Four plates and a small dish.
   A writing-table; effects sent to the agency of the
      National Domains.
8 *bis.* Belonging to Bazire:
   Two glass cups.
   A box.
   Three small fruit baskets.

9. Belonging to Roland, condemned·to death.
10. A backgammon-board, belonging to Castellane, who has escaped from the said prison.
11. Mardeuil, condemned to death.
12. Fécamp,·   „   „
13. Mohaux,   „   „
14. Choiseau,   „   „
15. Dupuis,   „   „
16. Champlateux (he had escaped from September).

The sitting broke up at two o'clock, having re-affixed the seals on the door of the entry of the said chamber, and concluded the present, and the citizens undernamed have signed,

BALLAY, GUIARD, BERTRAND, MOUSSET, VIGNIEUX, MINIER, *Secretary*.[1]

Conciergerie.—Return of 25*th Germinal, by Richard.*

Wife of Camille : Belonging to the wife of Camille, six hundred *livres* in *assignats*, a pocket book, a gold ring with five circlets, another gold ring with a woman's portrait.

Wife of Hébert : Belonging to the wife of Hébert, three hundred and fifty *livres* in *assignats*, a knife with a horn handle ornamented with silver, a pair of scissors, and a portrait of the traitor Hébert set in gold.

Camille : Belonging to Camille, a gold collar buckle.

Deposited on the 18*th Germinal, year two, by Richard.*

Danton and others : Belonging to Danton and others, seven hundred and forty-seven *livres* five sols (sous) in *assignats.*

Return of 19*th Germinal, by Auvray.*

Westermann : Belonging to Westermann, four thousand seven hundred and fifty *livres* in *assignats.*

[1] ' Archives of the Police Prefecture.' This interesting document is unpublished. The sitting, broken off at two o'clock, was resumed after three hours' interval. Among the relics of the nobles (house of Noailles) were found certain ' *church books.*'

To Camille Desmoulins, condemned :

A copper candlestick in bad condition, and a tin coffee-pot.

An earthenware water-jug and basin.

An earthenware chamber utensil.

Three bottles, a small earthen saucepan and pot ; sent to the office.[1]

No. 19.

ORDER FOR THE ARREST OF LUCILE DESMOULINS.

The French Republic, one and indivisible.

LIBERTY, EQUALITY, FRATERNITY, OR DEATH.

COMMITTEE OF PUBLIC WELFARE.

Minute of the Order.

Paris, 15th Germinal, year II. of the French Republic,
one and indivisible.

The Committees of Public Welfare and of General Safety jointly decree that the wife of Camille Desmoulins be at once imprisoned in Sainte-Pélagie, and the seals put upon her papers.

The members of the Committees of Public Welfare and General Safety,

(Signed) DUBARRAU, COUTHON, C.-A. PRIEUR, CARNOT, VOULLAND, B. BARÈRE, BILLAUD-VARENNES, ROBESPIERRE.[2]

---

[1] *Unpublished.* 'Archives of the Prefecture of Police.' Documents destroyed.

[2] These minutes are entirely in Dubarrau's handwriting.

No. 20.

CAMILLE DESMOULINS AND ROBESPIERRE.

Extract from the ' Mémoires de Charlotte Robespierre.' [1]

One of the gravest charges against my brother, Maximilien Robespierre, was, that he sacrificed Danton. I do not know whether this accusation is well founded ; all I know is that my brother loved Camille Desmoulins dearly, they having studied together ; and when he learned his arrest and incarceration at the Luxembourg, he went to the prison with the intention of begging Camille to return to the real revolutionary principles which he had abandoned for an alliance with the Royalists. Camille would not see him ; and my brother, who would probably have assumed his defence, and perhaps saved him, if he could have persuaded him to abjure his political heresies, abandoned him to the terrible justice of the Revolutionary Tribunal. Now, Danton and Camille were so intimately united that he could not have saved the one without the other ; if, therefore, Camille had not repulsed him when he held out his hand to him, Camille and Danton would not have perished.

.... Camille was as much a friend of Robespierre's as of Danton's. My brother's friendship for him was very strong ; he has often told me that Camille was perhaps the one of all the prominent revolutionists whom he loved the best, after our younger brother and Saint-Just.

Desmoulins was a true patriot, and was more virtuous than Danton, without being so much so as my two brothers ; he had most amiable qualities, but also several defects, which were the cause of his death : he was proud and irascible ; once offended, he never forgave, and he used the formidable weapon of his biting and sharp criticism [2] against those of whom he thought he had reason to complain.

Men who were far from valuing him for his patriotism and

---

[1] Chapter V.

[2] Here is a fresh example of this peculiarity of character noted by Charlotte Robespierre, and by so many other contemporaneous writers. In a dialogue in the fifth number of the ' Accusateur Public ' by Récher-Sérisy, I find a conver-

his talent, and who were jealous of his fame, calumniated him and accused him of being sold to the aristocrats; no more was required to let the fiery Camille loose upon those who attacked him, and upon those who, without attacking him, followed the same line of conduct as his calumniators. This is why, instead of refuting the imputations of certain members of the committees who were his personal enemies, he attacked the committees in a body, censured their acts, called in question the purity of their intentions, and even associated himself with the aristocrats. Calumnies were redoubled, or rather, falsehoods brought against him when he was irreproachable, turned to truths when he ceased, through resentment, to be blameless. Day by day, he separated himself more widely from his old friends, and made common cause with Danton, and allowing himself to be blinded by the praises lavished upon him by the aristocrats because of the hostility between him and the most terrible of the revolutionists, he became in reality the associate of the aristocracy.

The unfortunate Camille was turning round and round in a circle ; the enemies of the Revolution were extolling him to the skies, vaunting his principles, his eloquence, and his moderation. All these praises caused him to be suspected by true democrats ; his enemies made weapons against him of them, and said, Camille is a counter-revolutionist. Camille, beside himself at this accusation, flung himself with still greater fury upon those who attacked him, and the aristocrats redoubled their praises.

sation between Merlin (de Thionville) and Rœderer. The latter remembers that Sérisy had dined with Desmoulins in company with Merlin.

RŒDERER.

' I have been told Sérisy was the friend of Desmoulins—Desmoulins, that infamous——'

MERLIN (*interrupting him*).

' Ah, you are right ; we all three dined together. I cannot in conscience slander Sérisy ; Merlin will never profane the sanctity of the table ; his inviolable attachment to it is well known. . . . And Camille infamous ! . . . You will never forgive even his dust for his charming speech about you. *It seems to me that Rœderer's head was intended by nature to furnish painters with a study for hatred, jealousy and wickedness.*'

This speech of Desmoulins has nothing charming about it, and probably was invented ; but it is certainly characteristic. (J. C.)

Then it was that Desmoulins published his 'Vieux Cordelier,' in which he arraigned all the revolutionists, and, in consequence, the Revolution. This was worse than a great imprudence on his part—it was a crime. My elder brother said sorrowfully to me on this subject, 'Camille is ruining himself.' He was deeply grieved at seeing him desert the sacred cause of the Revolution, and, at the risk of compromising himself, he took up his defence several times ; several times, also, he tried to reclaim him, and spoke to him as to a brother, but in vain. At one of the sittings of the society of the Jacobins, when a storm of reproaches and accusations fell upon Camille Desmoulins and his 'Vieux Cordelier,' Maximilien began to speak, and while energetically blaming the works, tried to justify their author. Despite his immense popularity and extraordinary influence, his words were received with murmurs. Then he saw that, by trying to save Camille, he was working his own ruin. Camille did not give him credit for the efforts he had made to repulse the accusations of which he was the subject ; he only remembered the blame Maximilien had heaped upon the 'Vieux Cordelier,' and from that time he aimed a thousand acrimonious diatribes at my brother.

No. 21.

THE DANTONISTS BEFORE THE TRIBUNAL.

Topino-Lebrun's Notes.[1]

Among the documents given in this book none are more interesting than the two following fragments, the notes taken at the Revolutionary Tribunal by Topino-Lebrun, a juror ;—notes written, so to speak, at the dictation of Danton and his fellow-prisoners ;—and those of Courtois (de l'Aube). These two documents are, to a great extent, unpublished. Dr. Robinet has made use of Topino-Lebrun's notes in his work upon

[1] François-Jean-Baptiste Topino-Lebrun, aged 31, born at Marseilles.

Danton. The fragments we give have been drawn up by us from the originals of Topino-Lebrun and Courtois, which formed part of the Archives of the Prefecture of Police, and which were placed at our disposal by the kindness of the late M. Labat. The senseless conflagration which devoured so much artistic, archæological, and literary wealth in May 1871, also destroyed the MSS. of Topino-Lebrun and Courtois, with many other documents preserved by M. Labat. These fragments are therefore of inestimable value now-a-days. We publish what remains of them after the copies made by us in 1867 and 1868. Not only the accusers, but the accused, speak in these papers. However unconnected Topino-Lebrun's notes may be, having been taken during the hearing, they are more complete, and besides, more truthful, than the report of Coffinal.

Topino-Lebrun's Notes.

Danton.—' I, sold ! a man of my stamp is priceless. The proof—was I silent when I defended Marat ? When I was proceeded against under Mirabeau, when I fought against Lafayette ? My address to the people to rouse them to insurrection on the 5th and 6th October ! Let him who accuses me to the Convention, produce the proofs, the semi-proofs, the signs of my venality. I have laboured too much; life is a burden to me. I require the commissioners of the Convention to receive my denunciation of the system of dictatorship. I was nominated administrator by a triple list, the last one a small number of respectable citizens. At the Jacobins I forced Mirabeau to remain at his post ; I resisted him when he wished to return to Marseilles. Where is this patriot ? Let him come ; I demand to be confronted with him. Let him come forward ! I prevent the departure of Saint-Just ! I ordered to be arrested for the affair of the Champ de Mars ! I offer proof to the contrary ;—read " l'Orateur." Assassins were sent to murder me at Arcis. One was arrested ; an usher came to put the decree into execution. I fled then, and the people wanted to execute justice on him. I was at my brother-in-law's house; it was surrounded, and my brother-in-law was maltreated. As for me, I fled to London, and returned when Garan was nominated. Legendre was offered fifty thousand crowns to assassinate me.

'When the Lameths became partisans of the Court, Danton resisted them at the Jacobins before the people, and demanded the Republic.

'Let patriots rally together, and then, if we cannot conquer you, we shall triumph over Europe.

'Billaud-Varennes has not forgiven me for having been my secretary. *What proposition did you make against the Brissotins?* The law of *publicola*. I carried the challenge to Louvet, who declined. I narrowly escaped assassination at the Commune. I said to Brissot, "You will bring your head to the scaffold!" and I reminded Lebrun of it here. It was I who prepared the events of the 10th of August, and I went to Arcis—for Danton is a good son—to spend three days, and say farewell to my mother, and to regulate my affairs. I have witnesses of this. I was seen there in the flesh. I did not go to bed. I was at the *Cordeliers*, although a delegate of the Commune. I said to the minister Clavières, who came from the Commune, that we were going to proclaim the insurrection. After having arranged all the operations and the hour for the attack, I lay down upon my bed like a soldier, having given orders that I was to be called. I rose at one o'clock, and went to the Commune, now turned revolutionary. I made out the death-warrant of Mandat, who had orders to fire upon the people; the mayor was arrested, and I remained there, according to the desire of the patriots.

'I still believe Fabre to be a trustworthy citizen.

'I swear that I did not give my vote for d'Orléans. Let them prove that I nominated him.

'I had four hundred thousand francs out of the two millions to make the Revolution! Two hundred thousand livres for secret service I disbursed in the presence of Marat and Robespierre for all the commissaries of the department?—This is a calumny of Brissot. I gave six thousand to Billaud to go to the army: I furnished accounts for a hundred and thirty thousand, and the remainder I sent to Fabre to pay the commissaries; he was cashier, and I only employed him because Billaud-Varennes refused.

'Fabre never to my knowledge advocated federalism.

'I would embrace my enemy for the sake of my country, for which I would give my body.

'As a minister of justice, I have carried out the laws.

'Marat had a fiery nature, Robespierre's was tenacious and firm, and I was of use after my own fashion.

'I only saw Dumouriez once, when he sounded me about the ministry. I replied I would only be a minister when the cannon roared.

'Saw Westermann on the 10th, sword in hand.

'The Brissotins have attacked me indeed!

'Brissot's device was to make people believe that we disorganised the armies in Belgium.

'I am refused witnesses; very well, I will not defend myself any more.

'I have also to apologise for any unnecessary warmth I may have shown; it is my disposition.

'The people will tear my enemies in pieces before three months are over.'

.   .   .   .

Hérault.—'Upon this little box (*sic*) [1] denies the fact. He was named for the diplomatic party with Barère. Declares that he was never mixed up in negotiations, denies having ever printed anything in diplomacy.

'I understand nothing about this nonsense.

'I saved an army of sixty thousand for the Republic. Worked with Barthélemy for the neutrality of the Swiss.

'Have never communicated with Proly about politics; and what is more, I ought to be confronted with him.'

Camille.—'Born at Guise, department of Verdain (*sic*). At the Panthéon.'

Danton.—'Whatever may be said, this is quite certain, and it matters very little to me; the people will respect my head; yes, even when guillotined!'

---

[1] Probably alluding to his seat, as there seems to have been but one chair (fauteuil) provided for the accused.

Westermann.—‘ From Strasbourg, a soldier from my infancy.’

Westermann demanded to be examined first. Observed that it was a useless form. *Danton.*—‘We are here, however, for form's sake.’ Westermann insisted : a judge questions him. Danton said : ‘ Provided that we are allowed to speak, and to speak freely, I am sure to confound my accusers, and if the French people are what they ought to be, I shall be obliged to ask for pardon for them.’ *Camille.*—‘Ah ! we shall be allowed to speak, that is all we ask. (Great and heartfelt joy of all the accused deputies). *Danton.* Barère is a patriot now, is he not ? (*To the jury*) : I instituted the tribunal, therefore I ought to know about it.’

Westermann.—‘ I shall demand to be shown naked to the people, that they may see me. I have seven wounds, all in front ; I have received only one behind—my act of accusation. *Danton.*—‘We shall respect the tribunal because,’ &c. (Danton pointed to Cambon, and said) ‘You believe we are conspirators ! Look, he laughs ! he does not believe it ! Write down that he laughs’ (*sic*).

First witness : P. J. Cambon, thirty-eight years old, deputy to the Legislative and the Convention.—The decree of December 15th to make . . . .

‘ Anacharsis said to me : “ Come and dine with me, dine with Dufour," &c.

‘ I knew the guillotined Abbé ; entered into my exile (*sic*) ; he was a canon and not refractory. This is only a joke. He was not put on his oath. He assisted me in my exile. On July 14th at the Bastile I had two men killed by my side. Illtreated by my relations, I went away to travel. I was imprisoned for three weeks in Sardinia ; I have come back.’

Fouquier.—‘ On account of the rebellion of the accused.

‘ Why did he go on the fourth day with Herman to the jury-room to persuade them to declare that they had sufficient evidence ? ’

Camille.—‘ At the time of his dispute with Saint-Just, the latter said that he would kill him. I denounced Dumouriez before Marat. D'Orléans first. I commenced the Revolution, my death will end it. Marat was deceived in Proly. What man is there who has not had his Dillon? Since the 4th number I have written only to retract. I have "belled the cat" with all the factions. I have been encouraged, written to, &c.—Have unmasked the Hébert faction. It is a good thing that some one did it.'

Lacroix.—' I have neither eaten nor drunk with Dumouriez. Danton, Gossin, and I together always for seven days. Bought nine hundred francs and six hundred livres' worth of table-linen. It was a good bargain.'

Danton.—' I have publicly challenged an explanation of the imputation about the four hundred thousand francs. The result of the report is, that nothing belonged to me but my traps and a flannel vest (in a carriage full of plate).

' Have I the face of a hypocrite?

' I aroused the insurrection by calling for fifty revolutionists like myself.'

Philippeaux.—' Newly arrived from my department, I knew nothing about intrigues. I voted for Marat.'

(' It is false; he neither voted for nor against.')

Westermann.—' While Dumouriez was in Belgium, I was in Holland. Abandoned, and with the enemy either side of me, I led my legion to Antwerp.'

Frey (the elder).—' The emperor owed him five hundred thousand florins.'

Frey (the younger).—' I was a child rather than a brother.'

Gusman.—' Of his long speech, Danton said: "He is building castles in Spain."

' Herman listened a long time, and Danton said: "They are polite to him because he is a foreigner." Gusman denied having given money to the people.'

Danton.—' Barère is the patriot now, and Danton the aristocrat? France will not believe that long.'[1]

---

[1] ' Archives of the Prefecture of Police.' Documents destroyed.

No. 22.

NOTES OF COURTOIS (DE L'AUBE).

(Unpublished documents, now destroyed.)

DANTON.

The arbitrary opinion of the moment may cleave to his memory, dishonour it even, if it were possible ; but this truly great man will enjoy the esteem of posterity when there are none left in France but Republicans.

It is from the passions and writings of his enemies that I shall draw materials which will one day form his panegyric.

Cannot Robespierre's skin be torn without making patriotism bleed ? (*See* VOLTAIRE, letter, p. 90, vol. xv.)

What is gained by passing for a giant from the Magellan before a group of Lapps ?

Danton said in his prison (according to Riouf's report) (*sic*) that Robespierre, Billaut, Collot, &c., were own brothers to Cain.

Words addressed to Chrysippus, and which can be applied to Danton : *Tua te vis perdet.* Thy strength is thy destruction.

Bayle (article ' Concini ').—This man's insolence is a sad example of the fatality which attends the French monarchy more closely than any other country in the world. Its Queens almost always remain foreigners at heart.

Danton.—He said to me one day, about a month before his downfall, 'A certain Pope, whose name I have forgotten (Pius V.), said : " Since I have been Pope, I despair of my salvation ;" and I say : If the representatives of the people permit to be debased . . . . if the tyranny of the Committees be not restrained, I despair of the Republic being saved.'

The day that Danton's death was decided upon at the Revolutionary Tribunal, three jurors, Topino-Lebrun, Trinchard, and Jambat went in search of David, to ask his advice in their difficult position. They added that they did not hold Danton to be guilty. 'What!' exclaimed this bloodthirsty man, 'not guilty? Has not public opinion already passed judgment on him? What do you expect? Only cowards could behave thus.' And so the death of this founder of liberty was resolved upon.

Philippeaux, the victim of his probity, died because he had tried to make truth heard even in the den of tyranny.

Danton.—A saying of the Emperor Constantine which is applicable to him: They durst not attack him in front.

Many deputies come to the Assembly and sit there the whole time of their mission without speaking, like shopkeepers who open shops in order not to sell. (A saying of Danton's.)

Robespierre.—His demeanour was sometimes as ambiguous as his words (witness the pressure of Desmoulins' hand on the eve of his arrest).

He had, indeed, the power to kill them, but was never able to prevent their writings and reputation from floating above their corpses.

He would never have remedied an evil the duration of which he found to be to his advantage.

He jested sometimes in a bitter and caustic manner.

Collot d'Herbois boasted in the rostrum, at the *Jacobins*, that he knew a *suspect* by only looking him straight in the face.

Nero projected the extinction of the senatorial body, which was not base enough for his taste; Robespierre demands from the two Committees in conjunction the disbanding of the Convention, because it is an obstacle to his designs.

Saint-Just entreated Lebas to kill him. The latter called him a coward, and told him he had something else to do, after which he killed himself. Why was it not said to Saint-Just as to Nero: Is it then so difficult to die?

Fréron has said that Robespierre dishonoured the Reign of Terror. The Reign of Terror, which makes the wicked turn pale, but secures tranquillity to the just man.

Imputed crimes are a legitimate part of crimes committed.

The Feast of Viala, the day chosen for the slaughter of the Convention.

A saying of Danton's: 'I have the sweet consolation of believing that the man who died as the *chief of the faction of the Indulgents* will find favour in the eyes of posterity.' He said, on the subject of the executions,[1] that when people went smiling to execution, it was time to break the scythe of Death.

Goupilleau de Fontenoy, sent to La Vendée as a commissary, dismissed Rossignol, a creature of Robespierre's.— 'If,' said Barère to him, 'it was a general like Turenne you had dismissed, you would be easily forgiven; but when a patriot like Rossignol is in question, it is a crime.'
Weigh well this saying, and compare it with the political canker maintained in La Vendée. (Courtois.)

At the time of the courageous attack of Lecointre (de Versailles) upon Billaud, the sitting ended late. Seeing this, a deputy called out: 'Make haste and decree the accusation; I have some people to dinner.'

---

[1] Here is an incomprehensible phrase: *Vous êtes tant qu'il vous plaira à la rigueur actuelle.*
This phrase is also untranslatable.

Danton called *scoundrels of stupidity* those men who, without examination, but led by bad temper or some passion of that kind, allowed themselves to sacrifice the staunchest defenders of the country to it.

Ambition may be compared to the horse of Sejanus, which broke the necks of all who mounted it.

Danton.—Immediately after the decree of accusation against him, a member of the Committee of General Safety met a deputy, and said to him : 'Did you think the Committees were on the point of giving in ?'

He said, on the subject of the *sans-culotterie*, enforced by the orders of Robespierre and the Committees, 'He who always uses the same materials ends by working his own ruin. If a man persists in stirring up mud, he rarely escapes being covered with it, sooner or later.'
He said, that if Billaud and Robespierre were in good earnest (they continually had in their mouths the words virtue and probity, which were the order of the day), they would infallibly found the Jansenism of liberty.

Billaud.—This man, strong through the weakness of the Assembly.
A dagger on his tongue.

Danton.—He wrote to me on the subject of the war of the North, of which the beginning was not fortunate, 'Whatever may be the evils caused by the present war, they will still be more bearable than slavery.'

'It is false,' he said, 'that a revolution can be successful when no one knows how to profit by it.'

As Robespierre sometimes affected to despise great political measures he had not invented, Danton said : 'This contempt for great conceptions which are not his own, does not presage success in the future.'

He said that revolutions were like long and difficult navigation, during which we must expect the wind to blow from all parts of the horizon at once, and that the open sea was often less dangerous than the port towards which we were sailing regardless of the thin line of breakers in which the vessel sometimes goes to pieces.

I have heard him say that Robespierre might perhaps conduct the piece up to its fourth act, but that he would, infallibly, fail at the climax of the fifth.

Robespierre.—No temerity, no daring.   Praises : the Duplay family overwhelmed him with them.

Barère.—Weak and frivolous, fearful.

Danton.—He would willingly have been able to withdraw from such a whirlwind, but how could he do so after having played such a part ?

The powers of Europe did not see that the Revolution resembled a great lawsuit, which does not often enrich those who gain it, and completes the ruin of those who lose it.

Barère.—It is this man, an atrocious coward, who was the first to attack Desmoulins on the subject of the 'Vieux Cordelier.'

David helped citizen Lesueur, the painter, his pupil, to paint the picture of the beheading of Louis XVI.   He (and all the artists have recognised his brush) placed in it the figure of the Duke of Orleans (Egalité).   Danton is behind, his hands extended over the Duke's shoulder, receiving a purse from him.

Some days after the downfall of Danton, Camille Desmoulins, &c., being at a sitting of the —— *Thermidor*, at which Robespierre made a cruel and ironical attack upon these unhappy victims of his barbarity ; I saw beside me (for caution kept me at a distance from the seats in the interior of the hall), a citizen who, at those parts of the tyrant's speech which were loudly applauded by the majority of the Convention, clapped his hands also with all his strength, and looked at me smiling.   I thought I could perceive that his applause was not sincere, and I replied to him by a smile which told him I was not duped by the part he was playing. He then came close to my ear and said in a low voice : 'Were it to cost me the pair of gloves with which I am applauding' (his hands were bare), 'I would willingly sacrifice them to be guaranteed the downfall of the monster who now occupies the rostrum.' I told him to restrain himself. He pressed my hand, his eyes were suffused with tears, and he disappeared.

Danton (after Marat's death).—An orator who aspires to be Marat's residuary legatee.

Concourse of scholars of painting and sculpture.—*David :* It is at the Revolutionary Tribunal that this matter will be judged.

Danton.—I often see ——— (?) who blackens my character, but I remember having seen him struggle against bad luck, and I pity him.

Preferred the charms of private life to public grandeur.

Danton killed by Robespierre is Pyrrhus killed by a woman.

About the committees of government Desmoulins said : 'The safety of the Republic is still far off. ' It wanted everyone.'
Marat.—'Great scandal !' he said ; 'it is a great scandal that we want.'
Robespierre the younger.—He was called the great howler, the national bellower. Desmoulins said : Ducos' least gesture is an epigram, and the very sound of young Robespierre's voice is foolish.

Desmoulins said of the opinions put forward by Robespierre the younger in the rostrum that they always came from the throat, never from the head.[1]

---

[1] 'Archives of the Prefecture of Police.' (Unpublished and destroyed documents.)
At the end of these notes I found, scribbled upon scraps of paper, the following :

No. 23.

REMORSE OF ONE OF THE JURY OF THE REVOLUTIONARY TRIBUNAL FOR HAVING VOTED FOR THE DEATH OF HIS FRIEND CAMILLE DESMOULINS.

The author of this account does not give the name of the juror in question.   He says that, while he was in court, Desmoulins never took his eyes off him ; he seemed to say, Would you dare to condemn me ?   The unhappy man had daring, or rather cowardice, enough to give his vote against his conscience.   He was punished for it ; remorse took possession of his heart ; he was a new Orestes ceaselessly troubled by the furies.   Two months after the 9th *Thermidor*, one of his friends went to see him ; he found him gloomy, pale, downcast, taciturn—no more that energetic man whose voice · was constantly heard in the popular meetings, and who swayed the multitude at his will ; one would have said he was himself about to meet the fate to which he had consigned so many.

P—— asked him the cause of such an extraordinary change.   N—— replied at first by a profound sigh.—

Danton.—In the conference which Danton had with Robespierre in the presence of Laignelot, he said, among other things : ' If you are not a tyrant, why should you treat the people otherwise than as you would wish to be treated yourself? So violent a state of things cannot last ; it is repugnant to the French temperament.' Robespierre's answer was in favour of the Committee.—' Danton's tears ' (Courtois).

LANTHENAS.

Vous faites donc aussi des plans de République ?
Et vous voilà parlant en profond politique.
Quel miracle !   Comment et quand s'est fait cela ?
—Vous m'en voyez, ma foi, tout étonné moi-même. ·
Je ne saurais vous dire au juste le quantième
Dans ma tête un beau jour ce talent se trouva,
Et j'étais médecin quand la chose arriva.
(Parody of *La Métromanie*, doubtless Fabre d'Eglantine's.)

It is unnecessary to point out the importance of these historical fragments, which, but for me, or rather but for the kindness of the late M. Labat, who allowed me to take copies of them, would have been completely lost.   (J. C.)

'Do you fear,' asked P——, 'the consequences of the re-action?'

'Would to God,' cried N——, 'that the 10th Thermidor had witnessed the fall of my head, or that the reaction had sent me to my grave! I have assassinated my friend! I cannot live; I am torn by remorse. Camille is perpetually before my eyes; even now, while I am speaking to you, he is there—I see him, I hear him. Here, in a river of blood, floats the body I have so often pressed in my arms; there, immoveable, lies his head, separated from his limbs. It reproaches me with my barbarity, and yet I breathe!'

At these words his eyes clouded over, his whole body shuddered; he foamed at the mouth; a continual grinding of his teeth gave notice of an approaching fit; his eyes closed, he fell down, writhed, rolled, and tumbled about on the boards, which he covered with blood and froth. P—— could not hold him; four men were hardly enough to prevent his dashing his brains out. After a violent convulsion, he slowly recovered his senses, and reproached his friends for the service they had done him in bringing him back to life.

Extract from the *Anecdotes inédites de la fin du dix-huitième siècle*, p. 116, 1 vol. in 8vo. Didot junior publisher, year IX. (1801).

No. 24.

SANSON AT THE HOUSE OF M. DUPLESSIS.

15th *Germinal.*—I have executed the commission poor citizen Desmoulins gave me. At his dwelling, Rue du Théâtre Français, the house-porter gave me the address of citizen and citizeness Duplessis, Rue des Arcs. I took care not to go upstairs. I sent for the servant; without telling her who I was, I told her that, having been present at Desmoulins' death, he had begged me to take a locket to his wife's mother. I put it into her hands, and went away.

I had not gone a hundred paces, when I heard some one running after me and calling ; it was the servant. She told me M. Duplessis had asked for me, and wanted to see me. I replied that I was in a hurry, and would come another day ; but at that moment citizen Duplessis himself came up. He was an aged man, of very venerable aspect. I repeated to him what I had told the girl. He replied that I must have something more to tell him, and that he had to thank me. I still excused myself by alleging my business, but he insisted with much eagerness ; passers-by stopped, and some looked as if they were about to listen. They might have known me ; I thought it was best to follow him, and I went with him. He tried to take my arm ; I drew it back, and as, in the narrow street, we could not make our way side by side, I kept behind him. He lived on the second floor ; he took me into a large room, handsomely furnished, pointed to a chair, and letting himself fall into an armchair placed in front of a table laden with papers, he hid his face in his hands. Hearing a child's cry, I perceived in one corner a cradle with drawn curtains. Citizen Duplessis ran to the cradle and lifted up a little boy, who seemed to be ill, and was moaning. Showing him to me, he said, ‘ This is their son.’ There were tears in his voice, but his eyes, as red as iron on the anvil, were dry. ‘ This is their son,’ he repeated. He embraced him with a sort of fury, putting him back into his bed, and said, with an effort : ‘ You were there, you saw him ? ’ I made a sign in the affirmative. ‘ Like a man of feeling, like a Republican ? ’ he went on, without pronouncing the word death. I replied that his last words were for those he loved. After a silence of some length, suddenly wringing his hands and turning pale, he cried : ‘ And she ? my daughter ? my poor Lucile ! Will they be as merciless to her as they have been to him ? Two to mourn—is it not too much for miserable old people ? We believe ourselves philosophers, sir ; we think we are fortified by reason against this idea of destruction . . . . what becomes of philosophy, where is reason, when it is our own child who is menaced ? when we find ourselves powerless to defend her, to fight for her, to shed our blood to save her ? . . . O my God ! to think that we shall not be permitted to receive her last sigh, that she will be struggling, will be in agony for two hours, while we shall be here, in safety, in this house in which she was born, amidst these things which she has played with ; before a hearth at which she has sat ! To think that perhaps, less fortunate than Camille, she will have, to bring us her last farewell, no other messenger than the wretch of an executioner who shall have killed her ! '

I felt a shudder creep over my body and my hair, and I turned cold. He walked to and fro in the room, shaking his white hair, which had fallen loose, his hands twitching, his eye haggard, his whole aspect wild. Passing in front of a bust of Liberty placed on the mantel-piece, he overturned it with fury, broke it on the marble, and crushed the pieces with his foot. I was at once shocked and aghast ; I could not find any consolation to address to him, not a word of hope to say, and regretted bitterly that I had yielded to the poor man's entreaties. At this moment a bell rang ; a citizeness in her fiftieth year, still handsome, but her countenance distorted by despair, entered and threw herself into citizen Duplessis' arms, crying out : 'Lost ! she is lost ! she is to appear before the tribunal in three days !' She was the mother of Desmoulins' wife. I was in terror at the idea of being recognised by this woman, whom I had bereft of her daughter's happiness, whom probably I should have to bereave of her daughter's self also, and I fled as if I had committed a crime. Never have I suffered more than in the presence of those unfortunate people.[1]

No. 25.

A LETTER FROM FRÉRON TO LUCILE.

I beg Madame Desmoulins to be pleased to accept the homage of my respect. I have the honour to inform her

[1] Charles-Henry Sanson's 'Journal.'

that my destination is changed, that I shall not go to the National Assembly because I am setting out for the country with MM. Danton and Saturne. Will she have the goodness to remember that she is to present herself at the Assembly, before ten o'clock, in the hall of deputations; that she is to send for M. La Source, the secretary, who will come to her, and will find a place for her by means of the commissary of the tribunes.

I renew the assurance of my respectful devotion to Madame Desmoulins.

STANISLAUS FRÉRON.

Kindest regards to Camille.

Monday, January 7th.

No. 26.

LETTERS FROM MADAME FRÉRON TO LUCILE.

(*Unpublished.*)

Coubertin : Monday morning.

How good you are, my dear Lucile, to take such pains to answer so punctually, and to relieve my anxiety! I rely upon your kindness to let me know any good news when you know it yourself. Neither my husband nor my brother has written to me; but, according to what you tell me, M. De la Poype will be with you immediately. Scold him well, I beg, my dear Lucile, and beat him even, if you think it necessary; I give him over to you.

Good-bye, dear aunt; I embrace you with all my heart. Do tell me about your pretty boy; is he well? We shall, I hope, see him at some time together. Be the first to tell me of my husband's arrival; it will be so sweet to owe my happiness to you! Fanny is perfectly well. I received most tenderly the kiss she gave me from you. My compliments to your husband.

FRÉRON DE LA POYPE.
Coubertin, near Chevreuse, Chevreuse.

To Madame Desmoulins.

Here I come again, beautiful and kind Lucile, to plague you with my complaints, and the frightful uneasiness by which I am tormented. The letter your husband had the kindness to write to me does not allay my grief; he tells me that my brother has given him news of my husband, but he had not heard from him before his departure. He has not been absent long enough to have had time to give us news of himself since he set out. I do not hide from you, dear Lucile, that I am in a frightful state; for pity's sake, try to restore composure to my heart; let me owe tranquillity to you.

They say the enemy is within forty leagues of Paris; if this is so, the country will not be safe. Will you promise to warn me of danger, and to receive me into your house? I count upon the friendship you have always been willing to show me, and I shall throw myself into your arms with the greatest confidence.

I beg you to give my compliments to your dear husband.

FRÉRON DE LA POYPE.

Coubertin, near Chevreuse, Chevreuse.

The 5th.

Madame Desmoulins.

No. 27.

LETTERS FROM THE WIDOW OF PHILIPPEAUX TO MADAME DUPLESSIS.

Concerning the Education of the Children.

(*Unpublished.*)

A business appointment which should have taken place yesterday, deprives me of the pleasure of responding to your kind invitation, dear friend; but as I am to be the only loser by that, I beg and pray of you to meet me to-morrow at the deputy's house, with whom I am to go before the Committee of Inspection, about the object we have in common. Bring with you, I conjure you, your dear little Horace. Let our two children come together in a place at which their unfortunate fathers loved to meet. Our hearts will at least be better able to confront misfortune together. Farewell, I can no longer see what I write. Farewell, I am going to leave these few words for you, this summons to meet me at the Rue de l'Echelle, at the house of the deputy Nioche, between a furrier's and a perfumer's.

Friendship and greeting:

2nd *Thermidor.* Widow PHILIPPEAUX.

29th Vendémiaire, year VI.

I had hoped, citizeness and friend, to have the satisfaction of seeing you, during the time you required for the conclusion of the little arrangements of which you told me. I can no more flatter myself with the hope of this pleasure. The interval has passed, and you have certainly started on your journey.

How many things I had to confide to you! How necessary your advice was to me, and how I have suffered since I saw you last! My health is very much shattered; the troubles I have to endure are beyond my strength, and it seems as if Fate took pleasure in multiplying them. My request for a stamp-office cannot be granted. I was advised to ask for a lottery-office; I did so; I ought to have one, but at what a cost! My uneasiness is extreme; I applied to citizen Reubel, who has given me proofs of his good-will, but as yet without effect. This undertaking makes my head giddy. A considerable sum is required from lottery-office keepers, and I cannot flatter myself I shall be exempted from providing it, as I asked the government for one through the instrumentality of citizen Reubel. Finally, to give you an idea of the journeys I have had to make, and that very often, at one time to the minister, at another to the administrators, I was obliged to go at nine o'clock at night to speak to the Minister of Finance; it was frightful weather that day. Happily I had my son with me to give me courage. I should never leave off if I gave you the details of the trouble I am obliged to take. I was worn out; knocked up, and reduced to removing into a hovel, for which I am asked a hundred and sixty francs. I have not yet decided; I am advised to manage the office by myself, and I am about to sacrifice my beloved tranquillity. I shall not be able to weep freely any more, nor enjoy a moment's rest! What a hard life mine is! now there is no limit to my unhappiness. I now know that no misfortune can be greater than that of living ! . . . Forgive me, I am letting myself be carried away by my sorrow; I should be unpardonable by anyone but citizeness Duplessis. The affection you have shown me encourages me to open my heart to you, which is relieved by this outburst. My friend has congratulated me on having had the satisfaction of seeing you during the holidays. This excellent friend knows you and appreciates you, and wishes I were in a position to enjoy your society often. She charges me to give you her best regards; I beg you to accept them with my loving homage.

I greet you.   Widow PHILIPPEAUX.

I have as yet received none of my pension ; I have been put off until next month. I perceive I have not sent you the whole of Condillac's works. I still have a volume that I found among my own books. Citizen Duplain told me you had this work in your library, so you will have the double copies. I can take back the one I sent you if you do not want it, and I will return you the price. It will not inconvenience me in the least to take it back. My son destined three little volumes for Horace, from which he will derive great pleasure when he has learned to read. I will send them to you at the first opportunity ; it is Auguste's idea, to please Horace. I hope he will make the same use of them this winter that Auguste did, and that he will soon be able to read quite alone. I embrace him, so does Auguste ; he has been with me for some days to recruit his health, which has not been good. Accept his tenderest caresses and his respects. We wish you good health.

My compliments and kind regards to Mademoiselle Adèle. If citizen Etienne is with you, I beg you to give him my compliments.

2nd Ventôse, year IX.

Since your last visit, I have seen my dear children twice. We projected a visit to you, and fixed it for the 5th of this month ; but the weather is so unfavourable, that without your sanction I shall not undertake the journey to Bourg-l'Egalité. It is not that I am afraid of the bad roads, but for fear that our children should not be so well amused as they expect. I have promised to consult you before deferring this delightful scheme. It requires no less than your authority to give my reasons weight, however good they may be. You would be amused at hearing Horace talk about his arrival : he is to rush in and embrace you, frighten his aunt and Mère Laneau, run all over the whole house from cellar to garret ; above all he is to make plenty of noise. He says all this with the greatest vivacity, and only quiets down when he remembers that he is far away from you. He is no longer the same child ; he said, with great calmness, ' For all that, I cannot get accustomed to not seeing mama. I cry every evening and morning.' Dear, too amiable child ; at his simple and touching sorrow my own tears fall ! . . . . You have been informed of the way in which we passed the 30th. I had much pleasure in making the day of parting pleasant, and in spite of the grand people at the house of little Agathe's mama, where we dined, I managed to amuse the little people, the half of whom I took back to sleep with me. The evening passed quickly away ; at ten o'clock they still wanting to go on with their little games. At last my carriage took us back, and at eleven o'clock our little friends were lying in their beds side by side in my room, where they slept well ; at nine o'clock in the morning they went back to the college, whither I took them, happy and contented, and they are quite well. They will write to you ; my son, Horace's secretary, is going to beg you to come and see him. In yielding to their eagerness to have you, you will crown my desires.

Accept the expression of my feelings, dictated by friendship.

I greet you.

Widow PHILIPPEAUX.

H H 2

I have not felt any inconvenience from the effects of my fall, except an indisposition that a mere nothing would cause. The day after I was in great pain.

Paris : 8th Prairial.

Madam,

I cannot resist the pleasure of letting you know hat I have just repaired the loss of my dear one's portrait. The artist has succeeded very well this second time ; it is even better than the first. It is a masterpiece. The skilful artist has employed all his talent, and has left me nothing to desire. Will you believe that I am not yet strong enough to contemplate that cherished image? My health is shattered ; my grief disturbs my reason. Oh, how much we are to be pitied ! If I did not know your feelings so well, I should fear to commit an indiscretion by breaking a silence which I attribute only to your continual sorrow. I have felt it no less, but the years fly past us imperceptibly, and accumulate. Shall I not have the pleasure of seeing you again ? Good citizen Becqueret told me he had given you my compliments, and I have received yours through him. No one can feel your remembrance of me more keenly than I do, and I shall hope to be always honoured by it. Is your dear Horace well ? My Auguste is quite well, and works as hard as ever. What consolation this child gives me ! I am in want of it, I assure you. I hope you are well, and I assure you of my warmest feelings for you.

I greet you.

Widow PHILIPPEAUX.

My friend talks to me constantly of you, and has told me many times to remember her to you. She has been very ill this winter ; she is better now.

Paris : 4 Frimaire.

Citizeness and friend,

Your letter gave me great pleasure. I received it the day I left my home ; I was in the midst of the confusion of removal. I needed this fresh token of your affection. I confess to you that I was oppressed by the fear that I had worried you by complaints. I did not know what to reproach myself with nor how to construe your silence; it would have cost me too much to accuse you of indifference. I covered your letter with tender tears, and my eyes are still wet as I call you my friend. Oh! what a precious title that is to me! Oh! how I value it! I desire nothing better than to be worthy of it.

At the time when I was in the greatest straits they were busying themselves at the Directory for my relief. Citizens Reubel, Merlin, and François de Neuchâteau have ordered a company of the saltworks of the Republic to furnish me with the necessary funds for the security and expenses of the lottery office to which I was nominated. The undertaking is of sufficient importance to induce these gentlemen to hasten to subscribe to this condition. By this means I am proprietress of an office. It is impossible, citizen and friend, to describe to you the state into which this unhoped-for happiness has put me; I could not understand it. My sleep has been troubled by it, my mind disturbed—no, I cannot describe the good and the evil I have felt. A sensitive heart escapes no detail of any position; mine, wrought upon by misfortune, could not bear so rapid a transition from poverty to ease! . . . So here I am at last installed; the office established and opened on the 1st *Frimaire*, that is, four days ago. I think I shall soon get accustomed to this new existence. I get on better than I could have thought possible. I give you minute details; they can interest only a real friend, and I cannot let slip any part of that title. I embrace you from the bottom of my heart, and assure you of my most sincere friendship.

Widow PHILIPPEAUX.

A thousand kisses to your charming Horace and to Mademoiselle Adèle.

No. 28.

SALE OF THE HOUSE IN BOURG-LA-REINE.

(Autograph document of Madame Duplessis.)

Madame Duplessis's final decision to the persons who presented themselves, in company with M. Palloy, about her property, situate Bourg-la-Reine, canton Sceaux, her patrimony formerly known as the 'Clos Payen.' The purchaser has every security ; all is in the greatest possible order.

The superficial area of this property ;—part arable land, part vineyard, and kitchen-garden, is twenty-one acres. A cement quarry could be made on it. It brings in from four to five thousand *francs* per annum. Ten acres are let with offer of lease for three, six, or nine years, at the option of the purchaser.

Madame Duplessis will not take less than fifty-five thousand *francs*, plus a thousand *francs* as bonus, and she gives up the crops already gathered in and in the granaries, the fowls and rabbits ; finally, what she has herself stored, making a total of . . . . 56,000 *livres*.

No other conditions will be accepted.

As to the payment, she is to receive seven thousand *francs* deposit, which will not be inserted in the contract of sale, but for which she will give a receipt, with the understanding that she is under obligation to return the money in the case of any dispute, which is not to be feared, as all is legalised. Twenty-four thousand *francs* to be paid after the expiration of the term and delay necessary for the execution of the contract ; as for the twenty-five thousand *livres* remaining, she grants two years, provided interest be paid her at the rate of six per cent. per annum.

An immediate valuation will be made of the articles belonging to the garden, tools, farmhouse, wine-press, ladder, and all except the firewood, with immediate possession, except of the part occupied by vendor, of which she retains possession until October 15th, in order to have time to find a dwelling in Paris.

I have forwarded this deed to my man of business.[1]

ADDITIONS TO THE APPENDIX.

The following extract from the 'Révolution,' No. 24 (page 507), contains a satire upon Maury, which sufficiently indicates the tone of all the others :—

A comedy in two acts, entitled 'J. H. Maury,' is about to be performed at the *Grands Danseurs du Roi.*

Dialogue between Maury and Rosalie.

MAURY.

—Ah! j'ai bien du chagrin!

ROSALIE.

Qu'as-tu donc, petit cœur?

MAURY.

Un décret, ce matin. . . .

ROSALIE.

Un décret? achevez. . . .

MAURY.

Pour prix de nos services
Vient de nous dépouiller de tous nos bénéfices.

ROSALIE.

O ciel! à ce malheur qui se fût attendu!

MAURY.

De l'éloquence en vain j'ai déployé les charmes,
A tous les bons curés fait répandre des larmes,
Cité commentateurs, et docteurs, et robins,
Il a fallu céder le champ aux Jacobins. . . .

---

[1] Extract from the *unpublished* papers of Palloy the architect, who pulled down the Bastille. We possess a great number of these documents, in which the author, in his political electicism, alternately sings the praises of the Reign of Terror, of the Reaction, of Atheism and of Religion, of the Republic, the Monarchy and the Empire. The *patriot Palloy*, as he called himself, is the life-like image of the worshippers of success and courtiers of fortune. But unfortunately the race has not died out with him.

Le vicomte de Mirabeau intervient.

MIRABEAU LE VICOMTE.

> . . . . Pour moi, je vais à la cuisine
> Voir si certain gigot commence à prendre mine.
> Je vous ferai passer six flacons de bordeaux :
> Mettez par là la tourte avec les fricandeaux ;
> Garnissez ce lieu-ci de cette matelotte.
> Le petit marmouzet a gâté ma culotte.
> Pour qu'il n'arrive plus un semblable malheur,
> Et montrer que je tiens la cuisine en honneur,
> Je m'en vais, mes enfants, endosser le costume.
> Otons le bel habit et le castor à plume ;
> Donnez le tablier, le bonnet de coton ;
> Eh bien, n'ai-je pas l'air d'un bon gros marmiton ? [1]

The following extracts are from the *Complaint of M. Malouet, deputy to the National Assembly, against Camille Desmoulins,* author of the ' Révolutions de France et de Brabant :'

To the Criminal Lieutenant of the Châtelet at Paris.

The petition of Victor-Pierre Malouet, deputy to the National Assembly, setting forth that during the past year he has been constantly vilified by Camille Desmoulins, author of the ' Révolutions de France et de Brabant.'

Malouet imputes to Camille 'the excesses and the violence of a populace, led astray by incendiary writings, and his title of *procureur général de la lanterne.*' He represents him as an enemy of order and of the public peace, a calumniator, a denunciator, who points out victims to the justice of the people.

If, in a State with a police system, each citizen suffices for the defence of his honour, society in general and the tribunals ought to watch over his safety.

It is in vain to impute the inaction of the tribunals in such cases to the silence of the legislative body on the license of the press.

The life of the complainant has been in danger. Pursued at Versailles, insulted at the door of the Assembly, over-

---

[1] All this is dull enough, and not worthy of the Athenian wit of Camille.

whelmed with anonymous letters, reduced to carry fire-arms with which to defend himself, the complainant attributes all this to Camille Desmoulins.

In No. 31 of the 'Révolutions de France et de Brabant' the complainant believes that there are symptoms of madness. He cannot believe that, if the author had been in his right mind, he would have threatened the complainant *to imprint lasting characters upon his cheek*, to call him *infamous*, and to state that he had been *driven out from among the galleys at Brest and his name struck off the list of convicts*. A man like Desmoulins ought to be more used to receive than imprint durable characters of this kind, and the extravagant statements which he makes can only be the result of madness.

The complainant begs that Camille may be seen and examined by the physician to the Châtelet, and taken to any madhouse which may be decided upon, as a violent and dangerous lunatic ; or, otherwise, demands that he be obliged to make full retractation in the presence of a witness, and be bound over not to molest the complainant in future.

(Signed)   MALOUET ET LEMIT, *procureur.*

To be placed before the *procureur du roi*. July 7, 1790.

(Signed)   BACHOIS.

I offer no opposition on the part of the ᵢking to giving action to the complainant's plea on the grounds set forth in the present requisition, and consequently I give him leave to summon the said Camille Desmoulins with the object named in the said requisition.

Given on July 7, 1709.

(Signed)   FLANDRE DE BRUNVILLE.

The following is taken from a contemporary pamphlet :—

Letter from an Impartial to M. Camille Desmoulins, author of the 'Révolutions de France et de Brabant.'

Sir,

I hesitated about writing to you ; I said to myself, What is there, what can there be in common, between Camille

Desmoulins and the Société des Impartiaux ?   I remembered what one of our members at Marseilles had said : There is a long distance between the steel of the assassin and the heart of the honest man ; but since you have cleared the distance, and your calumnies have reached us, we must answer them.

We are indulgent towards error, but implacable towards cabals ; we hate brigands who have recourse to the lamp-post ; we execute ambitious men who make use of brigands ; and we despise journalists who devote themselves to the praise of the ambitious, of brigands, and of lamp-posts. The author concludes by saying : Every honest man may be admitted to the sittings of the ' Impartiaux,' presented by a member, 'if you cannot find anyone to present you there exceptionally.'

M. Emmanuel des Essarts.

A poet of rare ability, and who has closely studied the revolutionary epoch, has described Camille in the following verses :—

Camille Desmoulins.

Effroi des Feuillants à l'œil terne,
Qu'il joue et qu'il déjoue, et qu'il bat et qui'l berne,
C'est l'Horace de la Lanterne.

Mieux encor, c'est Camille, un accord singulier
De poëte et de cordelier,
Pour aimer sans égal, sans pareil pour railler ;

Riant d'un rire qui m'effare,
Jetant sur l'avenir les lueurs d'un grand phare,
Tour à tour sifflet ou fanfare.

Souvent au fer de lance aiguisant ses chansons,
Trempant de venin les soupçons,
Il enfonce ses mots comme autant de poinçons.

Il tue alors tous ceux qu'il blesse :
Le Maury, le Veto, la cour et la noblesse,
La force et même la fabilesse.

Sa verve meurtrière est toujours à l'assaut ;
Gare au méchant et gare au sot,
A l'honnête homme aussi. . . . Gare à toi, cher Brissot.

Tel un dieu d'Orient, funeste
Et bon, fait alterner l'abondance et la peste,
  Fécondant ou broyant d'un geste.

Tour à tour c'est Ménippe aboyant au passant,
  Aristophane éblouissant,
Diogène parfois éclaboussé de sang.

  Mais bientôt par une éclaircie
La Liberté visible à sa verve associe
  L'âpre accent de la Boëtie.

Il lance un *fiat lux* impérieux et fier,
  Rêvant sur les débris d'hier
Une Lutèce aux pieds caressés par la mer ;

  Une Grèce parisienne,
Sous nos brumes du Nord, lumineuse et païenne,
  La république athénienne.

Et tous heureux, et tous ravis, et tous chantants,
  La pompe des arts éclatants,
Et les Muses faisant abdiquer les Titans.

  Voilà le vrai Camille, une âme
Enfantine, et mobile, et folle ; oiseau de flamme,
  Esprit de faune et cœur de femme !

Unpublished Poems on the Revolution.

Something remains of the history of Desessarts the
actor, who was chiefly distinguished, however, by his quarrel
with Camille Desmoulins. Denis Dechanet, called Desessarts,
who was formerly a *procureur*, acted the parts of financiers,
dotards, and spies remarkably well. He had come from
Marseilles to Paris to replace Bonneval at the Comédie
Française. He made his first appearance on October 4, 1772,
as Lisimon in 'Le Glorieux,' and Lucas in 'Le Tuteur.'
He was received as a Sociétaire on April 1, 1773. 'Good-
nature mingled with bluntness, frankness, gaiety and keenness,'
such were, according to the testimony of contemporaries, his
qualities. In Molière's comedies he was excellent. But he was
so stout that when he played 'Orgon' a table had to be
made on purpose for him to hide underneath it. In the *rôle*

of Petit-Jean, in 'Les Plaideurs,' he excited general hilarity by the line,

Pour moi, je ne dors plus, aussi je deviens maigre !

In the 'Réduction de Paris,' by Desfontaines, Desessarts played the 'Prévôt des Marchands' *attenuated by famine.* Many anecdotes were told about Desessarts, of which Lablache was afterwards made the hero. The former, having challenged Dugazon to a duel, Dugazon took a piece of chalk from his pocket, marked a circle with it on the stomach of his adversary, and said: 'Let us fight fairly; all outside the ring is not to count.' 'How on earth is the fight to come off?' cried Lamazurier. The absurd duel ended in a breakfast. Desessarts died at Barèges, aged 59 (Brumaire, Year II.) of the shock caused by the announcement of the death of a comrade. Beneath the portrait of the former *procureur du roi* these words were placed : '*I would rather make men laugh than ruin them*' (Galérie Historique des acteurs du Théâtre Français, par P. D. Lamazurier, 1810, vol. i. p. 227). In Saint-Just's poem, 'Organt,' the following verse relative to Desessarts, whom Loustallot calls a *ridiculous monster*, occurs :

> 'Organt vit là Molé, dont le talent
> Est d'écorcher Molière impunément,
> Et Desessarts, *le Sancho de l'Ecole*,
> Qui croit l'Olympe assis sur son épaule.'

Desessarts was used to sarcasm ; he ought to have been bucklered against the jests of Camille.

The following is the text of the letter referred to by the author, and used in the prosecution of General Westermann. It was written by one Baré, a soldier in the line, and is a curious document :

De Saint-Maixent ce 24 juillet 1793 lan deuxem
de la Respublique fransaise.

Mon cher père et ma cher mère pour faire responce a votre laistre an date du 18 que jai resu le 21 que jaités de bivac je nets pu vous faire responce plus to sai pour main formée de les ta de votre santee pour la mienne elle ay fort bone epour vous faire quelques dée taille de notre si tuation quar je nets pas en core tous marquée comme nous somme de pui paris en na rivent à Nior on nous a mi couchez dans les glise Notre Dame sur la paille aprée avoire fai san dits lieux pour nous repausée tandise que les autre couchez chez le bourjoits car lon donne la prée fai rance au parisien pour couchez sur la dur encore aprée san nous avon raistée 8 jour dans les glise à Nior aprée ce la nous avon couchez deux jour dans les lit apree cela nous avon parti pour allée à Tours quand nous a von arrivez à potier nous avons resu *ordre de retournet à Saint Maiscent* et de la apartenait pour re juindre *l'armée de Vestermane* qui ai tes allée à Chatillon arrivez a partenait le lendemain nous avons resu ordre de partire a quatre heur aprés midi pour bellessuire trois eur aprée nous avon batu en retraite car *larmée de Vestermane* ai tes des faite il ne raistes plus que sa cavallerie pour linfanterie il nan avez plu nous avon retournet sur les auteur de partenait ou nous a von bivacquee deux bataillon que nous aition a troisheur du matin le *generalle Vestermane* ai venu nous passets en re vue et nous lavon restée au bivac le len de main on nous a fai prendre une autre posision don il a eu du mal en ten due car ai ten des sandue dans un font on na criet soi dissen a la traïson don le genetrall fut instrui et on lui a vai di que saites notre capitaine Rouy tandiquil ni ai tes pas quil aites allee a lhaupitalle pour conduire un homme qui avait resu un cou-defusi au bra dan la pres. midi comme je cherchai a diner dan partenait le commendan de notre bataillon celui qui avai dit au genetralle que saités notre capitaine me dit voit la belle affaire vot capitaine et le capitaine Baré von avoire la taite cassée moi qui ne savai rien de cela je lui demande pour coi il me dit quil avai dit que nous aition traïs moi je reste aimu et surtous quan je vie le genetralle Vestermane au sito passes a vec sa cavallerie qui san nallai au bivac je di a un de mais camarade que si on nallai faire mourire mon capitaine jallai desertee puiquil naité plus permi de parlée car je vie le genet-ralle qui *ajissai en maitre absollu* san assamblee le consaille de gere et san vouloire entandre le capitaine Rouy qui lui disai quil ne savai pas ce con voulai lui dire le genetralle Ves-termane *agisan en despote lui dit qu'il* voulles faire un aiscemple et lui dit maitee vous a jenous don le capitaine le fit ausito lorsque le grenadier aites pree a tirer et que le chasseur a chevalle faisait fron a notre bataillon don le genetralle leur avaidit que siles vollontaire branlai quil les ache par morsau aussito que le capitaine fu a jenou son fils se jeta dans les bras de son pere en disen quil voulles mourire avec son pere au sito un commendant dun bataillon dorlean dit au *genetralle* que les troupes demandai grace pour ce capitaine il n'an avai pas besoin pusquil na pas fait de faute voiet comme la libertee raigne je vous le laise a pensee nous aition tous consternes de voir un gugement au sibien rendu ce pendan comme par mis erricorde le genetralle dit au capitaine re le vai vous cette homme qui na vait pas manquée na vai pas besoin de son pardon car on ne fai grace qua un coupable il fallu passée par la de pui ce moment ce genetralle ne pouvai plus nous soufrire nous a von quitée Partenait la maime nui pour re tour net a Saint Maixent ou le genetralle fit maitre la troupe dans des li et *notre bataillon de parisien par préferance* il nous fit loger ale vaichez et voila trois semaine que nous isomme ce qui fai voire que les parisien son aimais je ne se pourcoi car il a des bourjoit quil en sont et tonnet car on a laugée jusqua 5 mille homme dans cette ville et nous n'aition pas 2 mille quand nous i avon arrivez et aprée sen nous ne somme pas encore 5 mille voila comme nous somme je croi quon net fachez de nous voire dans sai païs nous somme presque tout mariet et pair de fammille et voila la rée compance con nous donne voila Vestermane parti pour paris le citoyen Daillac quil la remplacée aprée sen sa net plus Daillac je croi que sai le genetralle Vajusquit et cé pourquoi je pri de me marquée si Vestermane ais à paris et quaice quil a de nous veau car je sui tous jour à mon poste mais si *Vestermane re venet* dans ce païs ci je serai au bliger de ment n'allée *car si savez ce que je vien des crire il me erée mourire* et cependant nous couchon tous jour partere de préfairance, autre chose je vous dires que je vien de re ce voire une laitre de ma femme qui ma fait grand plesir pour le cabinet que vous me dite je vous pri de faire comme pour vous. Marquée moi ou elle aura louet jespere ce pen dan aitre de retours sou peu, je vou pri de prendre bien garde a qui vous montrerée ma laitre je fini mon pere et ma mere de tous mon cœur. Votre fils.

E.-P. BARÉ.

'Marquee moi ce qu'il a de nouveaux au sujet de Vestermane et de Paris.'[1]

The following is the text of Lucile's last letter to
Fréron :—

24 Nivôse l'an deux de la République une et indivisible.

'Revenez, Fréron, revenez bien vitte. Vous n'avez point
de tems à perdre, ramenez avec vous tous les vieux Cordeliers
que vous pourrez rencontrer, nous en avons le plus grand
besoin. Plut au ciel qu'ils ne se fussent jamais séparés ! Vous
ne pouvez avoir idée de tout ce qui se fait ici ! Vous ignorez
tout, vous n'appercevez qu'une foible lueur dans le lointain
qui ne vous donne qu'une idée bien légère de notre situation.
Aussi je ne m'étonne pas que vous reprochiez à Camille son
comité de clémence. Ce n'est pas de Toulon qu'il faut le juger.
Vous êtes bien heureux là où vous êtes ; tout a été au gré de
vos désirs, mais nous, calomnié, persécuté par des ignorants,
des intrigants, et même des patriottes, Robespièrre (*sic*) votre
boussolle, a dénoncé Camille aux Jacobins ; il a fait lire ces
numéros 3 et 4, a demandé qu'ils fussent brulez *lui qui les
avoit lus manuscrit. Y concevez-vous quelque chose?* Pendant
deux séances consécutives il a tonné *ou plutôt crié* contre
Camille. A la troisième séance on avoit rayé Camille. Par une
bisarie (*sic*) bien singulière, il a fait des efforts inconcevables
pour obtenir que sa radiation fût rapporté, elle a été rappor-
tée, mais il a vu que lorsqu'il ne pensoit pas ou qu'il n'agis-
soit pas *à leur* la volonté d'une certaine quantité d'individus,
il n'avait pas tout pouvoir. Marius n'est plus écouté, il perd
courage, il devient faible. Déglantine est arrêté, mis au Luxembourg ; on l'accuse de faits très-graves. Il n'était donc
pas patriotte ! lui avoit si bien été jusqu'à ce moment. Un
patriotte de moins c'est un malheur de plus.'
Ces monstres là ont osé reprocher à Camille d'avoir épouser
une femme riche. Ah ! qu'ils ne parlent jamais de moi, qu'ils
ignorent que j'existe, qu'ils me laissent aller vivre au fond des
déserts, je ne leur demande rien, je leur abandonne tout ce
que je possède pourvu que je ne respire pas le même air qu'eux !
(*Ici,—détail qui donne je ne sais quoi de sinistre et de trop*

[1] National Archives. Trial of the Dantonists.

*vivant à ce document qui sent la mort,—Lucile laisse échapper
de sa plume une tache d'encre, et cette plume allant mal; elle
essaye de la façonner en traçant en marge des barres, des zigzags qui rendent cet autographe plus étrange et plus précieux
encore.)* Puissai-je les oublier, eux et tous les maux qu'ils nous
causent, je ne vois autour de moi que des malheureux. Je suis
trop faible, je l'avoue, pour soutenir un si triste spectacle. La
vie me devient un pesant fardeau. Je ne scais plus penser.
Penser, bonheur si pur, si doux. Hélas, j'en suis privée. . . .
Mes yeux se remplissent de larmes. . . . Je renferme en mon
cœur cette douleur affreuse, je montre à Camille un frond
serein, j'affecte du courage pour qu'il *ne perde pas le sien* continue d'en avoir.

Vous n'avez pas lu à ce qu'il me parroit ses cinq numéros.
Vous y êtes cependant abonné.

Oui le serpolet est *cueilli* tout prêt. C'est à travers mille
soucis que je l'ai cueillis. Je ne ris plus, je ne fais plus le chat,
je ne touche plus à mon piano, je ne rêve plus, je ne suis plus
qu'une machine. Je ne vois plus personne, je ne sors plus. Il y a
long tems que je ne vois plus les Robert. Ils ont éprouvé
des désagréments par leur faute. Ils tâchent de se faire
oublier.

Adieu, lapin, *tu* [1] vous allez encore m'appeler folle. Je ne
le suis pourtant pas encore tout à fait, il me reste assé de raison pour souffrir

Je ne saurois vous exprimer la joie que j'ai éprouvé en ap-
prenant qu'il n'étoit point arrivé de malheur à votre aimable
sœur [et à Paris] j'ai été tout inquiette lorsque j'apris la prise
de Toulon. Je pensois sans cesse quel seroit leur sort?
Parlez leur quelquefois de moi. Embrassez les tous deux
pour moi. Je les prie de vous le rendre en mon intention.

Entendez-vous, mon loup qui crie Martin, mon pauvre
Martin, *te voilà, viens que je t'embrasse*, reviens bien vitte.

Revenez, revenez bien vitte, nous vous attendons avec
impatience.

[1] Crossed out in the MS.